War Virus

Book 1

Daniel Magill

ProActive Content Fiction

War Virus – Book 1

Copyright © 2026 ProActive Content, LLC

All rights reserved.

No portion of this book may be reproduced, distributed, or transmitted in any form or by any means, including photocopying, recording, or other electronic or mechanical methods, without written permission from the publisher or author, except as permitted by U.S. copyright law and in the case of brief quotations embodied in critical articles and reviews. No portion of this book may be used by or for any AI programs, software, or other entities or systems.

In case you missed it, no part of this book may be used or reproduced by any information storage retrieval system. This book was not written to improve the AI algorithm's novel-writing ineptitude.

The story, all names, characters, and incidents portrayed in this production are fictitious. No identification with actual persons (living or deceased), places, buildings, and products is intended or should be inferred.

For permission requests, contact the author on X (Twitter) @dmagillwrite

Written by Daniel Magill

Book Cover by 100 Covers

Ordering information: Visit the author's website at danielmagill.net where you can purchase more books as well as story feedback and consultation services.

Publisher Information

ProActive Content, LLC

Seattle, Washington, United States of America

Library of Congress Control Number: 2026907433

First Edition

ISBN: 978-1-969279-03-4

Contents

War Virus

In the distant past, humans spread across half the galaxy. They found nothing but mostly empty worlds.

Among thousands of frozen wastelands and gas giants, only a few hundred planets could sustain life or be adapted to facilitate it.

Both Wester and Peterson Territories had billions of people, limitless natural resources, and a vast galactic gulf between them known as the Meridian Zone.

This planetary desert was completely barren of habitable worlds, save for those seven precious ones that constituted the perpetual war front – Risner, Kora, Lavoisier, Cinque, Terrasol, Portia, and Rita.

It was war as a way of life...

Part 1 – Risner

1

Dog Killers

The battlefield reeked. The stench rolled over the nameless rock-littered plain on the planet Risner.

Squad leader Thomas Shipp drank in the smell of all the dead Wester soldiers. It wasn't a pleasant odor like his wife Pretoria's perfume that she saved for the nights they could be together. But this one had its own brand of intoxication. The smell of victory. The scent of ground taken back. The essence of realized and deserved vengeance.

The odor reminded him of a story his Battlefield Combat instructor at Space Force University shared with the class on the final day. In the story, a blood-soaked soldier, wounded in battle on the planet Lavoisier, had holed up alone in an underground pod for six months. He never showered, wanting to preserve his water. When finally rescued, he emerged victorious and justified – because he survived.

Shipp took long, deep breaths, full of satisfaction. He indulged all his senses with the victory his forces had just won. The silent Wester corpses at rest in the soft breeze. The still-warm Mossamer-24 clinging to his hands. His soldiers' cooling electric pulse rifles quieting down around him. Licking the salty sweat from above his lips.

Without the dead, the terrain would have looked like most of this Meridian Zone planet – unremarkable at first glance. But with its uneven ground and occasional ravines, dips, and rises, small armies could approach with stealth and lie in wait. And that's what the three combined squads of Peterson Space Force ground soldiers led by Shipp, Karel Rothman, and Hosh Faraday had just done.

Shipp's armored boots trampled the dust and pebbles as he gathered with his fellow squad leaders. He mused about how many men and women had probably died on this same terrain over the last several hundred years of the Meridian Zone War.

"Probably as much ground up bone here as native sand," quipped Faraday.

"As long as more of it is Wester bone," Shipp replied.

Shipp thought of Pretoria, and wondered how she would react to the news of his utter annihilation of this Wester battalion. His favorite part of life on Risner was that little curled smile she would crack for him whenever he told her of the Westers he had dusted.

Dusted.

That's a good word for what we're doing here, thought Shipp. *From dust you came, and to dust you will return. That sounds like a saying I must have heard somewhere.* Shipp knew that if they could turn enough Westers on Risner back to dust, they could establish a more permanent base here. Start mining the erbium and vanadium. Get the water production going again.

Shipp's Peterson regiment headed back to their base – which was much newer than the closest Wester one whose reinforcements they had just wiped out. The soldiers re-traced the same path they took to get here to eliminate any chance of encountering leftover Morse mines – or rodents, as the Petersons called them. Of course, rodents were normally reserved for assaulting fortified bases. But the Westers were too stupid to understand that, and often wasted them by using them as conventional land mines. The only problem was, if you ran into them and your comrades were too bunched up, you could lose half your squad in a flash. The Peterson Mech Specialists could usually detect rodents from a safe range, but who wants the stress?

Shipp smiled to himself as he recounted his latest combat statistics. The Petersons went in with 145 and were walking out with 124. A 14.5% loss. Very costly. Some excellent soldiers died, including Gugbe, one of his best friends and part of his elite core.

But for a battle that lasted about fourteen hours and resulted in the deaths of 224 Westers, it was one of those ultra-efficient tactical masterpieces – a work of art that filled Shipp with a profound satisfaction. Faraday's battlefield genius shined. His squad of 48 only lost two soldiers. Shipp's lost five. Rothman had the most risk-prone task in this offensive, so her squad took the most losses, making a total of 21 across all three squads.

The soldiers trekked for about thirty minutes.

"Take a rest," Faraday ordered. They spread out in groups of two or three. This was standard procedure, in case some rogue Wester rat hiding nearby fired a hive bomb or a dual cannon rocket.

Faraday, Shipp, and Rothman huddled together to contact the main Peterson base on Risner. They were about six kilometers out. Shipp did the talking. He spoke to Yesler Vonn, the Commander of the Peterson Space Force on Risner, and Barnon Torres, the captain of the ground force.

"Vonn," the Commander's voice crackled. "How's your starry battlefield looking?"

Shipp gave Faraday and Rothman a look they immediately understood – *good thing we're not talking to General Renwar*. Nobody much liked Tap Renwar, as he was too indecisive in combat situations. But he was extremely good at managing a warzone base, and experienced leaders who could do that on any of the seven Meridian Zone planets were hard to come by. But they all loved Vonn.

"14.4% losses. Westers lost ten times as much. 10.6 kill ratio," Shipp reported.

"You get the sensors in place?" Vonn asked, surprising Shipp by showing little reaction to his good news. Shipp took it in stride, assuming Vonn had a reason.

"Heat and motion sensors embedded across a 7.4 square kilo area. You've got eyes on your south and southeast flank now."

"Why don't I have the signal? It's all dark here still."

Shipp shot a confused glance at Rothman and Faraday. Rothman scowled and took over the conversation because she led the sensor distribution operation.

"All units were functional. You should have gotten a steady flow of eyes over the last couple days," Rothman began.

Vonn interrupted, "Could they have Metalheads already? Doesn't seem likely."

"Jonas that. Hold on."

Rothman gave Shipp a puzzled look. Shipp whipped out his wrist monitor and ran through several pages of diagnostics and settings. He worked fast. The monitor lit up, dotted with lights over an expansive area on a map. He showed it to Rothman.

"We're seeing them all live on our tech," said Rothman. "Must be a connection issue on your end."

"Fireballs," swore Vonn.

Rothman could hear Torres grunt in angst and march out of the command center to investigate. Vonn called after him – "Tell Renwar. He'll figure it out."

One of the planet's suns descended below the horizon, and the light faded. After about two hours of darkness, the other sun would rise from the northeast.

"Let's get back," said Shipp. "I don't want to be out here when daylight returns."

Rothman spoke to Vonn again. "We're heading back. Should be there in an hour or so."

"Jonas," Vonn replied, and Rothman's comm headset went dark.

Shipp stood up and spoke calmly to the unit, but loud enough for everyone to hear him. "Rest is over, let's finish the trek. No lights. Stay alive."

Immediately, like a chant from a psy-ops clarity session, all 124 men and women whispered in unison, "Save your friend." And without another word, the unit rose in the failing light and began the last leg of the journey.

The planet's surface basked in utter darkness. The Peterson base sat on the other side of a steady incline, barring it from view, though it was nearly impossible to see at night with the naked eye. Shipp gazed up at the stars, a vast array of spectacular shimmering beauty. He loved starlight. The songs and poems from Peterson history that mused about starlight had burrowed deep in his heart. The ideas and the people most important, most valuable, and most precious to him always seemed to come alive in his mind when he was surrounded by nothing but starlight.

And the enveloping, comforting darkness found on the seven Meridian Zone planets had few peers in the distant Peterson Territory.

Alone in the dark, with no one but your fellow soldiers in arms – this was what Shipp signed up for when he committed his life to the Peterson

Space Force. No distractions. No certainty of tomorrow. No comfort. Just incomparable gratification from fighting to protect those billions of people and ensure their continued prosperity and expansion across this quarter of the Milky Way.

After about twenty minutes of walking, Shipp's brain trip into starlight reverie got interrupted when his comm came alive again.

"You guys there? Shipp? You there? This is Gugbe. I'm in a pit... You there?"

Shipp halted. He raised his arm and paused the progression, turning back to face his soldiers as he listened and responded.

"I hear you Gugbe. What happened?"

"Got... blown against a rock... dual cannon.... How long was I out?"

"Hold on, we're coming back to get you."

Shipp gathered everyone close enough so he could speak in a low voice.

"I just got a call from Gugbe. Not sure why his vitals weren't registering, but he's alive."

Shipp spoke into his comm again. "Can you walk Gug?"

"I think so... Don't have a clear sense of path to... Rita... rodents. Swirling sand... Hold on..."

There was a pause. Shipp waited, a bit uneasy at Gugbe's odd language and speech rhythm. It didn't sound like him. Rita was another of the seven habitable Meridian Zone planets, and Petersons and Westers both agreed it was a worthless pile of granite. Gugbe served there before transferring to Risner. Gugbe's silence worried Shipp.

Rothman closed on Shipp and whispered to him.

"Ninety minutes to sunrise. You go back and get him now, you won't make it back before light."

Shipp nodded in understanding.

"What's the word Gug?" Shipp asked. "You okay?"

Still nothing. Shipp waited as concern grew on his face.

"He stopped talking." Shipp tried again. "Gugbe? You hear me? You still with us?"

More silence.

"He's not answering."

Rothman knew what Shipp had to do. She didn't hesitate, placing her hand on his shoulder.

"Take four and go back for him. I'll keep my squad here until you return. Faraday can take the rest back to base. Go save your friend."

"Four?" Faraday exclaimed. "What if the Westers sent reinforcements? Take your entire remaining squad. How many you have left?"

Shipp knew his numbers. "43."

"Take them all," Faraday said. "Mine will return to base. Rothman stays here."

The three leaders agreed with the plan and separated.

Shipp gathered his core group of most trusted soldiers – Mixie, Zemmer, Blasé, and Ramad. Together they led the way for the rest of the squad, trotting along and trying to shave off a few minutes in the return trip, but not so fast as to be winded when they got there.

"Ramad," Shipp said about ten minutes from the battlefield. "Take ten spotters to that rise and position yourselves. You'll have a good view of most of the area."

Ramad split off with ten others, and the rest kept pushing forward.

"Mixie, you have Gugbe's last location yet?" Shipp asked.

"He was on the eastern flank. Farthest from us," she replied. "We know he was against an embankment."

"Who was fighting alongside Gugbe?" Shipp asked the group.

"I was," said Zemmer, along with several others. "I remember dual cannons hitting our spot. I can probably get us close enough to start searching bodies from there."

"Slow down," Shipp ordered. "Hit the dirt."

All 32 soldiers lay flat at once. Shipp hadn't seen or heard anything, but that didn't mean no one was out there. And he didn't want any enemy Westers to think he was unaware of them if they were. It was an act of unpredictability, to make anyone who might be watching take a pause on whatever they might be planning.

But Shipp and the Petersons had won this battle decisively, and it would surprise them if more Westers had already returned to the battlefield. They wouldn't want to risk losing even more soldiers after such a costly defeat.

Still, stealth and caution prevailed. The Peterson's Core Principle – 'stay alive and save your friend' – didn't just apply when someone was hurt or in danger. It applied before and even in the absence of a threat. Shipp didn't want to get picked up by a hidden sensor from the nearest

Wester base. He also had to minimize the chances of their heat signatures showing up on the monitors of another transport ship or some rogue ground assault vehicle.

"Arise and advance," Shipp ordered after five minutes. "Slow. Spread out."

The group disbursed into groups of two or three, far enough apart to avoid mass casualties in case of an attack.

Shipp directed his remaining soldiers. "Zemmer, Mixie, Blasé. You're with me. The rest of you – take positions. You decide best possible vantage. Hold still. Watch."

As his squad spread apart and staked out positions in and around the corpse-ridden battlefield, the stench saturated the air and filled their nostrils and lungs again. Some of Shipp's soldiers planted among the dead. Others stationed around the perimeter. Shipp left the specifics to them, based on what they could see and hear, and what the terrain demanded.

"Zemmer?" Shipp asked.

"Over there I think," Zemmer pointed to a slanted incline that appeared to be mostly dirt, angling up at about 70 degrees, too steep to climb. It was near the far eastern edge of the battlefield, closest to the Wester base that sat out of sight to the north from here.

"Gugbe," Shipp whispered on his comm. "Gugbe you there? We're here. Raise your hand if you can't talk. Turn on your uniform strip."

Peterson ground force uniforms had a line of phosphorescent fabric running from the neck to both wrists. It could be lit up with a click of the thumb against the palm, and the light would last for a minute or so.

"No sign of rats," Ramad spoke in Shipp's comm.

"Jonas that," Shipp replied. "Search bodies."

Mixie, Shipp, Zemmer, and Blasé spread out and began examining Peterson corpses. There weren't many, since they had only lost 21 compared to over two hundred Westers. So finding any Petersons at all took some time in the blackness.

Shipp found a Peterson corpse first. It wasn't Gugbe. Blasé found one a few minutes later. Not him either. Then Blasé found another one. Still not him. With no light, it wasn't easy to distinguish Peterson from Wester until they got close enough to see the uniform. To do that, they used a small light affixed to the forearm that they could quickly switch on and off.

Mixie reached another Peterson body, pitched headlong on its face. She knelt next to it and rolled it over. It was Gugbe. She shone her light on his face.

"I got him," she called out.

Shipp, Zemmer, and Blasé immediately turned to find her. She lit up her arms, and they darted through the corpses to reach her.

As they approached, they could hear her talking to Gugbe. "You with us Gug? Hey, it's Mixie."

She started rubbing his face, neck, and shoulders. His eyeballs moved under his lids, but they didn't open. She noticed his helmet had a huge chunk torn out. Mixie knew a dual cannon blast couldn't cause such localized damage.

Shipp and the others reached her.

"He's alive," Mixie said, "Head damage. I'm guessing hive bomb, maybe wizard."

Shipp examined Gugbe's helmet. He knew just about everything you could know about Peterson Space Force weaponry, and the Westers used the same technology. "Hive bomb, yeah," he confirmed. "Shine the light in there please."

Zemmer shone his light at Gugbe's helmet where the blast had ripped part of it away. Shipp could see no exposed skull. His head was intact.

"He's got some kind of blackout, but we can save him," Shipp said. "Mixie and Zemmer grab a leg. Blasé and I will get the torso." Then, switching on his comm, "How much time we have Ramad?"

"Sunlight in 34 minutes."

"Listen everyone," Shipp activated his all-squad comm channel and spoke to the 43 of them. "We're not going to make it back by night's end. Once we get back to Rothman, we'll all go together. Don't bunch up. Keep your comms on. We should have enough distance from the Westers to get ample warning from base if they fire at us."

Next, he called Rothman and updated her on the situation.

"We'll be here Shipp. Bring him back," she replied.

When Shipp reunited with the rest of his squad, he disbursed them in groups of four, and directed them to trade off carrying Gugbe every five minutes to prevent anyone from getting too exhausted. Gugbe was a big guy.

Knowing their average ground speed, Shipp estimated this method saved two minutes on the return to Rothman. Sunrise had begun when Rothman greeted her fellow squad leader and rejoiced at seeing Gugbe rescued. The horizon glowed behind them with a brightness that overwhelmed the bloody landscape in their wake. While Shipp knew an attack from the Westers was even more unlikely at this point, you could never, ever, let your guard down.

Including Rothman's group, over sixty soldiers helped save one. The Peterson Way.

***

The final return to base went without incident. As daylight brightened, Shipp felt great relief at having rescued Gugbe. He imagined one day sharing a victorious future with Gugbe, Mixie, Ramad, Blasé, Zemmer, and some of the other men and women with him now. Though they didn't attend Space Force University at the same time, Gugbe and Shipp had become close friends since arriving on Risner a few years back. Losing him would have permanently stained an otherwise successful mission.

As Shipp walked alongside his core group, Rothman angled toward him.

"Pretty lucky, the soldier you were closest to is the one you were able to go back and save."

"I can't imagine the Westers doing what we just did," Shipp replied.

"Reminds me of your story about the dogs. You ever tell them that one?" Rothman asked.

"Dogs?" Mixie's ears perked up.

"Just never came up," Shipp said to Rothman.

"Tell them. Your squad should know the moment their leader chose the greatest profession in the galaxy."

Mixie, Ramad, Zemmer, and Blasé walked alongside Shipp as he talked. A few other soldiers lingered behind, wanting to hear it too.

"I don't remember which planet it was, somewhere in Wester Territory," Shipp began. "They had an annual canine competition."

"Canine?" Ramad asked.

"Dogs," said Zemmer.

"What's a dog?" asked Ramad. "Is that a pet?"

"Yeah," Shipp confirmed. "I forgot your planet didn't have any non-essential animal life allowed. Mine was a dome too, but there were about ten dogs that I knew of. Anyway, a canine disease broke out on the Wester planet. This was centuries ago by the way. Pet medics arrived and found a way to cure the dogs and wipe out the disease. But the Wester government didn't want to pay for it."

"Cheap flametards," said Zemmer.

"Not money," Shipp corrected him. "The war. They felt the canine competition was distracting people from the Galactic War, making them interested in things other than killing Petersons."

"So what happened?" asked Mixie.

"They used the disease as an excuse to send in troops. They killed every single dog on the planet during the competition, including all the ones brought from other Wester planets. And they killed the dog owners too."

Blasé nodded in understanding, "To suppress interest in pets on all their planets."

Shipp nodded. "I was just a kid when I heard that story. I cried when my aunt told it to me. To this day, I cannot imagine living in a place with so little respect for life – human or animal. Westers are sub-human."

Rothman smiled and sighed, loving Shipp's story every time she heard it. "That's why we go back for Gugbe," she said. "That's what makes us superior. If he were on their side, they'd have let him die."

Rothman angled back to her squad. Shipp trudged on in silence, thinking about his story again. Even though it had been raging for five hundred years, his consuming passion was to end the Westers and win the war, something most thought impossible. But in the last fourteen hours, he was now 224 dead Westers closer to that goal.

The Peterson base came into view. The nearly impenetrable space-black walls resembled huge slabs of obsidian in the fresh sunlight. The perimeter was defended by partially obscured automated underground units and samarium shielded bunkers, in addition to thicker samarium shields protecting the structure.

Shipp felt conflicted. With the base so near, his hopes grew for Gugbe surviving and returning to fight alongside him. But he needed medical attention. As eager as Shipp was to celebrate the battlefield win with his best and closest friends, including his wife Pretoria, he knew that any celebration in a five-hundred-year war was premature.

When they reached the entrance to the base, Commander Vonn welcomed and commended Shipp at the door – a very unusual action for the leader of the fledgling Peterson presence on Risner.

"Squad Leader Shipp. You've enforced the Core Principle to perfection."

Vonn and everyone else extended their right arms, hand turned upward, elbow slightly bent – the Peterson salute of a helping hand.

Shipp lowered his head in humble acceptance, not expecting to celebrate something he did without hesitation or dispute. Then he gestured to the other sixty standing around him.

"It's for all of us."

2

Retaliation

The main Peterson base housed several hundred permanent soldiers and administrators. About twenty kilometers to the northeast and southeast sat two outposts, each defended by a couple hundred more Peterson soldiers and support personnel. Two lakes and several rivers near the northeast outpost provided ample water and a stunning array of local flora. The southeast outpost stood near a more barren area. Farther south from there, Shipp and the Petersons fought their recent battle.

Shipp's mission had been to annihilate a group of Westers after Peterson Space Force Command reported their landing during a brief space battle between two Peterson and two Wester attack ships above Risner.

As it turned out, the space battle had been a diversion by the Westers to facilitate the landing of a large contingent of reinforcements using three transport ships. The Petersons had proven very successful in establishing and defending their Risner forces ever since launching their attempt to re-take the planet several years back, and the Westers had been backpedaling ever since. But the enemy still occupied the majority of the planet.

One of those three transport ships suffered damage from a Peterson attack ship, forcing it to land several hundred kilometers from the Wester bases on Risner. Shipp, Faraday, and Rothman went out to meet and destroy that group of soldiers before they could reach safety. Mission accomplished.

The victorious Peterson soldiers went various ways once they entered their base. Shipp headed straight for the main hall, where he knew his three best friends in the galaxy would be waiting. Above the entrance to the main hall, he walked under these words etched into a metal plate:

Stay alive. Save your friend.

All Space Force University students had to take a full year course devoted only to the Core Principle and all its depth of meaning.

What is required to keep yourself alive? What skills must you master? What knowledge must you gain? To what extreme lengths will you go to keep yourself and your fellow soldiers alive, in battle and against geography and weather? How many different ways can you save someone? You can save someone's mind, in addition to their body. You can save their confidence. Their motivation and passion. Their dignity. How much value in human life is expressed by this active verb 'save'? How does the impetus to save influence strategic battle planning and decision-making? What does the 'friend' label imply about your fellow soldier? And its singular rather than plural nature speaks to the essential, personal value of each individual. Shipp loved all of this. The Core Principle coursed through his veins and breathed in his lungs.

"There he is. Him and his 10.6 kill ratio."

Shipp turned and saw his closest friend, Cameron James, smiling and waving him over. Shipp couldn't contain his glee, and bared his teeth with an all-in smile that would make his dentist proud. James was joined by Shipp's wife Pretoria and Roy Horman, Shipp's roommate from Space Force University.

"11.2," Shipp corrected him. "Gugbe was presumed dead with the 10.6."

"Dress it up all you like," James chided.

Shipp gave James a hearty embrace.

"Great to see you," Shipp said. "How's your stomach?"

"Getting better. At least I'm not contagious, they said. Next time I'll be back out there with you."

Shipp could tell from James' remark that his friends had been planning to roast him about the 10.6 figure, since it fell short of the 13.7 Risner record he set last year. And that wasn't just the record since the Petersons re-established a beachhead here several years back. 13.7 broke the all-time Risner record for a single mission, going back over three hundred years since they started tracking this particular metric.

Roy Horman went next, "I heard they're thinking of sending you back to SFU to teach classes, since you seem to have hit your peak," he chuckled, never to be accused of holding a straight face when telling a joke.

Shipp replied, "Faraday's the one to blame, sir. He left his Mossamer in the bathroom again."

Everyone laughed. Pretoria gave Shipp an embrace and a kiss. Roy followed with a quick hug, and then all returned to their seats. After an hour of conversation about the mission, Gugbe, and updates about the base, Shipp turned to Pretoria. "How are the outposts doing?"

"I had the southeast one ready to assist your team if needed. We sent twenty extra soldiers and supplies there after you called in about the larger Wester forces. They're flush with overflow."

"So you had to short-change the northeast?"

"We short-changed ourselves for the time-being. The outposts are more vulnerable. But we can manage okay here until our ships get through."

"I just hope we get the Beasts up to full strength soon. Isn't that your job Roy?" Shipp needled, though his question was very serious.

"Looks like they can't be repaired," said James as Roy shook his head.

"Neither of them?" Shipp clarified.

"Vonn and Renwar are tearing their hair out over it," said Horman. "What's left of it."

Shipp chuckled. "How many does that leave us then? Fourteen you said?"

Pretoria spoke up, "I've ordered five more, if my transports ever get through. After that, we'll be just one short. Attack ships keep patrolling too close to risk a landing."

"Seems like they never leave the space around Risner and Kora empty for very long," Shipp said.

"Well, at least we've got the full battery of Krocks," James said. "They won't risk attacking us from the air."

Relaxing with his best friends in the main hall, Shipp drank his Fuel, a specially formulated power packed drink given to every soldier once a day, but only available at the base. Returning soldiers always got one immediately. James watched his friend, a man he respected more than anyone else in the universe, down his nutrients.

"What was it like to lead this mission?"

Shipp knew what James really wanted to know. Did this live up to Shipp's life goals? Was this battle a defining moment? To strike such a costly blow given so small a window of opportunity? Shipp hedged. He needed to win every time. The only way to win this war was to gain something every time you went out there. No failures. No setbacks.

"I'm disappointed in our losses, but–"

Pretoria raised her hand. Someone was speaking to her comm. She listened. The others waited. Her eyes flushed and her mouth opened, wanting to talk but waiting for the comm message to end. Finally, "We have a transport coming. Tomorrow!"

"What?" Horman exclaimed. "Not possible to get here that fast."

"Not the one I ordered. This one was assigned to Cinque, but we're getting it instead because of our unexpected battle. I guess our attack ships managed a temporary opening to divert it here."

"What are we getting?" Shipp asked.

"24 new soldiers, bunch of equipment and stock. I gotta go. LaSalle is waiting."

Pretoria ran off to meet with General LaSalle, who led the administrative team. Pretoria was his number one. But then she stopped, came back and kissed Shipp, and then trotted away again. Shipp blushed. Even after a few years of marriage, he still wasn't used to having such an excellent woman loving him, of all people.

James and Horman both smiled at him but said nothing.

"So how many of those 24 do we get?" James asked.

"We lost four in the battle," Shipp said. "Almost five before Gugbe."

The next day, Shipp and numerous other Peterson soldiers and admins exited the south entrance of the base to watch the transport ship land. It landed about three hundred meters from the base, settling down in a flat area further to the south, away from the ravines and canyons to the west.

The bustle commenced.

The hulking main door of the transport ship lifted open. Swarms of admins and soldiers exited the ship while the Risner swarm approached. Lifts, crates, weapons, boxes, luggage, and more got catalogued, carried, and ferried from the ship to the base.

Pretoria and LaSalle met with the transport ship general and went over some figures.

"That's General Renwar over there," Pretoria pointed, "And General Torres next to him."

"You mind telling me whose head you went over to get us from Cinque?", asked the transport ship general. "I was hoping to see a friend."

"We don't do that," LaSalle said. "Space Force Command did. We need it more. It's the right call."

"I'd just like a little more notice next time."

"Then get a new job," LaSalle said, having no patience for squabbling. "This is war. We just fought a battle."

At that, he nodded to Pretoria to continue working with the general while LaSalle returned to the base to supervise the re-stocking process.

The 24 newly arriving soldiers shuffled toward Renwar and Torres.

Shipp, Faraday, and Rothman stood to the side, appraising the latest Space Force University graduates, the first to arrive on Risner in over a year. The three squad leaders each held small monitors, scrolling through dossiers on each soldier, trying to match faces and names with a few of them as they walked past.

Shipp also wanted to make eye contact with a few of them, which he did, nodding when they noticed him. One passing soldier stretched out her open hand to the three of them with the Peterson salute. They all returned it. Shipp scrolled through the faces and found her. Juthelle. Good first impression, Shipp noted. She cared about the Peterson Way.

Standing about halfway between them and the Peterson main base, Generals Renwar and Torres began debriefing the new arrivals.

"I'm General Tap Renwar, I've been serving under Commander Vonn over fifteen years, with him on Kora before we came here. I oversee combat operations across the three outposts. No matter where you end up, we'll be getting to know each other. This is General Barnon Torres."

Torres spoke next, "I lead the combat squads for the main base. If you end up at an outpost, you'll have a different general in my position. I also served with Vonn on Kora. We're a tight unit, just what you want when advancing a beachhead on a hostile planet."

"For a couple days," Renwar resumed, "You'll be assigned temporary domiciles. After that, most of you will end up staying here at the main base for good. The rest will head for the northeast outpost. Once we're done debriefing, I'll lead you inside and show you around."

He looked at Torres, who gave the first order to the new arrivals, "Your first task is to begin learning the local geography. I hold weekly trainings. You can never know it too well. You need to spend the first week swimming in it, 30km in all directions. I slept outside the base my first three months here. I placed half the sensors we have around the base. I've named the rocks and the trees. Before long, you need to know them too. You've got maps on your handhelds, which are waiting in your quarters."

Shipp smiled while listening to Torres. He gestured to Rothman and Faraday. "You guys know the joke about Torres right?"

"Of course," said Rothman. "He was raised by ants, but he killed the queen and took over because she got lost in her own hive."

Faraday and Shipp both laughed.

"He is good though," Shipp said. "He knows the view depending on which side of the rock or tree he's looking around. I love the detailed knowledge."

Back at the new soldiers, Renwar continued, "Commander Vonn will be out in a moment. For now, let's go check out the western ravine and canyons, which Torres wants to show you."

In an instant, Shipp, Rothman, and Faraday all heard an alert in their comms. Incoming. Faster than the speed of sound, dual cannon missiles careened toward and impacted the ground to the east of the Peterson base. The explosions sent up clouds of dirt, plus some rocks and a the branches from a solitary tree that had lived its final day.

Shipp's battlefield senses kicked in and he knew immediately what to do. "Head back to the transport ship! Stay away from the base! Everyone!"

Shipp yelled at the admins hustling around the area, and Rothman and Faraday joined him. Shipp looked at Pretoria, who stood partially up the ramp of the ship. "Get inside!"

Torres and Renwar appeared stunned and a bit indecisive, something Shipp had grown to dislike about both men. He ran toward them as the 24 new soldiers scattered. Not all of them heard Shipp's command due to the noise of the dual cannon shelling, which continued in intensity.

Shipp scanned the eastern sky. He saw waves of tiny missiles arcing and careening down toward the Peterson base. Some hit unprotected bunkers outside the base. Others impacted samarium shields and did minimal damage. Automated counter-fire launched from defensive turrets surrounding the Peterson base and intercepted some of the incoming missiles.

Shipp reached Renwar and Torres.

"We need to get to the ship, not the base!"

They both realized the wisdom of this, and tried to order the 24 to follow. But five of them had already begun running toward the base. Right into the line of fire.

Shipp prepared to run after them, since none of them yet had comms and couldn't be reached over the cacophony. But then, he saw Juthelle, the new soldier, already dashing toward the other five. She couldn't have heard Shipp's order. He watched her race over and direct them west, down in the ravines behind the base. Shipp approved – she was leading them to safety.

Shipp, Torres, and Renwar corralled the other eighteen and directed them back toward the transport ship. They made it safely inside and closed the huge door. They waited. The shelling continued for another couple minutes, then ceased.

"Hold here," Torres cautioned. "Wait for a second assault."

Shipp agreed, and eyed Rothman and Faraday. "Everybody get inside?"

"Far as we know, yeah," said Faraday.

"You think this is a response to our victory yesterday?" Rothman wondered aloud.

"Most likely," Renwar said before Shipp could say the same. "But they can't do much damage like this. They're just letting us know they're not happy, and that we better not leave our base again anytime soon."

"Kind of bizarre though," Shipp said. "Seems like a waste of munitions. They know they can't beat our shields with dual cannons from that distance. No chance."

"They did land two other transports. Probably had a surplus," Torres surmised. "Thought they might catch us off guard."

A new soldier listening to the conversation spoke up. "Why are we safer here? Isn't the base covered with more Blackhead than a transport ship?"

"Ships have more," Torres answered, "More importantly, they probably don't know our transport ship is here, so there's little chance they'd target anything this far away from the base. If we made it inside the base we'd be fine. But its perimeter is the most dangerous place to be."

"Why don't they fire K-rockets?" the soldier asked.

"Don't want to waste them when it's just a barrage from a distance. Unless they're planning an actual assault, all they're going to do is damage a few of our shields and bunkers," said Torres.

"And," Shipp added, "Everyone keeps as many surface to air K-rockets as possible to fight off attack ships. If we knew they'd just unloaded a few dozen Krocks, we would report that to Space Force Command and they'd send an attack ship against the Wester base. The rats know we'd do that, so they won't risk depleting their arsenal without cause."

"So this is an example of a battle with no deaths," the soldier said. "At SFU they told us this was common."

"Correct," said Renwar. "It's common only because we know what they're likely to do and not do, and they know the same of us. Standard procedures. Systematic defenses. That's why the war moves slowly. If something new or different happens, like the damaged Wester transport ship that crashed a few days ago, you have to pounce on it. Might not get a chance like that for years."

"Which we did, and took out 224 of them," Shipp declared.

Ten minutes later, no more dual cannons fired. Renwar called Vonn to confirm it was okay to emerge and continue the offloading process. Shipp scowled. Another example of Renwar always needing Vonn's approval before taking action. It was his greatest flaw, by far. Vonn gave it. The doors opened, and Pretoria resumed directing the supply disbursal.

3

New Leader

Shipp, Rothman, and Faraday sat together in a small room, looking over printed versions of each new arrival's dossier.

"Find your two yet"? Shipp asked Faraday.

"I've got six I'm interested in, but since you both need more, I'm going last this time. Take your picks first."

"Karel?" Shipp switched to her.

She sighed. "I know I want this one. Marsh. Look at his scores in the SFU simulations. Off the charts."

"Good choice," Shipp said.

"You don't want him?" she asked.

"You should get first choice, like he said. Since Gugbe survived, I only need four now. You need fourteen.

Rothman nodded, thinking about her losses again. But then she gave Shipp an eye.

"You want someone else don't you."

"I don't want anyone yet until we meet them in person."

"But you have your eye on someone."

"Don't we all."

She sighed. "Alright I'll take Marsh for my first."

"He's yours," said Shipp.

Later that day, the three squad leaders stood before the 24 new soldiers in the only meeting room in the base other than the main hall large enough to hold them all. Each leader pitched their vision for combat, for Risner, for the entire Galactic War, and for anything else they wanted to share that would give new soldiers an idea of which squad their skills, values, and personalities aligned with best. This was another facet of the Peterson Way, and Shipp loved it. Minimize conflict. Maximize unity. Prioritize relationship. Those ideals guided which soldiers joined which squads.

Rothman spoke first since she needed the most new soldiers. When she finished, Shipp went next. First, he looked around the room at each Space Force University graduate, making eye contact with all of them. Then, he spoke.

"The Core Principle. Say it."

"Stay alive. Save your friend," the 24 voices said in near unison.

Shipp affirmed their response. "I believe in that with all my heart. I live by it. I'm willing to die for it. Every one of you matters to me. Every one of you is worth more than a thousand civilians put together. You're doing the most important work in the galaxy. You're fighting to win against rats who want nothing more than to devour and destroy everything we've built in our quarter of the galaxy. Every Principle you learned at SFU, I live by. My squad lives by them. We breathe them when we sleep. We consume them when we eat. But..."

He paused, making sure his audience was listening.

"That's not the number one reason I'm here. I'm here because I'm part of the Final War Generation. The Meridian Zone War may have been going for five hundred years, but it can end. And if you're with me, you believe it will end. With us as the victors."

The room murmured a bit. Shipp let them ponder his extreme minority beliefs. Then he continued.

"I know about 'war as a way of life.' And that's all we know. All we've ever known. But ending the war isn't just about taking the seven Meridian Zone planets. We can do that. We must do that. But it doesn't stop there. One day, we need to take the fight into their Territory. Sack their military space stations. Destroy their weapons manufacturing. Annihilate their attack ship construction sites. Wipe out their vanadium and erbium mining. And most of all, obliterate their Blackhead manufacturing facilities. That's what winning the war looks like. Once we take the Meridian Zone, they'll be on their heels. We press forward. We become the aggressors. We don't stop until we're finished. We can do it – in this generation. But it begins here. On Risner. A planet where this base and our two outposts are all we have."

He looked around the room again. He noted Juthelle, her eyes wide, her gaze fixed on him. She looked hungry. He continued speaking.

"I want to be there when the war ends. When the last base falls. I want to go so far into Wester Territory that we re-discover our planet of origin," he paused, then finished his presentation. "I love the Space Force, because you don't have to fully agree with me to be in my squad. I know this is not a popular view. Whatever inspires you to fight, it's a good reason. This is my reason. If it's yours too, I want you. I see no reason to fight a war you don't believe you can win. Let's win it in our lifetimes."

Shipp took a seat. Faraday stood up next and gave his presentation. Once he finished, Torres directed the new soldiers to the main hall, where they'd be able to spend a couple hours meeting the three squad leaders and key members of their squads. After that, Shipp, Faraday, and Rothman would make their final selections.

In the main hall, Shipp's first instinct was to find Juthelle. He found her, staring straight at him once he entered the room. He approached.

"Juthelle Brickson. Right?"

"Yes, and I'm–"

"I have a question for you. Why'd you take those five soldiers down the ravine when the rats attacked?"

Juthelle looked puzzled. Shipp wondered if she was confused by the question, or surprised he went straight to a tactical discussion. Her answer made it clear.

"Isn't that the right call? I knew before we got here the Wester base was east. They can't hit us against the west side of ours. Safest place to be since our guys were already so far from the transport ship."

Shipp nodded. "Very good. I'm impressed you could think so crisply minutes after landing here for the first time. You already knew where to go. No hesitation. And you did it to save your friends. That shows tactical understanding, research initiative, and leadership."

"I want on your squad," she said.

"I also want to say," Shipp ignored her, "I appreciated your salute. You're the only one who gave it. And I know it was sincere."

She smiled.

"Last question. What's your stance on the Final War Generation?"

The hunger filled her eyes again. But this time mixed with pain. He noted it, but waited for her response.

"I want on your squad," she said again.

He approached her and embraced her, speaking into her ear. "You're on it. My first choice. Come meet my other leaders."

Shipp led Juthelle over to James, along with Mixie, Zemmer, Ramad, and Blasé. They waited at a round table. Shipp and Juthelle sat and he introduced them.

"My other best leader is Gugbe. He's unconscious. Nearly died in our last battle before you arrived. Guys? This is Juthelle Brickson. What do you prefer we call you?"

"I like Juthelle. Or Elle."

Mixie smiled at her. She instantly loved having another woman who appeared to have a strong chance of joining Shipp's core squad.

Shipp began, "Juthelle has elite skills with the wizard, the electric pulse, and the AX-15. She rated number one in her class with the wizard. I don't have anyone with that level of proficiency on that weapon, other than me. But there's two main reasons she's joining us. She believes in Final War Generation, and because of the leadership and initiative she showed during the surprise attack. So, talk to her."

"Where you from?" Ramad started.

"Maxwell."

Mixie beamed. "I'm from Maxwell too. Which hemispheres?"

"Southwestern. City of Umber."

"I was northwestern, in the capital. I've been here almost two years. Shipp is the best leader you could ever work with."

"I concur," said James. "Shipp's my best friend. And his is the best squad. We're thrilled to have you. We'd love to hear your story if you want to share it. Or, we can give ours first if you prefer."

"I'd like to hear yours," said Juthelle, evading again the chance to share something of her past.

"You guys talk, I have to get back. Need three more," Shipp said, rising and departing, leaving James to lead the discussion.

"How'd you meet Shipp?" asked Juthelle. "And what's his first name?"

"Thomas Shipp," said James. "I met him our third day at SFU in beginning level combat strategy. The presenter was talking about how the Core Principle applies to basic combat, and why rescuing and saving fellow soldiers is as important as killing the enemy. We can't win the battle if we lose too many of our own."

"Which presenter is that?" Juthelle asked. "Sounds a lot like Carpath."

"Yes, Carpath. I'm glad he's still there," said James. "When he said that, I told him about a news report I'd seen in my early teens. It takes 658,438 Petersons, on average across over 120 planets in our Territory, to produce and support a single Peterson soldier. I told Carpath that's how valuable each of us is."

"He gave that stat to us," Juthelle said. "It was part of his presentation."

"Yeah, we talked about it a lot, and why it's true."

"Why is it true?" asked Blasé.

James nodded to Juthelle to answer. She did.

"Meridian Zone is thousands of light years from the edge of our Territory. Just to get here, we need all the ships and the manufacturing and resources and personnel to build them. We need our uniforms, food, ordnance, weapons, enough to last for months since resupplies can be infrequent."

Blasé nodded and put the rest together. "Training. Communication. Strategy and intelligence. Coordination with other bases and other Meridian planets, Space Force Command. Stations."

"Exactly," Juthelle was enjoying the freedom to express herself right out of the gate. "If the whole war were fought on one planet, we'd still need all that, but the scale is so much smaller. You can travel around a whole planet in less than a day. This war is across the galaxy. So it takes far more people to support each soldier than in a localized conflict."

"You got it," said James, returning to her original question for him. "And Shipp got it too. After class, he asked me about all this, and we just went from there. I'm from Fincher. My parents both lost relatives to the Westers and wanted to fight, but they couldn't meet the qualification standards. When I heard this stat on the news, I told them I would qualify."

"What'd they say?" Juthelle asked.

"There were happy with my goal, but then told me how hard it was to qualify. I'd never cared much about physical endurance or fitness, and I was kind of a loner at the time. But after that, I changed. Fitness. Academics. Leadership opportunities. I started studying the war, the weapons, history, famous battles and generals. After two years, people noticed. And when I got my SFU acceptance letter, my parents cried. Even my dad. I'd never felt so much pride and admiration from them. I got a big sendoff from my school. 800 students gave me an ovation. My picture is behind etched glass with nineteen others from our school who've made it to the Space Force. My whole district came to a big celebration the day I left Fincher."

"That's awesome," Juthelle said. "Do you guys all know this story already?"

"Some of it," said Ramad, liking Juthelle's interest in their squad. And maybe liking her too. "I knew where you guys met, but not the sendoff part."

"Well, I'm sharing it because she asked how I met Shipp. When I told him about my sendoff, he realized he'd lost something important and it was too late to get it back. He grew up on Saul. It's a dome planet. Manufacturing parts for space stations and vessels. Only 300,000 people. He got his acceptance letter, and his parents wanted the whole planet to celebrate. But he didn't want a party, and turned it down over and over. He just wanted to get his hands on the weapons, and get here."

"The celebration isn't just about him. It's about the people sending you off," said Mixie. "So he regrets it now, I'm sure. I wish my parents had done that."

"Shipp loves that stat about the 600,000. It speaks to how important we all are. And why saving your friend means so much. You're saving 600,000 people when you save one soldier," James said, exhaling, feeling a sense of contentment at sharing all this with everyone.

"I've been wanting this my whole life," said Juthelle. "I lost a grandfather I never met, and an older brother. My other brother is on a space station. I also lost... someone else."

At this, she turned silent. Whoever this person was, the wound was still raw. The others could see it, and they didn't press her.

"It's alright," James said. "We're glad you're here."

Renwar interrupted the chatter around the room. "Okay everyone, time for nutrients. Then we want the new arrivals to get some rest. You'll all know your assignments by tomorrow."

That night, Shipp, Rothman, and Faraday divvied up the remaining soldiers. Shipp was thrilled with all four of his new ones, but Juthelle excited him the most. If she was as good with the AX-15 as her dossier said, and if her other soft skills were as good as he'd already seen, she'd be a perfect fit to add to his core group, especially if Gugbe wasn't able to return to combat.

Renwar sent the four soldiers not chosen by any of the squad leaders to the northeast outpost since it had fewer than the southeast one. The next day, they departed on a Beast, and Pretoria sent with them a huge re-supply.

4

12 Westers

Running. Breathing. Sweating.

Trampling the Risner terrain one breath at a time, Shipp's fully restored squad of 48 soldiers jogged eastward in full combat gear – toward the Wester base. Except James. He was over his stomach virus, but the medics didn't want him exerting himself this much just yet. Each soldier had one weapon strapped around their back, another attached to their combat suit, and another in their arms. Ready for war.

This was just a fitness run, but Shipp was all business. He wanted his squad to remain perpetually in the best shape of their lives. Age didn't matter. You run. Fast. Hard. And long. And run they did. The terrain here consisted mostly of low rolling plains, punctuated by an occasional shrub or tree, and dotted with boulders and rocks. But mostly dry ground. The Wester base wasn't visible, but it would be if they kept going in this direction. After a few kilometers of nonstop running, Shipp slowed to a walk and halted.

Everyone caught their breath. But only for a minute. Then Shipp began his instruction.

"See that tree over there? Torres named it Stinkface. Ask him why if you care. Stinkface is important because our sensor web extends about twenty meters beyond it to the east. So if you're ever out here and you see Stinkface, you know to stop heading east. Know the sensor web boundary. It's in the rocks. Bushes. Trees. Some underground. Westers use the same tech."

"What about that tree?" Juthelle pointed to another one north of their position.

"That's Claw," said Shipp. "We have a sensor buried in the trunk. Heat and motion, like the others. If you stand next to Claw and look north, you'll see a low point beneath two hills in the distance. Let's go."

They marched up to Claw and scanned north.

"Pass that point and head east, and you'll reach the northeast outpost. Do not head east until you cross the river, which you can't see from here. But it's there. As far as we know, no Wester sensors beyond the river."

"Can you cross the river on foot?" asked another new soldier.

"You'll get wet up to your waist."

"And how do you know for sure there aren't Wester sensors in our web?" asked another new soldier. Shipp looked at Mixie to answer.

"We'd detect them when their soldiers enter our web, and if that happens, we send out a DSE to hunt for anything they planted," Mixie answered. "That's also how we know where their web begins. Because of when they destroy our sensors."

Without a word, Shipp took off running to the north. The rest of the squad followed on a two-kilometer run. They ran near full sprint until they reached the river. Shipp noted the breathing of his squad. Most were ready for more. But the four new soldiers doubled over. Hands on knees or behind the head. Sucking water.

"You four are going to need to level up. You get caught out in the open here, running is your only way out. Ground force soldiers are in better shape than anyone in the galaxy, pound for pound. Everyone else, you can hydrate too."

Shipp pointed out more geographical features, and then took his squad back west. A few kilometers later, he stopped again.

"Look south through your vision-enhancers, you can see our base. We're directly north. We're going to head southwest from here, and we'll end up in a maze of canyons and crevices. These are on both sides west of our base, with the big ravine sinking down between them, about a forty-meter drop from the cliff west of the base. We'll navigate the crevices, run down into the ravine, up the other side, and back into the base from the south entrance. Let's go."

Two minutes into the run, Shipp had just reached the beginnings of the canyons when his comm flashed.

"Hold," Shipp announced.

Everyone stopped and waited while Shipp listened.

"I got an alert. Silent Alert. Just went off. There were two of these while we were gone on our last battle. Both tripped sensors from the northeast, not far from where we just were. Very strange timing. We're abandoning the run. Head straight for the base. It's five minutes away at full speed. But we're walking because we need to stay alert. Spread out. No sound. Comms off. Stay alive."

"Save your friend," came the collective response.

Juthelle sidled up to Shipp and whispered to him, "Isn't it dangerous to run us that close to the edge if the Westers are showing up there?"

"Good question," Shipp whispered back. "Why are we here?"

"To win the war," she whispered without hesitation.

"Then it's more dangerous for them," he answered.

***

Inside the Peterson base, the Silent Alert tripped. Total blackness. Even though just an arm's length apart, no one could see each other until they activated their infrared vision enhancers. All anyone could see was the pulsing red beam encircling the walls just below the ceiling. It pulsed for five seconds and then went dark.

During a Silent Alert, nothing more than a whisper was permitted. Laughing was prohibited. Sex was prohibited.

Only whispers.

Most of the time, nothing would happen. But until the generals and Commander Vonn could determine the nature of whatever tripped the Alert, the whole base would be like a black hole on land. A void of lifelessness.

General Torres intercepted James on his way to his assigned defensive position.

He whispered, "Come."

James knew what Torres wanted with only one word. During a Silent Alert, squad leaders, generals, and commanders would often congregate in the Command Center. There, they would coordinate surveillance and strategic operations as they evaluated and prosecuted the Silent Alert. Sometimes squad leaders didn't need to be there. This time, they did.

Shipp was one of the three squad leaders at the main Risner base, with Faraday and Rothman being the others. But because Shipp was out on his fitness run, his role fell to his most trusted alternate. For him, that was Cam James.

James followed Torres to the Command Center, built in the center of the base and insulated by sound barriers which allowed for more natural conversation even during an Alert. He was joined there by the alternates for Faraday and Rothman, and the base leadership team.

"All alternates?" James asked.

"We want you three here again just like the last two Alerts, for continuity. Looking for patterns," said Vonn.

Commander Yesler Vonn led the entire Peterson Space Force on the planet Risner, which at the moment consisted of this base and the two outposts. At age 46, Vonn had amassed an impeccable reputation as one of the best and brightest leaders still in active ground duty. After leading the Peterson campaign on the planet Kora for six years, they assigned him to lead the re-establishment of the Peterson presence on Risner, and re-take the planet. Vonn possessed the perfect blend of combat experience, strategic planning, and administration. He could lead, he could fight, he could manage, and he could plan the victory celebration – if it ever got that far.

Everyone gathered around The Table. Vonn and Renwar waited like dark statues in a room lit only by monitors and small track lights.

The Table depicted the web of heat and motion sensors, on which all their battlefield analysis depended. In this war, no satellites orbited above in space. Wester and Peterson attack ships would just shoot them down, and that technology had been abandoned centuries ago. Aerial drones and atmospheric sensors would suffer the same fate. To see anything, both armies had to implant and conceal as many sensors as they could without being detected.

The problem was, the Westers had their own sensor array, and where the sensor arrays intertwined, that's where conflict could happen. One force might be out with a squad using Dolton Sensor Eradicators, better known as Metalheads or DSEs, to find and destroy enemy sensors. But the other force might be out trying to plant new sensors at the same time.

One side would plant sensors, the other would plant more, then the other would destroy some and plant their own. The other would return and destroy those and plant new ones themselves.

Back and forth.

A battle of sensors and Metalheads. War as a way of life, in microscale.

This seesaw positioning often caused Silent Alerts. But as James discerned soon after arriving, this Alert was different. As Vonn studied the data and consulted with various specialists, Renwar caught everyone up.

"We detected a group of twelve Westers moving into our sensor array, about twenty minutes after Shipp's squad ran through," Renwar began. "So we tripped the Alert. Can you find them on The Table?"

Always training. Always teaching. Every moment. Something to do and something to learn, all at the same time.

James and the other two alternates quickly found them. Twelve red dots pulsated a good distance away from the main Peterson base, but quite a distance from the Wester base too, which appeared on The Table in its known location even though it had no Peterson sensors nearby. The breadth of the sensor web was represented by a faint green hue covering those sections of the map. The sections without sensors were just black, other than geographical features.

The Westers had walked into the Peterson sensor web from the east, in a straight line from their own base toward the Peterson one, fairly close to Stinkface and Claw. Renwar continued.

"The weird thing is, they just stopped. They appear to be immobile. Just sitting there. Haven't moved for at least five minutes."

James looked up. "And that's strange? Just five minutes?"

Torres interjected. "In this part of the field, I don't think we've ever seen Westers immobile for that long. Not the entire group that close together."

Vonn entered the conversation. "Westers are always moving. Just like us. No one stands still that long in the web. The other thing is, twelve is an irregular number. Wester squads out planting sensors or running Metalheads usually have four to six. I've never seen a group of twelve that close together just sitting like that, ever. Not on Risner."

James commented, "Sitting still is scarier than moving."

Vonn clarified. "Anything different from the norm is scarier than the norm."

Alesha Shim, Faraday's alternate squad leader, chimed in.

"Why not just attack them out in the open like that? They don't have sensors on us in that area, right? Easy surprise attack, and we'd have the numbers. Shipp's got 48 out there right now."

Vonn looked around to see the others' reactions. Most were waiting for him to answer.

"Good question," he answered, intoning that he wanted someone else to take a stab at it first, but that he knew the answer. Always training, even in tense moments.

James gave his take. "Makes sense to me. Shipp could divide into four groups. Attack from three directions, with a fourth on watch."

Torres countered him. "Just like we have the surprise, they could have the surprise from their end. Look how close they are to the edge of our sensor web. Probably thirty meters. Close enough that other Westers could be waiting beyond."

"But we could take them out with a hive bomb or a dual cannon," Shim countered. "They're unguarded. How could they be watching us from that distance within our own web?"

"They might have an attack ship nearby," said James.

"Flypaper," said Torres.

"Wouldn't they have attacked Shipp if they had a ship above?" Shim persisted.

Vonn nodded approvingly, pleased at the conversation.

"Good." He paused to let them think some more. "What's the third core principle of combat?"

All three alternates spoke in unison, "Never under-estimate the enemy."

"And that means," said Vonn, "Unusual behavior should never be responded to carelessly, impulsively, or based on assumptions that don't have the benefit of sufficient information. Nothing that appears to be calculated can be responded to as if random."

"Okay," replied James. "I see that. They're certainly up to something. It's a deliberate act. So the plan is to stand back and observe them?"

"For now," concurred Renwar. "They can't approach without us knowing it, and they know it. Whatever they're doing, it's a safe bet they're waiting to see what we do in response."

Shim spoke up again. "What if us having no response is what they're hoping for?"

"That," Vonn nodded, "is why we're on Silent Alert. And we'll stay on it for at least two more hours. Maybe more. If they haven't budged by then, we'll re-evaluate."

5

Beautiful Starlight

An hour later, Shipp's squad returned and changed out of their combat gear. They couldn't shower because running water was prohibited during a Silent Alert. So, they returned to their domiciles. Shipp found Pretoria waiting for him in the dark, lying on their bed. He exhaled and lay next to her.

For Shipp, James was his rock. Horman was his escape. And Pretoria was his life. Being with her pacified him, gave him respite from the ever-present drumbeat of a forever war. He felt her hand next to his. So much softer and cleaner than his sweaty soldier hand.

"Wow." Shipp whispered in awe as they lay next to each other in silent blackness.

"Tired? How was the run?"

"Great. The four fresh ones were pretty winded. But I tell you, this girl Juthelle. She's gonna be great. Outstanding addition. The people coming out of SFU are of such high quality. To the core. Superb human beings."

"Glad you found someone you like."

Shipp lay silent for a bit.

"You stink," she needled him.

"I'm just getting started."

Her quiet laugh relaxed him. They lay in silence a few more minutes.

She broke it. "Still glowing about your mission?"

"Mmm," Shipp muttered.

Pretoria realized Shipp would never use the term 'glow' in a situation where twenty fellow soldiers just died. She tried again.

"What I mean is, did you achieve warfare satisfaction?"

She coined the term 'warfare satisfaction' a couple years back, and it struck a chord with her husband. He would never be happy in this war, never truly satisfied until it ended. It wasn't just about losing soldiers he had come to love as brothers and sisters. He carried a much deeper burden. Pretoria and Shipp realized some time ago that they and the current generation shared centuries of a psycho-emotional, even spiritual burden their forbears had laid upon them through five hundred years of the Galactic War.

The idea of warfare satisfaction was that it had limits far beneath those of true fulfillment and contentment – something most of them had never felt, and probably never would. Warfare satisfaction was a temporary respite from the savages of endless hatred and brutality. An episodic relief.

Finally, Shipp answered. "I am satisfied, but that's not it." He paused. "Every time I see you, all I think about is how much I love you. I'm so glad we're here. Every day I'm amazed you came with me. And we get to share everything. We get something that doesn't belong in a war."

He rolled his head to look at her, even though they couldn't see each other. She could sense his gaze through the black.

"Best decision I've ever made," she purred.

Pretoria knew Shipp had never gotten over her decision to choose a life with him rather than her other military career options. It seemed the one insecurity about him she could never stamp out. As if he wasn't worthy of her love. So, she took every opportunity to reinforce it.

"Someday, we'll both achieve what we set out to do," Shipp said.

"I already am."

"I know. You know what I mean."

Pretoria decided not to answer.

"Sorry," Shipp said. "I know you hate talking about it. I think I'm worried about Gugbe."

"It's okay. I'm worried too. I can't imagine how Trusha is feeling. He's a great man."

"That's another thing that amazes me," Shipp continued.

"What's that?"

"Every single soldier in my squad is the best version of themselves they could possibly be. And Vonn. And LaSalle. Every single one. Losing Gugbe would be like killing a work of art, you know?"

"That's true of every soldier. We're all works of art," Pretoria mused. Inside, she warmed with joy. She loved listening to Shipp's heart expressed so tenderly.

"You're the best work of art of all."

Pretoria made that one really easy for him, and he didn't whiff on it. She smiled and laughed to herself, so quiet he probably didn't even hear it.

"I wish more Petersons thought that way about each other," Shipp said.

"Me too."

They lay in silence for a while.

Pretoria broke it. "Will we be able to retrieve the bodies of the lost?"

"You might be able to send the southeast outpost after them."

"I'll work on that tomorrow."

Pretoria felt Shipp's hand caressing hers. As she thought of the twenty dead and of Gugbe, she felt the same thing as Shipp. The limits of warfare satisfaction. Undeserved happiness. Her husband had the right perspective on this war. We fight to end it. To stop the carnage of Peterson brothers and sisters. And we don't celebrate beyond reasonable limits until that day. She married her prince, and he was everything to her.

Shipp and Pretoria got married soon after landing on Risner. They wanted to finalize the union after starting their active service, not at the University. Pretoria insisted on that, because the war would be their life, and she wanted their fellow soldiers – their new friends – to see them wedded. Plus, their sterilizations kept getting delayed, right up until a few days before leaving SFU, and they didn't want to get married while still recovering from their surgeries.

Space Force marriages were forbidden to have children. Marriage was encouraged, but the military didn't have the capability to care for children in hostile zones. Because a military career could go on for decades, anyone choosing this life knew they would not have children. Pretoria made this agreement with herself, and never looked back. Shipp was the greatest man she'd ever known, and he was worth the sacrifice. One day, he would become a general, probably a commander.

As the spouse of a soldier, she chose to do something greater than have a family. She chose to give her life and marriage to the advancement of the Peterson Way against the Wester aggressors. And Shipp did the same. Just like friendships were encouraged, marriages were encouraged as long as the couple could serve in the same location. You couldn't have one on a space station and another on an attack ship. And you couldn't have one on a Meridian Zone planet and the other administering a space station.

Pretoria was a superb administrator. Her gift for details, organization, and systems management showed up way back at age seven, and her parents nurtured and encouraged it. At age nine, Pretoria got to plan the annual Space Age Anniversary party at her school. By age eleven, the school's admin took the week off before the party, because Pretoria could spearhead the whole thing. By seventeen, Pretoria had set a goal for herself: Join the Space Force and become the lead administrator on one of the Central Frontier space stations by age 30. It was a lofty goal. Only thirty-eight military space stations existed, and only eleven sat near the Central Frontier – the region bordering the Meridian Zone.

But she was that good. And when Shipp met her, he celebrated each achievement of hers that brought her closer to that goal. In Shipp she found a man with even more personal drive than her, something she never thought possible.

And so, the stage being set, a familiar, unexpected, but entirely predictable problem arose. That ancient dilemma, one that goes all the way back to the time when humans only lived on one planet called Earth, now buried somewhere back in the corner of Wester Territory, just a distant memory for the Petersons.

Love.

Pretoria fell in love with Shipp. And Shipp fell in love with Pretoria. As their time at Space Force University neared its end, they had some hard decisions to make. She was in admin. He was in combat. She wanted to lead a space station. He wanted to fight on the front lines of the Meridian Zone.

Both wanted the other to do what they set out to do.

Shipp considered altering his plans. He sought a path that would still allow him to achieve his goals from a space station. Pretoria considered altering her plans. She wanted to lead a space station, but what she really wanted was to help win the war.

And that's what decided it for her.

Without even trying, Shipp won her over with his Final War Generation idealism. Roy chided him for this all the time. James admired him for it, but didn't share his confidence.

Pretoria had never considered it until meeting Shipp. But the more he talked about it, the more it inspired her. She wanted to surpass the limits of warfare satisfaction. She realized that for Shipp, the Peterson Space Force wasn't just a career. It was his very reason for existing – because this war needed to be won, and now was the time.

Once the Westers were destroyed and annihilated, beaten back far into their own Territory with their forces so depleted that they could never rebuild them, peace could prevail. The idea of winning, of settling on Meridian Zone planets, of building instead of destroying – that's what really pulsed within Pretoria all this time. "I want to build things," she realized. "Leading is building. And building is leading."

Pretoria discovered that if she were able to lead and build on the front lines, she would be helping build something new, something that would last forever when they won the war. She didn't follow Shipp to Risner just for love. She followed him to battle because of what he believed, that intangible driving force inside him that no instructor could teach. And once she latched on to his idealism, they were inseparable.

But Shipp never could fully accept it. He couldn't believe anyone, especially a woman he loved, would abandon her lifelong goals to go with him somewhere new. But Pretoria always had the same answer whenever this came up:

"Goals aren't etched in stone. They're drawn with starlight."

It was a quote from a famous book written a couple hundred years back by some motivational idiot. But Pretoria changed it. The original said 'written,' not 'etched.' She liked etched better because of the sense of permanence. And it just sounded better, because etched evoked a better parallel with drawn.

Pretoria loved the line. She always smiled when saying it, and giggled a little at the sound of it. And then her smile would make Shipp smile.

Mostly because after months of hearing it, he still didn't have a clue what it meant.

But 'starlight' is a beautiful word, revered by many Petersons, but by Shipp and Pretoria in particular. It was a word that deepened their bond back at SFU. Back then, Pretoria and Shipp shared one of their favorite life experiences in an observatory room at the very bottom level of the space station. From there, you could view the surrounding space as a 360-degree panorama. Pretoria only went there two times with Shipp.

One night during an off day, they wandered down to the observatory. Standing on the glass floor, their feet and entire bodies were surrounded by stars, blackness, and the planet Triman, which the SFU station orbited.

Another man showed up and broke their solitude. At first his intrusion annoyed them a bit. He was older, in his fifties, and not an active soldier. He was a support worker who helped facilitate some weapons training courses and also performed cleaning duties.

The man began to tell them about an amazing visual phenomenon that happened every so often on the planet Triman. He discovered it several years back in this very room. Ever since then he came down here on the specific dates and times he had mapped out for when it might occur.

Triman's sun had to be at the perfect angle. At most, this visual delicacy could only occur for a few weeks during each Triman year. To see it, the particular section of the planet where it happened needed to have few if any clouds. And, the SFU station had to be at the optimal position in its orbit. The man had figured out that with the right cloud cover, he might only see this sight one day per year.

After hearing all this, Shipp and Pretoria realized they were here on a very special day. On that day, Triman rotated below them, without a cloud in sight.

They waited.

The man sat there, barely moving. Waiting. Waiting. Slowly, the sunlight crept around Triman, a small planet well-known for its massive mountain ranges divided by huge canyons and ravines. Some of the biggest in the known galaxy.

The far side of the planet basked in sunlight, and the near side facing them remained dark.

Then, a streak of light flickered across the planet. And then another. Over a period of a few minutes, streaks of light broke through the canyon-sized gaps between a massive north-south mountain range. It looked like fingers of light reaching across the planet.

Then, the mountains began to glow. As the sunlight baked the far side of the mountain range, but kept them backlit from the station's vantage, the edge of the mountains turned yellow, then orange, then red. The red line looked as if someone had drawn it with a pencil across the planet's surface. By this point, the fingers of light now stretched thousands of miles beyond into the darkness on the near side of the planet.

The fingers of light weaved through mountains, shifting their shape every so often as a new mountain was summitted by the sun. A finger would bend in one direction, and then in another, then combine with a different part of another finger, and then vanish. Trembling almost as if alive. It looked like a hand of light massaging the planet. Eventually, fingers began merging as the sun rose over the mountain range.

At this point, the man smiled with anticipation. His mouth opened in awe. He stood and leaned against the glass.

The finale was coming.

Once the sun reached the right spot, all the remaining fingers of light got suddenly consumed as light burst across the planet's surface. In the blink of an eye, a whole section of the planet became bathed in light. The man exhaled in a gasp of wonder. His eyes filled as he beheld the beauty of this vision he had discovered. His voice deepened and wavered as he finally spoke.

"You're the only other people I know who have seen this," he said. He stood in silence at the wonder, pondering whatever memories and pains this celestial wonder seemed to pacify, if just for the moment. Then, he turned to leave.

"Thank you," said Shipp. "Thank you very much sir." The man nodded and left.

Pretoria leaned against Shipp, and they continued gazing out into space, saying nothing. His hand tightened around her waist. This starlight moment deepened their bond, because it seemed to indicate their shared destiny, just like the light crawling over Triman's mountain ranges. They were destined to follow each other into battle, wherever that may lead.

***

Back on Risner, as the Silent Alert continued, Shipp and Pretoria lay next to each other in the stillness for a couple hours. Barely moving. Touching each other's hands now and then. Whispering light conversation. But mostly just breathing in the silence.

Even though galactic peace remained a far-off distant hope, this moment offered a tiny measure of it.

Shipp thought about her face, even though he couldn't see it. He remembered how beautiful she looked that day on the observation deck. He thought about that moment often. Female beauty hadn't been a priority for most of his life, and he had set it aside as best he could once he committed to SFU. But in that moment and others during his second and third year especially, Pretoria had impressed upon him that she was a woman meant to be in space, among the stars. Not planet-bound in one place her whole life.

Finally, after a couple hours, the wall lights turned back on. Silent Alert over. Shipp and Pretoria turned their heads to each other and smiled. Shipp made his move. But she held her hands against him.

"I love you," she said. "But you still stink."

Shipp grinned. He arose, undressed, and hopped in the washer. He re-emerged minutes later and lay on the bed next to his wife. They embraced, kissed, and entered into passionate love.

6

Peterson Response

Several hours after Vonn ended the Silent Alert, the twelve Westers finally departed. Shipp met up with James to be briefed on recent events. By now, every soldier and admin on the main base and both outposts knew the situation. The actions of the enemy on this day had everyone guessing. The strange behavior had no equal in the history of the war.

Shipp learned the twelve Westers sat there, almost motionless, for over five hours. Vonn sent out automated sentry bots to observe them and confirm they were actually human, and not some kind of android technology. An unlikelihood in the extreme, but they had to be sure. Android soldiers had been tried about two hundred years back, with limited success. The cost of production never measured up to how much less capably they performed in combat. After a few decades of trying to make them work, both territories abandoned the idea.

But anything was possible. Maybe the Westers had a breakthrough in android technology. When the small bots came within sight of the enemy soldiers, they confirmed it:

The Westers were human.

The puzzling nature of that behavior kept the generals talking for hours. Shipp and James both attended most of the discussion. It was extremely rare for the generals to hold closed-door meetings and not allow anyone else in, and this was no exception. Even in high level strategy meetings, anyone could take part unless they had other assigned tasks.

Questions – even basic ones – weren't seen as distractions or interruptions. Brand new soldiers had permission to listen and at times participate. Vonn had the final say. His orders were followed. But the Petersons placed an extremely high value on a knowledgeable, informed military. Strategic planning could, at any moment, depend upon a single soldier who happened to be in a particular place, or have unique on-site intelligence that no one else had. That's why they held such high standards for acceptance to Space Force University.

You had to have brains and brawn to make it in the Peterson Space Force.

But equality is impossible. There would always be certain soldiers who, for whatever reason, seemed to have an extra set of giftings. Natural talent, keen insight, the ability to think clearly even in the most tense situations, superb use of weaponry, emotional resilience – all these and other traits could not be spread equally among the forces.

And Shipp had distinguished himself, beginning at SFU, and again since arriving on Risner. A rising star, he had earned deep respect among his squad and the generals.

Discussion dragged on. Faraday, Shipp, and Rothman interacted with the generals – Vonn, Renwar, and Torres – as well as LaSalle who took notes.

"We sent sentries and Metalheads out to the exact spot they were sitting," noted Renwar. "Just dirt. They didn't plant any rodents or sensors. Didn't discharge any chemicals. No digging. They really just sat there."

Torres added, "For five hours and fourteen minutes."

"New opinions?" Vonn asked.

"I still think it was a head game. They're just trying to get our comets crossed," said Renwar.

"Toying with us? For five hours?" said Torres.

"Why not? We've got centuries."

"I said new opinions," Vonn interrupted. "Yes, that's possible. I don't buy it though."

The room was silent for a couple minutes while everyone entertained new explanations.

"Maybe they were cannon fodder," Faraday broke the silence.

Shipp and Rothman laughed. Renwar, Torres, and even Vonn didn't seem to get the reference. Shipp picked up on it.

"You guys don't know cannon fodder?"

They shook their heads.

"We had a history presenter at SFU talk about that. It was an ancient battlefield strategy used back on Earth, I guess. Generals would send some of their own soldiers into situations where they knew the soldiers would get killed. They did it purely to aid in achieving a larger combat objective."

"They sacrificed their own soldiers?" Renwar asked, incredulous.

Shipp nodded. "Barbaric, right? Our presenter wanted us to understand how poorly soldiers used to be valued, and how much we've evolved since then."

"Cannon fodder. I never heard that before," Vonn confirmed. "Very interesting. You think the Westers might be willing to kill their own soldiers just to achieve an objective?"

"Just an idea," Faraday replied. "We all know rats don't value life like we do."

Everyone concurred with that.

Shipp thought of another interpretation of the Westers' behavior.

"I think it was a decoy. They knew we'd fixate on their guys. Somewhere, the rest of them were up to something else."

Vonn's head snapped in Shipp's direction. This was new. Somehow, it rang true to him.

"Yeah."

Renwar noted Vonn's concurrence with Shipp. "Okay, what? Where should we look that we aren't already looking? We've got sensor webs around both outposts and the main base for hundreds of meters."

Shipp was ready. "I don't know. But we should stock up the bunkers with extra ammo, extra firepower, and extra weaponry. We should prep the Beasts. If they're going to try something new, we need to be ready."

"What if they're out beyond the sensor webs?" asked Rothman.

"What if they are?" responded Faraday. "You wanna take squads out to look for Westers we don't know are there, and if they are, they'll have the advantage because they're probably hoping we do exactly that?"

"I'm not suggesting a course of action." Rothman replied. "We can't surveil the entire planet. They could be anywhere outside our array. The question is, what are they doing there? Building a new outpost of their own?"

"Right, but why would they need to decoy us like that if they're doing something we can't see anyway?" said Faraday.

"You're right," Shipp agreed. "Doesn't make sense."

Vonn jumped in. "It does makes sense. As long as we're fixated on their little fireless campout, it gives them some extra cover. They did it deliberately."

He turned to Shipp.

"We'll take Shipp's lead. Arm up the bunkers. Especially with Krocks for surface to air. Send out roving patrols from the outposts, but remain within the sensor web."

And with that, increasing the weapons and ordnance supplies in the bunkers became the task of the day. And the next day. And the next day. Weapons that had been concentrated inside the main base got disbursed among the array of sixteen bunkers that littered the areas around it.

Torres managed the overall weapons dispersal. Shipp received charge of half the bunkers, and Rothman the other half. Faraday's squad would remain within the base in the event of an attack. Rothman and Shipp's squads would fan out among their bunkers if the situation called for it.

Shipp delighted himself and his entire squad with the weapons dispersal task. Shipp loved weapons. His enthusiasm for them was contagious.

First, Shipp increased the supply of AX-15's to twelve per bunker, each with eight extra ammo packs. He doubled the number of propellers, also called wizards, from one to two. Currently, all the bunkers already had a 5cm wizard. Shipp added a 10cm one to go with it, plus an additional 5cm one at the bunkers nearest the western edge of the sensor web. He feared an attack from their backside, even though the terrain of canyons around the deep ravine was much more difficult to traverse.

He doubled the rations of prop-plusses as well. More commonly called hive bombs, Shipp knew that in certain combat situations this was the most useful weapon and he didn't want them to be far away. He also added a MagTon rifle to alternating bunkers. Currently, there were zero since it was less likely they'd use this weapon on Risner's open plains and rolling hills. But Shipp wanted them available.

Next, he assigned three pulse rifles to each bunker, as these could be highly effective in certain situations. The pulse rifle had played a huge role in their last battle, immobilizing large swaths of the 224 Westers since they weren't wearing combat suits, making them easy to kill.

Shipp also bolstered the supply of dual cannons to six per bunker, up from the current two. This weapon had proven to be one of the most useful in ground combat on Risner, due to the uneven ground.

Shipp's favorite weapon was the Mossamer-24, which combined the traditional rounds of the AX-15 with an electric pulse function and a smaller version of the Blackhead piercing K-rocket launcher.

For those like Shipp who could master its size, shape, multiple functions, and the reloading procedures, the Mossamer-24 could enable a single soldier to infiltrate and annihilate an entire enemy camp. Shipp put three Mossamers at each bunker. Though only about half his soldiers rated proficient with the Mossamer, he didn't want any of them to be without it.

The last major ground assault weapon employed by Shipp in preparation for a Wester assault was the one that struck fear into attack ships – the Kampraseuth rocket launcher. It had a terrible name, because 'rocket' sounded so menial. The Petersons called them Krocks. Who knows what the Westers called them. Shipp wanted two Krocks at each bunker, but Vonn overruled him on this, considering them too valuable to leave that many exposed. He authorized one per bunker. Shipp had to acquiesce.

Shipp also worked with Pretoria's team to construct four additional bunkers, two north, and two south of the base. He had Juthelle lead the other new members of his squad to construct one of them. On the third day of preparation, Shipp joined her and the others and helped them work.

"How old were you when you knew you wanted to be in the Space Force?" Shipp asked her while they worked.

"I was ten," she answered. "My oldest brother got accepted to SFU. I knew I wanted to follow him."

"Is that the one you lost?"

"Yeah."

Shipp honored her loss with some silence.

"You never wanted to do anything else?"

"No. Did you?"

"No. But I never realized how great an achievement it is to get here until it was happening. I remember, when I was leaving Saul for SFU, I was on a transport ship, and I met this guy, a neurosurgeon. He was, I guess, envious when I told him where I was going."

"Totally. He didn't qualify?"

"He said he couldn't meet the physical stamina thresholds. Tried and failed all three times. Before that day I knew people looked up to soldiers. But this guy was like 45. Talented. Smart. Successful. And he was jealous of me, an 18-year-old military student."

"All the best students in my school wanted to make it to SFU too. Most didn't," Juthelle said.

"You pass your first time?"

"Of course I did," she smiled at him, knowing by now how much Shipp valued confidence and a high self-worth.

"We have the best job in the galaxy," Shipp said.

"What's this?" Another soldier drew their attention. He pulled something from the wall of earth. A small metallic object. Shipp ambled over to take a look.

"I know what this is," Shipp said. "You just found this, right here?

"Yeah. In the dirt."

"This is a sensor, but it's at least two hundred years old. I studied these in a manual a couple years back."

"Does it still work?" asked Juthelle.

"Doubt it. But even if it does, it's not connected to any systems."

"How do you know?"

Shipp got their attention and held it up.

"Because this one was made by the Westers."

Shipp's revelation floored them. So did the implications. It meant that the Westers, over two hundred years ago, held this very ground. But the Petersons knew they also used to hold it, about forty years back, so this Wester device came from before that.

"I wonder how many times this ground has changed sides," Shipp mused.

At that moment, Mixie and Ramad ran up to him, excited.

"Gugbe's awake," Mixie beamed.

"He's standing up and walking. He remembers everything," Ramad added.

A wide smile spread on Shipp's face. "Is he approved for combat again?"

"Yes!"

"Let's plan a meeting with the six of us," Shipp said. "We'll welcome him back, update him on everything that's happened since. You set the time and place."

"Jonas," Mixie said and started to leave. She turned back when Shipp called her out.

"Mixie. Make up something fun for us to do for him. Be creative."

She smiled, "Right."

A few hours later, Shipp, Mixie, Ramad, Zemmer, and Blasé waited in a small meeting room when Gugbe opened the door. The base didn't have much in the way of decorations, but Mixie had worked with Pretoria to create a sign saying "Welcome back, rat killer." Gugbe loved it, and he got hugs and backslaps from his friends. They didn't lay a finger on his still-bandaged head.

When the initial joy died down, Mixie presented Gugbe with a wine allotment reserved only for special occasions. She had won permission for this from General LaSalle, and secured six of them from Pretoria. Gugbe received the first pouch, and once he sipped it and breathed in the fragrance, the others opened and drank theirs.

"Thank you guys," said Gugbe. "They told me I was out for days, but it felt like a nap. I'm so glad to see all of you."

"How do you feel?" asked Zemmer.

"About normal. My head hurts a little, but only on the surface. None of you got hurt? How many did we lose?"

"Well, from our squad—" Shipp began.

"That is classified," Mixie interrupted. To Gugbe, "We've got a prize for you."

"Oh yeah?"

"No it isn't," Shipp smiled at her, wondering what she was doing.

"You have to answer some trivia," she explained. "I've got ten questions. If you get seven right, you win something beautiful."

"Seven!" bellowed Shipp. "You're making it easy on him. That's not the Peterson Way."

"They're hard questions."

"So give him three guesses. I say he has to get all ten. For that prize?"

"Riding me hard again, eh Shipp," said Gugbe.

"I carried you for like five kilo—"

"Shipp!" Mixie stopped him again. "You're spoiling my trivia."

"Oh, I see. Battle trivia. My favorite."

Mixie then began quizzing Gugbe, making him guess things like the kill ratio, the number of dead Westers, who carried Gugbe back, who found him first, and various other details from the battle in which he nearly died. With three guesses allowed for each question, Gugbe answered six correct. Mixie decided this would be a fun way to debrief Gugbe on the battle.

"Well, too bad you don't get the prize," Shipp smacked his gums after the last question. "What a shame."

"What was it?" Gugbe wondered in deadpan.

"You'll never know. Go back to your domicile. We're done here."

Shipp knew Gugbe suspected a trick, like something in his room waiting for him. Gugbe arose and opened the door. Behind it, an admin named Trusha stood waiting. Gugbe smiled at his flame. She gave him a sultry hello, then threw her arms around him, kissing him repeatedly.

Afterward, he turned back to his fellow soldiers, grinning. "My prize?"

Shipp shook his head. "Mixie, you were supposed to tell her to leave when he failed the trivia."

"I think my comm is broken again," she feigned annoyance.

Shipp and the others laughed.

Then Shipp called Gugbe back in, "Thank you Trusha. We actually need him for longer. We're going to have a real military meeting now."

"No problem."

Trusha pulled the door shut, and Shipp and the others updated Gugbe on the Silent Alert and everything related to the strange behavior of the Westers.

7

Wine and Blood

It took several weeks for Shipp's weapons dispersal plan to take shape. Spreading the weapons around went fast. That was the easy part. The real work involved developing procedures for what to do if an attack came, and then training on it. Who would be expected to go where? If that soldier was dead or incapacitated, who else would take over their role? Which bunker was each soldier assigned to? Who was in charge? Who was responsible for communication between each group and with the main base?

Why hadn't this already all been done? Because a war that had lasted over five hundred years didn't look the same as one lasting five years or five months.

Everything became about the minutia.

This war rarely saw any grand battles or epic conquests. It was about holding ground. Making the enemy decide not to attack even after they spent months planning it. Destroying enemy sensors with Metalheads. Keeping clear lines of sight. Surveillance. Training. Fitness. Preparation. Nonstop preparation. You could spend five years preparing before you finally got to do some actual fighting.

But that's why precision planning was so critical. And that's why they created whole new procedures for every scenario. The Westers had struck first. They didn't fire a shot, and nothing happened. But they *did* something. And that forced a Peterson response that in all likelihood, the Westers would never experience.

This war was like a game of chess, except the pieces hardly ever reached the other half of the board. Just a bunch of positioning, posturing, and preparation. And then after everything was in place and the assault was ready, something else unexpected happened, and everyone returned to the starting positions and began again from scratch.

For this round of preparation, Shipp broke his squad into groups of six, with one person in charge of each group. James led one group, and Shipp took charge of one as well, in addition to coordinating the full squad. Shipp's squad included his elite crew of Mixie, Zemmer, Gugbe, Blasé, and Ramad. He spread the four new soldiers among four different squads.

If a surprise attack did happen, each soldier's first task was to find their team of six and head to their assigned bunker, unless the situation dictated a revised course of action. And multiple scenarios for revised courses of action got developed in extensive detail.

Shipp drilled his team on knowing the bunker locations. He forced his squad to walk blindfolded between them until they could still find the nearest one. It all depended on the angle from which you left your current bunker, and your awareness of specific natural features in the area such as a bush, a boulder, or a root in the ground.

They drilled. They prepared. They role-played. They simulated. The Peterson forces did this for months.

But the surprise attack didn't come.

Two months went by. Then three. Then four. No attack. And no more Westers sitting around motionless. But Vonn still considered the entire operation a huge advancement. Because now, the station was better prepared, no matter what might happen next. After the first month, he ordered the outposts to implement smaller versions of the same plan.

Shipp reached a point where he longed for the Westers to attack, because he was so confident in his plan. Pretoria reminded him of how clever and cruel the Westers were. And he knew it. Don't get overconfident. Ever. But his plan had so many redundancies built in, he could not imagine a scenario where they wouldn't be able to fight off an attack.

One late morning, Shipp, Pretoria, James, and Horman sat around the table sharing their weekly pleasure drink.

Each soldier received one 'pleasure food' per week. It could be food or drink. Officially, it was called a nutritional reward, and soldiers could pick from a variety of choices, while supplies lasted. The pleasure foods led to Pretoria becoming known as the queen of the base, because soldiers would request particular pleasure foods, and it was up to her to secure them, if possible. And she came through time and time again. Lately however, no re-supplying transport ships had arrived for months due to attack ship activity in Risner's vicinity.

These four friends usually chose drinks. Today, with fitness training completed, they had a couple hours to talk, laugh, and encourage each other to stay strong, stay tough, stay alert, and stay whole.

Wholeness – being known, being loved, being cared for – the Petersons considered this an essential component of the long deployments typical of ground forces assigned to planets in the Meridian Zone. You could spend years here. This was your family. Even if you went "home," you didn't really go home; you went to an orbiting space station. Very, very rarely a soldier might get a break on a non-combat planet.

The Space Force became your life, and everyone knew it when they signed up.

Wholeness meant inner equilibrium. It meant you know why you're here, why it matters, and what you have to do the next day. It meant emotional balance. Physical health. Social engagement. Honesty. Vulnerability. Healthy and rich relationships took high priority. Base protocols built in time when soldiers and admin could count on seeing the same people regularly.

Today, the four friends discussed planets they had visited in their former lives. After James finished his story about a planet he visited as a child, Pretoria spoke.

"I've been to Maxium. With Thomas, not long after we met."

"Maxium," said Horman. "I've heard amazing things about that place. Never got to go."

"It was worth every moment. It's got these huge marble formations that go down hundreds of feet into the ground, just unbelievably beautiful."

"That's a dome planet, right?" asked James. Shipp nodded, then added, "Only a few thousand people live there. They've got greenhouses and have planted vegetation within the domes, but the oxygen produced can only support a certain number of people without using tanks."

"All the best sights are outside the dome," resumed Pretoria. "The guide took us to this one spot where the marble is so clear, that when the sun hits it at a certain time of day, the whole rock fills with light, and you can see all the way down, through the rock."

"Wow. What color?" asked James.

Pretoria looked at Shipp. "We argue about the color. I say it's a dark lavender. He says light maroon."

Horman laughed. "Sounds like you both have it wrong. Surely there is another color that is, in fact, dark lavender and light maroon."

"Sangria," said James.

The other three turned. Huh? "Since when do you know anything about colors," taunted Shipp. "Did you take a painting elective at SFU?"

"He was the only one in the class," quipped Horman. "And he still failed."

"Did you just make that up, Cameron?" asked Pretoria. "I thought sangria was a wine."

"James doesn't drink alcohol, remember?" Shipp reminded her.

Once the chiding finished, James explained, "I had a cousin, a good friend of my dad, who died on Lavoisier when I was ten. About fifteen years ago I guess. Wow. Anyway, in his case, they were able to get his remains sent back to his family."

Everyone's smiles faded, and they listened intently.

"I remember going to their house, and seeing this box. It was about a half meter long. My little brother asked how his whole body could fit in there. I was old enough to know it couldn't, but I couldn't quite figure out how to explain it. My mom told me most of his body had been incinerated down to ashes, but that they probably kept a few of his bones intact, so the family would have something to see and hold on to."

"I've never heard of that," said Shipp, intrigued.

"I remember they opened it," James continued, "and inside there were four thin, long bones, his ulna and radius from both arms. Plus four of his fingers, the metacarpals still connected. No thumb. Then a jar with the ashes. His mom picked up the finger bones and held them. She had this peaceful smile on her face."

"So rare your family ever gets to see you again after this," said Pretoria. "What a gift for them."

James nodded. "Anyway, the box was coated with a soft kind of paper with a deep red color. And the two sets of arm bones were held together left and right with ribbons of the same color. My dad told me it was sangria, which the Peterson Space Force uses for situations like this because it's like a blend of wine and blood."

"Wine and blood," mused Pretoria. "Wine and blood."

"The royal life," said Shipp. "Cam, I never knew that about you. Thank you."

Pretoria snuck in the last word. "The marble was still dark lavender."

Just at that moment, the main lights went dark. The emergency lights flashed, and the Battle Alert audio blip started to sound. It was a quick, one-eighth second burst of sound, every two seconds, to alert everyone of an imminent battle and to immediately find their commanders and get briefed.

Explosive impact from dual cannon fire shuddered outside the base. Shipp, James, and Horman jumped to their feet.

Pretoria stood up, smiled at her love, clasped his hand in hers, and said, "See you later."

He replied, "I love you."

8

First Attack

Shipp fastened his headset and listened to Renwar calmly relay the situation to the three squad leaders.

"We're taking enemy fire from the west side of the base. They must have circled all the way around us while remaining outside the sensor web. So far dual cannon volleys and traditional rounds. Looks like they're trying to break our exterior barricades and samarium shields, which we extended after the first volley. Or possibly bait us to come fight them out in the open. No action on the east."

Renwar paused.

Shipp, Rothman, and Faraday all said "Jonas."

Shipp realized Renwar was probably listening to Vonn – the real architect of whatever plan was forthcoming. Hence the delay. Renwar really was a button-pusher when it came to actual battles. Too bad. But he decided to give Renwar the benefit of the doubt, since whatever they knew, they barely knew, because the attack was only minutes old.

Finally, Renwar continued.

"Implement Shipp's defense plan, formation Kora."

"Jonas that."

Formation Kora meant Shipp's 48-soldier squad would break into groups of six to the south of the main base, in selected bunkers among those they had constructed and armed. Rothman's squad would do the same to the north. Faraday's squad would remain at the ready in the base.

Shipp's squad assembled around him, fully armed and ready to fight and defend their right to occupy Risner. Shipp relayed the orders. Mixie,

Zemmer, Gugbe, Blasé, and Ramad followed Shipp outside to their bunker, about ninety meters from the main base.

As they exited, another volley of dual cannon fire impacted the samarium shields surrounding the west side of the base. Most of the explosive power from the missiles got repelled outward, with fire leaping away from the Peterson base. It looked as if the Westers were basically firing blind at the structure. But eventually, they knew the shields would weaken and they would be able to inflict damage on the main structure. They also probably couldn't see the Petersons spreading out north and south of the base because of the sizable drop in elevation to the west.

This natural height advantage was one reason the Petersons built their first base at this location, because it made the Westers unlikely to attack from this side. With one side 'defended' by the terrain, the Petersons could focus their defenses on the other three, which included the nearest Wester base to the east. And yet, here were the Westers, attacking from lower elevation on the west.

The deafening dual cannon explosions assaulted and buckled the base's samarium shields. Shipp watched and listened as he jogged toward his crew's bunker, trying to puzzle out why the Westers would choose an attack from this side. Even if they broke through the detached shield structures, dual cannons wouldn't be able to penetrate the exterior Blackhead-coated walls of the actual base. That would require Krocks.

Shipp's crew reached their bunker as dual cannon fire continued to shell the base. They heard one of the shields fracture, that familiar sound that always made Shipp think of a huge piece of glass breaking while a vehicle decelerated. His crew unearthed the extra weaponry.

Shipp broke out his Mossamer-24 and peered through the scope. He had chosen this bunker for his crew because he could see partway down into one of the small canyons to the west, and farther beyond to the lower flat ground on the distant horizon.

"Eyes out. Tell me what you see!"

All five of his crew followed his lead from different spots around the bunker.

Zemmer called out almost immediately:

"Pack of rats huddled beyond the canyon. They're far away. 1.2 kilos."

Shipp hustled around and prostrated himself next to Zemmer. Through his scope he could see them. About twenty Westers. Shipp zoomed in. They were reloading dual cannons. He got on his comm.

"Torres. We got about twenty rats 1.2 clicks to the west beyond the canyons. Dual cannons."

Torres replied, "Jonas that. Which canyon?"

Torres had named all the canyons. Shipp replied, "Looks like it's, uh... the Arrowpoint Canyon. We can see them through that canyon on the flatter ground beyond. Triangulate that from my position."

"Jonas."

Shipp waited while Torres, Renwar, and Vonn calculated the approximate location of the Wester soldiers based on Shipp's position, through Arrowpoint Canyon.

Soon, Faraday and twelve soldiers burst out of the southern main base entrance armed to the teeth, and took position behind the remaining samarium shields. Moments later, they fired a volley of dual cannons and hive bombs – enough to do significant damage if they hit the heart of the Westers.

Shipp and Zemmer watched through their scopes. The Westers scattered. The dual cannons impacted just beyond the main group. The hive bombs exploded. Shipp's lip curled as he could see at least two Westers fall. He updated Torres.

"You were about ten meters beyond the heart of them with the cannons. Hive bombs nailed a handful."

Just then, all the Petersons startled. Their eyes searched the sky at the distinct sound of Krocks launching, at least four of them. The thin white smoke trails rose up from somewhere to the north of the Westers that Shipp's squad could see.

He barked into his comm:

"Get Faraday out of there! They just launched four Krocks!"

Too late.

The rockets careened at lightning speed and impacted near the front of the main base, pretty close to where Faraday's twelve soldiers probably were. The sound of the metal twisting and warping made everyone pause. Did they break through the base's wall? It was hard to tell from Shipp's vantage.

"Eyes out everyone! Don't get distracted!" Shipp yelled to his eight crews.

More of Faraday's squad bolted from the southern entrance to help their fellow soldiers. Shipp and Zemmer confirmed that the Westers were divided in at least two groups, but they could only see one of them. And the one they could see began advancing forward, out of their sight below the rim of the ravine. The other group resumed dual cannon fire, eventually taking out two more samarium shields. Most of the western side of the base was now exposed, and with Krocks, the Westers would succeed in breaking through the walls.

"Move up everyone. Bunker fifteen. One five," Shipp ordered.

His six-member crew broke out of their bunker and high-tailed it to the bunker farthest south of the main base. Shipp ordered his other crews to also move south and west to new bunkers, as far from the main base as possible. Once there, Shipp had almost no time to settle in when they heard the hollow thunking sound of MagTons being fired and flying through the air. That meant the Westers had succeeded in breaking through the wall.

"They're targeting the hole they just blew in the side of the base!" Shipp yelled into his comm.

"We've already evacked, that area," Torres replied.

The MagTons flew inside, impacted, and exploded. Shipp could see fire pouring out of the base.

"Torres! They've got two groups, at least! Group farther north fired the Krocks. They're probably getting ready for a second round. We have to advance now!"

"Negative Shipp. Can't risk losing that many in open combat. They're baiting us out."

"If we don't go now, they'll just keep launching Krocks."

"Don't go down that canyon Shipp! Stay back. They will either advance or stay put. Fire from your positions."

Six of Shipp's eight crews began firing dual cannons. Shipp called Rothman, since her squad was north of the base.

"Karel, don't reveal your position by firing. Keep out of sight. Hold your fire. We're hitting them from here."

"Jonas. What about–"

Four more Krocks deafened everyone for a moment, and tore into another section of the main base. Rothman resumed.

"Shipp? I'm blind here. Hold on, Renwar's calling." She disconnected. Shipp called Torres.

"Torres! They're gonna rip apart the whole west side with those! Fire back!"

Torres turned on his comm to reply, and Shipp could hear Vonn screeching at someone. Shipp heard something about lost visibility. But the last attack must have damaged the base's comm tech.

"Shipp! Wait for orders. We need to ------"

Shipp turned to his crew.

"We're going now. Westers don't know these canyons like we do."

Shipp called James. "We're going down Arrowpoint. Your crew with me. Remaining crews stay back and provide cover fire when we need it. Tell them to break out the Krocks and prepare to target on our signal."

"Jonas."

Shipp, James, and ten other soldiers met and jogged toward the narrow, rocky, and descending canyon. Shipp got a call on his comm from Torres.

"Turn around."

Shipp turned. Torres stood about twenty meters back near one of Shipp's other crews at their bunker.

"We can't risk losing twelve of you for this. We're sending out four Beasts and will douse them with Krocks and cannons," Torres said.

"What if you can't navigate to wherever they're holed up? They'll just keep shelling us from long range."

"Don't tell me what I already know."

"Then let me go. I'm not about to stand around while our only base on this planet goes up in flames, and we have the tactical advantage."

"I don't have orders to let you go."

"You don't need them. It's situational chain of command." Shipp's favorite line in the Peterson Space Force code.

From this new position, Shipp scanned the base and realized he could see into the exploded section. He peered through the scope on his Mossamer. Part of Pretoria's office was exposed. He didn't see her. She was probably with Vonn. But it didn't matter.

Nostrils flaring. Face flushing. He stared down Torres so hard that even twenty meters away, Torres realized he couldn't stop him. And Shipp had correctly cited the rule of situational chain of command. He had intel the leaders didn't have. And he had autonomy to act on that intel.

Shipp led his soldiers down into the canyon. About halfway down, it split into two. Shipp took his crews left, knowing they'd be more concealed from the Westers who were still to the north. They made their way down toward the end of the ravine, and then ascended the steep crag, using footholds and old tree roots to reach the top.

From there, they finally had a good vantage.

They could see two Wester camps – the one Shipp's crew had seen previously, and another one about 125 meters north. Both camps were protected by hastily constructed samarium shields. Not as strong as Blackhead – not even close – but strong enough to withstand AX-15s.

Renwar squawked on Shipp's comm.

"What the flame are you doing Shipp? You're way out of the zone."

"Doing what I came here to do. You better send Rothman's squad to the two rat groups camped in the plain, because I'm about to let them know I'm over here. The northern one is probably firing the Krocks."

"Shipp – "

Shipp disconnected and spoke to his crew.

"Who's the best shot with the Krock on the Mossamer?"

Mixie spoke up. "I am. Besides you."

Shipp took her word for it without question.

"Mixie and I are gonna take out both shields. The rest of you will hit them with AX fire."

Shipp and Mixie prostrated on the ground and positioned themselves to fire their Mossamer Krocks, and the other ten soldiers prepared to fire once the shields were hit.

"You take the one to the right."

"Jonas," Mixie replied.

After a moment of specifying their targeting and preparing to use the Krock attachments on their Mossamers, Shipp asked Mixie if she was ready. She affirmed.

Shipp and Mixie unleashed their Krocks, and they bulleted straight toward the two shield barriers. Both direct hits. The explosions caught the nearby Westers by surprise. About thirty fled immediately. Shipp's other ten soldiers immediately followed with AX fire. One group of about twenty Westers ran north toward the canyons, away from Shipp's position, as Petersons from the bunkers near the base pelted them with AX fire and dual cannons. The other ten ran west away from the Peterson base.

But then, before Shipp's crew could fire on them, four more Krocks launched from somewhere else to the northeast of the Westers they could see. All four hit the main Peterson base again.

The launch startled all twelve Petersons – especially because these were full-scale Krocks, not the smaller ones on Mossamers. It also meant a third group of Westers was stationed in the northern canyons. Beasts would be useless.

"Sir," asked Zemmer. "What do we do?"

Shipp had to call it in.

"Renwar! Torres! The Krocks aren't coming from either group I can see. They're somewhere in the canyons to the north. Where the flame is Rothman?"

No reply.

Shipp changed his comm channel to call Rothman. She answered.

"Karel – where are you? The Krocks are coming from a canyon near your position."

"Renwar told us to hold here."

"He doesn't have the intel I do. You gotta take those out now. I've got thirty rats between me and you."

"Jonas that. We'll get 'em."

By this time, the surviving Westers who had fled north were out of sight, and the ten who fled west had regrouped and were preparing to fire. At Shipp's position.

"Get down the hill now!" James bellowed.

All twelve Petersons practically fell down the backside of the crag into the ravine as the Westers fired a dual cannon volley. Shipp's crew got to its feet and ran west as explosions erupted from the top of the crag they'd been on, and in the canyon right where they fell. The Petersons halted. Most assumed the plan was to turn around and retreat east back to the base. But Shipp stopped them.

"Those ten rats aren't safe yet, and we've got the advantage."

All eleven soldiers affirmed him. He replied, "Stay alive."

They responded, "Save your friend."

The twelve Petersons darted west through another smaller ravine. Not long afterward, more dual cannon fire pelted the hill they'd been on and the areas around it.

Shipp could hear more volleys being fired from the north, but the battle was out of sight.

"The Krock Westers are firing Mags and wizards. They might be out of Krocks," Shipp huffed as they double-timed it down the ravine.

"Or Rothman is on them," suggested James.

The crew reached the end of the next ravine. Shipp gathered them together.

"You guys know this terrain. We've been here a hundred times. Mixie. Which way you think those ten are headed?"

Mixie thought about it, and recalled the maps she had studied.

"I think they'll head west to that river and then turn south."

"Zemmer? Gugbe? Anyone else?" Shipp asked. Even in battle. Always training. Always learning.

Blasé answered, "I agree about the river. But why not go north since the rest of their guys are going that way?"

"Good question. James? What's the answer?"

James smiled at Shipp's method. Just like Vonn did it.

"Because they don't want to be caught dead in the same place together. They want to retreat in different directions. They'll assume we went back to base."

"That's right." Shipp replied. "And we're going to catch those ten when they emerge from that little grove of trees due west. Mixie, you take point since this was your idea."

Mixie smiled and took the lead. The group hustled through ravines, up inclines, and around rock formations. They reached the end of the rocky area. About fifty meters ahead, a river flowed north and south, and a grove of trees sat about 45 degrees from their position, toward the northwest.

"Down," ordered Shipp.

All twelve lay flat on the ground.

"AXs and Mossamers only. Be ready."

A few minutes later, the Westers began to emerge from the grove of trees, just as Mixie predicted. But way more than ten. More like thirty.

"Shipp?" asked Mixie.

James lay in a position with a better vantage. "They must have had a staging ground near the river."

Shipp smiled. "Great. Higher body count."

"Twelve against thirty?" James asked.

"Yeah," Shipp said. "Twelve against thirty. Target the ones parallel to your position. On one knee on my command."

Arrayed side by side about one body length apart, all twelve Petersons prepared to attack. Once all the Westers had cleared the trees, Shipp gave the order.

"Fire."

All the Petersons got up on one knee. Red laser lines from eight AX-15s spread across the chests of the oncoming Westers. Then, those and four Mossamers unloaded on the unsuspecting enemy soldiers, plastering the group from one end to the other. Bodies collapsed. Armor failed. Blood. Pain. Terror.

"Advance!" Shipp ordered.

They stood up and advanced on the Westers. Any fleeing stragglers got shot down. Anyone writhing on the ground got put out of their misery. Moments later, just quiet and still. More corpses to rot in the Risner suns.

Shipp's crew looked around in all directions. All twelve survived. Only a few shots had fired back in their direction, and only Blasé took a minor hit along his bicep.

Shipp looked at James and grinned. "Twelve against thirty."

Then he nodded James toward the grove of trees. James took his meaning.

"Crew up," James said to his group of six. "Let's scope out the trees and make sure nothing got missed."

Shipp got back on his comm. "Rothman. Give me a status."

Rothman crackled through, "We hit the rocket launchers, but they were well shielded by the terrain, and most of the rats fled once they saw us. Base is safe. Structure and surroundings took damage. They hit us all over the place, not just the main site."

"Did you catch a look at the other twenty who were headed your way?"

"They went well to the north. We didn't want to get that far from base since you've already taken the lead on that."

"You lose any?"

"No, we're whole."

Shipp updated her on what his crew had achieved. Then James returned and gave Shipp the thumbs up. No more Westers in the area.

When Shipp and James returned to the Peterson base, two things surprised them.

First, no one congratulated him. His group of twelve had met a surprise attack with aggression, rather than the predictable defensiveness the Westers had no doubt counted on and that Torres and Renwar had ordered. And yet, the other Peterson soldiers just stared. They seemed to be waiting. Or perhaps they were recovering their equilibrium, since this marked the first direct Wester attack on the Peterson base since its re-establishment several years prior.

Second, the damage was far more severe than he anticipated. The walls got hit by multiple Kampraseuth rockets, and numerous MagTons broke through and caused extensive internal damage. Shards of metal dangled from warped blast marks, fumes wafted upward, and supplies littered the surroundings. Two base support personnel got killed, including a mechanic who had been working on Risner since the beginning.

It was a great loss. Admins hardly ever died.

Shipp walked south to collect the other soldiers in his squad from their bunkers. The remaining crews had acted independently, as Shipp had trained them. Two crews of six rushed to aid Faraday's soldiers who were caught by enemy fire. Two more crews ran back into the base to save anyone who was injured from the blasts.

Another crew, which Torres had joined, had stayed in their bunker to coordinate with the others. Shipp darkened in dismay when he found them. The bunker had been hit by hive bombs and dual cannons, and they must have detonated close by. The shrapnel from the bombs killed three men and one woman in the crew. Only three survived, two badly injured.

Torres was among the dead.

“Flame it.” Shipp knelt in the dirt, placing a hand on one of the dead men’s ankles.

Zemmer spoke up. “Looks like it isn’t safer to stay back.”

“It’s never safe. Not until all the Westers are dead,” replied Shipp.

Shipp pulled some debris off the head of the dead woman. Only then did he realize who it was.

Juthelle. Gone in her first battle.

Shipp lowered his head at the shock of seeing her. He breathed slow and heavy breaths. Mixie closed her eyes. Ramad glared and scowled, as he had become good friends with Juthelle and developed romantic feelings for her. Shipp’s core group mourned the loss of the prized soldier they had welcomed just a few months ago.

Shipp had been raised his entire life to hate, loathe, and despise Westers. Over the centuries of war, Peterson writers developed a whole lexicon with different words for ‘hate.’ Different words for different contexts, intonations, and emotional states of mind. They were rats. Psychopaths. Mentally deranged. They had lost any sense of moral consciousness or respect for life. In this moment Shipp’s hatred mutated into detest. He could feel it in his extremities.

There was nothing to be done for them. No way to fix them. No way to appease or negotiate anything. Just exterminate them.

9

Awarded

"Well done."

Commander Vonn patted Shipp on the shoulder and affirmed his battlefield decision-making. He went on to commend Shipp's aggression in the face of attack, which likely stalled what the Westers had envisioned to be a much more destructive onslaught. By forcing two of the three Wester squads to flee earlier than they planned, it was easier for Rothman to fight off the one firing the rockets.

And with 38 confirmed Westers dead, compared to thirteen Petersons, Vonn surmised the Westers probably felt even more frustrated than them.

But it was a bold strike. And it inflicted great damage on the structure – damage that would require more resources to repair than they had on hand. LaSalle put Pretoria in charge of securing the necessary resources from Space Force Command, which would require a transport ship to pass safely through hostile space. But none of that worried Vonn as much as the other news that none of his soldiers yet knew.

The Westers had staged a simultaneous attack on the northeast outpost.

"They launched it at the exact same time?" Shipp said, partly to himself.

"As far as we can tell," replied Vonn, in the hearing the dozens of Petersons standing among dead soldiers and rubble from the damaged base, "The first dual cannons fired at us launched at almost the exact moment the rats fired on the outpost. They targeted poorly and were caught in the outpost's sensor web, which was farther out than they realized, so not much damage to that structure."

"Why would they execute two attacks and risk thinning their forces? Do they have more numbers than we believe?" queried Rothman.

Vonn replied, "They might. Our best guess right now is that the Westers have been planning, for some time, to eradicate our presence from Risner, and this is just the first stage of a prolonged offensive."

Vonn continued, "With Torres dead, I'm promoting Shipp to Field Commander in his place. He'll still be in charge of his squad too. I want all squad leaders to debrief with me in the Command Center now. The rest of you – attend to the injured. Restock the bunkers. Rest up."

Shipp approached Vonn, "Can I check in with Pretoria? Is there time?"

"You can have ten minutes."

"Thank you."

Shipp found Pretoria working busily with several assistants. General LaSalle popped in for a moment, then hurried off to another room. Pretoria's assistants updated her on damaged structural components and equipment while she tabulated figures and amounts. It was a frantic environment with multiple voices talking over each other, but purposeful and directed.

Pretoria's even keel kept everyone else on task.

She smiled at Shipp on seeing him, and they briefly embraced.

"I heard about you. Twelve against thirty."

Shipp smiled. "They never had a chance."

She sighed. A pained look, almost forlorn. But not because of Shipp's battlefield risk-taking. "We lost two really good people. Trusha. She was so good."

"Trusha was the other admin who died?"

She nodded. Shipp could see in her eyes the pain of losing one of her team. This wasn't supposed to happen. He deflated and sat down for a moment. "Does Gugbe know yet?"

"I doubt it. You should be the one to tell him."

Shipp nodded, staring at the floor. "We lost Juthelle too."

Pretoria sat next to him and leaned her head on his shoulder. "I'm so sorry. It happens so fast. I don't think I ever even got to meet her."

Shipp waited for a moment, then spoke again.

"I saw your office through the explosion. Glad you weren't in it."

Pretoria gave him a knowing look even though he wasn't looking at her.

"I was."

Shipp jerked his head to her. Stunned. Kind of like that feeling you get when playfully tossing a Morse mine in the air and then noticing it's armed. That pit in the throat. He realized how close he came to losing her. He kissed her and looked deep in her eyes. Kissed her again.

"I love you, starlight."

She grinned at him. Both of them took the attack and its aftermath in stride. They appreciated getting this moment to re-center themselves, together. This was war as a way of life.

Moments later, Shipp strode in the command center, full of focused anger. His nostrils flared, twitching involuntarily. Vonn, Renwar, Rothman, and Faraday awaited him. It was Shipp's first meeting with Faraday since the attack. Faraday gave him a bear hug.

"Way to go man. Taking it right down their throats. Brilliant stuff."

"I just did what had to be done," said Shipp.

Renwar interjected, "You and your eleven soldiers will be awarded commendations for Battlefield Bravery. Your names will be sent to Space Force Command and from there, to all the planets in the Territory. Your families will know you are fighting bravely and helping secure the Meridian Zone."

"Thank you sir. We need to better defend our west side."

It wasn't Shipp's first award. But it was his first for Battlefield Bravery, one of the highest honors for a living soldier.

"Stay alive," said Faraday.

"Save your friend," replied everyone else in the room.

Vonn then began the debrief of what happened.

Faraday's squad lost six soldiers. Shipp's lost three in the bunker, along with Torres. And the two base personnel. That angered everyone the most, because it revealed a much greater vulnerability than they anticipated.

Shipp's two injured soldiers would recover, as would all the other injured. But one of Shipp's men wouldn't be able to fight because a piece of shrapnel from the hive bomb had entered his right eye, removing his depth perception. He would transfer off Risner at the first opportunity.

The northeast outpost lost one soldier. As far as they could tell, the Westers who attacked them didn't lose any. That battle was mostly fought from the fringes, as neither approached each other because of the sensor web, and neither could safely attack without leaving their defensive structures.

"It's very clear," Vonn continued, "That this was a well-planned attack, and that they intended to inflict heavy first-strike damage on our facility. They used two separate squads in the lower plain to engage us, and a hidden third group in the canyons to use Krocks. Had you not intervened, the ones in the plain probably would have advanced on us, along with the other twenty they had back by the river. We project this attack will be followed by another, which they will hope happens before we can repair and re-organize. But they underestimate us."

"Did this have anything to do with the twelve rats sitting around a few months back?" Rothman asked.

"We've been discussing that," said Vonn. "It's possible they were feeling out our sensor web. Renwar thinks they had a second crew to the west of us at the same time, and we couldn't see them. Had we engaged the one to the east, that would have confirmed for them we had no sensors to the west. I think he's right."

"And since we did nothing, they gambled on it," Faraday surmised.

"Possibly," said Vonn.

"So where do we go from here?" Shipp asked.

"Pretoria's rebuilding work is top priority on our end," Vonn replied. "I need you three to start roving patrols, nonstop. And yes, we need to enlarge the sensor web west of the base – all the way to the river if we have enough tech. Renwar will update me on your progress."

Rothman, Faraday, and Shipp knew what this meant. It meant this mission was up to them to make happen. No one would be giving orders other than the occasional check-in.

"We're on it," said Rothman. "We'll work out the shifts and brief our squads."

Shipp halted them and turned somber. "Let's meet in 15 minutes. I need to talk to Gugbe first. He lost his love. Doesn't know it yet."

While Faraday and Rothman started planning the mission, Shipp went outside and found Gugbe. He waved him over and brought him to the east side of the base, where they could be alone. They sat on an old fallen tree.

"What's up Shipp?"

Shipp had never needed to have a conversation like this. But he knew it was part of the job. That didn't make it any easier. *Where do I start?*

"You performed with outstanding conduct today," he began.

"Thank you. It's an honor to fight alongside you every time."

"They're going to give us medals for Battlefield Bravery," Shipp told him. "Every planet will know."

"I remember hearing those stories when I was a kid, weekly war reports," Gugbe smiled. "Weird to be on this side of it. Doesn't feel the same."

Shipp smiled too at the remembrance of childhood, back when the vilification of Westers bled through their entire upbringing, and any news about Peterson advances was greeted with celebration. "People on my planet called those updates the Rat Review."

Gugbe laughed, "The Rat Review. That's vintage. I especially loved reports about attack ships. I loved attack ships as a kid."

"You almost never see your enemy on those," Shipp mused. "Maybe someday we'll serve on one and find out which is better."

"I had three attack ship toy models," Gugbe recalled. "I would pretend each was flown by my three favorite generals. My favorite was General Ainesh. You ever heard of him?"

Shipp nodded, "Yeah, he was in a lot of war reports. I haven't heard the name in a while though."

"That's because his ship got destroyed while protecting two transports near Portia," Gugbe said. "I remember because I was twelve when it happened. I was working after school with my parents in the field."

"You were on Remmo, right? The farm planet?" Shipp confirmed what he recalled as Gugbe's home planet.

"Yeah, almost all agriculture. We grow food for six or seven other planets. The report came on the harvesting tech's monitor. My dad saw the story and brought me over because he knew I loved General Ainesh. Ship wrecked. No survivors. No way to recover them."

"What was his ship's name?" Shipp asked.

"The Shatterer," Gugbe answered. "Ainesh and the Shatterer."

Gugbe smiled at the memory. Ainesh's death was one of the driving forces that led him to pursue a career in the Space Force. But being in the war was a lot different than fantasizing about it as a 12-year-old. The conversation halted. An extended silence. Shipp knew he had to break it with the reason for the talk.

"Armand," he began, "There is one piece of news that isn't good."

"What's that?" asked Gugbe. He really didn't have any idea.

"Trusha died in the attack."

Shipp looked him in the eye, gave him a moment, then rubbed his shoulders. The sudden awareness that he would never see her again hit Armand Gugbe all at once.

"I know she was special to you."

Gugbe sat silent for a bit, and then spoke, deftly shaking his head, "I never planned to love anyone when I came here. But she was... there was something about her. The way she laughed. The way she walked."

Shipp listened. And waited when Gugbe stopped. And listened again when he continued.

"One time she came to my room because my lighting unit failed. She brought a new one. When we turned it on, she just had this look, this smile. I told her she was the prettiest thing I'd ever seen. It was funny too, because she and I both knew that wasn't true. But it didn't matter, you know? She became the prettiest one in that moment, for me."

"Admins," Shipp lamented.

"Out of the whole base and they got her," Gugbe raged inside at the absurdity of the odds.

Shipp nodded. "You know what they always tell us when we lose a friend."

Gugbe knew, but it didn't help much now that he was living it. "Use it."

"Use it," Shipp said. "Never let your grief go to waste. I'm using mine for Juthelle. Next time we go out to fight, I want you next to me."

"I'll be there."

Shipp stood up. Gugbe followed his lead.

"Take today off, okay? Take some time to mourn. Get with your downtime group – don't spend it all alone. I'll be briefing the squad in a day or two. Until then – let me know if you want to talk some more."

10

All In

Mixie Shem grew up on the planet Maxwell, the second most populated planet in Peterson Territory with 2.5 billion inhabitants. She came from a large family, with two brothers and three sisters. Rarely did Peterson families have more than three children, and Mixie didn't know anyone with more than four.

Most couples had fewer children due to the pervasive feeling that resources could run out if they weren't careful. This deeply ingrained generational trait dated back to the earliest days of the Territory, when Jonas Peterson led the first colonists to this quarter of the galaxy. Colonizing new planets entailed enormous risk for everyone involved, and resources were always an issue. That uneasiness about not having enough still pervaded the thoughts and habits of many Petersons, even though centuries had elapsed.

Being so large, Mixie's family was well known in her sector of Chorn, the capital and one of the biggest cities on the planet. But she didn't grow up in need or want.

Her father taught at a teen preparatory school. He also coached the disc team, a sport that involved 7-on-7 teams where players passed a 6cm magnetized disc among teammates and tried to score goals. The Peterson Space Force developed the game in the early years of the Galactic War, believing it taught teamwork and developed strategic, fast-paced thinking. It caught on quickly on the more populated planets.

Mixie's mother worked for the planetary government for most of Mixie's childhood, coordinating construction projects. But when Mixie was eleven, she left that job and started a business manufacturing, repairing, and selling personal comm units.

With her parents both working stable, profitable jobs, Mixie's family always had plenty, and more to share. The main thing that kept the six kids from falling into complacency was the same one that motivated nearly every other kid to live inspired lives – the Meridian Zone war. News about it could be found just about anywhere. Everyone cared about it. The threat was real, and kids were taught about killing rats before they were old enough to read.

One summer day when Mixie was sixteen, she and a group of friends were enjoying an afternoon sweet drink at a post. Summers in Chorn on the planet Maxwell were especially nice. The post's monitor switched from its female-skewing entertainment programming to a war update. The teens watched as the newscaster delivered a devastating narrative about a ground war battle on the planet Risner. At that time, the Petersons were attempting to regain a foothold on the planet for the first time in decades, and their latest attempt led to a huge battle that cost the lives of 113 soldiers.

The newscaster concluded, "Peterson Space Force Command has committed to make another attempt at planting a permanent base on Risner. They have tasked Commander Yesler Vonn to lead the effort. Currently stationed on Kora, Vonn is one of the most decorated leaders in Peterson history."

"113 in one battle," Mixie marveled.

She and her friends fixated on the monitor as the update concluded. It was followed by a presentation from a friendly woman in a ground war suit much like Mixie would later wear.

The woman spoke, "There is no greater call or purpose in life than to do what I did – join the Peterson Space Force. You get to personally fight against the Wester aggressors. You get to protect our home worlds. Your planet. Your family and friends. If you qualify, your name will be etched in galactic history. Most applicants don't qualify. You must be smart. You must be fit. You must be mentally and emotionally strong and resilient. And you must be teachable. Is that you? The best age to apply is between 15 and 20 years old, but anyone up to age 30 is eligible. Will I see you next in the Meridian Zone?"

Mixie and all her friends watched the monitor, yearning to act. It switched back to the previous production, but they all turned away and began talking about applying. A few knew they'd be turned down.

"I'm not strong enough," one said.

"I don't think I'm smart enough," said another.

"I'm gonna try no matter what. At least I'll know I did everything I could," said a third.

"What about you Mix?"

Mixie stared back at the monitor, "I going all in. I already planned it," she declared.

When Mixie got home that day, her parents were saddened by her decision to apply for the Space Force. Not the reaction she was expecting. Her spirit deflated as they spoke.

"There's so much I was hoping to do with you," said her father. "You'd be so good at so many things."

"Like work with me at the company. We're doing really well," said her mom.

"But this is more important than any of that," Mixie said. "My friends' parents are all starry excited about them applying. I thought you would be too. Didn't you tell Rim he should apply?"

Her father came closer and embraced her, and then spoke softly to her.

"I know why you really want to go," he said. "The truth is, Rim won't make it. But you probably will."

Mixie struggled to understand why her parents wanted Rim to apply, knowing he would fail, but didn't want her to in case she succeeded. They must have battled with some selfish desire to keep their whole family together, even if it cost the Space Force a great soldier. Encouraging Rim to apply would give the appearance that they were happy to send their children to the war. But that wasn't the Peterson Way, and they should have known it. She wished they'd been happy for her, instead of thinking about losing her.

"We just lost 113 soldiers on Risner. The Westers own that planet. We have to retake it," Mixie told them.

"You're right, we do," said her mom. "It's hard for you to understand until you have kids. We just love you so much, and we know how capable you are. You can do anything. You're not like other girls."

"So I should take that and use it where it's needed most, and that's the Space Force," Mixie replied. "Right?"

"If that's what you want," her father said, "We support you all the way."

Mixie relieved at this, but the prickly feeling of their initial hesitancy gnawed at her. It never went away.

Within two years, her parents proved correct. Rim failed to qualify, and Mixie succeeded.

Six years later, her parents received a message that Mixie was being deployed to Risner, to serve under Commander Vonn. Her parents felt bittersweet at Mixie's celebratory language in her message. Their most excellent daughter was exactly where she wanted to be. And they feared they would never see her again.

A package arrived from Peterson Space Force soon afterward, telling them what to expect now that they had offspring in the war. It confirmed the salary Mixie would be earning, and explained how her money would pass to them if she ever died in combat. But two thirds of soldiers survive, they were told, and usually end up either working at Space Force University, joining an attack ship, or transferring to an outpost. Mixie would be free to return to Maxwell if that's what she wanted.

Upon her arrival at Risner, squad leader Thomas Shipp chose Mixie for his squad. Very soon, she endeared herself to him with her quick decisive thinking, elite weapons skills, and calmness under pressure.

11

The Plan

Six months after the Wester attack, a Peterson transport ship broke through and reached the surface of Risner.

They offloaded the supplies and personnel needed to finish reconstructing the damaged portions of the base. They also replenished food and medical supplies, and all the other basics needed to sustain and expand the Peterson presence on the planet. And of course, they brought additional weaponry and ammunition.

Best of all, they brought a fresh supply of soldiers. And, they took away the injured ones and a few who were concluding their service. All three squads on the main base were made whole again, and Vonn now had an extra forty soldiers in reserve. The two outposts received six more soldiers each.

Such a swift reconstruction marked a superb achievement, and Pretoria won the praises of Vonn, Renwar, LaSalle, the other base administrators, and the soldiers. She had to lead the effort while LaSalle oversaw fortifications at the northeast outpost. Her leadership in accomplishing so much within six months even earned commendations from Space Force Command.

And not a moment too soon.

Just two weeks after the replenishment, the Westers attacked the southeast Peterson outpost. Once again, the attack proved short-lived, just like the one against the northeast outpost in the last battle, and for similar reasons. The Westers couldn't penetrate the sensor web far enough without compromising their own safety.

No one died on either side.

Two months later, they attacked the northeast outpost, with similar results. Three weeks later, the Petersons lost a bunch of their sensors. The Westers were likely using Metalheads to detect and destroy the Peterson sensors.

This was a risky move, even though the mechanics of it were fairly simple.

Metalheads detected the signal produced by a sensor. Once located, they zeroed in and exposed it either by digging it up or ripping it from wherever it might be. Either way, once the soldiers operating the DSE got close enough, they could easily destroy the sensor.

Why were DSEs risky to use? Because the instant a sensor got taken out, the enemy base would know it. One downed sensor could be considered a malfunction, maybe. But if a second one went down, there was only one explanation. Your enemy is taking out your sensors, and you know exactly where they are. Depending on the location, distance, and terrain, it wouldn't be hard to find and attack their forces.

This time, the Westers succeeded at wiping out so many Peterson sensors because they did it in two phases. First, they unearthed but didn't destroy a bunch of them during the attack on the outpost, while the Petersons were occupied.

Then, in a well-planned and flawlessly executed mission, they sent out a group of soldiers to destroy all the unearthed sensors. In little less than an hour, the Petersons lost fifty sensors. The Petersons spent several weeks replacing the lost sensors, which meant they couldn't launch any counterattacks at risk of spreading their forces too thin. It also reduced their supply of sensors, delaying Vonn's goal of extending the web westward all the way to the river.

Because the Westers had so many more soldiers than the Petersons on Risner, Vonn mostly played a defensive battle. "Our goal," he told his soldiers almost every day, "Is to hold this spot, grow our forces, and eventually expand our presence on Risner." It was a long game, but it ensured the Petersons wouldn't lose what they had established here, even if it meant they launched very few planned attacks against the Westers.

Two years passed since the big Wester assault from the west.

And in that time, as Vonn predicted, the Petersons got attacked repeatedly, eleven times in total at the main base or an outpost. They lost a total of two soldiers in that time. Their defenses were getting stronger, more agile, and more spread out.

Vonn's plan was working.

They also continued to struggle getting transport ships through to the surface of Risner. Attack ships from both Territories constantly patrolled the space, jockeying for position around the various Meridian Zone planets.

During these months, Shipp drew even closer to his core squad members. Mixie was an outstanding soldier in all respects. Gugbe was a rock, fearless and with great battlefield vision. Zemmer's marksmanship had reached elite levels. Ramad's initiative and leadership capabilities grew. And Blasé's strategic planning abilities began to shine, along with his impressive physical endurance. He was a machine.

Shipp, James, Pretoria, and Horman also deepened their friendship. The four of them were becoming a powerful unit, built on bonds of love and respect no university or training program could deliver. One day, Vonn told Shipp privately that if he and Pretoria ever wanted to lead the Risner forces, Vonn would promote him and take LaSalle and Renwar to a different planet.

Shipp flushed at the vote of confidence. His Space Force career was accelerating, and his lifelong belief that he could help win the war for good grew even stronger.***

About fourteen months after her last successful resupply, Pretoria succeeded in landing a second. With this one, she increased the supplies of arms to a sufficient level that Vonn felt the Petersons could stage an attack. A few months later, after two more ineffectual Wester attacks, Vonn gave it the green light.

He called Shipp, Rothman, and Faraday into the Command Center, and together they and General Renwar began working out the details. They spent four weeks developing the plan of attack.

Attacking the main Wester base would be more difficult than anything they had done since re-establishing their presence on Risner. The Petersons would be attacking a larger, more established, better defended, better armed base that probably had three times as many soldiers.

But Vonn had consulted with Space Force Command, and they agreed the Risner campaign needed to advance. If they could destroy their closest Wester neighbor, they could plant a new main base in the vicinity, and then triple their outposts after that. That would mean control of the whole region. And besides all the expansion potential, these frequent Wester attacks needed a response. They needed to know the Petersons were strong enough to launch an attack, not just defend.

Vonn's goal for the battle was simple: Maximum damage, minimum losses.

As part of the planning, Shipp found himself consulting with James, who was not just his best friend, but a trusted military mind. Shipp loved James for his level-headedness. He never panicked. Shipp knew he would always give a straight and honest answer, and not in a belligerent or arrogant way. He also had more empathy and emotional insight than Shipp, and knew when to back off.

Shipp never had a brother, and he always thought of James as the closest thing to it.

The boldest aspect to this mission included a plan to enter the Wester base – an extreme rarity. If they could lure out enough Westers, and engage and kill them, they could then go in, plant MagTons, and detonate the structure from within.

James had been working on adding Blackhead to the leading edges of four of the Peterson Beasts, each of which could carry twelve soldiers. Normally, it would be suicide to try to attack the base with Beasts, because they could only move so quickly on the uneven ground, and they were easy targets for K-rockets. Beasts were better for rescue missions than assaults.

But with enough Blackhead in the right places, while a K-rocket could still inflict damage, it shouldn't be able to destroy them in one shot. Plus, if the Westers were too occupied fighting other Petersons around their base, the Beasts could quickly bring a great and sudden increase to the size of the Peterson forces.

The beauty of this plan was, if the first group of attacking Petersons failed to secure enough of an advantage to justify a base invasion, the Beasts would hold back within the Peterson sensor web. They would be ready if the situation justified it – maximum damage. But they would stay back if it didn't – minimum losses.

Once the four assault vehicles were equipped to withstand all attacks except K-rockets, Shipp, Faraday, and Rothman concurred that the rest of the plan was ready to execute.

They would launch the assault in two days.

Shipp spent most of the day before the assault with Pretoria. For part of that day, she was working, and he even joined her and assisted in small ways. For the rest of their time, they spent it alone, eating a meal and talking about their future as they lay in their room.

Pretoria showed him a private comm from Kora, which the Petersons held about as securely as the Westers held Risner. Three new Peterson bases were planned, and they had reached out to Pretoria to gauge her interest in leading one of them as the chief administrator.

Kora was a beautiful planet, easily the most scenic of the seven Meridian Zone planets. And being more secure, it also seemed like a good move to make after thriving in a hardened warzone on Risner for several years. It also conflicted with Vonn's offer to Shipp, which he had shared with Pretoria a few months back.

"Wow. First Vonn offers us Risner. Now Kora," Shipp said.

"I know. I don't know which one sounds better," she replied.

"When do you have to decide about Kora?"

"They're not sure." Pretoria answered. "They won't need the admins until the bases are built, which will be several months for each. So we have time to decide. But if you can take out the Wester base, that will give us room to expand our foothold here."

"I want to wipe them out."

"You'll have done about the hardest work there is. Expanding a beachhead. On Kora, you can help completely claim the rest of the planet for us. So you get to experience both extremes," mused Pretoria.

"That would be truly wiping them out, wouldn't it," considered Shipp. "It sounds like you want Kora more."

"I don't know. I've always wanted to see it. Feels like there'd be more variety there. You don't want to stay in one place your whole career right?"

"I'm not good at stuff like this. I came here because they sent me here. If we can reclaim Risner and hold the other planetary regions we have now, we'll own about 70% of the Meridian Zone. That's possible, in just a few years. I kind of feel like staying here is more important."

They talked about the broader war strategy like this all the time. But now, with a Kora leadership position opening, the situation had changed. Pretoria summarized:

"Advance Risner. Done. Secure Kora next. And then, you could move on to Lavoisier, which is where I know you've always wanted to fight. And finish your battlefield career there. I think that's a terrific plan. And, I can always hold my space station dreams over your head."

Shipp laughed, and she laughed back.

Then Shipp reminded her of her own line, "Goals are drawn with starlight."

She smiled and giggled at him, "You are correct, my sweet hero. But what do you think of that plan? Fight and win on three planetary fronts."

Shipp thought about her idea. Vonn's offer had compelled him, but it almost mattered more for what it said about Shipp's ability to lead. Vonn and LaSalle could continue leading here for twenty more years. They didn't need to leave.

Shipp looked at his wife and then answered. "Pretoria – I love it. Let's do Kora next. You get the admin post, and they'll transfer me and my core unit there to keep us together. Rothman or Faraday can take over here."

She smiled at him, and they turned off the light.

12

The Assault

Under cover of night, Shipp and Rothman brought their full squads to each outpost – Shipp to the south, Rothman to the north. The next night, after eating and hydrating, the soldiers emerged from the outposts and moved toward the outskirts of the Wester sensor web. They knew its border, because they'd painstakingly outlined it over the last couple months using Metalheads, but without unearthing or destroying any of the sensors.

Faraday's squad departed the Peterson main base and waited in the four Beasts near the edge of the Peterson sensor web. Though invisible to the Westers, his squad could join the other Petersons within minutes. The only thing that could mess up this part of the plan would be if a Wester attack ship entered Risner's atmosphere and saw them. The chances of that were almost nil.

Shipp and Rothman directed their crews to begin working the Metalheads.

South of the base, Mixie ran point with one group of six, James with another, and Ramad a third. North of the base, three of Rothman's best leaders took Metalhead groups from her squad. Each member of each group – 36 soldiers total – directed their own individual Metalhead device via remote control.

The area around the Wester base was mostly flat, with slight rises here and there, but few trees or rocks. That meant the enemy's sensors had to be buried, which meant the DSE's could dig them up. The little army of Metalheads began its rolling assault on the Wester sensor web. Each Metalhead needed to find between five and ten sensors.

Before he died, Torres had always insisted that the south end of the Wester base offered the best attack route. He believed its uneven terrain would permit you to advance within 200 meters of the base and still have sufficient cover from the land. And that's where Shipp intended to lead his squad into the Wester base once the intervening sensors were disabled. He waited just outside the Westers' sensor web. Motionless. Alert. Ready to do what hadn't been done in his lifetime.

Ramad found his first enemy sensor, and the first of the assault. The attack on the Wester base had begun. His device dug a hole and exposed the sensor, but didn't touch it. Instead, it planted a small explosive partially inside the hole.

Shipp listened as the six Metalhead squads updated him on their progress. Little by little, the number of sensors located and armed with explosives ticked upward.

Ten.

Fifteen.

Twenty.

Thirty.

After about three hours, they had planted explosives next to 242 Wester sensors. The other sun was dawning.

Shipp ordered all the Metalheads back, and waited. He called Rothman.

"Ready?"

"Jonas."

He called Faraday.

"Set?"

"Jonas."

Shipp gave the order to detonate. Like popcorn, little pockets of dirt exploded all around the terrain over the next ten seconds.

"Boom," said Shipp. "Come on out, you rat bastards."

Two Westers emerged from the eastern entrance to their base. Each held a hive bomb rifle. Shipp spotted them.

A group of six Petersons from Rothman's squad had planted itself far east of the Wester base. Shipp ordered them to fire. Moments later, three K-rockets lasered toward the two Westers from the east, smashed the shields, and exploded. Dual cannons followed, crackling more Wester samarium shields. Three more K-rockets. The two Westers ran back inside for cover, but only for a moment.

The assault from the east quickly increased in ferocity when Rothman's remaining crew began a full-scale barrage from the north. Dual cannons and MagTons exploded against the Wester samarium shields, the walls, and the foreground.

As hoped, Westers emerged and returned fire against Rothman's squad. Not as many came out as the Petersons expected. But it was the signal they were hoping for. She called Shipp.

"Move forward. Go in and take it! We have their attention!"

It was now Shipp's job to take 24 of his soldiers through the destroyed sensor web, enter the structure, and start killing from within. His other 24 would remain outside for now. Shipp called Faraday.

"We're closing on the base. Roll up and merge!"

Shipp advanced in stops and starts. He reached the rise 200 meters from the base that Torres had spoken about. He waited there until he saw Faraday rolling up over the rises to the west. He directed his squad forward as Faraday arrived on the Beasts. The combined Peterson squads poured into the base, firing at closed doors, open doors, and everything that moved.

Mixie and Ramad blasted into what looked like a weapons supply room, soon joined by six more Petersons. They unleashed AX fire in all directions, killing a couple Wester admins.

Shipp and Gugbe bolted through hallways, planting MagTons on doors which detonated behind them as they kept running. When they reached the end of each hall, they turned back to fire on anyone who emerged from the blown apart rooms. No one came out.

Blasé and Zemmer ascended a stairwell with six other soldiers, firing ahead of themselves the whole way up onto a second level of the base, killing several Wester admins along the way. No soldiers returned fire, and most of the rooms were empty.

Shipp and Gugbe eventually circled through the interiors and found themselves back in what appeared to be the main hall of the Wester base, where twenty other Petersons waited.

Shipp got nervous. He could hear intermittent fire above him from Blasé and Zemmer's crew. Some sporadic screaming. A few Wester soldiers continued fighting Rothman's crew outside to the north. But even that was dying down. Rothman would finish them off soon. Shipp nodded James toward that entrance in case any of them tried to retreat inside.

Not much moved. Eventually, Mixie and Ramad rejoined him, as did most of the rest of Faraday's squad. This included Shim and Horman, who was happy to finally be on the same combat ground as Shipp.

Where were all the Westers? They had encountered a bit of resistance in a few rooms, and killed several base support personnel. But only eleven Wester soldiers ran out to fight against Rothman. Where were the rest? Where were the leaders? The base seemed almost abandoned. Utter lunacy.

Rothman eventually joined Shipp and Faraday inside. She directed parts of her squad to wipe out the rest of the Wester sensor array, and ordered the outposts to send more soldiers to speed up the process.

"Where the flame did they go?" she wondered aloud.

"This way," Shipp said, and led her into what appeared to be the Wester Command Center. It looked quite different from theirs. Except The Table. A dead guy slumped over it.

"That guy," Shipp told Rothman, "Was the only one in here. I think he's a tech. There were no commanders."

"They wouldn't just abandon their own base. Let's search every rathole until we find them," she said.

"Jonas that," Shipp replied. He called Vonn and updated him. "Strange. We found the base almost deserted. We're checking every room."

"Shipp? That's very disturbing," Vonn said. "Renwar and I will talk it over. Be careful. Watch for traps."

"Jonas."

Over a hundred Petersons spent the next couple hours rifling through every room in the base. Any locked door got blown aside. They found no more Westers. They killed about thirty in all – eleven soldiers and the rest support personnel.

"I've seen enough," said Shipp. "Bring in the big boys."

Faraday's vehicles had brought enhanced explosives. No one expected it to be this easy, but they weren't going to miss the chance to destroy the base. They unloaded the explosives, and Shipp directed his squad to plant them throughout.

"If they come back, they're going to find a burnt-out hole no good for anything more than a campfire. Burn it to the ground," Shipp commanded. "Faraday, your squad can return."

"Jonas," and Faraday's squad prepared to roll back to the Peterson base. Horman waved at Shipp and left with Faraday.

Shipp and Rothman's soldiers began planting MagTons and other explosive devices on support beams, inner walls, corners, ceilings, and anything else that looked like it might be providing support to the structure. Some explosives were V-E upgrades, rarely used. These would be able to blow through the exterior Blackhead-coated walls, enough to hopefully crumple the building.

An hour later, Mixie reported to Shipp. "We're ready."

Rothman's comm crackled. It was Faraday.

"Anyone! Rothman! Are you there?"

"I'm here Hosh, what is it?" She could hear AX fire through her comm. Shipp leaned in.

"They're coming through the floor! They're pouring into the base Karel! Get back here now! Get bac---"

13

Patient Destruction

Shipp and Rothman looked at each other for less than a second. Then, they both yelled to their squads to evacuate immediately and return directly to the Peterson base.

On their way, Shipp hit the detonator, and the Wester base exploded. Multiple small explosions peppered the air, cascading into larger and larger ones, until the entire structure erupted in flames. The sounds of twisting, clanging, crunching, yawning metal screamed across the landscape as most of the structure fell. Only segments and shards of the Blackhead-coated walls remained intact.

It was a beautiful sight. Something the Petersons had been longing to see for decades, since before Vonn led the effort to re-take the planet.

But Shipp, Rothman, James, and every other Peterson soldier missed it. They raced back toward their own besieged base. Not a single one looked back. They made it about halfway there and then halted, as some of their soldiers collapsed from exhaustion.

"Get hydrated," Shipp ordered, gulping air himself.

He scanned ahead. He could see smoke escaping from one side of their base. Sporadic AX fire and wizards could be heard from the distance, along with occasional explosions from inside the base. He and several others peered through their scopes. Faraday's soldiers were in a firefight against Westers. The Westers were fighting from *inside* the Peterson base.

"So what, they drilled a tunnel?" wondered Rothman. "How'd they know we were going to attack them?"

Shipp looked around at his squad.

"We don't have time to figure that out. Gugbe, what do you see?"

Gugbe had kept nonstop watch through his scope the whole time. "Faraday's losing. He's in our bunkers."

"Is anyone coming out the east side toward us?" Rothman asked.

"Yes. At least twenty Westers holed up there," replied Gugbe. "Looks like they're in our main hall."

Shipp settled on a plan.

"Okay, we need to do two things. Save our friends, and kill all the Westers. The base is expendable. The rats have no base to return to. If they go back down their tunnel, they'll die inside, and they probably know it. They're fighting to the death. And we're going to give it to them."

He continued, "Rothman – you attack the Westers from here. Defend Faraday. My squad will curl around the southern edge and approach from the canyons to the west. We'll get inside through the emergency escape door, enter the base, and save our friends. Comm silence."

Rothman nodded. "Got it. I'll call the outposts to send us more Beasts."

Shipp's squad had a long run – about three kilometers to circle around the south without being seen. It would take about fifteen minutes for the outposts' four assault vehicles to reach Rothman. Running briskly, his squad should be able to make it in that amount of time.

"Squads – formation Rita," Shipp ordered.

Fanning out into eight crews of six, Shipp's squad ran hard, ran quiet, and ran focused. They looked forward. They glanced toward the base to the right. Then forward again. Soon, they dipped down in elevation, and their base fell out of sight.

Angling north again, they passed familiar shrubs and elongated rock formations, and made it as far west as the entrance to the southernmost canyon – not Arrowpoint. Torres had named this one Comet Canyon, with the 'tail' of the comet being nearest to the Peterson base. From that point, Shipp expected to have a good opportunity to assess the scene and make his next move.

Once they reached it, he did.

While his squad caught their breath and re-hydrated, Shipp scoped out the terrain.

Though he couldn't see them from here, he could hear diminished counterfire from Faraday's squad. That meant he'd lost a number of soldiers. Too many. Still, several continued fighting from various bunker positions. But the growing periods of silence cast an unnerving fear on Shipp's squad. Westers were probably trying to get intelligence information from Vonn and Renwar, or calling in reinforcements to help fight off Faraday and Rothman.

The time to strike back was now.

"Shipp," said Mixie, "We put sensors in this canyon. If they have access to our tech, they know we're here."

Shipp looked at James. "I want them to know. That way they'll fight us first."

Shipp directed four crews – half his squad – to reinforce Faraday and renew the assault from the south. The other crews – his own, James', and two others – would sneak in through the emergency escape door not far from here, enter the building, and eradicate the Wester infestation.

While Shipp's crews made their way to the escape door, the other four crews clambered toward Faraday's squad and assessed the situation. One of his leaders called back to Shipp.

"Faraday's dead. So is Shim."

Shipp took it hard but in stride. "Okay, you take charge. No Krocks."

Shipp called Rothman on his comm.

"We're set. Give me an update."

"Outposts are here. We've been hitting them hard. Almost out of munitions until the reinforcements got here."

"Go forward."

Rothman's crew launched dual cannons from afar, and the assault vehicles bumped over the uneven ground toward the base. AX fire erupted in all directions.

Shipp led his group of 24 down low underneath an overhanging ledge to the west of the base. He pressed a series of keystrokes on his wrist keypad. The dirt in front of them burst upward and slid down, exposing a circular red light with a curved handle jutting outward. Shipp placed his fingers around the handle and pulled. The light turned green, and a door opened. Stairs led downward into the dark.

Shipp turned to his group. "Stay close to your crews. When we get up, we separate and infiltrate. Use your tactical intuition. Kill 'em all."

Down into the dark stairwell they plunged. Quickly they reached the bottom, a flat track that ran for about ten meters before reaching another metal stairwell going up about two floors. They ascended and reached another flat section that went perpendicular to the flat one below.

Breaking into two groups, with Shipp leading one group and James the other, they stepped quietly toward the ends of the walkway, each of which led to a door with a keypad lock. Shipp glanced at James. A quick nod. They punched the code into the pad.

Zemmer pushed open Shipp's door, and Shipp burst in the room, Mossamer trained ahead of him. Empty. He ushered the other eleven in and pressed against the next door which opened into the command center.

"Leave that door open in case we need to retreat," Shipp whispered regarding the door they had just come through.

Muffled AX fire and wizards kept pounding the exterior on the east. Shipp could hear Krocks firing now. Full size ones, not Mossamer attachments. He looked at his crew.

"That's them, not us. Let's go."

He pushed open the door and found three Westers pouring over their Table, which was turned off. The Westers looked up in surprise. Shipp mowed them down. Zemmer, Gugbe, and Mixie ran past Shipp and flanked across the room. Blasé, Ramad, and the rest entered the Command Center and left the door open just a crack. This 'false' door had been completely obscured from inside the Command Center and made to look like part of the wall. The Westers had no idea it was there.

With only one known entrance into the room, the Petersons could defend from here.

Shipp scanned the room. Vonn and Renwar lay dead on the floor. The first Peterson generals to be killed in action in over fifty years. But before they died, Vonn apparently succeeded in turning off The Table, which protected all their remaining soldiers and other Peterson intelligence. Shipp grieved, but couldn't dwell on it yet. He used it.

"Wizards ready," Shipp ordered.

His four best propeller shooters came toward the door of the sound-proof room. Gugbe prepared to open it.

"Watch your targets. Rats only," said Shipp.

Gugbe opened the door slowly, knowing the Westers would think it was just their own guys. Ramad, Zemmer, Blasé, and another soldier walked out and fired 5cm wizards at two Westers who were communicating with their soldiers elsewhere.

More Westers who heard the sound ran in, and Shipp, Mixie, Gugbe, and others plastered them with AX and Mossamer fire. More firing could be heard in other rooms. Probably James' crew. Shipp led his crew through a hallway, turned left down another, and approached the entrance to the main staging hall. This hallway had three doors, all of which entered into the same large room from different locations.

Shipp divided his crew into groups of four. Here, the doors had small windows. They could see Westers feverishly working to fight against James as well as the Petersons attacking from outside. In the middle of the room, a large hole in the ground revealed the tunnel through which the Westers had infiltrated the Peterson base.

Another Krock fired outside. It was close.

A group of six Westers ran in and back out of the building. At least twenty more fought Faraday's squad and Shipp's other half to the south. Others hoisted more weapons and soldiers up from their underground shaft, using a mechanical lift with four legs spread out across the hole and hastily bolted to the floor.

How many soldiers did they have? For now, it didn't matter. Shipp led his team.

"Mixie. You take out the lift. MagTons. Hit the lift, then fire straight down the hole with rodents. Zemmer, you take the group to the south fighting Faraday." To his own group of Gugbe, Blasé, and Ramad he said, "We're going outside."

All three groups burst through the doors.

Mixie's group pelted the Westers working the lift, then fired MagTons at the legs of the lift. They attached to the metal and exploded. The lift buckled and teetered toward the hole. It was disabled but didn't fall.

Zemmer's crew hit the backsides of the Westers fighting Faraday and James with Mossamer and AX fire, killing a couple dozen very quickly. Shipp's group exchanged fire with the remaining Westers still in the building, but the rest ran out front toward Rothman's position.

Shipp ran outside after them, just in time to see another Krock fire at one of the Beasts from the Peterson outpost. The Wester rocket zipped toward it with that high-pitched telltale sound, and incinerated the vehicle, sending it tumbling over itself in flames.

Shipp, Gugbe, Ramad, and Blasé took position behind Wester supplies and unloaded on the Westers who were now caught between both groups. James and his group joined them.

Mixie and her crew aimed rodents down into the dark hole, and fired. The three-part explosion of the Morse mine rang through, and the Petersons dove for cover as fire and smoke billowed up and out the hole. They could hear Westers screaming from way down in the hole.

James yelled to Shipp on his comm through the noise, "More rats are inside!"

"Let's go get 'em," replied Shipp.

He waved his crew to follow. They searched through the hallway and found James' crew exchanging fire with Westers holed up in the mess hall. Shipp took Gugbe and Mixie with him, killed two Westers on the way, and reached the other side of the mess hall. In the room beyond it on the far side, he looked through a window as Westers blew through a wall with rodents.

On the other side stood Pretoria and her team, including General LaSalle. Her arms stretched out horizontally, as if to protect her team. Steady gaze. But only for a moment.

Still too far from the door, Shipp watched helplessly as a Wester commander ordered her soldiers to fire on the unarmed support personnel. They gunned them all down.

Incensed and desperate, Shipp raced to the door and burst through, followed by his squad. With James attacking from the perpendicular direction through another entrance, they caught the Westers from both sides and killed ten more. Their unfamiliarity with the Peterson base had made re-taking it fairly easy.

Shipp entered the room where his wife and her crew had stood.

The Wester commander who had given the order to fire on them was still alive, hugging a wall. She threw down her weapon.

Shipp searched the floor with his eyes. Bodies bleeding out. Dead. Dead. Dead. LaSalle dead. Shipp took a couple steps forward. He recognized his wife's shoes. Her legs. Her hands resting next to her hips. Her lifeless body greeted him from the floor. With every inch of her corpse coming into view, Shipp felt rage pulse throughout his body. His eyes filled with watery wrath. His breath shortened.

Finally, her face. Blood spattered but still beautiful to him. His fingers began trembling as he fixed his gaze on her for what seemed like forever. Gugbe waited and watched, making sure no other Westers survived while also monitoring Shipp. Wishing he could do something for his friend and commander.

The Wester commander who ordered the execution stood rigid against the wall.

Finally, Shipp breathed and looked ahead. He turned to see the woman who killed the only lady he had ever loved. The Wester commander sensed something was off here. She held her hands out, away from the rest of her body.

Shipp threw down his weapon, and approached her. She eyed him, uncertain. Nervous. He stood in front of her, peering into her soulless eyes. Without a word, Shipp unsheathed his knife, and slashed her across the throat.

The Wester commander, still alive and in shock, clutched her throat as blood spilled out in red vengeance. Shipp threw open the door facing west and dragged her staggering body toward the exterior patio overlooking the ledge. Once there, he grabbed her by the back of the neck, and looked menacingly into her eyes as the life drained out of her.

Then he threw her over the ledge, where she plummeted about twenty meters to her death.

Shipp looked back in the direction of his wife, enflamed with the prospect of eternal grief. There had to be a way to save her. To reverse what just happened.

Gugbe stood up from a kneeling position next to Pretoria's body. He looked at Shipp with intense devotion and love. Shipp walked toward him, never breaking his gaze, tears welling up as he neared. Gugbe rose, put his arms around Shipp, and said just three words through his own shared tears.

"Use it, brother."

14

Architect Elliss

Shipp looked down at his dead love. She was gone. Executed in cold blood by Wester rats. Her beautiful face as calm as ever. Even in death, no panic.

Shipp had never considered the possibility that she might die, even on Risner. He knew he might die, but not her. Especially after the close call a couple years back. It couldn't happen twice. The idea was so foreign that he couldn't process it. The shock froze him in time.

The Wester AX rounds had broken cases of pleasure food behind Pretoria and her team – including wine that dripped, trickled, and bled across the floor. Shipp watched the wine mix with Pretoria's blood. Sangria. Waves of rage and grief rose and crashed over and around him. His dreams died. His mind darkened. Starlight turned to supernova. He whispered to himself, so faint Gugbe barely heard him even though standing right beside him.

"Royal..."

Shipp stood silent for a beat.

Then, he looked at Mixie. Heartbroken for him, but ready to die for him, she wondered what he wanted from her. He strode toward her and ripped the Morse mine rifle from her hands. Marching back to the main staging room as if there was only one place left to go in the entire galaxy, Shipp reached the hole in the floor leading straight down to the Wester tunnel. He could hear Westers still scratching around down there, like ants.

Shipp tore off his combat suit. Quickly donned a Wester suit while Mixie, Gugbe, James, Zemmer, Ramad, Blasé, and the others watched.

He rubbed his hand through the blood of the Wester soldier whose suit he now wore and wiped it across his chest. Then, he jumped in the temporary manlift the Westers had installed on the side of their hole, and lowered himself down. Alone.

James took charge.

"Don't leave this spot. He comes back up – make sure no one shoots him."

In the vertical shaft, Shipp descended to the bottom and reached the horizontal tunnel that surely led all the way back to the now smoldering Wester base. He hurried past the bullet-ridden corpses killed by Mixie, and the weaponry and supplies she destroyed. In short order, he reached a group of seven more Westers, two of whom were badly injured.

One was talking on a comm.

"...I'm not sure. Dogs have regained control upstairs I think bro." Then, he saw Shipp approaching. "Hold on, General. We got one more grunt just made it down, ya."

They looked at Shipp, not realizing he was a Peterson.

"Anyone else left up there eh?" one of them asked, in that stupid accent they all use.

Shipp shook his head. "Anyone else left down here?"

"Just the op relay back there, ya. General Elliss says the dogs incinerated our base. Eh?"

Shipp nodded. "Yeah. We did."

He aimed his Mossamer at the speaker and shot him through his head, and then gunned down the other six before they had time to blink. He approached the dead Wester who had been on his comm. He held the Wester comm to the side of his face.

"General Elliss. Do I have you to thank for this? Ya," Shipp said, mocking their way of speaking.

Dead silence. Then, a response.

"Who is this? What just happened?"

"One day, Mr. Elliss. You're gonna find out. When I rip your heart out and feed it to you."

Shipp dropped the comm device, and aimed Mixie's Morse mine rifle into the dark tunnel before him. He emptied it, firing all nine remaining rodents, and then dashed back toward his own base and up the lift.

Shipp reached the splintered interior of the Peterson base where Mixie and the others waited. He ripped off his Wester disguise, and kicked it down the hole. Some dust from the Morse mine explosions made its way up the hole in response, almost like an underground monster had belched in gratitude for all the lives it just claimed.

***

Two days later, the Petersons assessed the damage. And buried their dead.

Faraday, Pretoria, Vonn, Renwar, and LaSalle. They worked together, and they died together. All five received honored burials, side by side. Burying the dead wasn't easy on a planet where little civilization existed. But there was no way to preserve the bodies long enough to send them home. No ships could come to their rescue in time.

The best they could do was use the trench digger and carve spaces in the ground for each person. But Faraday, Pretoria, Vonn, Renwar, and LaSalle were buried separately from the other dead soldiers and admins, near the more permanent rocks approaching the canyons. They marked each grave with a plaque, engraved on the rock shelf behind them.

Shipp knelt on the freshly dug mound where his only love would be lost forever. He ran his fingers through the earth in a mournful caress. His future wiped clean. Mixie cried for his loss, and wondered how Pretoria's death would affect the only squad leader she'd ever known.

James was the only one brave enough to approach Shipp and kneel next to him. He wrapped his arm around him. Shipp broke, leaning into his friend and weeping while his surviving squad looked on, with full respect and unity.

When Shipp regained himself, he and James stood up together.

All the surviving Petersons stood there waiting. Because now, Shipp was in charge. All the generals and Faraday were dead. It was just Thomas Shipp, Karel Rothman, and the two outpost commanders back at their bases.

Shipp realized they were waiting for him to give orders. He found his mind, enough to deliver them.

“Get what we can, load up the vehicles, head for the outposts. Rothman north, mine south. Base personnel and extra soldiers go with her. Come back here later and reassess.”

It took several trips back and forth, but eventually, they determined what happened. Apparently, the Westers had spent years digging this tunnel, one little section at a time, to prevent any chance of the Petersons detecting their work. The hole beneath the Peterson base had been there for at least a year, waiting to be used at the optimal time.

It appeared as if the Westers had deliberately provoked the Peterson assault by attacking them in several low-risk battles over the last two years. Their goal had been to make the Petersons think a more threatening offensive would be coming against them. That fear would eventually drive them to attack the Wester base. In other words, they were baited – with a plan that took years to realize.

At the first sign of the Peterson attack on their main base, the Westers headed through their tunnel to take out the Peterson base. In the couple hours it took to cover the underground distance between the bases and get all their weaponry positioned, the Petersons were wiping out sensors and planting explosives in the mostly empty Wester base. The Westers even opted to sacrifice some of their own people so they could infiltrate and destroy the Peterson base, knowing it was the only established one on the planet.

“Cannon fodder,” Shipp observed. “Animals.”

The Peterson assault on the Wester base was extremely effective. They obliterated several automated defense systems, including over half the samarium shields. The Westers probably thought these would perform better than they did. They certainly hadn’t counted on losing their own base so fast. But the Westers were willing to let it be attacked while the bulk of their forces traversed the tunnel.

An underground assault was unprecedented in the five-century Galactic War. Nothing like this had ever been done before.

At the southeast outpost, which Shipp used as the de facto Peterson main base, they communicated the aftermath of the battle to Space Force Command. The main base had lost all but three admin support personnel. All the reserve soldiers died, and Faraday’s squad had only eight members left, two severely injured. Five Beasts were destroyed by Wester K-rockets, including two from the outposts that were filled with twelve soldiers each – all dead. Rothman's squad only lost three, as she attacked from a distance. Shipp's squad lost five.

Shipp's friend Roy Horman was among the dead from Faraday's squad.

With about a hundred soldiers remaining from the main base, plus those at the outposts, the Petersons still had a sizable force, ample supplies, and plenty of weaponry. Their most immediate concern focused on a possible retaliation from the next nearest Wester base fifty kilometers to the east. The Petersons were now much more vulnerable. Outposts should not exist independently.

Shipp pressed Space Force Command to send a colonization ship and begin rebuilding the main base. A colonization ship only lands one time. The ship itself provides some of the materials to construct a new base. That way, the entire ship can be stocked with everything needed.

But Shipp's real reason for getting Space Force Command here was much simpler. He wanted off this rat planet. Forever.

Part 2 – Lavoisier

15

LI

Flight had a soothing effect on Shipp. He hadn't expected any effect at all when he first arrived here. But now, rumbling through the sky on his fifth flight since transferring from Risner to Lavoisier two months prior, he realized this was probably his favorite part of his new assignment.

The motion relaxed his mind, and he could drift off in peace without effort, though still fully alert. He discovered he didn't like talking to others during flights. He much preferred listening to the sound of the soft engines. The humming, pulsing vibration reminded him of a song he used to hear back in his teenage years, a song he'd forgotten all about until now.

In addition to the sounds, the flight would sway from side to side, almost like a huge hand was moving it along like a child plays with a toy shuttle. Shipp felt safe, almost invincible, while in motion through the air of this poisonous, filthy, dirty, wonderful planet.

James went with him on every flight. They had become inseparable. They bunked together. Shared meals. Discussed strategy. Processed grief. And James had learned the same thing about Shipp during flights. Leave him alone. Let him be at peace here, the only place he seemed to find it.

Shipp wasn't doing well. Too often, he internalized his grief and told James to "not worry about it." But James worried about it. He knew the Peterson Space Force's psychological training taught soldiers to channel their grief into focused rage, and to not allow lost loved ones to impair their judgment.

But Shipp was doing more than that. Some moments, he seemed determined to forget her completely, and just go with the flow of the moment. Especially on flights like this one. But other moments, he would find a place to be alone and just sit there, unmoving. James didn't think either one was helpful. Shipp needed to talk about it with someone, and James knew it had to be him. But most of the time, Shipp wouldn't go there, and James didn't press.

The ship's flight commander, Mansa Li, barked over the comm to the 28 soldiers on board.

"Touch down in five. Gear up."

Every soldier on board immediately reached for the breathing face shield resting below their chins, and affixed it over the nose, mouth, and eyes.

Lavoisier was just rocks and dirt. No life. No water. Poisonous air. If you exited the flight without breathing protection, you'd be dead in minutes. But the flights were sealed such that no air could escape or enter. And they were slightly pressurized so that if any slight openings existed, like a worn off screw or a cracked seal, the interior air would flow outward, and no exterior poisonous air could enter.

But even with all that protection, each soldier's breathing gear had to be ready at all times. If an air alarm sounded, or if the flight got attacked or malfunctioned and had to land without warning, the first task was for each soldier to shield their face.

They'd be landing in just a few minutes. The flying units rarely flew much higher than fifty meters off the ground. If they did get shot at by Westers, flying low would increase the chances of a successful crash landing where everyone could stay alive – the Core Principle of the Peterson Space Force.

Shipp's underground Lavoisier base had just two flights, and every time a flight departed from the base, they faced the risk of being shot down should they encounter any properly armed Westers. The flights were not well armored and made easy targets for a K-rocket or a MagTon. So the Petersons only used them when they had an extremely high degree of certainty that no Westers would be in the vicinity of the flight path.

The flight decelerated and descended, making a soft landing in a huge plain extending for several kilometers in all directions except one – a vast canyon to the west.

The hatch opened, and all the soldiers exited except one. That one remained behind to monitor movement and stay in touch with their only underground base in this hemisphere, which they left about thirty minutes ago. Shipp breathed deeply, almost as if he were ingesting the poisonous air in a final moment of satisfaction after a mission well done.

James nodded him over, and off they went, just the two of them. Shipp nodded at Gugbe and Zemmer, who went off as a separate pair. Ramad and Blasé had also come to Lavoisier with Shipp, but they weren't on this particular flight mission.

Mixie stepped off the flight and paired up with Shelsie, who had been on Lavoisier for over two years. Mixie smiled and gave Shipp an affirming nod as they parted. Shipp ignored her and looked the other way. He'd been ignoring her since they arrived here, and Mixie didn't know why. Neither did Shipp.

All 28 soldiers marched off in pairs, lugging huge packs on their backs.

Lavoisier was much smaller than Risner, and had almost nothing in common with it. For Shipp, that was the best thing about it. Some places featured rolling hills. Go another few kilometers and you might find sharp, craggy cliffs. Certain regions were bound by ravines where the ground had split at some point in the long distant past, and which had eroded into canyon-like formations that sunk hundreds of meters down.

One such ravine lay to the west. The mission today was to complete the planting of Rock Eyes between where the flight landed and the ravine. They headed out with packs full of Rock Eyes. If successful, they would return with packs empty.

Each soldier had about three hours of oxygen. They were given two and a half hours to plant every Rock Eye in their packs. By spreading out in twos, soldiers could protect each other if either person's breathing unit failed, and they could cover much more ground. Who would plant which Rock Eyes, and where, had been marked out in excruciating but necessary detail back in the base before they left. Upon landing, no orders needed to be given because every soldier knew what to do and where to go.

The Petersons' current plan with Lavoisier was to work methodically, taking over individual sections of the planet by covering them with Rock Eyes. These devices functioned much like the heat and motion sensors on Risner, except these resembled local rocks which littered the ground everywhere.

With the last four flights, they had covered quite a bit of ground approaching the ravine dropoff that was now just a few trots away. On this fifth flight, they expected to finish planting Rock Eyes the rest of the way. Once completed, with the canyon as a western border, the Petersons would have surveillance across a 400-square-kilometer region of the planet, with their underground base about 6km from the eastern edge of that region. After today's mission, they would map out the next area to cover.

Two hours and fifteen minutes later, Shipp placed his final Rock Eye and strode over to James, who had just one left after he finished with his current one.

"Moving like sludge, Cam. Got rocks in your shoes?" Shipp needled him.

James stood up after activating the Rock Eye, "Just waiting for you so I can tell you face to face how terrible your work was today."

Shipp's eyes glistened as he managed a short laugh. He needed levity like this more than water, and James usually held a reliable supply. But then James got serious.

"Actually, I think you forgot to turn on one of your Eyes. Looks like a dead zone in this area. Perhaps a bit too eager to finish first again."

James showed Shipp a screen filled with dots. One notable area on the screen had no dots.

"Weird," noted Shipp. "Let's check it on the way back. Get your last one done first."

"Jonas that."

James planted his final Rock Eye, and they trudged back toward the flight, stopping in the dead zone area. Sure enough, one of Shipp's devices sat there, unactivated. He bent down, lifted up what looked like any old rock in the desert, and pressed an invisible button. A small latch opened on the side. The latch had been completely concealed by all the exterior rock-like features. Shipp flipped a lever inside the latch and a light came on.

James looked at his screen. The dot appeared. "Well done loser. I mean soldier."

"At least it's not a dud," Shipp replied.

All 28 Petersons returned to the flight within two hours and 35 minutes. The hatch closed, the air pressurized, and they removed their breathing shields. Li returned to the flight command room and fired up the engine as he spoke over the comm.

"Congrats soldiers – every Rock Eye successfully placed and activated. We've got about 30 minutes to return. Make sure your breathing units are turned off so no air is wasted."

Li was so good. Shipp had gained instant admiration for him the first time they met. It was one thing to be so attentive to detail, and so consistent about it. Li was a great communicator. But in addition to all that, he was a great pilot. He had been on Lavoisier almost four years.

Before Shipp's first flight, there was a mechanical failure causing a frustrating delay. Li wasn't scheduled to fly that day, but he came to help when the other pilot called him. Six soldiers, including Shipp, were scouring over blueprints and staring down an opened access panel at one of the mechanical junctions.

Li looked inside the junction, reached in, and tapped a light ray a couple times.

"One of your stabilizing wires is shorted out. Can't make any turns without it, so the flight's computer won't let you start the engine." Always training.

Li then leapt into the flight, clanged around a bit while talking to himself, unintelligibly to the rest of them. Minutes later, several beeping sounds informed the other soldiers the problem was fixed. Li hopped off the flight, carrying a bad wire between two fingers.

"It's good now. When you get back I'll show you what I did."

And with that, he went back to whatever he'd been doing before. Shipp couldn't stifle a grin. He loved smart people. Efficient people. Focused people. Li was the complete package. From that point on, he wanted Li as his pilot for every flight he was assigned. Li happily obliged, and they started becoming friends.

Li's flight touched down on a flat slab of orange rock. No base in sight. Just dirt, rocks, and rolling hills as far as the horizon in every direction. But this slab of rock wasn't rock. Compressed air swooshed around the flight from the border of the slab. The edges of the slab rescinded, and the flight began sinking into the ground. The rock slab was a landing platform.

Once submerged under the ground, another slab slid above the flight and sealed against the surface, replacing the one the flight was still sitting on. Underground now, the flight was enclosed in a cylindrical, six-centimeter-thick polymer shield, with ventilators ringing the upper and lower borders all the way around.

The poisonous native air began to filter out the upper vents, as clean air replaced it from the lower ones. It took about ten minutes. Once Li's board flashed, he opened the doors and the soldiers shuffled out, funneling through the only door in the entire cylinder. This was the permanent home for this flight. The other one sat in a similar chamber on the other side of the underground base.

The Petersons had perfected this model for underground base construction on Lavoisier. They had six others in operation, all in the quarter of the planet bounded by the northern and western hemispheres. Shipp's base, called LUB-7, was the only Peterson base in the southern or eastern hemispheres. LUB-7 was the Peterson Space Force's latest attempt to expand the area under their control. The next stage of the plan involved founding a sister base about a hundred kilometers from this one within the next two years.

In addition to the seven LUBs, they had a larger number of older, much smaller underground units. Those were more like life capsules, and they dotted the planet, interspersed among the bases. The life capsules were the previous version of Peterson underground technology. They abandoned it decades ago, except for emergencies, and some were now uninhabitable. The life capsules had no flights or any way to house them. They had sleeping quarters for between ten and fifteen, but more than that could fit if necessary. No one currently occupied any of the life capsules.

Much older than the life capsules were the original surface domes, built for mining purposes, not combat, by both Petersons and Westers before the war. The domes enabled the mining of the rich deposits of vanadium and samarium which made this planet such a prize. The domes were abandoned centuries ago since they were so easily damaged and rendered uninhabitable by military weaponry, unable to seal off the poisonous atmosphere. Now, covered in dust, the remaining domes looked like diseased versions of Lavoisier mountains, complete with sharp edges, overhanging eaves, and useless interiors.

Shipp and James entered the social zone of LUB-7 and sat down to relax. Several other soldiers did the same at other tables. Li smiled when he saw Shipp and James, and joined them.

They wouldn't relax long.

General Stimara Loshea passed through and commended all the soldiers. She had been leading LUB-7 – short for Lavoisier Underground Base – the last two years. Every time Shipp saw her, he looked away. *Why did she flaunt her long hair like that? What kind of soldier draws so much attention to her appearance?*

When he first met her, he was surprised by it, but figured maybe she felt some reason to make herself look good for the arrival of her newest crop of reinforcements from Risner. But she looked like that every day. She made her face look attractive too. Her clothing always seemed one size too small from top to bottom. It was distracting, and Shipp was growing to resent it.

Loshea found Shipp, James, and Li, and headed straight for them. She sat in the only empty chair at their table.

"We received news about Risner while you were out."

"Save your breath," said Shipp.

"No," she replied. "Save your friend, not your breath."

Shipp scowled. Was this an attempt to be clever or cute? Why was she using the Core Principle of the Peterson Space Force as a punchline?

Loshea looked directly at Shipp. "Look at me, colonel." He looked. "Your friends on Risner are all dead. You need to know."

"No, I don't," replied Shipp, trying not to flinch at the devastating news. "I'm here to locate and destroy the Wester underground bases I know are here but that you haven't been able to find in over two years. I don't have time for stories from a dead planet."

He stood up to leave. She rose and stepped in his path.

"Your anger is commendable. I value it, far more than you realize. It's why I made you a colonel upon your arrival. What I don't commend is your dismissive attitude of your senior officer. There wasn't a hint of this in your record. You have a problem with me, Colonel Thomas Shipp?"

He looked her in the eye.

"I'm here to find the Wester base. That's all I care about."

He stepped around her and headed down a dark tunnel toward his unit's quarters. She watched him leave. Then, she sat down and faced James, and waited. James finally spoke:

"He took it real hard when she died. Still is."

General Loshea nodded. "I know. So did I when I lost mine." Loshea's husband died when a Wester attack ship found its way to an exposed Peterson space station, and wiped out half the inhabitants. Li lost his brother in the same attack, and came here with Loshea afterward. He always spoke highly of her to Shipp.

But James didn't think Loshea quite grasped the depth of Shipp's loss, or the recency. It was only six months ago. He tried a different approach.

"She was his starlight, General."

Loshea nodded ever so slightly, and seemed to lose herself in thought for a moment. She then relayed her respect without a word, and James acknowledged it. After a pause, she continued.

"I'd like to share the update with you, and you can pass it on to him."

"Sure."

Loshea began with the Space Force Command transport ship that arrived on Risner three months after Pretoria died. That ship brought reinforcements, fresh supplies, and arms. It also served to honor Shipp's transfer request to Lavoisier. After unloading its cargo and personnel, Shipp, James, Mixie, Gugbe, Zemmer, Ramad, Blasé, and about twenty other soldiers loyal to him boarded the ship and came to Lavoisier.

Karel Rothman was promoted to replace Shipp on Risner.

Plans were in the works to bring a colonization ship and resurrect their destroyed base. But the Westers correctly ascertained that the remaining Peterson outposts didn't have sufficient anti-air K-rock defenses, which had been neutralized at the wrecked main base. Two weeks ago, the Westers sent a wave of four attack ships straight through Risner's atmosphere, and they annihilated both outposts with their far more destructive K-rockets – the extra-large ones only used by attack ships.

Not a single Peterson was left alive on Risner.

Loshea finished, "Your friend needs to know, especially about Rothman. I was told by Space Force Command to be sure he knows what happened to her."

"I'll tell him," James promised. "But before you go, I have a question."

"Go ahead."

"Why did several guys in Unit 2 laugh when Shipp mentioned the Wester underground bases on this planet?"

Loshea demurred a bit. Then, she answered.

"LUB-7 has been here for four years. One through six have been here for almost fifty. No one has ever seen a Wester underground base. We see temporary domes go up and come down as they come and go. We see squads in motion now and then. But we haven't seen evidence of any bases of the sort you described. We figure they're using old life capsules."

"So you don't think there are any expanded bases or tunnels. And neither do the others," James pressed.

"I think the Wester assault you encountered on Risner was exceptional. Could they have used that type of technology here? I never would have thought so before hearing your account. Now, I'm not so sure."

"Why aren't the others open to it then? It's quite logical to me, and I never use that word."

Loshea's response surprised James. "Live underground for four years, and you'll understand."

With that, she stood to leave. "Sergeant Li, always a pleasure. Excellent flight work today."

"Thanks for the update, General," Li responded. Loshea left to attend to other tasks. James and Li looked at each other. Li broke the silence:

"You think Shipp is impaired because of Risner, and Pretoria?"

James shook his head, curling his lip.

"Not as far as the rats are concerned."

16

Phantom Bases

LUB-7, like the other six Peterson bases on Lavoisier, was built to house three squads of soldiers and a team of administrators. That enabled them to operate with nonstop active-status personnel.

When Shipp and the twenty soldiers from Risner arrived and a few others left to end their service, Loshea had to reshuffle the squads to balance them out at 28 each. The numbers took a few weeks to settle. During that time Shipp got himself stationed on Li's flight squad. In addition to those 84 soldiers, there were 21 administrators and support personnel, plus General Loshea and another general who worked alongside her.

Because battles were so rare on Lavoisier, the generals seldom ventured out from LUB-7. That usually left the flight commander functionally in charge out in the field.

As on Risner, any soldier who wanted to sit in on strategic planning meetings was permitted, and Shipp took this opportunity from day one. The day after his little scruff with Loshea, he was right back in the next meeting. Up to this point, though he had attended at least forty meetings, he had mostly listened, soaking up the rhythms and terminology of Lavoisier. If he spoke up, it was usually to ask a question.

But it was that one question he asked a few weeks back that caused a stir throughout the base. He asked, "Have you ever developed a mission strategy to locate any expansive Wester underground bases or tunnels?"

Loshea seemed intrigued at the thought but said nothing. However, Shipp interpreted her silence as 'no,' because the likelihood seemed so miniscule to her and several others at the meeting. Most seemed to think the Westers were still, at best, using technology similar to the life capsules, along with temporary domes. Less permanent and more versatile. The other general, Strim Lom, scoffed at the idea immediately, and took every opportunity to ridicule or minimize it from that point on. Shipp loathed him, and yearned for another leader like Vonn. Whereas Risner had been everything Shipp had wanted and expected from his Space Force experience up until the Wester attack that killed his wife, Lavoisier seemed frayed by more typical human failings.

Today's planning meeting started off well.

They posted a display on the wall monitor showing several hundred square kilometers around LUB-7. On it, the advantage provided by the Rock Eyes was resounding. A whole swath of land leading up to the large western ravine now sparkled with surveillance dots. Combined with the Rock Eyes and other surveillance already in place, LUB-7 would be impossible to approach within ten kilometers in any direction without being spotted.

"Beautiful work," General Lom affirmed. "A DSE-proof sensor web."

Loshea had also done well in constructing a battery of about thirty automated, modified AX rifles encircling LUB-7. These weapons were also concealed underground, but were built to emerge and attack any approaching Westers. The rifles could swivel within about a 45-degree range, and they could be operated remotely from within the base. Since LUB-7 was all alone in this hemisphere, Loshea had made its defense a priority since her arrival and promotion.

"I think we should expand to the north next," Lom continued.

Shipp took this opportunity to assert his first mission proposal since arriving on Lavoisier.

"I think now is a good time to start getting serious about finding the rat infestation on this planet, and wipe them out. By expanding our foothold, we could control this planet within our service time, and actually start mining it."

All heads turned in Shipp's direction – the two generals, several admins, and about ten other soldiers. Predictably, Lom butted in.

"Wherever the rats are, our current approach will expose them eventually."

"That's too slow. It will take decades to cover the whole planet with Rock Eyes," responded Shipp. "We need to analyze the planet's terrain and locate areas most probable for an underground base. Let's start with places where we might build one."

"I've been on this planet for seven years," said Lom. "I've been in every LUB at least once. The Westers we encounter are dropped off from space or hiding in capsules. We've seen them do it – from land and from space."

"You have no surveillance on over three fourths of the planet."

"We invented this tech, and the Westers haven't found any of our bases, so they couldn't have copied it," said Lom, the frustration mounting in his voice. He wasn't used to being disagreed with, and it irked him.

Shipp stood and walked to the wall screen.

"They have their own underground tech. I've seen it. I walked inside it." Shipp paused. "I killed rats in it. They used it on a planet that has no need for underground bases. I think they perfected it here where they do need it. And then one of them got smart, and they adapted the tech to Risner."

Lom approached Shipp, and countered him with a barrage of sensible objections, "Where do you propose we start looking, on the three fourths of the planet where we have no surveillance? How do you propose to find a phantom base that may or may not exist, with just a few hours of oxygen supply at a time, using one of two irreplaceable flights?"

Shipp kept a measured tone.

"This is how we win the war."

Some laughter escaped from a few soldiers around the room. Lom smiled. "Win the war? Are you one of those?"

"If you don't think we can win the war, then what the flame are you doing here, General?"

Loshea had let it go to this point, but she stepped in when Shipp undermined Lom's authority.

"We all want to win the war," she began. "But it won't happen in our lifetimes."

"Not if we don't find their underground bases," Shipp said.

"Colonel Shipp," Loshea said.

But he interrupted her. "Who wins the war? The side with the most attack ships. That's it. That's everything. Once one side wipes out the other side's attack ships, that side rules the space front. You rule the space front, you win the war. How do we build the most attack ships? We start mining Lavoisier again and triple production of Blackhead. How do we start mining Lavoisier again?"

Shipp looked around the room. The answer didn't need to be spoken. Shipp could see he had caused a few of the listeners to at least think differently about the war.

"We can do both jobs at the same time," Loshea said. "Let's find an area that has underground base potential, and make that our next Rock Eye mission."

"As long as we connect those areas back to the ones we've already planted," said Lom, a man too driven by a need for closure, for completion. And it was distracting him from the real mission. Shipp despised Lom even more from that moment on.

Li spoke up. "Question, General. Have all these Rock Eye sensors failed to detect a single rat? We've plastered the land with them. I confess I don't come to all these briefs, but I haven't heard of a single active signal. Where have we seen their soldiers already?"

Loshea signaled to an admin to put the data up on the screen.

There were Rock Eye regions, and Rock Eye clusters. The regions all connected to LUB-7. Outside of those regions, they had planted a few clusters here and there, before they started pursuing Lom's strategy of blanketing the entire quartile.

"We started planting Rock Eyes more than three years ago," Loshea began. "In that time, the sensors have tripped a total of 26 times. The purple dots represent sensor activation incidents."

Everyone studied the screen.

Li quickly synthesized the display and made the key observation, "You've got 17 of those 26 all near this cluster to the northeast." He pointed on the screen. "Either they like landing their troops in that area, or there's a base nearby."

Shipp flushed with focused rage, and looked straight in Lom's direction.

"You've been sitting on that intel for how long? Vonn would have been all over this." Shipp didn't wait for an answer. He kept calm and just took charge. "Find three areas with base potential near there. We head out tomorrow. I'm on the first flight out."

Everyone left the room except Loshea and Lom. He waited for her response. And he got one.

"You should go with them, General Lom. Get some fresh air."

17

Seek and Destroy

They didn't head out the next day, because even Shipp knew some degree of planning needed to happen first. But four days later, they were airborne.

And even though General Lom was on board this flight, Shipp got command of the battlefield units. Lom would lead the small group of soldiers who would stay with the flight should a ground battle commence. If they did find a Wester base nearby, there was a high probability of combat, and they couldn't risk losing one of their two air vehicles.

Li piloted, as usual. For this mission, Shipp brought all the soldiers who wanted to kill Westers most, plus his core unit. That meant James, Mixie, Gugbe, Zemmer, Ramad, and Blasé, plus several more who had come from Risner. Mixie's new friend Shelsie came too, and enough others until the maximum of 28 had boarded the flight.

Flying low, they traversed ridges, slopes, and rock-strewn vistas. Just light brown everywhere. Beautifully ugly, thought Shipp. Li flashed the alarm that they would be landing soon. Then Mixie shouted to the whole squad: "Westers! I got two rats off starboard. Armed with conventionals."

Shipp, seated on the other side, nodded to James to survey the landscape, and then he addressed the squad.

"Stay put. Remember – we can't overload one side. Watch your own views and take in the terrain. We'll be walking it very soon. When we land – arm up, grab one Rock Eye each, and head out. General Lom – you run point from here with five others. You pick the five. Defend the flight at all costs."

"Already done," replied Lom.

"Landing on the other side of the ridge at 330 degrees. Thirty seconds," announced Li.

Everyone affixed their breathing shields. The flight circled around and set down just on the other side of a low ridge that overlooked a plain. The Westers had been spotted in a gulley on the other side of that plain. They took off running when they saw the Peterson flight.

Li landed just far enough back from the ridge line that a Wester emerging from the gulley on the other side of the plain shouldn't be able to see the flight. But they all knew it was only a matter of time before the Westers would locate them.

Now outside the flight and leaving Lom and five others inside, Shipp addressed his 22-member squad. "James – tell us about the terrain."

James gave a quick summary.

"From where we sit, the Westers are to the south, running along a gulley toward the east."

Everyone looked east. In the distance sat a small cluster of moderately elevated hills – high by this planet's standards. Leading up to that was an increasingly craggy landscape. The gulley was really just the first of many rivets in the terrain leading toward the hills.

James relayed this to the squad, and then interjected his assessment.

"With all those ridges and gulleys, you've got a series of ups and downs. Very gradual though. No one's going to fall off a cliff here, but if we get caught down in a gulley by a bunch of Westers on a ridge, we're dead. So we stay high. But not too high."

Shipp affirmed James' instructions.

"Not too high. That means just off the top of a ridge. Don't walk the highest point. You don't want to be seen from both sides below if you can help it."

"Jonas that," several soldiers responded. Shipp continued:

"Remember – your goal is twofold. Plant your Rock Eye and watch for rats. Kill them if you can. But the main objective is to ascertain where they're coming from. Pay attention to their movements."

"What about hostages? Or is it kill on sight only?" Zemmer asked.

"That's a battlefield decision for each of us," replied Shipp. "But if you take a hostage, you make sure that rat is subdued and disarmed. Check for blades."

The 22 soldiers rose over the ridge and hustled down the other side to the plain. They headed southeast, toward an estimated point the two Westers would be approaching, assuming they kept running straight. The idea was to start surveying the area they were running toward, because if a base existed in this area, it lay in that direction.

Mixie approached Shipp. "That area isn't one of the ones we identified as a potential base zone."

"I know."

James noticed Shipp's curt reply and lack of tactical response. Very unlike him. Then Shipp turned away from Mixie, who was right next to him, and searched for Gugbe.

"Gugbe," Shipp said. "Plant your Rock Eye here."

Gugbe prepared his device.

While he did, Shipp divided his forces, "This is hard core. Remember your training. Some of you haven't fought a real battle in years, right?" A few of the Petersons who were Lavoisier veterans nodded.

"Neither have these rats if they've been here a while. But we have." He nodded to his Risner comrades. "I want two groups of six and two groups of five. Always keep another group in sight. One leads, the other stays farther back and on a different ridge. Stay alive."

"Save your friend," came the callback.

Shipp took Zemmer, Gugbe, Blase, and two Lavoisier veterans. He put James in charge of a group of five, Mixie in charge of another group of six, and Li the leader of the last group of five, which included Ramad.

"James and I are going left. Mixie and Li go right – beyond the gulley where we saw the two rats. Stay on your comms at all times. Eyes open in front and behind. Plant your Rock Eyes as you go. Remember we have about three hours of air."

They split into four crews.

Shipp's crew veered toward the direction of the Westers, so James veered slightly away. The idea was to reach the edge of the plain and then assess what they could see beyond it. Mixie led her crew straight toward the gulley, double-timing it so she could parallel Shipp as best as possible. Li took his crew alongside hers, about ten meters apart.

Shipp's crew approached a slight rise that led to a series of gradual ridges and ravines. They flattened to the dirt and crawled up to overlook the area beyond. All six laid out next to each other so each could scope the terrain.

Silence.

No movement.

They saw no Westers. So they stayed put, waited and watched. Shipp knew they had time to be still because it would take Mixie and Li longer to get into a parallel position since they had to go farther south.

James' crew hedged up against a small section of larger rocks, keeping Shipp within sight. James ordered his crew to survey the areas to Shipp's left, to protect him from any ambushes from his backside. Both crews huddled here for about twenty minutes, before Li crackled through the comm.

"We're set. I can see straight down three ravines. No rats. But there are recent footprints in one of them."

Shipp replied, "Which one?"

"From your position, the third ravine to the south. The walls get steeper the farther it goes toward those hills, and it looks like it branches out about two hundred meters away."

"Jonas." Shipp pondered Li's better vantage intelligence, and relayed all this to James so his own crew would hear everything. "What do you think, old pal?"

James smiled and shook his head. "What are you asking me for, point man? Do your thing."

Shipp addressed his crew and laid out the strategy, but kept his comm on so James would know their plan.

Then, Shipp took the lead with Zemmer in the rear. His crew proceeded single file along the upper left side of the nearest ravine. They could see over that ridge to the right, but would not be visible to anyone walking at the bottom of the ravine below it. Farther to the right, the ravine with Wester footprints was separated from them by two other ravines. James and his crew began advancing down the ravine just to the south of Shipp's, keeping one between him and the Wester-traversed ravine. James' crew walked along the upper right slope. That meant one full ridge and two ravines stood between his crew and Shipp's, but since they were walking along the upper half of the slopes, they could see each other.

Shipp's orders were clear and being followed.

To the south, Li and Mixie followed a similar pattern, with Li on the other side of the ridge bordering the Wester ravine, and Mixie one more beyond him to the south. A couple Petersons from each crew planted Rock Eyes as they went. The larger hills and mountains in the distance crept closer, and the ravine walls grew steeper and taller. Gugbe relayed the current status back to Lom at the flight.

More walking. Looking ahead. Looking left. Looking right. Different members of each crew were assigned to focus in certain directions and trust their fellow soldiers to be doing the same. Finally, Shipp's crew approached an area where the ravines seemed to branch off and change directions.

"Whatever you do," Shipp spoke in his comm to Li, James, and Mixie, "Do not get caught at the bottom of a ravine. Stay on the slopes. Ravines are for rats."

Shipp's crew reached a point where two ravines on each side merged in front of him, so he had to descend. He led his crew down one slope and back up the other side. But he never took the whole crew down at once. Two at a time ran down and back up the bordering slope. James observed from his own ridge.

Zemmer caught sight of movement down a ravine in the distance. He called the crew's attention to it. Two Westers had crossed a ravine, heading to the south. Shipp's crew increased their pace, and the others followed suit. Shipp informed Li the Westers were probably heading in his direction. Moving quickly, they closed the distance to where the Westers had been spotted. Li spotted them again, racing down a ravine directly away from him, about fifty meters away.

His crew fanned out, got on one knee each, and prepared to fire down the ravine. Two soldiers fired four hive bombs, while the others fired AX rounds. The hive bombs whizzed through the ravine. One banked off the side. Each approached the fleeing Westers and exploded near the targets.

One Wester fell, but the other picked him back up and they kept moving. The Peterson AX fire increased in accuracy as the Westers approached a turn. Right at the turn, one Wester got caught by Ramad's AX-15.

"Wow, nice shot," Li said.

The Wester stopped his forward motion, got turned around by another shot, and then blasted multiple times in the chest and head. He collapsed. The other Wester escaped around the turn.

"One down," Li informed Shipp.

Shipp's crew ran at a brisk pace to reach the ravine where the other Wester had escaped. But they ran into another ravine intersection that forced them to run down theirs and back up the other side of the next one. This slowed their approach. Shipp let them catch their breath once they reached the upper slope of the other side. Then, they peered over the summit of that next ridge.

AX fire pelted near their heads almost immediately, and all six hit the dirt.

Shipp looked back at James. "What do you see?"

"Can't see anything. Ridge line is too high."

The Westers had to be in a ravine or on a slope somewhere on the other side.

Shipp split his crew. He, Zemmer, and Gugbe crawled left. Blasé and the other two went right. All stayed on the outer side of the ridge, which curled around slightly like a crescent moon, with the curvature bending away from James. If the Westers were in that ravine floor, Shipp reasoned he could surround them from both sides.

Shipp crawled up to the summit of the ridge to get a better look. Zemmer and Gugbe came alongside him. The ravines were starting to feel like a maze. Several possible avenues lay before them, and a clearing of sorts lay before them on the other side. No Westers. Shipp stood up.

When he did, an automated turret rose from the clearing floor, rotated in his direction and fired. Shipp caught sight of it and flattened before it could target him.

"It's an automated AX cannon! Hit it with rodents!"

Gugbe, Zemmer, and the other two Petersons hurled Morse mines toward the turret's position. Each mine hit the ground and then began their three-stage chain reaction explosion. As the rodents hit the ground in the clearing, Shipp stood up to become bait for the turret.

The turret rose up. The first Morse mine explosion blew upwards, clouding the view of the turret. The second explosion blew outward, and the third and final explosion blew up and out with even greater force.

The rodents that landed closest to the turret did extensive damage to it, impairing its ability to fire and turn. Zemmer prepared his MagTon rifle, and fired one at the turret. The weapon attached to the turret's metal, and blew it to pieces a second later.

Shipp looked around at his crew. All alive and unharmed. "Well done. Move forward. They're guarding something in this direction."

Shipp also took this opportunity to plant his Rock Eye. James crackled through the comm.

"Shipp – you got a bunch coming your way, down three different ravines ahead of you. At least ten. Recommend you pull back toward us."

Shipp didn't hesitate. He and his crew raced back down the slope, up the other side and over the ridge. Then, they laid out again and looked back in the direction James had indicated. James had moved his crew forward and to the right.

That meant James and Shipp were now doing what Shipp had done with his own crew moments earlier. They had two crews facing the same direction at the same distance to a potential target coming from the area behind the turret's position.

"They probably have all these ravines mapped out and memorized," James cautioned. "Presume they know how to catch us from behind."

"Li," Shipp called. "Get your crews heading in our direction and watch our backsides. The Westers seem to be based somewhere to the northeast of our position."

But Li came back with a disturbing response.

"Negative Commander Shipp. We have six to eight rats approaching our positions from due east. Don't want to be surrounded."

"Jonas that. Follow your tactical determinants," replied Shipp, telling Li to do whatever he needed based on his on-site intelligence. The Peterson Way.

"There they are!" Zemmer called out.

Several Westers emerged from different ravines ahead of the Petersons. But they quickly fell out of sight, guarded by the ridges. The Westers now occupied the clearing where the turret had been.

"That clearing where they are now – they can't come out of that without climbing that ridge, right?" Shipp conferred with his crew.

Gugbe read Shipp's subtext. "Fire dual cannons into the clearing now!"

Four Petersons set up their cannons and fired a volley into the clearing. It went too far. They quickly adjusted and fired twice more, plastering the clearing.

"Hold your fire," Shipp ordered. "Watch and listen."

It was hard to hear though, because Li and Mixie were now engaged in firefights with Westers near their positions. Both armies were heavily protected by the terrain and no one had a good shot at the enemy.

"James," Shipp called. "Fire a dozen rodents into the ravine just to the north of my position. Set them on a one-minute delay."

"Jonas," James called back on the comm.

"If they did find a way around," Shipp told his crew, "They will have to come through the ravine to our left."

His crew understood.

We're the bait. And we're going to run along the ravine floor – what Shipp had said never to do at the beginning of the skirmish. But now, the tactics had shifted and it was the right call, so no one questioned him.

James' crew fired twelve Morse mines, and they landed inside the ravine to Shipp's left, separated by about five meters from each other. Shipp and his crew raced down to the bottom of the same ravine, and barreled west, leaving the rodents in their dust. James paralleled Shipp's vector along his own ridge, with one ravine between them.

Six Westers had indeed found a way around the crescent-shaped clearing and saw Shipp and his crew far down the ravine when they rounded a corner. Shipp was at least a hundred meters ahead of them. But being in the same ravine, the Westers could see them straight ahead. They chased them for a bit, and then started firing with traditional rounds.

Shipp knew the risks were too high.

"Hit the dirt!"Everyone fell to the ground.

The Westers were closing fast, but were now passing through the waiting Morse mines, unaware of their looming demise.

Ten seconds.

Nine.

Eight.

Shipp and his crew rose up to one knee and started returning fire. This surprised the Westers, and they stopped the pursuit and tried to find cover.

Detonation began.

One after another, the Morse mines exploded. Most missed the actual Wester soldiers, but with mines exploding all around them, they lost their bearings and became terrified and disoriented. Shipp's squad ran straight for them, AX-15's blazing, and gunned them all down. A complete one-sided slaughter.

Gugbe turned back toward Shipp as dust blew across his face, and gave a huge grin, so big you could see it through the breathing shield.

"Yeah boss. That was vintage."

Shipp nodded, then gave the next order.

"Let's head back to that clearing and re-assess."

They clambered up the ridge to their left and marched cautiously back toward where the turret had been. Shipp and his squad returned to the clearing, now strewn with fragments from the automated turret. They stayed on the ridges surrounding it, and planted a Rock Eye. James' squad paralleled them again on another ridge.

Half a kilometer to the south, Li and Mixie continued to battle a group of Westers. Shipp asked James to catch him up on their status.

"There's a group of at least ten rats holed up in an area they can't get close to. They've launched dual cannon volleys but the Westers seemed to evade them somehow. Not sure how they could know where they would land. But they keep returning fire. So far no confirmed kills on either side."

Shipp nodded, "I think we have them on the defensive since we're fighting two fronts. Looks like we've cleared ours out for now. We'll catch the other group from behind. On the way, plant the rest of your Rock Eyes. The base has got to be nearby. Watch out for new attacks. If there's a base entrance, they can send more our way."

Moving toward a position behind the Westers fighting Li and Mixie required some tact. They didn't want to give themselves away, but also didn't want to take too much time getting there. Plus, they had to keep their eyes open in all directions.

One ridge and one ravine at a time. Sometimes straight paths. Sometimes curved. Never bunched up too close, but never too spread out.

Shipp and James headed south. James went slower, as he planned to remain north of the enemy, while Shipp would position his squad farther east behind the Westers attacking Li and Mixie. They'd have them from three sides.

With one more ravine to cross, the terrain appeared to flatten out beyond it to the south. Shipp's squad ascended the slope toward the crest of their current ridge.

When his squad of six approached the crest, their heads became visible from within the ravine before them. Six Westers awaited them from down in the ravine and fired at first sight – too early as it turned out because they only hit one Peterson soldier. And fortunately for Shipp, his squad wasn't immediately in the Westers' direct line of sight. The Westers were about ten meters to the west, so it took a moment to aim in their direction. But they seemed to know the Petersons were coming.

The Wester attack struck and killed the Peterson soldier closest to them, one of the Lavoisier veterans. He fell to the ground dead just as Shipp and the others hit the dirt. Shipp immediately called James on his comm.

"There's a whole nest of 'em in the last ravine! We just lost one!"

But James called back with worse news.

"Another squad coming toward your position in the ravine behind you. You'll be boxed in on both sides in about thirty seconds."

The Westers who just fired on them didn't wait. They fired an array of Morse mines toward Shipp's position, exploding on impact. His now five-person squad was forced to flee farther to the east, away from James and the other Petersons.

Zemmer fell, his calf punctured by one of the rodent blasts. He writhed in pain, but scrambled back to his feet before collapsing again. Shipp ran back to save his friend.

"Gugbe!" Shipp yelled. "Fire wizards toward the oncoming squad and cross the last ravine. Burn south and circle around the far side to connect with Li!"

"Shipp!" Gugbe yelled back. "You two can't stay here alone!"

"We won't be – do it!"

Gugbe, Blasé, and the other Peterson fired a series of wizards in the direction of the oncoming Westers James had told them about. James heard Shipp's plan, and supplemented it with a dual cannon volley.

The oncoming Westers had to halt and take cover, especially as they heard the dual cannon missiles approaching.

Shipp rolled himself and Zemmer down that same ravine, picked Zemmer up on his back, and clambered up the other side. The ravine wasn't straight, so he was able to make this move without the oncoming Westers seeing him, because they were busy avoiding the missiles from James.

Meanwhile, Gugbe, Blasé, and the other Peterson soldier had to cross the last ravine, where the six Westers who had attacked them were waiting. But they were fifty meters west of their position. They scrambled down the bank, and fired AX and Mossamer fire toward the Westers, who had to hit the dirt to shield themselves.

Gugbe got his group up the other side of the ravine and to the flatter terrain, where they dashed south, looking back now and then to see if any Westers were pursuing. None were. He called Shipp on his comm:

"Shipp – I think we're in the clear. We're about to circle back to Li."

But Shipp couldn't respond. He was trying to make his way to James, but was being attacked by the new group of Westers who seemed to know he had crossed their ravine even though he was sure they hadn't seen him. They might have surveillance here too.

Shipp's position was being pelted with AX fire and the occasional rodent, but they couldn't get close enough to target him well. He situated right against a large rock to the east and a smaller rock he could see past toward the south, on a flattened section of a ridge.

James fired several volleys back and forth with the Westers attacking Shipp. Were he alone, Shipp could make it to James. But Zemmer could barely walk.

"James," Shipp called him. "I can't get to you with Zemmer. You gotta come to me."

"Jonas," James called back. "Watch out for rodent fire. We're coming."

Shipp trusted James, and knew he'd get here. The problem was, what if the six Westers from the ravine Gugbe just crossed decided to come in his direction too. They would intercept James, and there would be two sets of Westers attacking them. This had been the Petersons' advantage earlier, but now it was them getting out-maneuvered.

Just as James and his squad surmounted another ravine and got a bit closer, Shipp saw the other six Westers ascend the ridge. They were coming his way.

"James."

"I see them Shipp. I can't get to you, and I can't hold them back from here."

The thought crossed Shipp's mind. *I might die next to this rock.* He dismissed it.

James' squad began unloading all sorts of firepower toward the six Westers. But the Westers made it down into the next ravine and avoided any casualties, and then returned fire toward James. James' crew was now caught in the same type of back and forth that still ensnared Li and Mixie, as far as Shipp knew. Firing blind from within ravines was a difficult battlefield.

"James," Shipp called again. "If more rats come at us from whatever base is near here, we're dead. Only one option left to get us out of here."

"I'll do it," James responded, already knowing.

Back at the flight with five other Petersons, General Lom heard the alert comm while scanning the distant battle with a scope. He tossed the scope and leapt into the flight to answer. It was James.

"This is Lom. I read you James."

"We need an air attack run now. My squad and Shipp are boxed in, flanked by at least two Wester squads. I'm sending you their position and ours. Get here now before more arrive."

"Jonas."

Lom and the others got on board, closed the hatch, and lifted off within thirty seconds.

Lom ordered two of his soldiers to man the ground weapons as he input James' positional data on his screen. Flights were equipped with the equivalent of AX rounds – meaning the same materials, but of twice the caliber. They could also drop rodents and a few larger explosives.

"Get ready to drop fire on those rats," Lom ordered his soldiers.

Lom had moved fast, but not fast enough for Shipp. As James fought off the six Westers from the southern ravine, the other group made its way toward Shipp from behind the large rock to his backside. He knew it, but he couldn't stop them.

Shipp armed up his six remaining Morse mines, and set them to various timings, ranging from thirty seconds to two minutes, and then tossed them around both sides of the rock. He didn't care if the Westers could see them, because it would delay their approach since they didn't know the timings.

He looked at Zemmer, "Flight is coming. When it hits the other crew, we're running in that direction, toward the attack. You just get down the ravine, and I'll get you up the other side."

Shipp knew he had to fight off all the Westers coming his way by himself. Not good. But his Mossamer was ready.

The first of Shipp's rodents exploded. He could hear Westers react. They ran down the ravine toward the north. They were close, but that was good, because Shipp intended to run in the other direction once Lom got here.

And there he was. Lom's flight approached, faster, faster. Shipp knew the Westers could see him too. The Westers fighting James turned to fire at Lom, and so did the Westers near Shipp, which gave away their position. They hit Lom with MagTons, which attached and punctured the flight.

Lom's crew fired back at the six Westers near James, and pelted them with AX fire and explosives. Shipp took his chance. He gave Zemmer a shove, and the injured Zemmer rolled down into the ravine.

Shipp broke out of hiding, whirled toward the rock he had been hiding behind, and started pelting it with Mossamer fire while running backward and falling down into the ravine. The Westers who had been approaching him ran down into the opposing ravine to avoid his attack.

Lom's run finished and he flew far to the east before circling back around. The Westers who had been attacking Shipp knew Lom would come back for them, and they dashed away from Shipp.

He was free.

Shipp slung Zemmer over his shoulder, and ran toward James' position. James headed toward the six Westers in the ravine who had been attacked by Lom to confirm they were all dead.

Shipp was much closer and he got there first.

To his surprise, they weren't dead. In fact, only two of them were. Two were injured, but the other two fired AX-15s at Shipp as he summited the ridge. Down he went again, and Zemmer screamed in pain as he landed on his injured leg and suffered a fresh AX wound in the shoulder. Shipp dropped his Mossamer, and scrambled across the dirt to recover it.

When he got to it, he rolled over and saw two Westers standing on the ridge, ready to fire at him and Zemmer. He was too late.

Pretoria's smiling, beautiful face flashed in his mind.

A split second later – both Westers heads exploded with blood, penetrated with AX fire.

James ascended the ravine and stood next to their dead bodies. He looked at Shipp, and cocked his head. James' AX-15 smoldered from the kill. Shipp exhaled and let out a whimpering laugh of relief.

"Don't even think about dying, you rat turd," James said.

18

Unknown Threat

"Where's the rest of your squad?" Shipp got to his feet and helped the grimacing Zemmer get as comfortable as possible. One AX round tore through the edge of his shoulder. And his calf was ripped apart, in very bad shape.

James pointed down the ravine, "There are two injured rats. We're taking them alive." Shipp nodded in agreement.

At that moment, Lom's flight flew over them again heading back west. Shipp and James could see blast holes and other damage. One engine was dead, and it wobbled with an unsteady trajectory.

"That's not good," Shipp observed. "Let's get outta here."

They each noted to themselves that Lom didn't fire on the group of Westers who had been attacking Shipp from behind the large rock. James and Shipp lifted Zemmer up with their shoulders so he could walk on one leg. They ascended the ridge, and saw in the neighboring ravine that James' squad had disarmed the two surviving Westers and marched them toward Lom's landing spot.

Twenty minutes later, Shipp, James, and the other soldiers reached the flight. Lom was furious.

"We can't make it back! How the flame are we going to get back? How'd you guys get into such a jam like that?"

Shipp laughed at him.

"This is war, General. Thanks for saving us. Why didn't you fire on the other Westers?"

"What other Westers? We didn't see any except the ones to the south with Li."

Shipp looked at James, and then back at Lom.

"Then they have a base. Couldn't have disappeared that fast. They went underground. Just like I said."

Lom nodded, finally acquiescing to Shipp's point of view. "Looks that way. Could just be a capsule though. Pretty odd place for one in those gulleys. What about Li? Help him finish those rats off too?"

Shipp shook his head, not even phased by the fact that a general was asking him for battlefield advice.

"We need more intel on the Wester base. For all we know they've got exits all around us. Let's pull back and retreat."

Shipp got on his comm, "Li – we're pulling out. Head west. Then meet us at the new flight position."

"Jonas," Li responded.

When Li and Mixie retreated, the Westers pulled back too, knowing that pursuing them would be foolish. Thirty minutes later, all the Peterson squads were back together at the grounded flight, including Gugbe and the rest of Shipp's squad.

Gugbe rejoiced at seeing Shipp and Zemmer alive. "How's he doing?"

"Fine for now, but we need to move. And blind those two rats for me. Can they walk?"

James' squad wrapped cloths over the face shields of the two Wester captives and affixed them with adhesive strips. With their hands bound, they could be led right off a cliff without knowing it. Lom could hold his tongue no longer.

"Move where?" Lom began. "You told me to attack. I didn't count on them disabling our only transportation. How do you propose we traverse the 20.2 kilometers we covered to get here? Walk?"

Shipp ignored him and waited for James to answer his original question. He did:

"This rat took an AX round in the shoulder and another in the hip. He can walk well enough." James shoved that Wester soldier aside as if he were a garment being tried on, and stepped over to the other one. "This one took a shot in his left quad. He's gonna need help."

"Maybe we should just make it easy on him," suggested Mixie.

Lom became more animated with angry panic each second he was ignored.

"Commander Shipp – I need to confer with you, now!"

Shipp held up a finger directing him to wait. He looked at Mixie, and smiled at her for the first time since they arrived on Lavoisier. She noticed, and sustained the eye contact. A nice moment of re-connection. Mixie still had no idea why Shipp had been ostracizing her since they arrived on Lavoisier. It heartened her to feel acknowledged again, as if a long lost relative had returned home.

"Mixie – I like your brain on this. It's tempting. But I need two captives for this to work." He turned to James. "Can we rig up a stretch for Zemmer and another for the rat?"

Lom took the hint.

"Shipp! You can't walk 20 kilometers on this planet! We have like an hour of air left. Each!"

Shipp looked back at him, acting puzzled.

"I thought it was 20.2." He looked at Gugbe. "Didn't he say 20.2?"

Gugbe smiled and nodded. Shipp finally approached Lom and faced him.

"General Lom. Of all people, you are the last one who should be panicking like this. You've been cooped up in that space pod prison for so long you forgot what the flame we're doing here. We've got O2 reserves on the flight and you know it. So what gives? Are your feet sore? We're the ones who've been fighting for our lives the last two hours."

Lom stood speechless for a moment, not expecting to be cut down so thoroughly in front of everyone. But Shipp wasn't finished.

"Peterson Space Force soldiers are supposed to be of one mind. Kill Westers. Stay alive. Save your friend. Tactical overrules command. Do I need to recite them all? You've been acting like you know this place, and there can't be a base, and we just need Rock Eyes everywhere, and all this conservative, tentative, one-square-centimeter-per-day cowardice. Meanwhile, the Westers DO have a base, and who knows how fast they're building it out and multiplying it!"

"There isn't enough oxygen on board for–" Lom looked around to count everyone, but Shipp already knew the number.

"24 plus two rats."

Showed up again, Lom marched into the flight to make his point. He went straight for the oxygen reserves to physically count the amount remaining. Shipp lowered his head, then looked to Li, and gestured at him to state what Lom should already have known.

Li spoke immediately, "For 26, we've got enough extra for about an hour more per person."

"How much is that in dispensing time?" Shipp asked.

"About 25 seconds," Li responded. Shipp gave the order:

"Everyone – add 25 seconds of oxygen to your tanks. Do the rats last in case Li over-estimated."

Li monitored the oxygen reserve as each Peterson hooked up to it and turned the lever for 25 seconds. When the Wester captives got a turn, the first one filled up for 25 seconds. But the second only got 17 seconds, and the tank ran dry.

From behind his blindfold, Li could sense the Wester's soup of panic, fear, and rage. Li just laughed. "At least now the rest of us will have a warning sign. Let's go, ratface."

Back outside the flight, Shipp gave the orders:

"We're marching back toward the base. Li will stay in communication about our position while they prep the other flight to come pick us up. We have about two hours of air. Li – when do you expect them to make the rendezvous?"

"Probably about an hour."

"Alright. So – all that useless panic notwithstanding, let's get the flame out of here."

They set off. But Lom couldn't live it down, and spouted another rule.

"Under no circumstances are both flights to be out of the base at the same time. No circumstances! Shipp – this isn't—"

"General," Shipp interrupted again. "We don't have two flights. We have one. And it's coming to save your life. Machines can be replaced. Soldiers can't. I'd think you'd know that by now. I don't want you to speak again until we're back with Loshea. You can tell her all the rules we've broken, while killing at least eighteen Westers, losing four of our own, destroying an underground turret, confirming the existence of an enemy base, and learning a whole lot more about our General second in command."

Gugbe, Mixie, Blasé, Ramad, and James stood silent. They knew to leave Lom alone. They knew Shipp took no pleasure in speaking to his general like this. And they knew Shipp wouldn't stand for any physical or verbal abuse from anyone in his unit – including against a disgraced general. He was simply telling Lom the truths he didn't seem to want to hear. Or perhaps he really was incompetent and tactically atrophied, as Shipp surmised, having been underground and in isolation, without any combat for so long. Either way, they just focused on the trek, with Gugbe and James carrying Zemmer on a stretcher.

But Shelsie didn't know how seriously Shipp took his allegiance to every Peterson – even the unreliable ones.

"You can speak to me, General," she chided.

"Quiet, Shel," Mixie scolded immediately.

Shipp exhaled and closed his eyes at Mixie's instant reaction to Shelsie's puerile comment. He realized how valuable and loyal Mixie had always been, and still was, and that he had been stonewalling her since Pretoria died. Why? Was he blaming all women for his wife's death? Was it because a woman killed her? How could he assume such an irrational perspective? Mixie was as good as anyone else in his squad, and he knew it. So why had it been so hard to even look at her the past few months? He didn't fault all men for killing Roy Horman or Commander Vonn. It didn't seem to matter how effectively the Petersons trained their soldiers. Shipp loathed himself – just for a moment – for falling victim to such a primitive, divisive mindset.

He turned to Mixie while they walked. Caught her attention again. He flashed her the Peterson handsign greeting – index finger and thumb extended. She smiled back and returned the sign. Mixie flushed with a renewed sense of acceptance at Shipp's validation. She didn't resent him for having excluded her for so long. Rather, she had been questioning herself, wondering what she had done. She still didn't know, but it felt great to be aligned once more.

An hour passed. They marched forward without a break. Soldiers took turns carrying Zemmer and the injured Wester. Then Shipp spoke to Li in everyone's hearing – the first words since Mixie had muzzled Shelsie.

"Li, you have an update?"

Li had been walking separated from the rest of the group, about twenty meters out, so he could talk openly to the base without weighing everyone down with the nuts and bolts of getting the other flight to pick them up. At Shipp's word, he angled back toward the group.

"They needed a little more explanation than they should have, and overloaded the flight the first time. They didn't get why it only needed a two-man crew. So they're about twenty minutes out."

"Plenty of time."

A moment later, Mixie spoke up, alarmed.

"Shipp. Something's wrong with my face shield. Getting blurry."

Shipp stopped. He and James walked over to her and examined the clear covering.

"I don't really see anything, mine is a bit fogged up for some reason. James?"

"Mine too."

"Shipp – that's what I'm telling you. It's not fog."

At this, Shipp realized they all had the same problem. He looked around and spoke up to everyone.

"Anyone got a clear view or are we all like this?"

He got a variety of answers, none of them good. Shipp then looked at the Wester captives. The one standing looked tense. Shipp took a few steps toward him. The Wester's hands were trembling. His breathing had accelerated too, as evidenced by his heaving shoulders. Shipp directed James and Mixie to triangulate around the Wester. Shipp ripped off the blindfold and got in his face. He looked terrified.

"Don't ratshit me. What's happening to us? What's happening to you?"

The Wester let out a terrified laugh.

"Whatever it is, it's 24 to 2. Not a bad way to go down." He kept laughing uncontrollably, but interspersed with a frightful wail. Whatever was happening, this guy knew it, and it was turning him inside out.

"Li!! Where's the nearest life capsule?" Shipp queried. He knew there used to be several in this area, because once LUB-7 was completed, all the nearby capsules were abandoned.

Li activated his wrist monitor. He pointed toward two small rises.

"There's one in the foreground of those mounds, about a kilometer away."

"Everyone! Follow Li. We got about one click to go, and we're running it – gear and all. Everyone move – now!"

"Shipp!" said Mixie. "Shipp it's getting worse!"

"I know! Run everyone!"

Mixie's face shield seemed to be worsening faster for some reason. It almost seemed to be crystallizing. If this kept up much longer, she wouldn't be able to see.

Shipp told Li to call the incoming flight, order them to return to base immediately, and tell them what was happening. He reasoned that whatever was happening, the flight may not be aware of it since it was pressurized. Unless their windows were also crystallizing.

"Almost there – don't slow down. Full sprint!"

The entire group followed Li, covering the kilometer in under three minutes. With all their gear, weaponry, and two injured men, Shipp was pleased.

Out of breath, breathing hard, and struggling to see through an ever more coarsening face shield, Li collapsed to his knees and brushed off the flat ellipse-shaped life capsule entrance. A grid of numbers lay on the surface. Li punched in the old code. The door slid open.

"Okay – we can fit three at a time in the hold. Gugbe – you and James get Zemmer in first," Shipp directed. "Everyone else, catch your breath. How long do these take?"

"It will cycle out the air in about 20 seconds, then the lower door opens," Li responded.

"So 26, that's nine groups. About four and a half minutes to get everyone in," calculated Shipp.

"Jonas that," said Li.

Without panicking, the Petersons watched James and Gugbe bring Zemmer down the ladder into the hole. The upper door slid shut. They waited. Three at a time, the process repeated. Shipp directed the next three each time. Toward the end, he had to send in the Westers one at a time with two Petersons.

After the other 24 were safe inside, Shipp and Lom remained alone on the surface. Their face shields almost white, they knelt with their hands on the door. Lom hadn't spoken a word since Shipp told him to stop talking.

"Shipp I can't see."

"Neither can I. I can feel the door, but I can't see the light to know when it's clear."

"Can you see the numbers?"

"I held my fingers on the keypad. I should be in the right position."

Lom said, “If one of us has to take off our mask to see the pad...”

“We’re both staying alive, General Lom. I’m sure it’s been 25 seconds by now.”

Shipp punched in the six-digit code.

Nothing happened.

Shipp tried again. Nothing again. The keypad was completely flat, so there was no way to feel for buttons.

“I think I’m out of position.”

“Shipp – you’re better equipped to lead this right now. I’ll take off my shield.”

“No you won’t. I’m just going to shift a little each way and keep trying.”

“You can’t do that. Our shields are going to crack in pieces any second now.”

“Lom!”

Suddenly the door opened below them. James stood inside wearing a fresh face shield. He helped Shipp and Lom clamber inside the pod. The air cycled out, and the inner door opened.

Shipp and Lom landed on the floor and ripped off their face shields. When Shipp dropped his on the ground, the formerly clear face shield shattered, with crystallized fragments spreading across the floor. He had been seconds away from... what, exactly?

19

Life Capsule

Shipp took a reading of the room. His soldiers were scared. Heads in hands. Trembling extremities. Eyes darting back and forth. Regaining normalcy. None of them had ever experienced anything like this. They weren't used to unknowns. What happened? What could have caused their face shields to disintegrate like that?

Shipp knew three things. First, he needed these 24 soldiers to regain their composure. Second, he needed to contact General Loshea and warn her. And third, he needed to get the Westers to talk, because it was obvious they knew what was happening right when it started.

"Everyone," Shipp began, "Just take a breath. We're all okay. Whatever's going on up there isn't down here, or something tells me we'd know it by now. James, go assess the oxygen generators. Take Mulsh and Amio with you."

Mulsh and Amio had been on Lavoisier for more than two years, and doubled as war science specialists. They knew war science like Shipp knew weapons. Shipp heard them talking once about the prototypical chemical properties of Blackhead. It was way above him. And Amio was assigned by Loshea as a liaison between the war science administrators and the soldiers, because he could easily understand both worlds. They fought in Li's squad in the recent skirmish.

James, Mulsh, and Amio were about to head down a dark hallway when someone interrupted.

"What about those rats? What about this hole you drug us into? This place isn't meant for 24. Certainly not 26. Fifteen is pushing it."

Shipp turned to see Lavoisier veteran soldier Filo Rawlic, sitting with his back against a wall and legs flat on the ground. Still breathing hard and dripping sweat from the run, the stress, and the terror. Rawlic had remained back at the flight with General Lom during the battle. Shipp knew little about him.

"I'm aware," Shipp replied. "One thing at a time. Let's get the O2 status first. Next up is communications. Li – can we get Loshea on this?"

He pointed to the main console. It was decades old and dusty. No one had set foot in this capsule for at least five years, possibly as long as eight.

"We should be able to, assuming it will turn on. But the basic tech isn't much different than what we use now."

"Whatever O2 they find isn't going to be enough." Rawlic continued. "All this to find an underground Wester base, and now we're stuck out here, couple dozen k's from our own with no way to get back."

Shipp remained calm. It took a lot to antagonize him, and he knew there was reason to fear. His job, as he saw it, was to assuage those fears, not minimize them. And he presumed Lom wasn't up to the task.

"Rawlic – you're right. We're stuck. For now. We solve the problem, one piece at a time. Right now, we're all safe. So just leave it at that, get some water and nutrients."

He then turned his attention to the Westers, who seemed to be hoping Shipp would forget about them. He didn't.

"Gugbe, take those two into separate rooms and latch 'em tight. Take off their boots and belts. Leave the lights off."

Gugbe took Ramad and Blasé with him, and they carted the Westers off to quarters in opposite directions from the central operations room where everyone else remained. Rawlic seemed to approve of this move. Shipp glanced at Lom to read his face. Lom seemed lost in thought, as if he was trying to anticipate what Shipp would do or say next, because he should be the one doing it or saying it.

"Lom," Shipp said. "If we can get Loshea on there, you talk to her first. But not until we have an O2 status."

A smart move, because Loshea had no idea Lom had mentally crumbled in combat. This gave Lom a renewed status in front of this group, and would leave Loshea completely unaware that anything had gone wrong. Shipp valued the role of appointed leadership, and now all the soldiers knew it.

Everyone waited. About ten minutes passed. James, Mulsh, and Amio returned.

On Lavoisier, underground oxygen was created through chemical reactions. Each base had a large room filled with reagents and laboratory equipment that enabled production of oxygen. The process was mechanized such that the oxygen got collected and stored under high pressure in large tanks. These tanks could refill the smaller tanks the soldiers took whenever they went out. Other generated oxygen got funneled into a slightly less pressurized holding room, and then slowly filtered out into the living spaces such that the ratio of oxygen to other gases was conducive to human health.

James needed to determine how much oxygen production capacity remained. Back when the life capsules were abandoned years ago, the Petersons took some of it with them to LUB-7, and left only enough for an emergency reserve in case anyone needed to return to the capsule.

Like now.

Except with 26 pairs of lungs in a space designed for 15, whatever O2 capacity remained would be used up fast.

"Amio's got the oxygen status," directed James.

Amio took center stage. As always, everyone got to hear this, not just the leaders. No secrets.

"Based on what we found, it looks like they left enough O2 reserves to last about six weeks, assuming fifteen people breathing it. We've got 24. Or 26 if you count the rats."

"Which we don't," interjected Rawlic.

Amio continued. "With 24, we're looking at about four weeks of oxygen. With 26, even less."

James spoke up. "And what about taking the four large tanks in there, going outside if that becomes possible, and walking back to the base, filling up each soldier's reserve as we go? Is that possible?

Amio nodded, "It seems reasonable. But as you said, it might not be possible to go to the surface."

"No one's going to the surface anytime soon," declared Shipp. He stood in everyone's view. "No one."

He rotated around to make eye contact with all 23 Petersons in the room. "We're not going anywhere until we talk to Loshea, and then the Westers, and see if we can figure out what just happened up there."

Rawlic jumped to his feet.

"And what if we can't? What if the rats won't talk? What if Loshea knows nothing? What if there's no way out of here?"

Shipp looked at him squarely and gave the only possible answer, as matter-of-fact as an administrator explaining how to use body sanitizers.

"Then we'll all die here."

Rawlic couldn't take Shipp's absolute lack of emotion. Shipp took a step toward him.

"You're a Peterson soldier, Rawlic. We just lost four men out there. They're dead. You're alive. You think that's some kind of special right you have? Any one of us could die in the next battle. If it happens down here or up there, what do you care?"

"Because up there at least I'm dying for something," he shot back. "Dying the way a soldier is supposed to die."

"Everything we do is dying for something," Shipp replied. "We now know there's a Wester base here. You – you and Lom – practically saw it from the air. Those rats vanished without a trace. We know they have some kind of new chemical weapon that eats face shields. And we're going to get all this intel back to Space Force Command – even if it means carving it on the doors and walls while we breathe our last breaths."

Rawlic studied Shipp, realizing he didn't know the full meaning of devotion.

"Shipp," Lom spoke for the first time in front of the soldiers since Shipp told him not to. "If that chemical weapon is planet-wide, then our bases on the other side of the planet are also vulnerable. You thought we were on the cusp of winning this planet. We might be about to lose it."

Shipp nodded. "Which is exactly why we need to get Loshea on comm. Li, how's it going?"

Li had been occasionally clanging around under the main console, muttering to himself now and then, but mostly just working and listening to the Peterson discourse.

"We have power, obviously, because the emergency lights are on and the O2 is blowing," Li said. "I think one of the wires is shorted out. Just looking for the problem."

"Got enough light?" asked James. Li nodded even though no one could see his head.

Shipp addressed everyone again. "Get some nutrients and water in your bodies, and take an hour of rest. Hopefully we can comm with Loshea at that time. No one rests in the two rooms with the rats. Gugbe – you go check on them and make sure they're still latched. There aren't enough beds for everyone. Be considerate. We'll rotate if we have to. That's it."

The hour felt like seconds.

Everyone rested except Li, because only one person could fit in the small space where he labored. Shipp and James did a quick weapons inventory at the top of the hour and then entered one of the sleeping quarters to rest too. It was just the two of them in the room, and they laid on bunks.

"You did good," James said. "Watching Lom self-destruct was really something. Hard to imagine anyone on Risner doing that."

"I know, incredible. I think Loshea was right though. Being underground for so long. This is a tough world," Shipp pondered.

He considered Rawlic, who seemed to be mimicking Lom's earlier panic with this newest chemical weapon threat. Followers take after their leaders. Lom was a bad leader.

"Saw you and Mixie," James said. "That was good to see."

Shipp shook his head, disappointed in himself. He put off a vibe like he didn't want to talk about it. But James wasn't ready to throw in the towel this soon.

"Does she remind you of what happened?" James queried gently.

"I just needed a break. I need a break maybe still," said Shipp.

"From Mixie?" James asked.

"Come on Cam, just forget it." Shipp said.

"Shipp—"

"Cam, I'm in control. I'm not losing my head. This is just grief. I'm not over it yet okay? That ought to be enough," Shipp interrupted.

"Your friends can't pay the price for your loss," said James.

Shipp's eyes moistened a bit, out of James' view. Pretoria invaded his mind again. He tried to shove her out. Mixie replaced her. He shoved her out too. But then Shelsie, and then Loshea. Then the face of the female Wester commander who killed his wife. Shipp thought of the faceless General Elliss he spoke to through the Wester's comm unit.

"Flame it," said Shipp, getting up to head back out.

"Lay down," James admonished, surprising Shipp with his firm tone. Shipp halted. "You've got forty more minutes to rest. You need it."

"Then stop talking to me about women. I'm dealing with it," Shipp said.

James had suspected this for several weeks as he watched Shipp stonewall Mixie. Now, Shipp had revealed the accuracy of James' intuition. James softened again.

"Let me help you deal with it better," James offered as Shipp lay back down. James continued, "It won't go away, but you can't keep shoving it down."

"You never lost anyone like this," Shipp said. "What the flame do you know about it?"

"I know how I'd feel if I lost you," said James.

At this, Shipp heaved a deep sigh and wiped away a couple tears. He lay there breathing deeply for a couple minutes. James let the silence linger as his friend processed his loss in safety. Finally, Shipp broke the silence.

"I know it wasn't Mixie's fault at all. I know that. I'm not going to ignore her anymore. I don't know what's wrong with me."

Shipp rolled on his side and closed his eyes. James let him enjoy some silence, considering this a win for the time being.

The end of the rest hour broke when Li swore angrily and hurled a driver out of his cavern, sending it clanging across the stone floor. Shipp and James arose, exited their quarters, and hurried over to get Li's report.

"Can't do it," said an exasperated Li. "The problem wasn't wiring. They took the receiver out. I didn't even think to check for that because why would you take the receiver?"

"Maybe at the time the new base needed an extra one for some reason," Shipp guessed. "Like for a flight. So where does that leave us?"

Li put it in plain terms. "We can send messages, but we can't hear the reply."

Shipp looked at James. A few others had arisen and were paying attention, including Lom and Rawlic.

James suggested the only course of action. "Well then, we need to tell Loshea everything we know and then solve our remaining problems on our own."

Rawlic growled at this, and was joined by a few other Petersons who didn't like the news. He and the others crowded near Shipp and James, waiting to see how they'd explain their way out of this one.

But Shipp didn't even acknowledge them. "Okay, do it. Li – update Loshea. It's time to talk to the rats. Rawlic, you're with me, Lom, and James. I do all the talking to start. If I miss something, speak up once I'm finished. Everyone clear?"

Rawlic didn't know how to feel. Instead of a conflict he seemed to expect and almost want, he got promoted to a critical task of the moment. Why? Shipp reasoned Rawlic's passion and desire to survive would make him an asset in this situation, and he wanted to capitalize on it. But Rawlic couldn't discern that through his simmering anger.

Shipp walked over to Mixie, and whispered something no one else could hear. When the conversation ended, Mixie nodded and headed down a hallway. The quartet of interrogators marched down the other hallway to the room with the first Wester, the one who had received less oxygen when they filled up before leaving the flight.

20

Interrogation

The Wester lay on the floor, latched to a post with his hands and feet bound. He had been dozing, but awakened when Shipp, James, Lom, and Rawlic entered the room. He spoke with the typical Wester dialect, which was sickening if not insulting. All those extra added syllables and sounds they always wasted. Barely a sentence without an 'eh,' 'yeah,' 'right,' 'uh,' 'no', or a whole rotting lot of other spurious sounds.

All the Petersons felt nothing but absolute contempt for this joke of a man. It was certainly a unifying force, which Shipp counted on.

Shipp began, "I'm gonna make this real simple for you."

The Wester turned his eyes toward Shipp.

"You can die quick and painless. Or you can die the most painful death we can dream up. And we have 24 pretty smart soldiers here who would be happy to put their minds to this problem. Either way, you aren't gonna live past this."

The Wester smiled a devious smile. He seemed to regard Shipp like an equal, as if he would have said the same thing were the sides reversed.

"Bro I'm looking forward to it, dogbreath," said the Wester.

Shipp smiled at the classic Wester insult. Rats and dogs. Each chose their own hated animal and attributed it to the enemy. Shipp always thought this was funny though, because dogs are of course infinitely superior to rats in pretty much every way.

"Woof," said Shipp.

Even Rawlic cracked a smile at this.

Shipp continued, "Your other rat friend is in a different room. I'm gonna ask you the same questions I asked him. If your answers deviate in even the slightest detail, one of you is going to suffer a very painful experience, and it won't be your last."

Shipp had to make clear how much pain he could inflict. His best outcome was to make the Wester truly afraid of the unknown. Otherwise, Shipp knew he would never reveal any valuable secrets. The Wester seemed at least a smidge unnerved by this. Shipp began:

"How long have you had underground bases on Lavoisier?"

The Wester let out a slow laugh, almost mocking. Shipp took this to mean they had established underground bases for a long time. Shipp looked at Rawlic and nodded toward the Wester. Rawlic smacked the Wester in the side of the head with his AX butt.

Not having a helmet, the Wester recoiled against the wall in pain, clenched his teeth and fists, and tried to rub his head. He couldn't because his bound and latched hands couldn't reach that high. Shipp let the pain linger.

"Laugh again," Shipp said.

The Wester sat silent and grim, submitting to Shipp in that moment.

"How long?" Shipp asked again.

"A while ya," the Wester began. Shipp and the others just waited, knowing this would make it clear they expected more, and that this was the most painless time to divulge it. The Wester gave a little more. "Several years. I don't know precisely, eh?"

"How many bases?"

"One," the Wester replied.

"How many soldiers in it?"

The Wester hesitated. Rawlic got ready to hit him again. But James stopped him.

"Hold on," James said. "One base? I don't think I believe that. How many entrances to this one base?"

"Lots, ya" said the Wester, attempting to instill enough fear to make them nervous about an assault. "Dozens." But his ploy had the opposite effect on James.

"I knew it. It's one base with tunnels spread out all over. Just like on Risner," James said.

Lom spoke here. "I don't think there's just one base either, tunnels or not. But we need to go punish the other rat for lying to us." Shipp turned back to the Wester and looked at him, as if awaiting a reply.

The Wester sat silent. The Petersons waited. Then, Shipp nodded them all out of the room. Once out, he directed them down the other hallway. "I don't believe him either about one base."

Passing Mixie, who waited in the hallway containing the room with the other Wester, the four men entered the room to find the second captive sulking, because he knew his fate. Shipp picked up on it immediately.

"You know how this is gonna end," he said.

The Wester didn't budge. Shipp continued. "Except, you don't know. Your colleague back there is a rat turd. We had to beat it out of him just to admit you have an underground base, which we already knew. You want this to end quickly, you answer us. You want the worst possible end to your life that you can imagine? Follow your friend's example."

"He talked?" the Wester asked.

"He told us you have six underground bases with dozens of entrances each, spread around the planet," Shipp began, truthfully reflecting only half of what the other Wester had told them.

At the mention of the word 'six,' the Wester's head twitched. With four Petersons studying his every tic and fidget, the Wester had a tough time remaining stoic. Plus, the realization of his impending death had apparently been eating away at him for a while.

Shipp concealed his suspicion. "Can you confirm your friend is telling the truth?"

"What are you gonna do if he's lying, ya?", the Wester asked.

"The one who cooperates the most will suffer the least. By far." Shipp meant it. He didn't have to lie at all here.

The Wester believed him. "Six is wrong bro. It's three."

"Very good," affirmed Shipp. Rawlic noted the Wester's extreme cowardice, and how Shipp had drawn out what appeared to be the truth with relatively little effort. Lom was impressed too, especially considering he had been the most skeptical about the presence of Wester bases.

"Where are these bases located, approximately? All near each other? Spread around the planet?"

The Wester talked again. "All around, see. One here. One in the next northern octet over, the other in the south near your bases on the other side, a few hundred k's away, ya."

'Octet' was a word Westers used to describe planetary regions. Planets were broken up into sixteen segments, with eight octets in each hemisphere.

"How do we find the entrances?"

"There's a whole bunch. I can't describe it without a map. Hidden in the canyons mostly."

"Last question," Shipp said, because this Wester was cooperating.

"What was eating away our face shields out there?"

The Wester eyed each Peterson quickly and then turned away and started glancing in random directions on the floor, as if looking for a hole in which to crawl away. Shipp slapped the Wester's shoulder to regain his attention. He got down on his level, face to face.

"You know what it was. You tell us now, and I promise you a painless death."

The Wester seemed to be searching the air for an answer, a way to explain it, a way to avoid it – something. He seemed almost panicked. His jaw began to quiver as if suddenly chilled. Shipp placed his hands on each of the Wester's shoulders.

"Why won't you talk? What are you so afraid of!"

"I don't know what it is! I don't know what it is ya! I swear I don't know what it is! Lo it's new and that's all I know! I swear ya!"

The Wester looked at him pleadingly. Shipp angled up at James, who ever so slightly nodded him out of the room. Shipp stood and all four Petersons trudged out. They entered another room to keep out of earshot of the rest of their soldiers. Shipp looked at Lom first, wanting his take.

Lom shook his head. "He seems scared. Just not sure if it's of us or something else."

Rawlic piped in, "Why's he got to be scared of anyone else when he knows we're going to end him?"

"Exactly," agreed James. "Why would he be scared? Only thing I can think of is he's afraid we won't believe him. But that just doesn't fit."

Shipp sighed. "Let's go back to the first guy."

Shipp barreled into the room of the first Wester, grabbed him by the armpits, and slammed him against the wall. James shut the door as soon as he, Lom, and Rawlic got inside and shut the door.

"You lying rathole. It's three bases, not one. Your cowardly friend just told us everything."

The Wester twitched at this. His eyes flashed with rage, and he started kicking. This proved difficult since he was still latched, so it looked kind of pathetic. Rawlic started laughing. Shipp cut him off.

"You tell me what's eating face shields up there, and you tell me now!"

The Wester spat in Shipp's face. Shipp flared in rage. He threw open the door and bolted down the hall. Came back with an axe. The Wester screamed. Shipp swung it and sliced the latch in half, freeing him from the wall.

"Hold him down!"

Rawlic and Lom held the Wester's legs while James held his arms as far apart as they could go. The chain connecting his legs and arms lay in Shipp's sights. He swung again, and cut the chain in half. The Wester was free.

Rawlic angled up at Shipp in confusion. But Shipp grabbed the Wester, yanked him out the door, and sent him hurtling through the hallway toward the other waiting Petersons in the central operations room. They all backed away. Just as the Wester regained his balance, Shipp was at him again.

He shoved him violently into the capsule tube that led to the surface, so with so much force that the backside of his head smashed into the cylindrical wall. Shipp sealed the door. He looked at Li and then back through the small clear window into the tube. The Wester got to his feet and stared back out at Shipp.

"You tell me what's happening up there, or you're gonna be our lab rat!" Shipp threatened.

The Wester looked up and realized Shipp meant it. He put his hands on the window and started screaming in terror, swearing, and slamming himself against the door. Shipp looked at Li.

"Can the door withstand that?"

"You want to find out?" asked Li, incredulous.

Shipp looked back at the delirious Wester. His face turned cold and firm. "Send him up."

Li opened the middle hatch, and began to plunge the Wester upward. His kicking and screaming increased. The middle hatch closed beneath him. They couldn't hear his movements anymore, but the outer hatch opened, and the Wester soldier would soon be up on the surface with nowhere to go.

Shipp turned to face the other 23 Petersons, including a stunned Rawlic.

"Anyone still have any doubts the Westers know what almost killed us up there? He's afraid of dying from that, not the atmosphere."

He looked around. Not a peep from anyone. Mixie caught his eye from the hallway. She gave him an affirmative nod to signal that unity was achieved.

"Gugbe," Shipp said. "Go kill the other rat. One shot. No pain."

Gugbe headed down the hallway without a word and followed Shipp's order.

21

3 Weeks Later

Shipp awoke from his sleep shift. This was the final day of his three-day turn sleeping in one of the actual beds, and he hadn't wasted it. Nine blissful hours. His best sleep since they got trapped in this overcrowded life capsule.

But his internal clock hadn't awoken him. He could hear commotion out in the central operations room. Shipp splashed water on his face, got hydrated, changed into his soldier gear, grabbed a nutrient kit, and headed out.

He found Rawlic, Mulsh, and three other Petersons arguing with Gugbe and Li. Rawlic was speaking, while the other four held AX-15s as if out on patrol. Shipp deduced that his attempts to unify the group three weeks back were about to come loose. The tension had been building over the previous week as their O2 dwindled and they had no more certainty about the surface. The sound of his soldiers arguing this loudly worried him.

"What's the problem Rawlic?"

"We all know the problem. We got one week left. Then we suffocate. And I don't see anyone doing anything about it the last three weeks."

Shipp remained unmoved. "Unless you can prove to me the surface is safe, I don't see a whole lot of options. We've updated Loshea alternating days."

"You don't even know if any of them are alive. They could all be dead," said Mulsh.

"All the more reason why we need to stay alive here," said Ramad. "It might just be us."

"And how do you intend to find out?" asked Rawlic. "Is your plan to just sit here and die? What if the surface is safe? Whatever was up there can't last forever. The Westers want this planet too. You think they'd unleash a weapon that would render it uninhabitable?"

Shipp gave this question some pause. He nodded at Rawlic. "That's a good inference. Makes sense. There might be a time limit of some kind."

Rawlic took a step toward Shipp. "You get it then. We can't just sit and die here when it might be safe up there."

"How do you want to test the safety? Last week we exhausted every idea we could think of. I'm not allowing anyone up there," Shipp declared.

"Go up fully protected. We'll know if the breathing shields are cracking. We've got eight new ones we can test out," suggested Rawlic.

"You're assuming it only affects breathing shields. What if it gets through clothing too but just takes longer?" Shipp countered. "How long until it affects our skin? It's a 14k hike back to the main base. That's two hours minimum on this terrain."

"Yep, and with the four big tanks, we can give each person three hours of O2. We'll make it," Rawlic pressed.

James stepped in. "You'll make it if your equipment protects you. What are you going to do? Stand there and wait while your O2 drains?"

"I'm not sitting here just to run out of air! I'm going, and no one's going to stop me," Rawlic said.

"I'm going to stop you," said Shipp, his voice rising. "We're going to wait until the last possible day before we even think about that plan. No one's going up there until then."

"You're not in command, Thomas Shipp. General Lom is," Rawlic said, minimizing Shipp by not stating his title.

Rawlic noticed James, an improving Zemmer, Gugbe, Ramad, and Blasé all coalescing behind Shipp. Rawlic nodded and smirked.

"Of course. The Risner rebels who think they can come here and take over our operation just because they fought off a Wester tunnel attack."

Li stepped over to Shipp and joined him.

"We are all Petersons. Don't make this tribal, Rawlic. We are one. There is one enemy, and he's not among us," Li said. "Shipp is right. There's no point in going up there. We can wait six more days."

"Not if something goes wrong!" Rawlic intensified. "You gonna assume your calculations were correct? Mulsh did the math, and even he says predicting gas volumes can be imprecise because of incomplete reaction mechanisms. One week is a guess. We might only have a few days!"

"The four large tanks are full and ready," responded Li. "If O2 drops sooner than we expect, we can start using the tanks then, and decide to try the surface. We have a surplus hour for all 24. You said it yourself."

Shipp looked at Lom, who seemed to have no interest in trying to mediate the growing tension. Shipp wanted to be sure.

"General? You got anything to say here?" Shipp asked.

All eyes turned to General Lom, who clearly wasn't prepared to navigate a situation like this. Lom rubbed his fingers through his hair and tried to avoid eye contact with anyone. He started licking his lips. Shipp shook his head. Lom had more nervous tics than a man walking naked through a minefield.

But Shipp waited. So did everyone else.

Lom finally spoke. "Maybe we should try General Loshea again. Or turn on the monitor and scan the surface for Westers, like we did last week."

Rawlic's response surprised Shipp. "Sure. You do that. Scan the surface again. I'm going to sleep."

With that, Rawlic headed down the left hallway, leaving Mulsh and his other allies facing off with Shipp and his. Division had arrived, and Shipp couldn't find a way to mend it. But Rawlic's earlier comment had stoked his curiosity. He approached Li.

"Hey Li. What do you think about Rawlic's idea that the Westers have a counteragent for whatever this contagion is?"

"Makes sense," replied Li. "He's right. They want the planet. They wouldn't want it impossible to inhabit. Besides, they're still here. The Westers have limited O2 as well. More than us, but not unlimited. They have to come out someday."

"Right. So the question is, does this thing die on its own, or do they have control over when it dies?" Shipp wondered aloud.

"If it were me?" Li conjectured, "I'd want control."

"Me too," agreed Shipp.

A voice behind Shipp interrupted their exchange.

"EVERYONE, stretch your hands out to the sides right now! Obey or die!"

Shipp turned to see two Petersons aiming Mossamer-24s in their direction. Four more Petersons, including Mulsh, jumped out of a side room and did the same, forming a semi-circle of five men and one woman around the majority of the remaining Petersons. Six Mossamers, at this range, could obliterate the room and everyone in it in seconds.

Rawlic sauntered back down from the hallway. He hadn't slept. They'd been planning this, probably for several days. Rawlic held a seventh Mossamer. The Petersons in the target zone, including Shipp, looked around and slowly raised their arms out to the sides. Rawlic got on the intercom at the main console and addressed the base:

"All remaining Petersons in the capsule – come out of your rooms now and step into the center of the circle. I count four of you missing. Out here, right now."

"A Peterson mutiny, Rawlic?" Shipp started. "That's unprecedented, in five hundred years."

"Really, Thomas?" Rawlic responded. "You think every single attack ship, every single ground war, every space station battle – all of them have recorded the actions of every soldier for five hundred years? When the situation turns against you, we do what any humans would do. We survive, and we take sides against those who oppose us."

Shipp began, "No one opposes anyone here. We're waiting six–"

"We're done waiting!" Rawlic bellowed.

"You go out there, you could die," James said. "You screw up the exit, you kill all of us too."

"What do you mean 'us too'?" Rawlic queried.

"We're not going," James said. "Even if you do."

"I hoped you'd say that," said Rawlic. He nodded to two of his men, who marched in the storage room and hulked out two of the four large O2 tanks. They lugged them around the semi-circle and placed them in the capsule tube leading to the surface.

"You won't be needing these then," Rawlic said, turning toward the tube.

"Oh yes we will," said Mixie, emerging from the hallway with an AX-15 in one hand and a pulse rifle in the other.

She took up position behind the semi-circle of rebels, so none of them had a clear shot at her. Rawlic seethed, but didn't lower his weapon. Neither did the others. Rawlic tightened his grip on his weapon. Shipp eyed him. A standoff. Petersons against Petersons. And Mixie was Shipp's wild card. He had anticipated a possible revolt several weeks back, and had told Mixie to stay out of sight as much as possible. He had her sleep in one of the unused storage rooms. Rawlic probably had forgotten about her. Now, she held the entire group of rebel Petersons in her sights.

"Well done Mixie," said Shipp. "Guys? You want everyone to die? It's that, or disarm."

Shelsie stepped out from within the group of captive Petersons, surprised to see Mixie after several weeks.

"I've been wondering where you were, Mix. Thanks for saving our tuts." Mixie smiled at her friend, and ordered all seven rebel Petersons against the wall opposite the main console. Rawlic, Mulsh, and the other five Petersons slowly backed against it and lowered their weapons.

"Set them on the ground," ordered Mixie. The seven soldiers complied.

But then, Mixie's head exploded with blood, as a shot from a smaller AX-9 went straight through her.

From Shelsie.

"We're getting out of here now," said Shelsie.

Mixie collapsed on the floor, dead instantly, eyes still open. Shipp roared like he was chained in hell, erupting in agonizing rage. He leapt at Shelsie, ripped her weapon from her hands, and beat her to death with it, losing all semblance of self-control. Blow after blow into her head, until she was barely recognizable. Her blood splattered all over him. Shipp cried as much as screamed and he smashed and pulverized her into the ground.

James tried to pull him off, but Shipp shoved him backward into Gugbe and Zemmer, and they all tried to subdue Shipp's vitriolic grief. Ramad and Blasé tried next. Shipp fought them off.

In the chaos, Rawlic and his allies regained their weapons and headed toward the capsule tube. They each affixed one of the eight undamaged breathing shields that had been found in the life capsule. With Shelsie dead, there was one extra. Rawlic held it up.

"Anyone? We got room for one more." No one budged. He shrugged, and tossed it on the ground. Then, Rawlic sent up the first four Peterson rebels, leaving just Mulsh, one other, and himself to wait for the next opening.

Shipp finally relented from crushing Shelsie, giving in to Ramad, James, Gugbe, and Blasé. He looked down at her smashed, unrecognizable face, and dropped the blood-smeared AX-9. His bloody hands trembled. He crawled over to Mixie, feeling his heart and soul ripped out and torn to pieces at the sight of another dead friend. He caressed her silent, blood-covered face, paying no attention to Rawlic. He ran his fingers over her eyelids to close them.

"Flaming comet tails," Shipp gritted as his vengeance around Pretoria returned in full force, then amplified. Helpless, he couldn't take his eyes off her corpse, wishing again for some way to alter reality, to overcome the finality of an undeserved death.

James watched Rawlic. As did Li, Gugbe, and Zemmer. James walked toward Rawlic and his allies, with something in his hand out of their view.

"You go up there, you might die," he told them. "I'm not going to stop you. But I want to give you something."

Rawlic raised his Mossamer warily. James held out his hand. A pair of Rock Eyes.

"Plant these two in your path so we can monitor you."

Rawlic sneered, "You're just as much of a coward as that excuse for a general over there." He gestured toward Lom, who lowered his head in shame.

James attached the Rock Eyes to Rawlic's pack. But unknown to Rawlic, James had already turned them on. Rawlic let him attach them, and then stepped into the capsule tube with the other two rebels. The door sealed. They lifted up past the middle hatch, which closed behind them. And then they were gone.

Shipp arose, his face, hair, hands, and clothes splattered with Shelsie's blood, and his left hand smeared with Mixie's. He hung his head, a disheveled spirit, and spoke in a barely audible whisper.

"I'm sorry. For losing control of myself. I'm sorry for letting you all down. I just... I never imagined a Peterson..." He turned to MIxie again, almost as if hoping this was a mistake, or a dream, and that she would stand up again. A tear ran down his face, carving a path through the blood. Then, he trailed off and trudged down the hallway, entered one of the sleeping quarters and closed the door.

Li ran over to the monitor and turned it on. He located the two Rock Eyes moving toward the distant LUB-7. The seven mutinous Petersons hiked briskly. Li and a growing audience watched the pair of dots move along the map at a steady pace. Over ten minutes passed.

Then, for a moment, they stopped.

The dots held in place. Unmoving.

They began traveling in the opposite direction, back toward the Peterson life capsule. James, Li, Gugbe, and all the remaining Petersons watched, leaning toward the monitor like cats. All except Shipp, who wasn't in the room.

The speed of the dots' return toward the life capsule entrance was twice what it had been when heading away. Rawlic was running back. There could only be one reason why.

Li looked at James, his speech halting. And then, he asked The Question. He uttered words unthinkable in the 500-year history of the Peterson Space Force:

"Do we save our friends?"

James felt his heart slam up in his throat. Never in his life, never in any of their lives, had they encountered or conceived of a scenario where they would have to ask that question, and not be instantly unanimous about the answer.

He looked at the bodies of Mixie and Shelsie. The blood on the walls and the floor. The two remaining O2 tanks. And he didn't know what to say.

"Shipp!" James called. "Shipp, they're coming back! The plague is still up there! What do we do?"

No answer from the dark, silent hallway.

James looked at Li. Then Gugbe. Then Zemmer. Blasé. Ramad. No one felt able to violate their first and most revered Core Principle. It had been implanted and cultivated as primordially as any belief, value, moral, or ethic could ever become part of a person. No one dared speak against it. But how could they let Rawlic and the others back in after their murderous mutiny?

"Leave the hatch locked," came a voice from the side of the room.

It was General Lom. The maligned general arose. He walked to the main console, and pressed the locking mechanism on the outer hatch, sealing the fate of Rawlic and the others. Lom muttered something unintelligible to himself, but held on to the mechanism as Rawlic's dot reached the outer hatch.

"Everyone leave," Lom ordered. "Go to sleeping quarters and take a rest."

At first, no one moved, still in shock at what just happened, and even more at what was happening now. Lom turned to them.

"Now!" he commanded, almost pleadingly as if afraid he might lose his newly discovered nerve. "Go rest! Leave me alone to this!"

Slowly, the other Petersons filtered down the two hallways, leaving Lom to see to the deaths of seven soldiers under his command. Which he did.

22

The End

21 hours later, Shipp emerged from his quarters. He had cleaned himself up, but still pulsed with grief and subdued despair. And embarrassment. Head down. Avoiding eye contact. The other fourteen Petersons were awake, conversing quietly. They seemed calm. Shipp glanced to where he had left Mixie's corpse. It was gone, and the area had been scoured clean. Same with Shelsie's. No trace of blood remained.

Shipp searched for James, and found him next to Li. Both of them stared back at him. They smiled softly and nodded him over. The other Petersons acknowledged him as he went, and seemed unbothered by his presence, in spite of having witnessed him murder one of their fellow soldiers. Shipp sat on the floor next to James and Li. All his body language craved an update, so they gave him one without a word from him.

"Lom cleaned up the room all by himself. It was spotless when we came out," Li began.

"What happened to the bodies?" Shipp murmured.

"With the rats, sealed and wrapped," James replied. "Amio did some calculations. With nine fewer people, we've extended our available O2 by a few days. Still nothing from Loshea, but Lom updated her on the mutiny, including his part in it."

Shipp irked at this. "His part?"

He didn't know Lom was the one who sealed the fates of the seven rebels. Li told him. Shipp seemed genuinely surprised, and stared in Lom's direction for a good while, as if re-sizing him up. Then, he summarized the current status.

"So, I guess we're all in this together then."

James and Li nodded. "They broke the Core Principle, which led to what you and Lom had to do as leaders. Everyone is with you," Li assured him. "Loshea has been informed. If she comes to a different conclusion, she'll have to deal with all of us, not just you and Lom. Unity has been restored in the capsule. If this is the last week we spend alive, we will spend it of one mind. We've lived together. We've fought together. And if it comes to it, we will die together."

Shipp breathed a huge sigh. James knew how important unity among the Space Forces was to Shipp, and had no doubt been talking with Li about it. Now Li understood it too. Of course, it was easy for him, because he shared the same commitment.

But then, Shipp seemed to flip to a new page in his mind, and redirected the conversation.

"I was thinking in there about what Rawlic said, about the Westers having some way to counteract whatever this thing is. If they do have a way to stop it, then all we have to do is wait until they appear on the surface, and we'll know it's safe."

Li read Shipp immediately. "We should be nonstop monitoring all the Rock Eyes we just placed in the last battle."

Before Shipp could answer, Li was at the console, punching up the coordinates for the newly planted Rock Eyes. He spent a few moments inputting codes. Then, the map of the region appeared on the monitor, with dots sprinkled around an area to the northeast. Shipp joined him.

"How many did we plant?"

"19 Rock Eyes transmitting from this region," Li confirmed. He activated the live view setting. On screen, they could see live footage from all 19 Rock Eyes. Each device featured cameras pointing in three directions that could rotate their lenses about 30 degrees each. That gave pretty good coverage of the surrounding areas.

Shipp located the one placed near where the automated turret had been. Then he studied the others.

"So, about half of these are in the two locations where each battle took place, right?" he asked.

Li nodded. "We have a good chance of spotting rats in either area, especially if the hostages were telling the truth about dozens of access points."

"Good," said Shipp. "We have about ten days to go. So we sit and wait." He stood thinking, and then spoke again. "I'd like to see Mixie receive a proper burial. And I want to see her face again please."

James nodded. "I figured you'd want that. Assuming we survive this, we'll carry her back to the main base and do it there. We used all the remaining embalmers on her."

Shipp put his hands on James' shoulders, and leaned his head against the middle of his back.

"Thank you Cam. Thank you."

Five days passed. Not a Wester in sight from any of the Rock Eyes. Amio emerged from the oxygen generation room with fresh calculations. Everyone turned their attention to him.

"I just used up the last of the oxygen generation reagents. Based on the masses of what's left, we have 4.76 days of oxygen. About 114 hours."

Shipp nodded. "Plus the two full tanks."

Amio nodded. "Yeah. And with 15 people, those are good for about two hours per soldier total, which is about how long it takes to hike to LUB-7. That's cutting it real close."

Li corrected him. "Our personal tanks still have about an hour left too. So we should have about three hours each."

"I hope so," said Amio.

Everyone seemed to accept the news for what it meant. Shipp headed back to his sleeping quarters. When he got there, he saw General Lom approaching. Shipp entered the room and let Lom in, who closed the door behind him. Shipp sat. Lom looked directly at him, not as intimidated as before. They hadn't spoken since Rawlic's rebellion.

"Commander Shipp," Lom began, "I've been trying to think of what I want to say, because I know we need to talk. As you've figured out, I'm not so great at this sort of thing. I'm a details guy. A planner. An implementer. A supervisor. And a warrior. But I think, tactically..."

"We all have our strengths, General," Shipp cut him off. "I really admire the action you took after I.... They needed a leader, and you stepped up when it mattered."

"We all know you're superior to me as a battlefield commander," Lom said. Shipp wasn't quite sure where he was trying to go here. But he let him talk.

"I guess what I want to say is, I think you're the best field commander I've ever seen. I'm glad you led this mission, and I'm glad you survived to this point. You can take my place if we get back," Lom said.

Shipp shook his head.

"I'm getting out of here the first chance I get. This is two planets that have cost me more than I gained. I'm done with the ground."

Lom misread him. "I didn't realize you were that close to...uh... Mixie." His struggle to remember her name didn't seem to register with Shipp at all.

"She was part of my squad for years on Risner. I knew her better than my own sister, who's six years older than me. She saved my life once. She stood by me through everything. She was immaculate on the battlefield. A superb marksman. She followed me here. And she held steady while I struggled with my wife's murder."

Lom nodded in affirmation. "You're blessed. I've never had someone like that."

"Mixie was loyal far beyond expectation. And to me, that's everything in this war. All we have are our friends and the hope of victory," Shipp concluded.

He choked up again at the image of the bullet piercing her skull. It played through his mind over and over, as if it just happened. He remembered touching her lifeless, bloody face. Tears filled his eyes again. He rubbed them out, but didn't mind Lom seeing his grief.

"I suggest you write an epitaph for her within the next four days," Lom said. "In case we don't get out of here. Loshea can get it back to her family."

At this, Lom left. Shipp turned toward the small desk in the quarters, and saw a writing tablet. Lom's idea was superb. Shipp wrote out his honor to Mixie right then and there.

A hundred hours had passed since Amio released his final calculations. The fifteen surviving Petersons were beginning to accept their fate. Several had already written final words to their families and to Space Force Command, as Shipp had suggested everyone do.

Shipp ran through another weapons inventory with Gugbe and Ramad. He wanted to confirm everything was ready if they discovered the surface was safe in time. That meant battlefield uniforms, nutrient units, hydration, and weapons. Everything needed to be ready to pick up and run at a moment's notice.

Each Peterson had fully refilled their personal O2 tanks while new oxygen continued to generate. It was much easier to extract it from the machine than the air in the room. After a brief recap, Shipp felt assured that everything was ready.

Except for two problems: Breathing shields and a plan.

For the plan, what would happen if there were Westers nearby? Should they engage them? This would use up precious oxygen. Next, what if they returned to their main base but found everyone dead and the interior contaminated? The Petersons had done their best to think through various scenarios like these, but with so many unknowns, it was hard to nail down strategies that everyone could commit to with a high degree of confidence. This was not the way Petersons usually conducted battle or engaged with a scenario.

And as for breathing shields, most of the remaining ones had poor to almost zero transparency. They salvaged the best fifteen remaining ones from the various dead and departed soldiers, but visuals would not be better than 50% for anyone, except for the lone brand new one Rawlic tossed on the ground before he left. Shipp didn't know how to decide who should get to wear it. So, they did a random drawing. Each soldier scribbled their name on scraps of packing material, and Shipp drew the winner. It was Li.

Six hours left.

Shipp ordered everyone to hydrate and eat. And he told them they would do so again with 30 minutes left. Whatever happened after that, no one would be short on energy.

Everyone kept checking the monitor, watching the live feeds from the nineteen Rock Eyes. Nothing budged.

Two hours left.

Amio got angry and slammed his helmet against the wall. Shipp reprimanded him. Had Amio actually broken his helmet, he'd have to find a replacement with even less transparency. In other words, keep your head together. We're not going to fall apart no matter what.

Lom shook his head in amazement at Shipp's commitment. Shipp would fight until the last possible second, doing everything there was to do. Shipp ensured that these fifteen soldiers would be ready, no matter what.

Five minutes left.

Amio and everyone else headed into the oxygen generation room and waited. They watched the oxygen production gauges, which slowly descended in intensity. No one spoke.

Four minutes. Three minutes. Two minutes. One minute.

The seconds ticked down to zero.

But oxygen kept sputtering out. 87 seconds later, it finally stopped. Shipp smiled at Amio.

"You suck at math."

Amio forced out a laugh. "Hey, at least we got more, not less."

Shipp addressed everyone:

"Okay, now the real clock begins. Breathable air within this space will last for a little while, and we'll breathe it for a couple hours. After that, we'll begin using personal supplies. The two large tanks will be our last resort. There's also a chance that the two tanks of O2 stolen by the traitors are still functional on the surface. If so, that would buy us additional time if the surface becomes safe. We're all in this together. We all live. Or we all die. But we will die like Petersons. Not like rats."

Everyone accepted Shipp's instructions, not picking up on the irony of being underground but determined not to die like rats. Shipp himself didn't pick up on it either.

More time passed, and pretty soon the carbon dioxide content rose to the point where Shipp had to order everyone to affix their breathing shields and start using their personal oxygen supplies.

"Stay calm. Don't breathe hard. No running. No exertion," Shipp ordered.

Their personal oxygen supplies could last up to three hours. After two hours, Shipp ordered everyone to eat and hydrate again. They would have to start using the tanks soon. He needed everyone to be ready.

But that hour ticked by as well.

One at a time, each soldier had to refill their supply from the large tanks. The first tank got drained completely, and then the second one too. Each soldier now had about three hours of oxygen left, and no other recourse.

They were three hours from death.

23

Fighting to Live

88 minutes later, James stood up and pointed to the monitor. A Wester soldier trudged around near one of the Rock Eyes. Suddenly the room filled with shouting and commotion. Shipp fired an AX round into one of the walls to quiet everyone.

"Keep your breathing calm!" Shipp admonished. "Excitement is valueless if we don't survive to enjoy it. Amio – what's the status?"

Amio updated his calculations. "Each of us has about ninety minutes of air left." He looked at Shipp. "That's not enough to get back."

Li couldn't stand the thought. "It is if the tanks up above are still usable."

He immediately crammed into the capsule tube. Shipp joined him and told the others to wait there. He and Li rose up in the shaft. For the first time in weeks, they stood on the surface of Lavoisier. It looked pretty much the same as before.

They looked down at the entrance. The Blackhead-coated plate that covered the life capsule entrance was dotted with tiny indentations. The ground around it was pocked with holes. Rawlic and the rebels must have fired their weapons to try to break back in, but were unable to penetrate the outer defenses. Shipp realized the reason. They had each taken Mossamer-24s, but they hadn't brought any Krocks with them.

What idiots, he thought. They were so fixated on leaving that they failed the most basic preparation steps. Unfit for the Peterson Space Force.

Shipp felt Li tug his arm. Shipp turned around and saw the bodies.

Sprawled on the ground in grotesque positions, Shipp counted five dead Petersons. It was hard to make out who was who, because their faces had been completely eaten away. It appeared as if some type of insect had chewed off their skin, muscles, and blood vessels. You could see bone. Their clothes were eaten through too, though only in parts. Apparently it took much longer for the contagion to get through fabric, but it still could.

"That must be the rat you sent up," said Li, pointing at a body farther away toward the direction of the Wester bases.

"Let's get to work, we don't have time," said Shipp.

They located the two oxygen tanks, about two hundred meters from the entrance. Rawlic's rebels abandoned them in their efforts to return to the capsule. Two other Petersons had tried to carry the tanks back at first, but left them behind at some point. Shipp and Li found their bodies about halfway between the capsule entrance and the tanks. They reached the tanks. The metal seemed intact. Li noticed a gaping hole on the underside of one tank.

"Looks like someone shot this one out for some reason," he surmised. "Probably just went mad."

Shipp hooked his oxygen tank up to the other one and opened the valve. The gauge on his tank increased.

"This one works," he said.

A few minutes later, Shipp and Li returned to the life capsule and updated everyone. One tank worked. With that tank, each Peterson would gain about sixty minutes of fresh oxygen, bringing their new totals to about 2.5 hours' worth.

"Is that enough?" asked Gugbe. Amio hesitated. So did everyone else.

"It's a hike," said James. "That means harder breathing. fourteen kilometers. Under three hours of air. We might make it. We might suffocate in sight of it. Are we just wasting time talking about it now?"

Shipp rose up and declared a new plan. It seemed to just come to him in that moment, but he had absolute certainty it was the right course of action.

"No." Shipp said. "We're not going back yet."

That got everyone's attention. And James could see it – Shipp had again become his best self in this moment.

Shipp continued, "We're going to locate and invade the Wester underground base, steal their oxygen, and then blow it up. Then, we'll go back."

Gugbe grinned. "Yes. That is a great plan. I'm with you 100%."

Shipp didn't wait for any discussion because there wasn't time. "Everyone, fill up your tanks with the amount of O2 Amio says, get your gear, and come face the console. Li and I will zero in our best guess for the location of the entrance. Then, we head to the surface."

Li, Shipp, and James quickly scanned through the footage of the Westers. In total, they saw four Westers at various points in time, three of which seemed to come from the same narrow canyon.

"There's an access point in this canyon. Has to be," said Li. "How do we approach without being seen?"

"We don't," said Shipp. "We also know there's an entrance somewhere in this vicinity, because Lom's flight passed over that spot and six rats vanished. Remember?"

James saw where Shipp was going.

"You want to do snake in the hole, from that SFU simulation we dominated," said James.

Shipp nodded and smiled. "That, combined with bait and switch."

Lom admired how well these two seemed to read each other's thoughts. He asked the logical question:

"Who's the snake?"

Shipp looked around, then back at James. "James and I ran this in a simulation. We took out the entire opposing force without losing one. Not a one-to-one correlation of course. You were the snake before. Up for it again?"

"Hissss," said James, drawing some cheers from a few other soldiers.

"Let's move," said Shipp.

"Wait," Li said. "If James' task is that important, he should have this."

Then, Li gave James his face shield, the only completely clear one they had. James hesitated, astonished at Li's sacrificial act. He looked at Shipp, then back at Li. But only for a second. It was clearly the best move. James took it, and gave Li his clouded one in exchange. Shipp marveled at Li. *This is a Peterson. I would die for him.*

The fifteen Petersons made their way up the capsule tube. They used up about 45 minutes of oxygen just to return to the earlier battlefield zone. Shipp used his comm to remind everyone what was at stake and to brief them on the 'snake in the hole' tactic.

"We've got under two hours to do this. James, branch off. The rest of us, we're heading to the coordinates we discussed. Break into twos and threes, surround it with a semi-circular array arcing around James' location. We fight off any attacks that come our way until James greenlights us."

Shipp broke off with Gugbe and Zemmer, who still wasn't able to run. Amio went with Li as the only pair, and the rest broke into three more groups of three.

The Petersons didn't have time to waste, and not just because of their dwindling oxygen. They also needed to get in the right position before a bunch of Westers emerged to fight them. But this time, they were familiar with this terrain.

It wasn't long before Shipp found himself at the exact same spot where he and Zemmer almost died before James saved them. They surrounded the ravines leading into the canyon where the base entrance had to be, and waited.

The Westers must have seen them, and had to know they were massing around this entrance. It was only a matter of time before Westers emerged from other access points. The one James monitored alone wasn't far, so it was a good bet. But if this gamble didn't pay off and the Westers didn't come out from that entrance, or if their guess as to its location was too far off, this might be the last battle ever fought by these fifteen Petersons.

But, it worked.

First, Lom's trio came under fire from the east, as did Shipp's. They were well shielded by the landscape for the moment, but this time the Westers launched Morse mines right from the start, much harder to evade. The first few landed off target, but it wouldn't be long before they zeroed in on the Peterson positions and flushed them out into the open.

Before that happened though, James watched in surprise as one side of a canyon wall cracked open.

"They're walking right out of the wall, not a hole in the ground. Get ready!" James called over his comm.

Four Westers emerged, one at a time. James rose up with a simple AX-15, and plastered them all. He threw that weapon down, retrieved his MagTon rifle, ran toward the opening in the canyon and emptied it, firing all eight inside the crevice.

As they exploded one at a time, fire burst briefly out from the hole.

"Snake in the hole!" James called out.

Shipp's crew, which was closest to James, fired their entire battery of dual cannons in the direction of the other attacking Westers. Hit or miss, this would make the Westers wary of emerging from their positions for at least a couple minutes. This gave cover to the other Petersons, who quickly dashed up and down the ravines and crests until all convened around James in the canyon next to the Wester opening.

Shipp quickly counted all his soldiers, and then nodded them in.

The groundbreaking nature of this moment was completely lost on all of them. No Peterson had ever entered a Wester underground base in five hundred years of war. These were the first. Of course, underground bases were relatively new as a battlefield asset, but that didn't make the moment less significant. These Petersons would be the first to see the differences in underground technology on Lavoisier.

Once inside, they quickly realized a key difference. The Westers' air cleansing station was at the bottom of a set of stairs. The interior within the canyon wall was filled with Lavoisier's atmosphere. James' MagTons had turned parts of this grating into useless shards of metal. But Shipp also noticed several dead Westers in the vicinity, and others who had tumbled down the mangled staircase the Petersons were about to descend.

Shipp led the way. Lom, taking up the rear, closed the door behind them and locked it from the inside. The Petersons noted an air purification door at the bottom of the staircase.

Li opened it, and every Peterson trained their weapons as the chamber opened. There was room for six inside, more than the Peterson life capsule entrance, but far less than their main base.

"Gugbe. You, Zemmer, and Lom stay out here. If any rats come through that door up there, it's up to you to stop them," Shipp said. "The rest of us will go through here in two shifts."

"Jonas that," said Gugbe and Zemmer in unison.

"Stay alive," said Shipp.

"Save your friend," his two Risner friends replied. Lom echoed it a second later.

Shipp, James, Li, Ramad, Blasé, and Amio entered the air cleansing chamber first, weapons trained at the interior opening that would lead inside the Wester base. The chamber had no windows, so the Westers on the other side had no idea they were about to be met by Petersons, unless they'd caught on to their plan from surface sensors. But it was a risk they had to take.

"Fire immediately at everything you see. Hives and Mags only. I'll do the Mossamer," Shipp ordered.

Once the chamber air purified, a blue light switched on and the inner door opened. As it did, the other five Petersons immediately fired hive bombs and Magtons. Explosions, sparks, and deafening roars filled the underground space. Shipp unloaded dozens of rounds from his Mossamer, firing in every direction through the billowing smoke, even though he couldn't see much.

"Out," ordered Shipp.

The six exited, and the door closed.

"Spread out and wait," said Shipp.

All six hugged the walls on either side of the entrance, and waited for the next six Petersons to come through. By the time they did, the room had cleared of enough smoke for an accurate situational analysis.

There were two dead Westers in the room, but that was it. It appeared as though the rest fled when hearing James' assault on the entrance. This was the best hope of their plan, and the Petersons felt relieved that it appeared to have worked.

The twelve Petersons broke into groups of three and went room to room, section by section, always protecting each other, never moving too far ahead or apart. They had one goal – find the oxygen generation room. All the potential intelligence they could gain here would have to wait for another day.

Ramad, Blasé, and another soldier rounded a corner and were met with AX fire from a group of four Westers. They retreated behind the wall at the sight of them. Shipp heard the firing.

"James – you're closest! Go support!"

But Ramad didn't need James. He had perfected his skill with the wizard. He fired six 10cm discs along the walls of the hallway. They ricochetted around and banked into the corner where the Westers huddled. Upon hearing screams and shouts, Blasé and Ramad burst into the room, unloading AX fire before the Westers could recover from the wizards. All four dead.

"Enemy neutralized," Ramad spoke into his comm.

"Well done," Shipp commended.

"Found it," called Li at almost the exact same moment. He and Amio had opened a door near the end of a hallway. Unlike the sleeping quarters around them, this door was blue instead of orange, with a large 'O' plastered on the outside. No reason to hide it, because neither side expected the other to attempt a mission like this.

Amio opened the door, and five Petersons darted inside. The room was empty. They found oxygen tanks, new breathing shields, and plenty of reagent material. Amio glanced at his gauge.

"An hour to spare," he observed.

"Everyone fill up and get a new shield. No time to waste," said Shipp, still waiting in the hallway with James. "Looks like we've seen everything in this area except whatever is behind that," he pointed to a black wall that stretched across a huge section of the area they were in. James approached it and shook his head.

"Blackhead."

Shipp nodded, and looked at Li. They had the same thought. It was probably a door, leading to other sections of the Wester base. The hostages had revealed there were dozens of entrances, but they hadn't revealed that various sections were separated by impenetrable doors. Underground, it would be suicide to launch a K-rocket at such a door. It might break through the door depending on the thickness, but it could also bring down the ceiling.

"They might be massing an army on the other side of this. Get filled up fast and head back out. Send in Gugbe, Zemmer, and Lom once you get there," Shipp called on his comm.

As each Peterson filled up, the others watched the Blackhead door warily, weapons ready to fire in case it opened. When Shipp finished filling up his oxygen tank and returned to the main room, the Blackhead door remained closed. He joined the last group of Petersons in the purification chamber.

Once through the chamber, they ascended the rickety staircase back to the surface level. Shipp unlocked the door but didn't open it. He turned to face everyone.

"If they anticipated us coming back out this door, they'll be waiting outside, and we'll be outgunned, just like the guys James cut down," said Shipp.

"But they don't know all we wanted was oxygen," said Lom, realizing it at the same moment he deduced Shipp had known it the whole time. "They think we're infiltrating the base."

"Most likely," said Shipp. "They probably pulled all their forces into the base and are on the other side of that door, deciding when to open it and what to prepare for. While they're deciding, we'll be running. Each of us has almost four hours of oxygen, and we filled up one large tank which can buy us more time. Is everyone ready to run?"

"Stay alive!" called out Gugbe.

"And save your friend!" replied the rest.

Shipp threw open the door. Not a Wester in sight.

They bolted through the canyon, up and down the crests and trenches, and headed west. After running for about ten minutes, they slowed to a walk. They would walk the rest of the way, knowing they still needed to conserve oxygen. The walk would take several hours. Zemmer's calf was in great pain, and his ability to walk at the desired pace became tougher and tougher. But they couldn't slow down, and he had to gut it out against the throbbing. A month in the capsule still hadn't healed it well enough.

About two kilometers from the main Peterson base, their oxygen gauges fell dangerously close to zero. Each soldier took about thirty minutes' worth of oxygen from the additional tank. This final air supply enabled them to reach the outer entrance to their main base. There was no way they hadn't been spotted, with all the Rock Eyes around the base, so Shipp didn't worry about going in unannounced.

Either all the Petersons inside had died from the plague, or they were ready to debrief them. But when the automated turrets didn't attack, Shipp knew Loshea had deactivated them.

Lom opened the outer door. The fifteen Petersons descended the ladder, and the air purified around them as the floor lowered toward the underground level. Through the glass enclosure, they could see General Loshea and the rest of the Peterson army, waiting and watching.

Once cleansed, Lom opened the inner door and went through first, then Shipp. They took off their breathing shields and helmets, and waited. General Loshea stepped forward and appraised them all, amazed and in utter disbelief.

"We thought you were dead."

24

Balance of Power

A day after Shipp's crew of fifteen returned, Loshea was satisfied with their detailed account of what happened over the last several weeks. Apparently, the life capsule communications console was even more dysfunctional than Li realized, because not a single message sent by Shipp or Lom had come through.

After Li's warning to the second flight about their face shields, Loshea had called the flight back. But after that, they never heard a word. Several weeks back, she sent four soldiers on a recon mission to check for any visual signs of Lom's campaign, such as smoke on the horizon. When their breathing shields started crystallizing, they quickly returned to LUB-7. A couple weeks later, she sent out two more soldiers to see if the same thing happened. It did. Fortunately no one died, but Loshea had seen enough to believe that whatever this chemical weapon was, it had probably killed Lom's entire unit.

So, she sent an emergency comm to Space Force Command, but hadn't received any definitive answer about help arriving. Plus, it was unclear what the help could do, because whatever was eating away the breathing shields might also damage attack ships and transport ships. And that was a non-starter.

Loshea concluded they might be here alone for quite some time. Not that unusual for Lavoisier, but still a bit unnerving considering this new airborne threat. When Shipp's group of fifteen suddenly showed up in the Rock Eye sensor web, everyone was shocked to see them alive.

She spoke to General Lom first, naturally.

Lom quickly realized Loshea knew basically nothing, including how he had failed to lead in several critical situations. But he still took the opportunity to laud Shipp's leadership and battlefield tactics. He left out some of his less shining moments. So did Shipp. In his debrief, Shipp focused on their victory on the battlefield, what they knew about the contagion, Rawlic's rebellion, Mixie's murder, and how they managed to survive.

After debriefing, Shipp retreated to his sleeping quarters. James, Gugbe, Zemmer, Ramad, and Blasé joined him, and the six of them rested and talked, trying to process the incredible events of the previous month. The subject turned to Rawlic's rebellion.

"I looked up what history I could find," Ramad said. "There's no record in five hundred years of a Peterson mutiny. What he did, and the fact he went so fast in that direction, so early in our captivity, makes me wonder how he qualified for the Space Force."

"Yeah, but the other seven went along with him," said Gugbe.

"There was something about being trapped there," Shipp mused. "Something drove them to do things they probably never imagined doing. It's funny, because we're trapped here now, basically. Life on Lavoisier is to be trapped underground. So why did it affect them so much and not us?"

"Resentment," said James. "Jealousy maybe. Some of those guys were already kind of against you, even before all this. They saw us as outsiders, not as Petersons. Lost their purpose. Lost their identity. Reality wasn't far behind."

"That says something about Loshea, and probably Lom too," said Shipp. "It never should have come to that."

"The virus," Blasé said. "It was... it's not fear of being trapped. It's fear of an unknown threat. They fed off the fears of the Wester hostages. Let it drive them mad."

"You know what I've been thinking," Gugbe said. "We barely had enough air to make it back here, just the fifteen of us. If Rawlic hadn't left, we would have run out of air and died."

The room was silent. Shipp was astounded. That meant, in a contorted way, that Rawlic's recklessness actually saved the fifteen who made it back.

"If you're trying to get me to revise my appraisal of them and make them heroes for sacrificing for us—" Shipp began before being interrupted by Gugbe.

"Not even close boss. I was thinking that if we had just let them go, Mixie would have made it back with us."

The thought distressed Shipp. Her death – what a waste. The memory he would never forget, her body collapsing – grief pressed within his brain and all his extremities.

"I miss her," Shipp whispered, closing his eyes and lowering his face. "I wish..."

The others kept silent. Each man pondered Mixie's loss in his heart. Shipp spoke again.

"But yeah, Gugbe is right. We would have died if they hadn't broken unity. We would have died together. Probably with just hours to spare. I wonder... maybe that would have been better."

"Better?" Ramad said, confused at how his commander could even pretend to wish for death over everything he had been fighting for all these years.

Shipp said nothing. James knew why. The others clued in. Mixie had been part of their squad for years. With the exception of James, the others in the room had fought alongside her since she first arrived on Risner. Ramad arrived with her on the same transport ship. Going on without her – it just wouldn't be the same.

Shipp's eyes enflamed as he replayed Shelsie murdering her yet again. Caressing her lifeless face. Mixie would be dying in front of Shipp a thousand times every year the rest of his life. At the hands of a Peterson. Unthinkable. Unimaginable. He remembered her performance on Risner, when she rose to the moment and helped fight off the Wester invasion of their base. To fight alongside someone so long. To trust them. To admire them. To mentor them. That's what Shipp longed for when he joined the Space Force.

"Mixie died for nothing," Shipp said. "I should have..."

"Shipp," Zemmer stopped his commander's descent into a crippled mind. "The people responsible for Mixie are still alive. The Westers invented that weapon. Whoever did that, and whoever chose to deploy it against us – that's who killed her. Rawlic, Shelsie, and the others may not have been fit for the Space Force, but their deaths are also because of the real enemy. Same enemy as always."

Shipp looked at Zemmer. He felt a flush of warmth in his heart. His skin pricked with goosebumps. Something shifted in his spirit at Zemmer's words. He looked at James, who nodded in complete agreement. Gugbe, Ramad, and Blasé all agreed too. Don't lose sight of the real enemy. But Shipp took their support and unity in a direction none of them expected.

"I'm gonna find him. I'm gonna find the rat who made this weapon. I'm gonna feed it to him. Right down his throat. I want all of you there with me when it happens. We gotta get off this rock."

The six men looked at each other in silent agreement. This was their new mission. Shipp had found a darker path out of his despair. His friends would follow him there. And the more he dwelled on it, Shipp began to realize this altered focus could also be the path he sought to end the war – with the Petersons winning it forever.

***

A day later, division among the base leadership arose about what to do next.

Shipp wanted to load up the other flight with quadruple the firepower and extra oxygen supplies, return to the scene, and draw out more Wester forces. The purpose would be to secure more hostages and intelligence, and ascertain the true nature and full extent of this mysterious contagion.

But Loshea wouldn't hear it. She was relieved that fifteen Petersons had survived. But the mutiny, the uncertainty of the Wester base layout, and the contagion told her that laying low was the smartest move until additional help and reinforcements could arrive.

Shipp was greatly relieved to learn that the six Peterson bases on the other side of the planet had also noticed the effects of the contagion and had taken similar precautions. Twelve Petersons died from it, because they were caught too far away from a base and couldn't get back in time. But it could have been a lot worse.

"This is a weapon, and they just unleashed it on the entire planet. Don't you see what this means, General?" Shipp pressed.

"Yes, it alters the balance of power in their favor, and we have to find a way to get it back, like we always do," answered Loshea.

"No," countered Shipp. "This isn't about balance of power. This is a war-ender. They could invade our Territory, launch this weapon on our general population planets, and wipe out billions in a matter of hours."

"I understand the risk, Colonel Shipp. But if we're going to do anything about it, we need a lot more help. You're talking about assaulting an unknown target, with an unknown number of soldiers inside, where they can see us coming and we can't see them. And, they have a weapon we don't fully understand. That's a really bad set of odds. That's not the Peterson Way."

"There won't BE a Peterson Way if we don't take this chance now. The Westers have to know we know about their weapon, so they aren't going to just sit around and wait. They're probably calling their commanders now and getting ready to set their world-ending campaign in motion," Shipp said. "It's now or never," he concluded.

Unlike most discussions, this one happened behind closed doors, at Loshea's insistence because of the extremely high stakes in play. Only Shipp, Loshea, Lom, James, and a couple other key personnel were present.

Loshea wouldn't budge, "Nothing in this war moves that fast. We can afford to wait a few weeks, a few months. Probably even years. They can't just march into our Territory without being spotted. We've got space stations, attack ships patrolling, detection webs. Space Force Command will develop a more comprehensive strategy than you or I can come up with in the few hours you're talking about."

"We know the terrain," Shipp replied. "We've been there. We can name specific canyons, valleys, crevices, and plateaus. It's not a blind alley. The fifteen of us are fully qualified to lead this. And, the rats don't need to invade our space with ships. They just need a weapon to fire that will carry this chemical to our planets. They can slip that through the webs."

"They don't even know where our colonized planets are! They've never been to our–"

Just then, the General of Administration broke up the conversation. "There's a ship landing. One of ours. An attack ship."

Loshea and Shipp looked at each other. She spoke first. "From our emergency comm?"

Loshea, Shipp, James, Li, Lom, and several others made their way to the surface to greet the attack ship's commander and crew. Attack ships weren't always familiar with the intricacies of Lavoisier's environment or the underground base procedures. So, Loshea typically took a team to the surface to help acclimate them. But this time, there was much more at stake than breathing clean air.

The attack ship's Blackhead-encased door eased open and lowered to the ground.

Shipp had never seen an attack ship this close. The entire ship was black, fully encased in God's Armor. An odd lack of symmetry, its form jutted out in various shapes and angles, almost like a kid stuck a bunch of geometric figures into a glob of clay and coated it in tar. No windows that he could see. Everything was run internally to protect the exterior of the ship, he surmised. What a beautiful piece of machinery.

Some condensed air and moisture escaped with a puff, and down the ramp marched three men.

The one in the middle was clearly the general, Shipp guessed. He walked like someone who knew he led one of the most fearsome and impenetrable weapons of war in all human history – combined. The presumed general had fierce eyes, so alive, alert, and focused that Shipp wondered for a moment if he ever slept.

The man extended his hand to General Loshea. "General Garrison, commander of the Sorcerer. This is my Comm Officer, Commander Harden. And this is Jennings, First Officer."

"Pleasure to meet you General," began Loshea. "Are you responding to our comm? We received no notice you were coming."

"That was at my request," said Garrison. "Didn't want to take any chance of a comm intercept. Not given the stakes you described."

Shipp wasn't going to wait. He interjected, "What stakes? What do you know about what we've discovered here?"

Garrison looked surprised to hear an unintroduced officer speak up like this. But he didn't seem to mind. Before Loshea could say anything, Garrison replied.

"An unknown biological or chemical weapon that seems to have infected the entire planet. Possibly killed a whole attacking force. Definitely killed twelve in the secured hemisphere. Frankly, General, I'd like to do whatever I can to flip the tables on this immediately. I'm here to make the Westers regret ever inventing that weapon."

Shipp was elated. Garrison could not have made a stronger first impression. Loshea probably detected that, and she tried to suppress Garrison's evident enthusiasm.

"We don't yet know exactly what we're facing, and the Westers have an underground network of bases and tunnels apparently far more extensive than we realized," she explained. "I'm currently waiting on Space Force Command for an officially sanctioned response strategy."

"I'm your response strategy," Garrison stated flatly. "You show me where these bases are, and we deal with them our way. Now. While the pickings are fresh and the threat is localized."

Shipp flushed with joy, adrenalin, and vengeance. Garrison could see it. He nodded at him in affirmation, as if to say that no more discussion was needed. But Loshea kept trying, "General, we don't know if the threat is localized."

Shipp butted in again, "That's why we have to act now. Before they send attack ships to protect it. Let me get more hostages – administrators this time instead of soldiers. We'll find out a lot more, because we'll have time. And with the attack ship, they won't have a chance."

"They have K-rockets. That gives anyone a chance," Lom spoke up.

"Not against us it doesn't, not on this planet," Harden said, speaking for the first time. "They don't have any external weapons."

"They have underground automated turrets," said Loshea. "How do we know they don't have Krocks of a similar sort?"

"It's a risk worth taking," said Garrison. "We can take a few hits. And we brought a Desert Raid." Loshea raised an eyebrow at that, and Garrison continued, "Trust me. You don't run an attack ship without taking risks. It's not like with ground wars, General. No offense, but whoever this guy is" – pointing to Shipp – "he's right. We're here to assess and then neutralize. We've assessed..."

He looked around, letting his unfinished sentence speak for itself.

Loshea said, "General, you're not in command on Lavoisier or over my base. We work together on this."

"I'm all for it General, 100%. As long as working together means destroying that base."

"You destroy that base, you might unleash more poison," said Lom. "What if you destroy whatever counteracts it too?"

"You misunderstand me, General. I'm not going to just blaze my guns and detonate the region, which we aren't equipped for anyway. As your astute officer here has made clear, we need rat hostages, not just corpses."

Garrison's bluster seemed matched by an admirable sense of order. He was a brawny brain – absolutely perfect to lead an attack ship. Shipp knew Loshea wouldn't be able to stop him. It was only a matter of time.

The group of soldiers and the attack ship's command crew entered LUB-7. Garrison made it plain what he had come to do. Loshea began to wonder if she was being overly cautious, or if this attack ship commander was in over his head. But she couldn't figure out how to slow his determination. And Shipp ate it up like candy dipped in Wester blood.

A couple days after their arrival, Garrison addressed the entire base personnel:

"Commander Shipp has created a detailed attack plan, in coordination with myself and commander Harden. This upcoming assault is the very reason your base exists. You're alone on this half of the planet. You're here to establish and advance the beachhead. This is how you do it. This isn't the time for timidity or pause or assurance. This is the time to act, because the fate of our worlds is at stake, perhaps more than at any other time in the last five hundred years. You have an attack ship backing you up, and we were sent here because of the urgency of this situation. And this isn't just any attack ship. I've been leading the Sorcerer for fourteen years. Six of my crew of have been with me that entire time."

Shipp was more impressed with every word that came from Garrison's lips.

"We have more kills than any other ship in history. We've destroyed more ships than any other ship in history. We're the best there is. That's why SFC sent us to you, at this moment."

Garrison looked around the room. He could tell some were absolutely with him, while others were unsure. The unsure ones were looking around the room, searching for their leaders for guidance.

"Commander Shipp is about to call you into service. Listen."

Shipp prepared the most important rallying speech of his young career. Over the last two days, working with Garrison had revived his passion for the war like never before. It now exceeded how he felt when he left for Risner from Space Force University. Garrison's strategic mind was brilliant. He was measured, methodical, and focused. He anticipated problems and complications, and built contingencies into his plans. Combined with an irrepressible thirst for victory, Garrison personified what Shipp had always wanted in a leader. He had found his next Vonn.

The clincher came when Garrison revealed that he believed the Petersons could actually win this war, in his lifetime. This was the first time Shipp had encountered someone who believed this as completely as he did. And it came from an attack ship general who had every other admirable leadership quality Shipp could imagine.

Shipp stood in front of everyone and made it very simple.

"Who do I want on my squad? Anyone who has lost someone to the enemy. If you've lost a relative, you're in this fight. If you've lost a friend, I'll follow you into battle. If you've lost a parent, you can be my commander. If you've lost wife, husband, or lover, I'll trust my back to you against a hundred rats."

Shipp surveyed the room. The same soldiers preening for Garrison ate up Shipp's words too.

"If you're ready for this battle, you step over here and prepare to board that flight," Shipp concluded.

In all, 32 Petersons stepped forward at Shipp's call, including every single one who had returned with the surviving fifteen. Except Zemmer, whose injuries disqualified him, and General Lom.

Garrison looked over his 'recruits,' nodded at them in admiration, turned to Shipp, and gave the command.

"Let's fly."

25

Attack Ship

Of course, it wasn't quite that simple. The battle didn't begin until two days later. But Garrison's exhortation did elicit a raucous cheer from the 32 Peterson volunteers. Harden and Jennings flushed with bloodlust. They didn't get to see this sort of thing very often because attack ships were crewed by about twenty, and rarely were all of them even in the same room.

By the end of the two days of preparation, every member of the squad was required to restate the plan verbally. They had to commit the key aspects to memory and demonstrate mastery.

Every one of them passed the test.

In addition, the only remaining LUB-7 flight had to be upgraded with additional oxygen supplies and extra weaponry for a sustained assault, if one became necessary. Li led that part of the preparations. Shipp would lead the ground assault once the flight landed, and the attack ship would wait unseen until the opportune time. Several possible scenarios had been worked up as to when that would be. They had one chance to take advantage of the element of surprise, and they weren't going to waste it. Having an attack ship backing you up in a ground battle was a rare luxury.

Finally, before the battle could commence, Shipp insisted on returning to the life capsule to retrieve Mixie and give her a burial. Li flew Shipp, Gugbe, Blasé, and Ramad to get her body.

Next to a hillside, so the burial mound wouldn't be too conspicuous, the four provided a final resting place for their betrayed and murdered friend. Her tomb would be easily reachable for any Petersons visiting

LUB-7. Once ready, James, Loshea, Lom, and several others joined Zemmer and Mixie's other best friends at the grave.

Garrison and Harden asked to witness the burial too. This greatly surprised Shipp, but he gave permission, deeply moved that these men who just met them would stand to honor one of his fallen friends. Ramad spoke first. Then Blasé, Zemmer, and Gugbe. Last, Shipp took his turn to eulogize Mixie. Even through his face shield, the emotion in his voice was palpable.

"When we say to save your friend, we mean any Peterson soldier. But for anyone who fought alongside Mixie for long enough, that meant so much more. She became a true friend. A friend is loyal. A friend is trustworthy. A friend is dependable. They show up when you need them. They listen. They strengthen. They encourage. And in Mixie's case, they keep doing all this, even when..."

Shipp faltered, knowing he needed to reveal more of himself here.

"Mixie kept being my friend, even when I unfairly put her at a distance for several months after we came to Lavoisier. I treated her coldly. I avoided her. Something in me resented her even though I had no rational or logical reason for doing so. I can't have those months back. But when I got over myself enough to see that she was still the same great person, she didn't return my resentment. She welcomed our friendship back like it never left. The way she died was... unforgivable."

He paused to finish, "I will miss you forever."

Harden, whose steely exterior made him seem like one of the toughest men Shipp had ever seen, teared up as Shipp concluded his eulogy. For a soldier he never knew. To Shipp, Harden's face looked older than his body. Creases, lines, and texture suggested a man who had suffered more than most in this war. Shipp surmised it may have been years since Harden last smiled. He could relate.

Garrison approached Shipp after he finished speaking and offered this, "That was very well done. Much appreciated."

Shipp concluded Harden and Garrison must have lived through a lot of battles and losses. These were the kind of men Shipp imagined fighting alongside when he joined the Space Force.

James embraced Shipp, "I'm proud of you. I know that was hard."

Shipp bowed and turned away from James, letting his growing list of losses fuel him. He was trying to 'use it,' as he prepared himself for the next battle.

***

Not long after Mixie's burial, the third trip back to the Wester underground base commenced.

Li piloted the only remaining flight in this hemisphere. If it got shot down and disabled, the Petersons would have no way to fly anywhere once Garrison left. But with the attack ship now in reserve, there was no need to risk taking the flight too close to the Westers. It would land several hundred meters from where they had previously engaged the enemy.

The biggest surprise, to everyone's delight – even those who didn't think this attack was the right move – happened when Garrison informed them he brought a Harris Shield Array.

A Harris Shield Array featured two cannons mounted on samarium-based foundations and shielded by a lesser version of Blackhead. Not quite as strong, but strong enough to sustain itself in a fierce battle. The cannons fired small supersonic mini-rockets that were loaded with a powerful explosive. In a typical arrangement, the cannons would be placed 10-20 meters apart. Between them, the foundations of the cannons produced an ultra-tough semi-opaque magnetic shield that covered the entire space, including the cannon towers themselves.

A soldier could stand behind this magnetic shield and be protected, even from AX fire. The shield could redirect and repel any known projectile fired at it. The only way to get through a Harris Shield Array was to attack the towers. The base at Risner used to have a Harris before Shipp arrived, but it had stopped working properly, and no replacement had ever been sent. This would be the first time Shipp used one in combat.

Li landed the flight after flying over the Wester base such that they would be noticed, but fast enough that he could safely escape before Westers emerged from any access points.

The 32 Peterson ground soldiers exited the flight. Two groups of four men carried each foundation for the Harris Array. They set it up about twenty meters in front of the flight, and spread the towers apart by fifteen meters. This was more than enough room for all 32 soldiers to be protected by the shield, with the flight protected behind it as well, once they finished assembling the towers and activating it.

Meanwhile, Garrison took the Sorcerer back up into space, to wait for his signal to act.

The Peterson ground force spread out into four groups of eight. The idea was to give the Westers the impression that they were launching another ground assault with multiple squads, similar to last time. The four groups approached their best guesses about where the Westers might emerge.

Shipp took his long-time crew of Gugbe, James, Ramad, and Blasé, along with Amio, Li, and Lavoisier veteran Durman. Durman, one of the fifteen who survived the life capsule, leapt at Shipp's call to arms. Shipp chose Durman for this crew because the Westers killed his dad on Portia when Durman was ten years old.

Shipp's crew quickly located the hidden entrance to the Wester base they infiltrated last time.

They waited. No movement. Shipp looked at James.

"They better not have abandoned the whole thing, little cowards," Shipp said.

"I don't think so," said James. "Far too much invested in a place like this."

Still nothing. Shipp didn't want to wait any longer.

"Let's go," he ordered. "We have to draw them out."

"Shipp," said James. "Pushing ahead too aggressively cost us a lot on Risner. Are you sure this is the time? We don't know all their access points."

Shipp considered James' comment for a moment. He was right. Too many unknowns. Shipp relented.

"Alright. Hold here. Eyes out."

More waiting.

Garrison crackled over their comms. "Run back – now! Head for the Array!"

At that, all 32 Petersons arose and dashed back toward the flight. Why? Because Garrison could see at least three dozen Westers emerging from multiple access points. He noted the locations from far above and out of sight. Then, he unleashed a weapon he had never used in combat – the Desert Raid.

From outer space, about two hundred half-meter cylinders shot down at hypersonic speed toward the Lavoisier surface, with spear-like tips on the lower ends. They impaled the ground in a mostly circular pattern in the vicinity of the advancing Wester soldiers.

Some Westers saw the cylinders thunking into the ground all around them. They halted, and cried out to everyone to return underground. But it was too late. Each cylinder sent an explosive shockwave into the ground, bursting clouds of dust and sand into the air. Then, the sides of the cylinders pried open, and an internal mechanism propelled a violent wind. Collectively synchronized, the wind from each cylinder aggregated and intensified, producing a sort of temporary tornado. The wind wasn't strong enough to knock someone over. But the point was to get so much sand and dust in the air that visibility would be practically zero.

While the Westers scrambled to find their way back underground, the Sorcerer descended from space, down through the sky, and hovered to the south of the dust cloud. At the same time, the 32 Peterson soldiers reached the Harris Shield Array and took cover behind the magnetic barrier. Five Westers were far enough out to be on the periphery of the swirling dust cloud. Knowing they couldn't enter it, they turned toward the fleeing Petersons and assessed the possibility of pursuing them.

The Petersons activated the cannon towers of the Harris Array, and then watched the Sorcerer descend and prepare to attack. Though no gun barrels could be spotted on the attack ship, from its hull about thirty hive bombs shot forth, larger than the ones used by infantry. Each bomb shot into the dust cloud and exploded. Those were followed with high-caliber AX fire, shooting in a spread pattern through the swirling dust.

A few automated weapons emerged from the ground and fired Krocks at the Sorcerer. It took a few hits, but quickly retaliated and neutralized the threats. Garrison guessed that if the Westers had anti-attack ship Krocks, many of them would be within the Desert Raid cloud or require manual operation, and thus be unmanned due to the sudden Peterson onslaught. His guess proved correct when their counterattack proved so inadequate.

At the same time, the twin cannon towers from the Harris fired five batteries at the Westers who had avoided the heart of the Desert Raid attack. The high-pitched squealing sound of the rockets launching eclipsed that of Krocks from a Mossamer, and caused several Petersons to flinch. In the distance, explosions from the Harris rockets kicked up even denser clouds of dust and debris around the disoriented Westers, and most of that debris then merged with the Desert Raid cloud. All five Westers died or were badly wounded.

At this, the 32 Peterson soldiers ran back toward the storm cloud. As they neared, Garrison ordered the Desert Raid to cease. The wind died down, and debris began to settle. As it cleared, Shipp's team found multiple dead and dying Westers. The four squads methodically searched the area, killing any soldiers who remained alive.

It was a flawless start to the battle. 0 to 36. The sort of thing Shipp lived for.

But now came the hard part. Garrison fed the four squad leaders the locations of the four access points he had observed from above. Shipp was amazed.

"Four holes, and four squads. We each take one. You all know what this is about. Stay alive," Shipp ordered.

He heard the reply in his comm from 31 soldiers and from Garrison and Harden in the Sorcerer. And with that, the four Peterson squads reached the access points, and simultaneously entered them.

26

Underground Assault

Shipp's squad of eight burst through a hidden door in a canyon they hadn't reached before. Three of the four newly discovered access points were of this nature. The fourth was a hole in the ground, more like the Peterson life capsule. As before, the cagey, metallic interior began with a set of downward stairs. The room was empty, with two levels down to the air purification chamber. Shipp's squad clanged down the stairs and reached the outer door.

"Remember – they don't know if we're Westers who made it back inside, or Petersons," Shipp whispered. "That gives us a couple seconds advantage. And that's all we'll need. Just try not to shoot too many consoles this time."

"Break into fours?" Gugbe confirmed.

"Jonas," replied Shipp. "You, me, Li, and Ramad. The other four follow us immediately once we clear the chamber."

James knew why Shipp wanted him and Amio in the second group. In case something went wrong, he wanted James to lead. And he wanted Amio's science expertise preserved depending on what they encountered inside.

Shipp and the other three entered the chamber. Li and Gugbe got on one knee and prepared their AXs. Shipp readied his Mossamer. Ramad held a pulse rifle since it was unlikely everyone inside would be wearing soldier's armor, and they would be defenseless against the immobilizing effect.

The planetary air filtered out and the breathable air blew in. Blue light on. Door open.

At the first crack open, Li could see several Westers waiting. He fired immediately. Shipp followed up, hitting more Westers to the right of the ones hit by Li. As the door fully opened, Gugbe started shooting to the left of the room, and Ramad sent a pulse into the most densely packed group of Westers. All five of them fell down and constricted into grotesque semi-fetal positions, unable to move. All the dead were admins except for two soldiers.

The Petersons stepped out as the door closed behind them, and they continued firing at anything that moved. They quickly discerned there wasn't much space to the right of where the chamber opened into the room. Just a wall of supply shelves. The Petersons backed against the shelves and waited. From there, they could see three hallways leading out from this main room, which housed several monitor consoles.

One hallway extended almost straight out from them for quite a distance, but then seemed to branch off in two directions like a T. Another hallway took a sharp right very close to their current position, and the third was a long and gradual left. The sharp right hallway was also the widest, and it cornered up with the consoles.

"Gugbe –watch the right," Shipp directed. "Li, the left, and I've got straight ahead. Ramad – switch weapons to wizards."

Tunnels like these were the perfect place to fire wizards, because they could bank back and forth down the halls, potentially taking out multiple enemies.

They removed their face shields and waited.

Moments later, James, Blasé, Amio, and Durman emerged from the air purification chamber. Immediately, Westers fired from around the sharp right corner. Gugbe fired back though he couldn't see anyone from his vantage. No idea how many were there. The Westers had basically fired blind, but they got lucky because James and his group had just exited the chamber, and were still closely packed together. Blasé got hit, and crumpled to the floor dead.

Seven left. Not good to lose such an experienced soldier so fast. Shipp burned with focused rage at the loss of another long-time friend.

"James!" Shipp roared. "Get over here now! Get away from there!"

James and the others fell in line against the back wall and along the console wall. As they did, the Westers fired blind again, hitting nothing this time. But Shipp knew they would be firing something worse than AX rounds very soon, and his squad was penned in.

Wizards couldn't bank around such a sharp turn. Shipp switched his Mossamer to Krock mode, aimed at the wall between them and the Westers, and launched. The explosion blew apart the wall and sent three Westers careening backward. Parts of the ceiling caved in. With all the noise and debris, it was hard to see if any Westers survived.

But Gugbe, James, and Amio advanced, firing continually, killing the three on the ground as well as the five still immobilized from the pulse rifle. This would prevent any direct attacks from the hallway, for the moment.

"Hug the walls!" Shipp yelled to them. The three of them held tight against the left wall, out of sight of anyone who might be coming down the gradual left tunnel.

Shipp, Li, and Ramad advanced along the right wall with the consoles until they could see down the left tunnel. Durman kept watch of the long tunnel straight ahead.

"Movement!" Shipp bellowed, as he saw something down the left hallway.

Ramad ripped a batch of seven wizards. The discs banked and cut their way down the hallway. It was hard to tell if anyone got hit, but this would keep them out of sight until the Petersons could secure the right hallway.

"Stay on them Ramad. Watch that hallway," Shipp ordered.

James switched weapons, and reached a more agreeable angle with the hard right tunnel. He could see around the corner through the debris, up to a certain point down the far side of that hallway. No Westers in sight, but he knew they could be up against the near side. James fired three Morse mines down the hallway, timed to explode in seconds. At the sound of his weapon going off, he could hear several Westers bolting away. They had been waiting just meters away.

The timing of Shipp's assault had so far been nearly perfect, except for the counterattack that cost him another longtime friend in Blasé. They caught the Westers unprepared for another internal invasion.

"James!" Shipp directed. "You and Gugbe get in that right hallway and watch. Durman keep your eyes straight ahead. Ramad and I will watch the left hallway. Li – you and Amio see if you can find a layout of this place on their console."

James and Gugbe entered the wide right hallway. It banked again about twenty meters ahead, with no doors between here and there. Several doors dotted both sides of the other two hallways, which were both about six times longer.

"This place looks like a maze," James commented. "The tunnels are way more complex than ours."

"Just like on Risner," said Shipp.

James got Shipp's attention and pointed upward at the ceiling. Shipp looked. Dirt and rock, native to Lavoisier, not refined metal like the Peterson bases use on their ceilings. They noted a few support beams shoved through parts of the rock.

"Their tunneling machine must be a lot different from ours," Shipp mused.

"Probably works faster, so they can build longer and more elaborate tunnels," James said. "And deeper."

Shipp refocused their attention. "We need to get our bearings. Where are we in relation to the room we got the O2 from last time?"

The five waiting soldiers started drawing mental pictures trying to piece together the surface terrain and imagine where everything was positioned.

"I'd say that room is maybe fifty to a hundred meters that way through the rock," Gugbe said, pointing back through the air purification chamber.

"I agree," said James. "It's a good bet the left tunnel eventually leads to that room, and the Blackhead door we saw from the other side."

"Good," said Shipp. "That means, if we can secure the left hallway and all the rooms in it and beyond, we can consider that section safe. If Li and Amio can't make any progress in the next minute or two, we're going down that hallway."

"Jonas," said several voices.

A couple minutes passed. Shipp looked at Li. Li shook his head. "We could figure it out in a couple hours probably, but this is just trial and error. We don't know their codes, their tech, or much else."

"Okay, scrap it then. James, Gugbe, Durman – hold your positions. The four of us are going room to room," Shipp said.

Shipp, Li, Amio, and Ramad crept down the left hallway. They counted five doors, two left, and three right, and then the hallway curved sharper to the left farther on.

"Ramad – keep your eyes down the hallway. We know there's something down there," Shipp said. "We'll take the rooms."

The doors were metal, as was typical, so AX fire wouldn't work, and neither would Morse mines, wizards, or hive bombs. Too much damage would occur outside the rooms, and they couldn't risk bringing down the ceiling. That hadn't mattered earlier when they were attacking the right tunnel, because even if the ceiling had crumbled, it would have just sealed off Westers from that direction. But here, they needed to secure this entire branch of tunnels.

The best approach was to first try opening the door, and then fire inside immediately. If locked, their only viable weapon was the MagTon. Amio shoved open the first door on the right. Shipp prepared to fire, but it was just a small storage closet. Next door, also on the right – Amio opened that one. Shipp saw light inside, and he plastered the room with Mossamer fire. Empty.

Third door, on the left. Amio tried to open it. Locked.

Li withdrew one MagTon and placed it against the door. He activated it, and it adhered to the door. Switching on the timer for five seconds, Li withdrew with the others, and they waited. The MagTon exploded and left a bent, twisted opening with metal shards angling out in random directions. It looked like a metal spider web. The door also dislodged.

Li strode up to the opening and without looking in, fired a hive bomb into the room. The tiny pebbles exploded in all directions within the room. They dragged open what remained of the door. It was a meeting room doubling as food storage. Empty.

Next door, last one on the right, unlocked. Just sleeping quarters, also empty. And the last door on the left was locked. It was an oxygen generation room. Li fired a hive bomb inside, which damaged some of the equipment.

"Amio – will this affect our breathing?" Shipp inquired.

"Highly doubt it. I'm sure they have multiple O2 rooms in a place this big. But if they have Blackhead doors separating each section, this might be the only one in this area," Amio replied.

"We can come back and use these smaller canisters that weren't damaged if we need to," Shipp said, pointing at a crate against the wall. "Let's keep going."

Back in the left hallway again, the four of them continued forward. Up ahead, the hallway widened into a room, angling to the left.

Shipp reached the last good corner he could hide behind, and prepared to look around it. Li pointed straight ahead. Shipp looked. It was the Blackhead door they were looking for.

Shipp held out a reflector to see around the corner to the left. He saw a group of Westers, not dressed as soldiers. Shipp concluded there must be another console on the other side of this wall.

"Admins," Shipp whispered. "Take as many alive as we can."

Ramad switched back to the pulse rifle. All four Petersons burst into the wider open space.

"Hit it! They're here ya!" screamed one of the Westers.

A Wester admin pulled a large lever on the console. Immediately afterward, Ramad pulsed him and he crumpled to the ground, immobilized, screaming something unintelligible. The other four Westers all had small AX-9 firearms, just like the Wester admins on Risner.

Two of them immediately placed the guns against their own heads and fired, killing themselves, baffling the Petersons. A third was about to do the same, but Shipp gunned her down with his Mossamer before she could. The last Wester tried to fire into his own head too but the weapon failed. He started screaming and begging, running away from the console toward the Blackhead wall, and then to the far corner of the room.

"Stop!" yelled Shipp. "We're not gonna kill you!"

"Please kill me please bro!" the Wester pleaded. The Petersons began to clue in. They realized what must have happened when the Wester pulled the lever.

"Uh, Shipp?" Li began. "Let's get outta here now!"

Shipp looked down at the immobilized man on the ground. The pulsed Wester's face started turning red. Blisters formed. Fast. Turning gross. That could only mean one thing. They released a batch of the contagion – in their own base. What rat turds. Only a Wester would do something so reprehensible as to thoughtlessly kill themselves and their own soldiers down the hall, who would surely die once the virus diffused through the hallways.

Shipp took several steps back. He switched his Mossamer to Krock mode, aimed up, and fired at the ceiling leading into the room where they found the admins. The explosion shattered the rock, which crumbled into the base as the roof caved in. The Petersons backed up more as dust and dirt blew against them. Shipp hoped to block off the contagion. Huge boulders, slabs, rocks, dirt, and debris spilled everywhere and piled up. It didn't completely seal off the room, but Shipp felt it was a good effort and would at least slow down the spread.

At that moment, they heard an intense firefight echo through the hallways. James, Gugbe, and Durman were being attacked. Shipp and the others bolted back down the hallway to save their friends. The lone surviving Wester admin followed in helpless terror. Shipp realized it.

"Li – latch and secure him! We'll handle this!" Shipp, Amio, and Ramad raced ahead. Li stopped running, turned, and clocked the admin across the shoulders, sending him to the floor. Being an admin, he was no match for Li, who quickly subdued and latched him using the same method as with the hostages in the life capsule – hands and feet bound together, and then a third latch connecting those behind the back.

"Face shields on!" Shipp called out to everyone as they reached the place where the three hallways intersected near James, Gugbe, and Durman.

Ramad, Amio, and Li complied, and Li found a spare in the weapons storage room and affixed it over the Wester admin's face.

But James, Gugbe, and Durman couldn't hear. They were exchanging AX fire with Westers around the corners at the other end of the short hallway, twenty meters away. James was on one knee on the side opposite where he needed to be, and the other two stood on the side closest to the exit through the air purification chamber.

The Westers fired a batch of Morse mines, which landed on the ground between the three men. Gugbe and Durman targeted the mines and fired at them, pushing them back toward the Westers. They exploded mid-hallway, jolting the walls and causing the ceiling to crumble again. Morse mines were not a good idea here.

More AX fire. Then wizards. One disc flew past everyone and banked off the wall right next to Shipp. It flew over his head, missing him by a few centimeters, and careened down the hallway, skidding past Li and stopping at the end of the hall. Soldiers on both sides so far had been able to protect themselves using the corners. But the Petersons had to get out, and that meant Shipp, Amio, Li, Ramad, and James had to cross the large space leading to the wide hallway.

Shipp tried to reach James and the others on his comm during a break in the battle.

"Put your shields on! All of you!"

This time they heard Shipp, and didn't question him. James, Gugbe, and Durman affixed their face shields, then resumed firing at the corners on the other end of the wide hallway.

Meanwhile Li talked to the hostage Wester, "What did you do back there? Was that the plague you just let loose? In your own base?"

"Ya bro," the Wester admin replied, struggling to move. "Gonna kill you all with it someday, ya."

"And yourselves, you stupid rat," retorted Li. "Maybe we go get a sample of it and replicate it, just like every other weapon you've developed."

"Good luck bro," mocked the Wester. "It's biological ya. You can't make it 'cause you don't have the source material."

"What source material?" Li pressed.

"They don't tell us that," laughed the Wester, partly from the pain. "Somewhere too far away from you."

Back at the intersections of the hallways, Shipp called James again.

"James! We got a hostage. Can we get outta here somehow? We can't get past the intersection without crossing right in their line of fire!"

More AX fire tore apart the walls at both ends of the hallway.

James heard enough to get the gist. "If you help, maybe we can all cross over!"

Shipp knew what that meant. He had four small K-rockets remaining. Shipp got on one knee, aimed as far down the Wester-occupied hallway as he could see.

"On my mark – everyone run across. Li – you ready with the rat?"

"Ready!" called Li, who soon crouched right behind them.

Shipp fired. The K-rocket impacted the far wall and exploded, causing the whole place to shudder. Shipp, Li, Ramad, and Amio bolted for the other side, yanking the latched Wester with them. James ran across too. But the Westers began firing immediately after Shipp's rocket exploded, which apparently hadn't hit close enough to deter them.

James cried out, spinning around as he got pelted in the shoulder. Shipp, Gugbe, Li, and Amio made it across and turned back. More screaming. The Wester hostage had also been hit, and Ramad took a shot in the hamstring.

James fell, and crawled back to his original spot, still on the wrong side of the hallway. Bleeding badly and clasping his shoulder. Shipp could see James took one in the calf as well. Durman and Li pulled Ramad to safety. They left the Wester hostage laying there, and the other Westers kept shooting, eventually killing him without realizing it.

Shipp swore at the loss of the hostage, then quickly re-focused on James, who was weakening. Shipp began boiling with desperate rage.

"Cam!"

Shipp grabbed Ramad's stash of Morse mines – all the remaining ones. He looked at Gugbe and Durman. They instantly knew his plan. Arm them all at once and toss the pack down the hallway.

Shipp spread the rodent belt on the ground. Eight in all. Li came over to help. Each man put his hands on two mines.

"Five second timer," Shipp said. "Ready?" They nodded. "Now."

Each man turned on two rodents at once. Shipp grabbed the belt and hurled it down the hallway. It exploded multiple times. More dust came down as well as some larger chunks of the ceiling. Some scary groaning sounds, as if Lavoisier was getting angry. Shipp, Gugbe, and Durman jumped across the hallway to get James. Shipp and Gugbe hung James over their shoulders and ran back across while Durman fired blind into the dusty hallway.

But then, the Westers fired their own K-rockets. Three at once.

One rocket impaled Durman and exploded him to pieces. The other two impaled and exploded the back wall and sent Shipp, Gugbe, and James hurtling toward the area they wanted to go, with ceiling chunks falling on them.

Li had already sent Amio with the injured Ramad into the air purification chamber so it would be ready for him and the other four. With Durman dead, just three now.

"Come on!" Li bellowed, as Shipp and Gugbe carried James the rest of the way.

They reached the chamber. Before the door closed, Shipp fired a K-rocket from his Mossamer at the console, and then used his pulse attachment to hit it in another spot, hopefully rendering it useless. Then, the chamber door closed them safely inside. The Westers wouldn't dare damage the purification chamber, as it provided the only way to retain use of their tunnels.

The other side opened.

Shipp looked up and saw Amio helping Ramad get up the stairway. Gugbe ran up to help, and Li stayed to help Shipp with James. Four soldiers saving two.

Amio, Ramad, and Gugbe reached the top of the stairs, and exited into the canyon.

Then, Shipp looked up in despair as he heard multiple AX-15s firing from outside. He watched helplessly as round after round tore into his three men up above. Gugbe fell backward onto the metal walkway, which clanked and shuddered.

Shipp left James with Li and raced up the stairs to save Gugbe as the canyon door tried to close on its own. Shipp, after observing the dead Ramad and Amio outside, pulled it shut and locked it. He stared down at Gugbe, one of his most precious friends.

Gugbe looked up at Shipp. He knew he wouldn't survive. Shipp started seething. Gugbe reached up with his hand. Shipp took it, holding it tight.

"It's okay," said Gugbe. "We had a... we had a historical run. We... you gonna take this planet."

Shipp tried to speak but thought of nothing to say.

"War as a way of life," said Gugbe as he smiled. "I'm part of the story now."

"You're part of my story. I'll never forget you. You didn't die for nothing," Shipp sputtered.

"The lady," Gugbe managed to say. "Your lady...she loves you." His eyes tilted upward and widened in astonishment, almost as if seeing a vision. Then, he said something Shipp would never forget.

"She put a hex on you Shipp. She put a hex on..."

Then, he breathed his last.

A hex? Shipp marveled, transfixed at Gugbe's last words. He sat immobilized by his losses, unable to venture out.

Li arrived, having rested James against the sides of the stairwell down below. He looked at Shipp, and knew how much Gugbe meant to him. Li grabbed Shipp's head and held it against his chest with one arm. Then, he called Garrison.

"Sorcerer, this is Li from Shipp's squad."

Harden answered immediately. "I got you Li, this is Harden."

"We just tried to come out and three of our best guys got killed. The rats are on the surface? How the flame did that happen?" Li fumed.

"Rats poured out six other holes after the Desert Raid and started hitting us with Krocks. We've been playing cat and mouse ever since, trying to keep them out of the four holes you guys are in. You're the first ones to come out. They must have a ton of soldiers down there."

"Jonas that," said Li. "Can you come clear us a path?"

"Yeah, hold on. Stay inside until our signal," Harden said.

Li trained his AX at the door in case any Westers opened it. Shipp did the same toward the air purification chamber door down below.

A few minutes later, they could hear huge hive bomb explosions, rapid AX fire, and K-rocket explosions. Then, they heard the Sorcerer fly over their position. That was the signal.

Li and Shipp lifted James and carried him outside on their shoulders. They quickly studied the area, now littered with bodies, and ran along the canyon. Staying low in the ravines, they put good distance between themselves and any Westers who may have returned to that area. Eventually, they made it back to the Harris Shield Array.

A scowling man they didn't know emerged from the flight. He looked annoyed, but he immediately walked toward them and lifted James from their tired arms, laying him on a sanitized stretch. He began attending to James' shoulder.

"I'm Locke, Chief Medic on the Sorcerer. Garrison wanted me down here just in case."

Shipp and Li lay down behind the Harris Array, exhausted, angry, grieving, and relieved.

Twenty minutes later, a second squad of Petersons escaped from the Wester base, with two hostages in tow and all eight soldiers surviving. The Sorcerer succeeded in driving most of the remaining Westers from the surface, or killing them. After another twenty minutes, both remaining squads emerged, one with seven soldiers alive, and the other with just two. The squad of seven had another hostage, making three total.

Once the Petersons cleared the area, the Sorcerer positioned itself to hover near one of the holes where the Westers had retreated, and fired a nuclear-tipped K-rocket straight down. It burrowed deep down and detonated, rattling the ground beneath them. They fired three more in the same spot. Then, they did the same into five more doors, three vertical doors in canyon walls and two holes going straight down.

Whatever remained of the Wester base, most of it had to be irreparably damaged.

The Sorcerer hovered over the flight, protecting the remaining Petersons as they made it back. Then, along with Locke, the 20 surviving soldiers and three admin hostages boarded, and Li piloted them back to LUB-7.

Garrison crackled across the comm.

"Outstanding and brave performance. I salute all of you with all my heart, in particular, the friends we lost." He waited with a moment of silence for about ten seconds, then continued. "We've got three Wester hostages and crippled their base. Now, it's up to the big brains to break down this virus weapon, replicate it, and defeat it."

Shipp lifted up his eyes at Garrison's voice. The mission was a success. He heard the words, but he couldn't feel the joy they should have produced. The loss of three more longtime friends from Risner, Gugbe, Blasé, and Ramad, left him looking back at the battlefield with a forlorn gaze as they flew away. His rage merged with grief, both of which softened at the reality of such a profound victory. He turned to James, who had been staring at him the entire time, almost like he was reading his mind. Shipp shook his head.

"This is life for us. War as a way of life," Shipp said, with a blank look on his face. "We lose some, but we win the greater fight. Lavoisier will be ours by this time next year."

He said the words. He even tried to mean them, and part of him probably did. But he couldn't expunge the ever-growing list from his mind.

Gugbe. Ramad. Blasé. Mixie. Rothman. Faraday. Vonn. Horman.

And her.

27

Notice

On the planet Maxwell, Mixie Shem's father got buzzed on his comm that someone was at his door. He'd been informed a representative from the Space Force would be visiting, and that he and his wife would want to be there. Their other four kids were grown up now, so the parents of five opened the door to greet their visitor.

Outside stood a middle-aged Peterson Space Force representative, holding a box.

"Mr. Shem?" the rep said.

Mr. Shem nodded, "That's me."

"I'm from the Space Force, may I come in?"

Mrs. Shem offered him a place at their table.

This wasn't the first time a Space Force representative had personally visited them. Several years ago, two reps arrived and informed Mixie's parents she had received the award for Battlefield Bravery, for her part in helping repel an attack on Risner. Her name and face ruled Maxwell's media for weeks, and her friends held a huge party in her honor. She received a second Battlefield Bravery award a couple years later for helping fight off the Wester infiltration of their base.

The Shems also received an update, not in person this time, when Mixie transferred from Risner to Lavoisier. They were heartened to know Mixie had performed with excellence for so many years, and felt great pride in her achievements. They knew her potential. But it was quite another thing to see that potential come to reality, especially in a way that rallied an entire planet around their family.

Today would be different. The rep sat down and opened the small box, removing several sheets of film with writing on them – the typical printed materials used on Maxwell and most Peterson planets. He sat in silence for a second and exhaled. Then, he looked at the waiting couple.

"Mr. and Mrs. Shem, your daughter Mixie was killed on Lavoisier," the rep began. "I'm very sorry to have to share this with you."

Mr. Shem's heart sank. He felt like he would lose his stomach. An emotional gut punch. He closed his eyes to stop the tears that formed from leaving their place. Mrs. Shem bowed her head and wept in silence. The rep gave them a few moments.

Then he continued speaking, "As you know, she was amassing quite an impressive combat record. She was a top-rated marksman, and performed at a high level in multiple battles. It's a very great loss for all of us."

The rep choked up while speaking, as if deeply affected by her death even though he never knew her.

"I have a letter for you. It's from General Loshea, the base commander on Lavoisier where Mixie was stationed. It details her combat history and Loshea's final appraisal of her. And there are some other records in here. You get to keep all this. There's also a letter from another soldier, her squad leader dating back to her time on Risner – Colonel Thomas Shipp. She followed Shipp from Risner to Lavoisier. He included some things for you as well."

Mr. and Mrs. Shem picked up the note from Shipp, and read it.

To the parents of Mixie Shem:

Mixie was one of my best soldiers from the day she was assigned to me. She fought by my side, never wavering, and never questioning. She performed exceptionally every time I asked anything from her.

Your daughter was brave, skilled, driven, focused, and completely trustworthy on the battlefield. She was my friend. And I failed to save her.

In the photo I included, you see her with my best squad from Risner. That's me with her on the left, then Zemmer, Ramad, Blasé, and Gugbe. All of these except Zemmer died on Lavoisier, but he suffered injuries that will force him out of the Meridian Zone. All of these were her friends, and mine.

Her death is hard to talk about. You'll be told she died in combat on Lavoisier, after we encountered a deadly airborne virus and had to hide out in an old life capsule. That's mostly true. There is a virus. Unfortunately, I'm not allowed to tell you how she really died.

But I want you to know she should still be alive. I'm enraged. I'm livid. I'm never going to get over it. I think about her death every day. I watched it happen, and couldn't stop it. But I promise you this – I'm devoting the rest of MY time in the Space Force to annihilate the Westers who were ultimately the cause of her death. Every single one of them. I'm going to hunt them down no matter where it takes me and crush the life from their eyes.

I wish I could mourn with you. Someday, I hope to tell you what really happened, in person. But more than likely, you will never see me or hear from me again.

-Thomas Shipp

The Shems finished reading and sat stunned. They turned to the Space Force representative in confusion.

"What does this mean?" Mrs. Shem asked. "Why is he not allowed to tell us how she really died?"

"I'm not sure what you mean. I haven't read any of these materials. They're for you," he answered dispassionately. She showed him the letter from Shipp. He read it, shook his head in bewilderment, and said nothing.

Mr. Shem picked up the photo, and treasured it. It was the first image he had seen of his daughter in four years. And the only printed one he had of her as a soldier. Tears bulged and ran down his face. There would never be closure now. Never. Only anger.

The rep stood up, nervous and unsure how to handle the contents of Shipp's letter. He tried to return to his script. "There's a lot more in there for you to look at, but you should read the letters first. A number of things will be happening the next few weeks. As hard as this is, what's best is if everyone in your family, and your city, and this entire planet, can mourn with you."

"But how did she really die? I want to know," Mixie's mother said again, more stern this time. "What does this mean?"

The rep blanched. Lost for words.

"Who do I talk to about this?" she asked him, off his wordless reply.

"Other officials from the Space Force will be coming here," he answered. "You can see the schedule of events in there. You should talk to them. I'm sorry. I don't know what else to tell you. I've never seen or heard anything like this before."

Mixie's parents were left waiting and wondering. And they would never get an answer, because no one on the entire planet of Maxwell, or at Space Force Command, knew it either.

Part 3 - Space

28

The Sorcerer Reborn

Shipp waited.

He'd been sitting on a bench for thirty minutes, waiting outside a meeting room on the 38th floor of Space Force Command, orbiting the planet Humman. This gas giant sat near the border between the Central Frontier of Peterson Territory and the bulk of the colonized planets. The Central Frontier was the buffer zone, devoid of almost any habitable planets, that faced outward toward the far-off Meridian Zone and the much farther off Wester Territory.

On a monitor across the hallway, Shipp watched updates from the always-on Peterson Territorial News. There was no sound. He saw a story about a Wester soldier taken captive who said the only reason he became a soldier was because his parents threatened to disown him if he didn't, since his three siblings had all joined the military.

Shipp shook his head at the callousness and lack of loyalty Westers seemed bred to. The Petersons positioned the war as the most aspirational occupation. Young people wanted to join. They weren't compelled to join. What a difference.

The men and women who joined the Peterson Space Force weren't the down-and-outs, or those with lower intelligence, or those hoping to get a better job later. They weren't inmates being offered a way to reduce their sentences. For Petersons, aspiring to join the Space Force positioned you as the elite, pursuing the most noble and respected career choice. The military leaders made more money than planetary governors. The soldiers made more than doctors and engineers. And when soldiers died, their families were generously awarded with honor and excessive financial compensation.

Shipp pulled a printed photo from his shirt pocket. In the photo, he sat with Horman, James, and Pretoria back on Risner, along with Gugbe, Mixie, Zemmer, Ramad, and Blasé. It was the only image he had with all his closest friends together. Only Zemmer and James remained, but Zemmer's injuries had proven too severe to remain on the battlefield, and they retired him to Space Force University and then probably a space station.

Li had developed into a priceless and unexpected new friend. Shipp wished he had known Pretoria. They would have clicked, because Li could think on a systems level like her. Now, only Li and James felt like brothers to Shipp. They were the only ones left. Today, the three of them sat on the cusp of a whole new set of friendships.

General Garrison, at this very moment, sat in a meeting discussing the final updates on what had been gleaned from the three Wester hostages captured on Lavoisier. And based on previous updates, Shipp anticipated the Sorcerer getting tasked with a very special mission, and he longed for a spot on the ship.

He wanted it with all his heart.

He was done with life on the ground. "I want to die in space," he now often thought to himself. On one occasion, he even spoke this out loud to James and Li.

James gave his predictable reply, "I don't want you to die anywhere." And Li said nothing, because he was coming to realize that nothing could repair the damage inflicted on Shipp's previous idealism. Though Shipp had mended his severing from Mixie for a short time before her death, the compounding losses of so many dearly loved and admired comrades had James worried about Shipp, even more now than after Pretoria's death.

Shipp's idealism was morphing into fanaticism.

His belief that the Petersons could actually win the war still persisted, but it had advanced into a fixation, an obsession. Shipp wanted to be the one to push the theoretical 'button' to annihilate the Westers entirely. Of course, no such button existed and there was no reason from the last five hundred years to imagine there ever being one.

James had begun wondering why his friend seemed to take the losses so hard. James had lost friends too – some of the same ones – as well as others. So had Li. He and Li talked about it several times. They concluded it might be harder for the person in authority to lose the friends under their command. They're friends, but in a way, they're also like students. Plus, Shipp loved the Peterson codes and principles more than almost anyone. His losses seemed to violate them, in his mind. He had failed to save his friends. His true friends. His lover.

For James, the losses were fellow soldiers. For Shipp, he felt tasked with their lives. Each time he lost one, it felt like losing a son or daughter. Especially Gugbe and Mixie. They had fought side by side for so long. They could read each other's thoughts in battle. You can't train that. You can't force it. It develops organically, beyond simple trust and experience. It develops out of friendship – and a shared vision of the war and why it's being fought.

Now, Shipp had holes in his soul that couldn't be bandaged. And he was filling those holes with vengeful, fanatical rage.

When Shipp crushed Shelsie's head after she murdered Mixie, James knew the old Shipp would never return. And he knew Shipp needed him now more than ever. He resolved to make protecting Shipp and being there for him his number one focus, even in battle. And he easily brought Li into the same line of thinking.

If there was to be a rebirth of a better version of Thomas Shipp, it would be with them by his side. Were they to leave him on his own for any reason, he'd have no one left, and the darkness would consume him. They alone stood in the way, and they knew it.

And it was clear that the men on Garrison's ship weren't of the same ilk. There was something different about these attack ship men. Something admirable. But also, something a bit less human. You got the sense that they would die for you in a heartbeat. But only if it was tactically beneficial. Then again, James and Li could be wrong about them.

It had been almost a year since the big victory on Lavoisier.

Not long after the battle, they returned to the same Wester underground base and discovered the Sorcerer had indeed destroyed so much of it that most remaining Westers had died from exposure to the atmosphere. They found only about twenty left alive after the nuke-tipped

K-rockets did their work. In all, well over a hundred dead Westers lay within the demolished base, with Peterson losses coming in at sixteen after all was resolved.

From what they could find within the Wester base, they determined the location of the next closest one. Calling in two more attack ships, they laid waste to it from the air, pummeling it with repeated K-rocket attacks, and the larger attack ship brand of Morse mines and MagTons. This success confirmed the primary vulnerability with underground bases: Being found. Once found, unless there were defensive ships in the area, a handful of attack ships could decimate an underground base with relatively little risk.

The third and final Wester base on Lavoisier, somewhere in the other hemisphere assuming the life capsule hostage had told the truth, couldn't be located from anything they could decipher. But if that really was the only base left, it was only a matter of time, and their isolation would eventually force them to call in help from outside.

After they helped finish off the second base, Shipp, Li, and James ended their service time on Lavoisier. They boarded the Sorcerer along with the three Wester hostages and returned to Space Force Command. It was the first time Shipp and James had been back in Peterson Territory since landing on Risner. Their first time on a space station in years. It didn't feel real.

But Shipp knew this was the way forward, and James and Li were united with him for life.

The trip back took a couple months. Shipp, James, and Li took the opportunity to start learning about attack ship technology. Just the basics. They were like sponges. What most impressed Shipp was how one got assigned to an attack ship.

No graduate came out of Space Force University and went straight to an attack ship. Only seasoned ground warriors who wanted a fresh start could join. And even that wasn't enough. You also had to be recommended for it. An attack ship assignment required elite level skill, mental toughness, and the ability to adapt quickly. You had to be eminently trustworthy, because you could be confined for months with the same crew, alone in space.

Even more interesting, every ship's general got to lay out their own crew requirements. One of Garrison's was that to be on his ship, you had to have lost at least one person very close to you – in battle. Childhood losses didn't count. Shipp, James, and Li were all accepted, on a preliminary basis. The problem was, the Sorcerer didn't have enough room for all of them.

So, Shipp had spent the last few months teaching courses at SFU. It was a welcome but temporary change. James spent most of his time learning about the various space vessels, and Li joined him, in addition to learning the basics of flying them.

But the whole time, all three friends looked forward to any results from the hostage interrogations. Experts worked on them month after month. The only thing more grueling than what the hostages were enduring was having to wait for updates. Teaching gave Shipp something else to think about that still aligned with his newly emerging life mission, or obsession – to eradicate life on all the Wester planets.

The hostages confirmed the existence of a weaponized virus. Then, they confirmed its biological origins, from some planet deep in Wester Territory. They weaponized it at a station orbiting the planet. But none of them knew its location.

Later, they confirmed that the Westers had developed a way to counteract the effects of the virus. But it wasn't a vaccine. They called it a countermeasure. It wasn't administered to each person. Rather, it was deployed, just like the weaponized version. Once deployed, it eradicated the virus. None of the hostages revealed how long that took.

Eventually, the Peterson intelligence experts decided they'd learned all they could. Two of the hostages were killed painlessly. The third, who never cooperated the entire time, was released into space.

Then, the next and much more difficult task arrived – what to do with all this information.

Shipp, Garrison, and Harden had begun collaborating about a possible strategic response. It would require traveling to Wester Territory for an extended, yearslong mission – something that hadn't been attempted in over a hundred years, and hadn't been successfully achieved in even longer. Invading at this distance presented multiple challenges.

That far from home, any ship would be on its own. Communication delays would be so lengthy that asking for any on-site assistance would be pointless. Supplies could not be replenished. Repairs would be impossible. That's why neither territory even considered the attempt anymore.

What would be the point? You'd just lose a highly valuable attack ship, and for what?

But this was different.

The virus posed the ultimate territorial threat. It was a war-ender. If the Westers figured out a way to deliver this virus to the Peterson planets, they could wipe out entire populations without firing a shot or risking one soldier. If they could infiltrate a space station or even SFU, they could kill everyone in the facility. This was the first significant shift in power in decades, and it gave the Westers a huge advantage.

The Petersons believed they had one of two choices:

First, they could find the virus and the countermeasure technology, and figure out how to replicate it so the Westers would know they had lost their advantage. This was the normal response to any new technological military developments. Any time one side won a decisive victory, they would assess the technology of the defeated. If they discovered any advancements or unique tech developments, that information was relayed to the big brains back in the territories, and the relevant upgrades were made. This is how the phrase "war as a way of life" found its way into the Peterson lexicon.

For the second option, since the virus appeared to be localized to one planet, they could figure out a way to neutralize it at the source, and simply end its existence.

Shipp was dissatisfied with both options, and his mind started pondering and searching for a third, more consequential strategy. But none of this mattered at all unless the Petersons could first figure out how to find the Wester planet that originated the virus, and then somehow – get there safely.

And that's why Shipp waited on a bench.

Garrison and Harden were making a pitch to Space Fleet Command, the branch of Space Force Command that administered the space vessels, which included attack ships, convoy ships, and transport ships. If they could convince Space Fleet Command to certify their plan, it would be brought to Space Force Command for final approval.

The plan, developed by Garrison, Shipp, and Harden, was to send a single attack ship into Wester Territory, specially equipped, on a one-way mission. The first goal would be to infiltrate a Wester facility and locate the planet containing the virus. Once located, travel to that planet, assess the virus technology from there, and if possible, destroy it and the station.

Garrison, Shipp, and Harden had developed several ideas for how to modify the Sorcerer to make this long journey. Shipp wasn't allowed in the meeting because he wasn't officially part of the Sorcerer crew or even part of the Space Fleet yet.

But he itched to know.

So he sat there waiting. For over three hours.

Staring at the image of his lost friends. Gazing out the window at the stars and the planet Humman below. Imagining what General Elliss – the Wester leader who led the attack on Risner that killed Pretoria – might look like. Shipp didn't just want to invade Wester Territory to deal with the virus. He also wanted to find Elliss. He imagined all the things he might say and do to him.

He replayed the image of the female commander who gave the actual order to kill Pretoria, the one Shipp threw over the ledge to her death.

With Mixie's loss, Shipp had no more women close to him. And he decided he didn't want any. There was something extra painful about losing them. Mixie's death had cut him deep, partly because of the way she died. In the ensuing months, he decided he wanted nothing more to do with women.

And the Sorcerer, as with most attack ships, was entirely crewed by men. Of the seventeen attack ships currently active in the Peterson fleet, fourteen had all-male crews, and two had all-female crews. Only one was mixed. Shipp decided this made sense, especially for the long periods of isolation you would spend on board. The mixed crew included four pairs of married soldiers, and that explained the exception well enough for Shipp.

His losses no longer served as fuel he could 'use,' as he had once said to Gugbe and as Space Force University taught them. For Shipp, his losses seemed etched into his soul. The final positions of their bodies came to him in visions as he tried to fall asleep at night. Their voices. Their faces. They called to him. They cried out to him.

Their families got notified of their deaths, and Shipp inserted personal words to the relatives of Mixie, Gugbe, Blasé, and Ramad. He had been too stricken with grief to do likewise on Risner. Pretoria's family never heard from him. But it felt trite. It didn't assuage Shipp's soul or give him peace. It just fed his darkening spirit. He wanted to kill every Wester he could find. And it no longer mattered where he found them.

Finally, Shipp's mental meanderings got interrupted when the meeting room door opened. Garrison and Harden filtered out alone. Shipp stood, yearning to hear good news. He couldn't tell from their faces what to expect. Garrison laid it out.

"There's good news and bad news. Which do you want first?"

"The good news," Shipp answered immediately.

Garrison nodded. "They approved the mission."

Shipp whole body pulsed with a flush of near ecstasy. The mission of a lifetime, actually happening. But then he halted his thoughts. *What if the bad news is that I don't get to go?*

"What's the bad news?" he asked.

Garrison sighed and then began, "They don't believe we can modify the Sorcerer to the degree necessary for a mission like this. So, they want to design and construct an entirely new attack ship. Something bigger and more powerful than anything ever made before. A super attack ship. Prototypical. Construction will begin as soon as possible. So, the bad news is, we have to wait. Probably for a couple years, because they're going to need megatons of Blackhead."

"But I'm in? James and Li are in?" Shipp wanted to know.

Garrison nodded. "I'm going to create a mission description and present it to my crew as well as to you three. This ship will need a bigger crew than a standard one, so I don't see any reason all three of you won't be able to get on board. I would take you in a heartbeat and be honored to have you."

Shipp beamed. He exhaled a breath of great relief, placed his hands on Garrison's shoulders, and gripped them tight. Then he looked him in the eyes.

"I'd wait five years to be part of this mission, brother."

Garrison replied knowingly, "I figured you'd say that."

Shipp turned to gather his things so he could go tell James and Li the news.

Garrison spoke one more time. "The ship is called The Sorcerer Reborn. I'm going with what works. But in the meantime, they're going to send us on another mission while we wait. I'll want you three on board for that, because you need space combat experience. Pretty much nothing in common with the ground wars."

Shipp nodded in agreement.

"So finish up all this teaching silliness and let's get on with it."

29

The Program

"What do you consider to be the most pivotal moment in all of human history?"

Shipp stood in front of a class of about forty third-year Space Force cadets. He taught this class once during the past year in addition to a couple advanced combat strategy courses, and had been looking forward to it again ever since. In this course, he could freely unleash his beliefs about the five-hundred-year Meridian Zone war.

"Boil it down to the essence. All of history, starting back on ancient Earth from what we know about it. The one moment. The one event. The one discovery. The one decision. What do you think?"

Shipp paced across the small stage and gave them a few minutes, occasionally making eye contact with some. Finally, someone spoke.

"The Hyper Trans invention," a female student named Timna suggested. "Soo Yung Wong breaks the time barrier."

Shipp nodded, "Great choice. Wong's brilliant innovation sits head and shoulders above any other technical invention before or since that time."

Shipp displayed a series of photos showing Wong working. In one photo, Wong was shaking the hand of a well-dressed, important-looking man in front of a tall white obelisk, a monument stretching a couple hundred meters in the sky, surrounded by parks.

"What's that thing?" inquired Warsh, another female student.

"Dunno," said Shipp. "These are photos from ancient Earth. Only a few remain to us."

Another photo appeared, showing a somewhat spherical device of great complexity.

Shipp continued, "Wong figures out how to leverage magnetic fields, gravitation, and relativity to facilitate super accelerated space travel, but without the Einsteinian consequences of age. The territorial schools don't talk about this much, but Wong's invention didn't just make long distance space travel possible."

Shipp paused and looked around. "It also saved humanity. Earth's resources were running dry. It was a fished pond, in terms of vital minerals and raw materials. Now, for the first time ever, humanity could discover and colonize planets that could sustain life, far away from Earth. They had catalogued hundreds of worlds, many of which held potential for human life. Now, they could suddenly visit them all."

Shipp paused again. "And this led to?" He looked around. Did anyone know? They should have learned this in a different course.

"The First Great Question," answered Maahir, a male student near the front.

Shipp nodded. "How do we choose who gets to colonize new planets? This question became the question of the era. While the techs spent decades developing spacecraft and other technologies to make the Hyper Trans fulfill its potential, the leaders of the day had to figure out who gets to go first. You can't send ships full of prisoners and rats into space, right?"

The students laughed at the reference to Westers. Shipp knew it was always a winner.

"Eventually, who did they decide to send?"

Lauric, another male student, spoke up. "The best of humanity. They had a long list of criteria, and they used it globally. It wasn't just about being smart. It was about being good. Sensible. Rational. Dependable. Trustworthy. Even-headed..."

Shipp held up his hand to stop the student, who clearly liked this topic.

"Good. It's a great story. Three hundred people per ship. Five ships. One disappears without a trace. But the other four make it to new planets, fully resourced and ready to build."

Shipp looked around, "These are our ancestors – the first space colonists. We come from them. That means, we Petersons come from the best of the best of ancient Earth."

The students ate this part up.

"But the Westers. They come from all the rest of Earth, as well as the best of the best. So they're intermixed with the average. The weak. The low. The deviant. The despicable. Westers are inferior to us for this reason. You all know this already."

All the students nodded. They'd been fed this since childhood, and understood it completely.

"Back to the original question," Shipp redirected. "All this is interesting. Important to know. And it all came from Wong's invention. But that's not the most pivotal moment in history."

Several students laughed nervously, surprised. They looked around the room while Shipp waited.

"Hyper Accelerator. The HAT, from Corpuz," said Malon, a male student piggybacking on the first idea, since it seemed so close.

Shipp nodded again, "Marianne Corpuz and the Hyper Accelerator Thrust. A contemporary of Jonas Peterson. Hundreds of years after the Hyper Trans has sent millions of former Earth residents to new worlds, Corpuz solves the problems that had been revealed through usage of the Hyper Trans."

He showed a photo of Corpuz, smiling, sitting next to a schematic of her idea.

"I like this photo," said Shipp, "Because there's this quote I like that some historian guy wrote about her discovery."

He put the quote on the monitor and then began reading:

"Corpuz wasn't just a scientific genius. She was a scientific artist. She took Wong's mechanical, physical work of wonder, made it work better, and made it look better. She took the greatest invention in human history, gave it a much-needed repair job, and then made it pretty. The HAT is the perfect blend of science and art. Its elegance and simplicity are matched only by its technical marvel."

Shipp smiled. Then returned to the previous photo of Corpuz next to her schematic.

"I like this photo, because her schematic itself is like art. And she's proud of it before it's even been made, because she knows it's going to work. She's done the math. And now she's got the paintbrush."

With the Hyper Trans, humans could cover celestial distances in months rather than centuries. But it could break down in several ways, and out in the vastness of space, repair jobs were difficult. The occupants of a broken-down space vessel could be stranded for months waiting for a repair team. Over time, they kept finding new ways it could break down, and it required too many technicians just to keep it operating.

Corpuz's upgrade, now known scientifically as the Einstein-Corpuz dimensional thruster, found a new way to begin the initial acceleration, when the greatest amount of stress was forced upon the Hyper Trans. The elegant simplification of the HAT required far less machinery, and took up much less room on the ship. And as the historian described, it just looked cool.

Shipp displayed a photo of an actual HAT drive.

"Aside from Jonas Peterson, Corpuz is my favorite person from history," Shipp said. "She's the reason the Peterson Territory has so dense a population. At first, they didn't realize how far superior her invention was to Wong's. She was 34 when she invented it. It was first installed in a space vessel eight years later. But it wasn't until her 70s that nearly all space vessels were equipped with HATs."

Shipp removed her photo and left the screen blank.

"That's forty years of waiting, before her vision was properly recognized and acted on." Shipp looked around. "We're facing the same kind of waiting. A five-hundred-year war. A war that yes, we can win."

Some students shifted in their seats, knowing this was a topic of disagreement. And Shipp wanted to be absolutely clear where he stood.

"In our lifetimes."

Students couldn't hold back their nervous smiles this time. But Shipp wasn't smiling.

"The war is ours to win. All it takes is gaining a tactical advantage. And right now, we have the opportunity to gain one. After I'm done with you twerps, I'm going on an attack ship mission that I believe is the most important in five hundred years. Right now, the Westers have the advantage. Our mission is to take it from them."

Shipp's conscience darkened as he thought about the people he lost, and the precipice of legend he now stood before. He regained his thoughts and continued.

"Corpuz's HAT was a great moment. But it's not the most pivotal one in history," Shipp declared.

Students began tossing out other ideas. And each time, Shipp expounded upon it. For ideas he anticipated, he had photos and other slides to use as part of the discussion. But at the end of each one, he would say, in the same monotone, "But it's not the most pivotal moment in history."

Over the course of this unit, which took several days as Shipp urged them to continue trying to come up with ideas, the students received a great history lesson about the war, what caused it, what came before it, and what was at stake.

Maahir suggested the moment the Space Age was officially enshrined as the new calendar, when the ancient Earth calendar was done away with. This happened after Jonas Peterson led the colonization of what became the Peterson Territory. The Wester government, known then as the Galactic Parliament, worked with the newly formed Peterson government, known as the Celestial Convention, to do away with ancient Earth time.

They still measured days as 24-hour periods, because it would be too hard to change and there was no reason to do so, though holding to that daily cycle took effort on some planets with different rotational patterns. People still had to sleep. But the governments agreed to designate the beginning of the Space Age as the year the first five colony ships departed from Earth using the Hyper Trans. That was 0 S.A. That marked 287 S.A. as the year the new Space Age calendar was born.

The old era of Earth, and all the history from that time, began to fade. Most languages faded over time too. Today, the Petersons had little remaining knowledge of Earth, and didn't even know where it was. They just knew it lay deep in Wester Territory, and that no one cared about it anymore.

Timna suggested the discovery of the Meridian Zone.

Shipp had to correct her on this.

"The Meridian Zone as we know it today was not discovered as that. It was simply known as the Galactic Void for centuries."

Shipp showed a slide depicting the whole Milky Way Galaxy, separated roughly into fourths. One fourth was labeled as Wester Territory, another as Peterson Territory, and the other half as Undiscovered.

"In old days I've been told they used to dream about finding crazy creatures and monsters on other planets. People would dream up all these bizarre evolutionary permutations."

Shipp showed drawings of creepy, silly, and fantastical aliens. The students laughed.

"But as you all know, we've taken over about half the galaxy, and it's just us. Only a couple minor life forms here and there but nothing sentient. The only monsters in this galaxy are the ones we left behind when Jonas Peterson settled here."

Shipp pointed to the area between the two Territories.

"This is the Meridian Zone, as we know it today. It's a relatively large area of space with no habitable worlds, except for seven all clustered near each other. You know their names. Kora, Terrasol, Lavoisier, Cinque, Portia, Rita." Shipp paused, not wanting to say the last one. Trying to keep stoic, the students started to wonder how he could forget the last one.

"Risner," said Jub, a male student, assuming Shipp wanted someone to complete his thought, as he had done previously.

"Yeah," Shipp nodded and spoke too softly for them to hear. Pretoria's face, covered in blood, flashed in his mind. He pictured the place where he buried her and marked the rock behind her.

He looked again at the image and pointed to the same area.

"When the Void was first encountered, they stopped colonizing beyond it, and instead spread out within the existing territory. Now, I'm sure one of you is thinking of saying the most pivotal moment is when Jonas Peterson led the first array of space vessels across the Void and colonized the first planet in our territory. A great moment for sure, but not the most pivotal."

Horace, a male student, suggested, "The destruction of the comm satellites?"

Shipp commended him, because this was a rarely considered idea, but a good one. When the Peterson colonizers first succeeded in reaching the other side of the Void and found a bevy of habitable planets, they realized the journey had taken several months. Quite a long time, and not one most people would want to traverse repeatedly. So, to maintain communication, a string of satellites was deployed to keep the Wester Territory in touch with the growing Peterson one. The Petersons prospered rapidly for decades as more and more ships traveled there to join them.

But then, in 385 S.A, a meteor shower tore through the Void, and destroyed four consecutive satellites. Once they ascertained what happened, neither territory wanted to foot the bill to replace them. And because the Petersons felt secure and self-sufficient by this point, both sides agreed to just leave it as is. Eventually, the remaining unmaintained satellites stopped working too.

Thus, from around 385 S.A. until the origins of the war in 516 S.A., not a single message was sent or received by the Petersons or the Westers. Each society had 131 years to develop in total isolation from the other.

And that's why, when they suddenly encountered each other on Kora in 516, they were like total strangers. It felt as if they had discovered a new race of humans. Each territory had decided, on their own, to explore the seven Meridian Zone planets. And once they found the enormous wealth of resources contained on them, both territories colonized them, and communication resumed. At first, this was a joyous reunion.

But tribalism is endemic to the human condition.

Whereas before there was cooperation, now, mistrust and uncertainty. Whereas before they shared, now they rivaled. One had more efficient mining methods on one planet. The other settled in what turned out to be a richer area on another planet.

Risner and Kora had abundant water supplies. Lavoisier teemed with vanadium, more than any planet yet discovered in the entire galaxy. It was in the planet's core. The rocks practically bled it. Cinque overflowed with iron, titanium, and samarium, another highly prized material because of its role in dome technology, as well as in Blackhead. Terrasol had zinc and holmium, another prized rare earth element, and massive underground ice. Portia turned out to have even more samarium than Cinque. They were astounded to find two planets with so much of it.

In 532 S.A., the first conflict broke out. No one knows who attacked first. But these were miners and settlers, so the attack wasn't severe. No weapons were present. But it didn't matter. The blow had been delivered, and retaliation was seen as the only possible response. From there, it escalated. Over five hundred years later, supremacy over these seven planets and the wealth of resources they contained consumed both territories.

Shipp returned to center stage.

"Lots of great ideas. Lots of pivotal moments. But there's one remaining. You're very close to it. It lies at the very heart of the war. What we want. What we need," Shipp hinted.

Timna finally put it together and figured out what Shipp wanted to hear.

"The invention of Blackhead," she declared.

Shipp held out his hands in feigned relief.

"Yes," declared Shipp. "The invention of Blackhead. Now, you are all free to disagree with me on this. Different people say different things. But I consider this the most pivotal moment because this is the reason we're fighting this war."

Shipp went on to remind them why Blackhead was invented. It wasn't for war. It was synthesized to combat the greatest threat to galactic travel. Space debris like comets, ice rocks, and small rogue objects had caused quite a bit of trouble for space voyagers. With a galaxy of resources, exhaustive scientific research sought to develop an 'invincible' hull for spacecraft.

It took decades. But Blackhead was the result. It was a unique blend that used vanadium and erbium as its primary metals. Combined with a unique blend of other raw and synthetic chemicals introduced at proper times and temperatures in the production process, Blackhead – known colloquially as God's Armor – was born. It was so strong it could withstand proximity-targeted nuclear blasts.

At that time, it protected space vessels traveling the vast interplanetary and interstellar journeys at extreme speeds. Space debris that used to pose lethal threats now felt like dust on the side of a road. Even larger space rocks and boulders just ricocheted off the surface of Blackhead-coated vessels.

Blackhead was essential to modern space travel. Thus, both territories needed it to survive. They used it for spacecraft, space stations, and ground facilities in hostile environments. They all wanted God's Armor to protect them. Each territory occupied well over a hundred planets. Different planets contained different resources, and some planets depended on others for various materials. Without safe space travel, all this would be at risk.

"But also," Shipp continued, "Blackhead is the key to winning the war, because it's the strongest defensive material ever constructed. This vanadium-erbium alloy with all the other minerals that are part of it, offers two promises in one. First – it allows us to fight against the enemy and protect our friends. Second – it makes possible the life we are fighting for, once the Westers are driven out of the Meridian Zone, and their military capabilities destroyed."

Shipp concluded, "It is our protection, and our salvation. It is God's Armor."

Timna wanted to agree with Shipp, so she added on her thoughts, "If Blackhead hadn't been invented, there may not be a Peterson Territory at all, is that what you're saying?"

Shipp nodded. "Basically, yes. Corpuz's HAT drive is legendary. But you still have to protect the ships. It begins and ends with that."

"When was Blackhead invented?" asked Timna.

"Somewhere in the early one hundreds. No one is exactly sure, because it got worked on and perfected over time. Even today, the stuff we're using on attack ships is better than the original colonizer ships. And we're making it far thicker on our attack ships than they did back then," said Shipp.

"What about K-rockets?" asked Horace.

Shipp nodded. "I love the story I heard in weapons training about this. As a brilliant mind once observed, the only thing strong enough to penetrate Blackhead is... Blackhead. That was Kham Kampraseuth, who fought on Peterson attack ships for years but got injured and had to retire. He devoted the rest of his life to developing a weapon that could defeat Blackhead-plated ships. Anyone know how it works?"

"I do," said Malon. At Shipp's direction, Malon explained K-rockets.

"They use the same Blackhead, using it to form the rocket's tip with wedges and jagged protrusions, angled with mathematical precision. Our weapons instructor calls it the bee stinger from hell. When properly targeted, they embed and propel their explosive power forward, creating a larger opening."

"And," Shipp followed, "Kampraseuth found a way to weaponize Blackhead itself, within the explosive material, which widens the damaged area even more. Still takes a lot of rockets to get through a thick surface. But it's the only way."

With that, Shipp began to wrap up another day of discussion. "I used to think that whoever could manufacture the most attack ships will win the war. Attack ships are far more powerful than anything on the ground. Last year, we incinerated two underground Wester bases on Lavoisier with attack ships. Those bases took years to construct. Attack ships are the difference-makers."

"Why don't you think that anymore?" asked Maahir.

"Because both sides have enough attack ships that unless we can find a way to destroy a lot of theirs all at once, both sides will always have enough. Plus, K-rockets and other defenses are very strong on most planets and Central Frontier stations. There aren't enough attack ships to win the war, and there never will be."

Shipp continued. "But we can win the war. And with my upcoming mission, we can take the tactical advantage and keep it permanently. That's all for today. Stay alive."

The class responded, "Save your friend."

The students logged their appreciation and began to file out.

30

Construction Begins

The next day, Shipp met with James and Li to attend a discussion about the design of the Sorcerer Reborn. The three of them would be spectators mostly, while Garrison, Harden, and other officers from the Sorcerer collaborated on the features and layout of this brand-new prototype.

"Remember," Garrison reminded the engineers, "We'll have almost no chance of repair or resupply. That means we'll need far more of everything. More weapons supply rooms, more provisions, more shield array ports. This isn't just about thicker armor."

Shipp, James, and Li had a lot to learn about attack ships, and that's why Garrison wanted them here. Shipp noted a poster depicting the basic design schematic of a conventional Peterson attack ship. Three levels, connected by metal stairwells at various junctures. The top level was the smallest. It included just the Pilot Room and Comm Room, which was a couple steps down and separated by a five-meter hallway. Easy enough to audibly talk back and forth, but far enough to divide with a sealed barrier in case the Pilot Room ever got too damaged to be occupied. If that happened, you could pilot the ship from the Secondary Pilot Station on the mid-level.

The Pilot Room was the only place on the ship with windows. Super thick and protected by multiple shield array ports, but large enough to get good visuals when helpful. Most piloting was done through the monitor tech and relied on a complex web of scopes and sensors embedded throughout the ship's exterior. The scopes made it possible to see in any direction.

In particular, the Light Ray Motion Sensors enabled the attack ship to 'see' much farther. Commonly known as the LR, these sensors beam out UV light rays in all directions and use them to track movement within a substantial range, even while traveling at HAT speed.

Shipp had already learned quite a bit about attack ship routines on his journey from Lavoisier to Space Force Command aboard Garrison's ship. Either the First Officer or Comm Officer manned the LR most often, especially during combat situations when tactical decisions had to be made without delay or hesitation.

So when Garrison brought up the need for more "of everything," he was including LR sensors. Losing a few sensors here and there didn't matter. But if a ship lost too many, you'd be flying partially blind. Alone with no chance of repair in Wester space, the Sorcerer Reborn couldn't afford that, so they would need many more LR sensors than a normal attack ship.

One engineer suggested embedding them a few centimeters beneath the surface of the ship, and then adding little circular nubs protruding from the surface – fashioned with Blackhead – to give extra protection to the LR sensor web. That would also make the whole ship resemble a freakish, prickly urchin.

"Excellent," Harden reacted to that idea. "We should do that with the scopes and shield array ports too."

"Can't do it with the ports," said Pushta Dons, the Weapons Officer on the Sorcerer.

Dons was a major asset to Garrison. He had been in space as long as Garrison and could easily take a spot as First Officer or even as General aboard another ship. But he didn't want it. He believed in loyalty to his crew and to Garrison most of all. Dons understood that the best attack ships maintained as much cohesion and unity as possible. The more they knew each other, the more they could operate with absolute faith in each other's abilities.

Dons continued, "Shield arrays wouldn't function with that additional external barrier. It would weaken the strength of the array. Need a smooth exterior, with the ports flush with the surface."

Harden accepted Dons' expertise. "Okay, then we need double the ports."

"Or triple," said Garrison. "It's a bigger ship. Triple the port density whenever possible."

The shield array ports in question functioned using similar tech as the Harris Shield Array. It essentially coated the ship with a repulsive shield that could redirect enemy fire to blunt the impact or even repel it. But unlike a Harris, these shields had to be permanently activated. Thus, tiny ports dotted the attack ship exteriors, and each one emitted the shield array barrier. On its own, one port would be worthless. The idea was to overlap the various ports. With the current tech, as more arrays overlapped, the protective strength increased exponentially.

Thus, two overlapping ports would quadruple the protective strength. Three would provide almost nine times the shielding. Typical attack ships had six or seven array ports overlapping at any given section of the ship's exterior. For the Sorcerer Reborn, Garrison wanted 15 to 20.

An engineer questioned the feasibility of such a high port density, wondering if so many holes – even though quite small – would compromise the integrity of the hull.

Dons agreed. "Can you test that? Build a surface and do a stress test?"

"That would be a costly surface," responded Jennings, the First Officer. "And it would greatly increase the construction time."

"Run the test in the simulation first," said Garrison, "Let's see what it predicts. If the error tolerance veers too high, we can look at building a test surface, or maybe just reduce ports by a measure."

At this, Shipp had to ask something.

"Question. Can't we build the interior skeleton of the ship now and work this issue out while that's happening? Why can't we start constructing the core sections?"

"Good question," said Dons. "The reason is because all the exterior elements of the ship – LR, scopes, shield ports, weapons ports – they connect with the interior of the ship, and each one plays a role in how the interior is designed so none of the connections ever get severed. These exterior elements are what keep us alive."

Harden added, "Basically, if you think of the HAT as the heart of the ship, and the interior walls as the bones, the relays for the exterior elements are like the blood vessels. We design the ship to be as certain as scientifically possible that the blood vessels will be protected and functional."

Shipp nodded, not sure he fully understood.

"Can't you just repair them if they get damaged?" asked Li.

"We encase them within the ship's structure," replied Dons. "The vast majority cannot be accessed at all while in space. And they never go bad, because nothing can disturb them except exterior damage. Once that happens, that sensor or port is done, so it doesn't matter. That's why we build in so much redundancy. Redundancy is easier than repair."

"You can't repair your own ship?" Li responded, incredulous.

"We can repair what breaks. These parts never break," replied Dons. He smiled at Li's reaction. "Hard to believe isn't it. But I've been in space for over twenty years. Never had a relay malfunction on its own. Not once."

Li looked at Shipp. They both grinned at the impressive tech. The attack ships really were the elite of the Space Force. The discussion between the engineers and the Sorcerer's officers resumed.

Shipp returned his gaze to the schematic of a standard attack ship. The top level contained just the Pilot Room and Comm Room. Below that was the mid-level and the lower level, both of which were much larger.

On the way back from Lavoisier, Garrison had told him the Comm Room was the most important room on the ship. Any new design had to include either an additional layer, or an extra thick single layer, of Blackhead encasing that room. From the Comm Room, you could talk to nearby ships and stations, send long-range messages when necessary, and communicate within the ship. The Comm Room also operated the LR, essential during battles. Each level had its own Comm Room, so they referred to the top-level one as Comm-1.

While each member of the crew wore personal comms in one ear, sometimes, like during a battle, the background noise interfered too much. The Comm Rooms provided an enclosed environment. In such a situation, the earpieces were better for receiving, and the Comm Rooms better for sending.

The mid-level of the ship housed all the dormitories, the waste recycling system, and the Medic Station, which included the nutrient supply. It also included Comm-2 and the Secondary Pilot Room, each on opposite sides of the staircase leading up to the top level. The mid-level also featured the Power Control Room, where the HAT drive occupied the central position in the ship.

A hallway ringed around the mid-level surrounding the Power Control Room, with sealable Blackhead barriers every five meters or so. The hallway branched out toward the exterior of the ship at four locations. Branches led to weapons stations. While the Weapons Officer – Dons – directed attacks from his station in the lower level, the point of having so many firing stations was that anyone on the attack ship could, at any moment, be called on to fire a weapon.

Both sides of the elliptical hallway were layered with Blackhead, meaning that the HAT drive was protected from outer space by at least three distinct layers – the exterior one, the outer edge of the hallway, and the inner edge of the hallway, plus the floors above and below it.

For the new prototype ship, Garrison and Harden advocated for at least six distinct layers – double the norm. With all the storage and cache space they would need, this seemed reasonable to everyone. All these layers achieved a singular goal – if one section of a Peterson attack ship became uninhabitable for any reason, they could seal off that area and continue to operate from the remaining sections.

The lower level contained the Weapons Supply Room, Comm-3, Fire Control, and the escape pod, which held up to four people. Fire Control was the largest single room in the ship. During an attack, up to six weapons crew members could be firing independently all in the same room. This proximity allowed them to speak directly to each other and not have to rely on comm tech.

Shipp, James, and Li met the bulk of Garrison's crew on the way back from Lavoisier.

At the top level, every attack ship had two pilots operating the ship, nonstop. The Sorcerer's lead pilots were Blake and Reeves. General Garrison could usually be found on the top level along with Comm Officer Harden, but Garrison would often depart to confer with Dons or other officers and crew. First Officer Jennings could serve in any capacity. He could replace the General, and could command from any level on the ship if called upon.

On the mid-level under normal conditions, you would find the Chief Medic, the Mid-Level Control Officer, and the Propulsion Supervisor, essentially the attack ship's mechanic. If an attack ship lost its PS, that meant serious trouble because he tended to stay on the interior of the mid-level during battles, the most protected part of the ship.

Locke, who Shipp, James, and Li met on Lavoisier, served as the Sorcerer's Chief Medic. Mackson was the Mid-Level Control Officer. And Yao the Propulsion Supervisor. All had served on the Sorcerer for many years. On most ships, including the Sorcerer, the Mid-Level Control Officer also had some degree of medical skill and could serve as an assistant to the Chief Medic. Wise to have more than one doctor.

On the lower level, the Weapons Officer could pretty much run the show. He had a high degree of autonomy during battles, including drills. For the Sorcerer, that was Dons.

These nine positions were considered essential to the successful operation of a Peterson attack ship. All the remaining crew served as assistants and second shifts in various capacities, mostly in Fire Control working under Dons. Most crew possessed multiple skillsets and could function as gunners, technicians, pilots, communicators, or several of these.

Attack ships never slept. If the General was sleeping, the First Officer was in command. And since no one served on an attack ship who hadn't spent several years in the ground forces, most of these soldiers were over thirty, with several over forty or even fifty years old.

Later, in a subsequent meeting, James studied the rough schematic of the developing Sorcerer Reborn.

"What are those spaces on the edges of the new ship?"

"Storage rooms and caches," replied Harden. "Just like the relays, some of each attack ship's supplies are housed in enclosed rooms, many of which cannot be reached from within the ship. These rooms are loaded up with ammunition and nutrient supplies."

"The idea," Dons added, "Is inner and outer layers of protection. The storage rooms are farther within the ship than the caches. So a batch of weapons gets sent from a storage room to a cache for a particular firing station. The cache room is much smaller. That way, if that cache room gets damaged, you don't lose your whole weapons supply, and the storage rooms can feed multiple caches. All this can be controlled from the Weapons Supply Room on my level."

Shipp wanted to confirm something. "So it's possible to fire your cache empty and have no more ammo at that station. What do you do – load more from storage or move to a different station?"

Jennings answered, "Depends. In Fire Control, you would reload the cache, assuming all the other firing stations are still occupied. If one of them is unmanned, you move to that station while Weapons Supply refills the cache. It takes a few minutes to fully reload most caches. It also depends on which weapons you're dealing with. K-rockets take longer than TI's and MagTons."

Shipp was pretty sure he got it. "But if you're on the mid-level, you'd move to a new station."

"Absolutely," confirmed Dons, "Because you don't know what's happening in Weapons, and until you talk to them on comm, you don't know how long it will be. And by the way, on the Sorcerer we call it the rock, not the cache. Cache is the tech term. When we say 'stock the rock,' that means refill your cache."

"Have you ever emptied all your caches at the same time?" asked James.

"I'd be a pretty ratty Weapons Officer to let that happen," Dons quipped. Garrison and the other officers all laughed.

"Just checking," added James. "I think I get it now. Those spaces are larger than on standard attack ships because we're going to need far more weapons and supplies."

All the officers nodded.

"And that's also why we need much thicker Blackhead, and more layers of it between all these storage rooms and caches. Hallways. Walls. Skeleton. Exteriors," said Garrison.

***

Weeks passed.

Shipp continued winding down his instructional duties, and the designs of the Sorcerer Reborn began to take shape. They kept hashing out details, day after day, sometimes 12-hour days of nearly nonstop collaboration.

As Shipp's final days of teaching approached, he got invited by Garrison to watch a cinematic from Space Force Command. It was from Olba Station, orbiting the planet Scimtar, an attack ship construction site recently modified and enlarged. The cinematic showed the skeleton of the Sorcerer Reborn being fit together. They could already see the central housing where their HAT drive would be installed.

Construction had begun. And the greatest mission of Shipp's life, possibly of anyone's life in the last five hundred years, was one step closer.

31

Carya

Shipp, James, and Li knew they would soon be sent on their first space mission as part of Garrison's current Sorcerer vessel. And by this time, with Li having spent nearly two years befriending Shipp, the three of them had become the strongest trio of friends any of them had ever known.

Li had come to care as much about Shipp's despair and the ruination of his soul as James did. Even a year after Lavoisier, Shipp seemed protective of his thoughts, and resisted attempts to get him to open up about his losses. He seemed to be nurturing them. Letting them wash over his mind and heart. Before they embarked on their upcoming mission, James and Li decided to visit Shipp's domicile.

Shipp was packing up, deciding what to leave behind and what to bring with him for several months in the confines of space.

In the middle of packing, he came across a box of printed photos from his time on Risner. He had none from Lavoisier – his desire to preserve memories died there. But he still had the ones from his previous station. The photos interrupted his packing. He sat down, studying a photo of Pretoria next to LaSalle and Vonn. In the photo, only Vonn looked at the camera. His wife and LaSalle were working on something. Vonn had an approving smile that Shipp interpreted as admiration for him, something Shipp valued and longed for from his leaders. He missed Vonn as much as anyone else he'd lost. He remained the best commander he'd ever served under. He was hopeful Garrison might finally measure up or surpass him.

When James and Li arrived, Shipp compacted the photos in his hand into a single pile and dropped it back in the box.

James noticed, "Can I see those? I didn't know you had that many."

"Not now," Shipp replied.

"You bringing those with you on the Sorcerer?" asked Li.

"Haven't decided yet," said Shipp.

James redirected the conversation, "Well, Li and I have written up letters to send to our families and friends. We did this when we got here last year. We're doing it again before we leave. Might not get another chance."

"That's great," said Shipp. "Good idea."

"So where's yours?" asked James, off Shipp's assertion that this was such a good idea.

"I don't need it," Shipp said. "My past is, that's my former life. I'm done with it. I'm going to die in space."

"Shipp," Li said, "You may not need it. Or, you may not think you need it. But they need it. They deserve to hear from us. If you were there, wouldn't you want to hear from your relative after all we've been through? It's so rare. It's precious."

"What do you mean I may not think I need it? You think I need to send this?" Shipp said, picking up on Li's deliberate emphasis of the word 'think.'

"These people are the reason we're fighting," said James. "It helps me to reconnect with them. So I remember."

"What helps me is to forget them, just like I have to forget everyone else I've lost," said Shipp.

"But you haven't lost the ones back home," said Li.

"I lost them when I arrived on Risner. That was my new home. That was my new family. And most of my family died there. The rest died on Lavoisier. Except for you two.""Your family is still alive on Saul, Shipp," James said. "I looked them up to be sure."

"My family is you guys. And everyone on Garrison's ship is about to join it, I hope," said Shipp.

James pressed, "Remember when you didn't let your relatives celebrate with you before you left for SFU? And you told me you regretted it after hearing my experience with that. It matters to them, not just you."

Shipp kept silent. He had a response, but didn't want to share it.

James wilted. He and Li realized how fully Shipp had committed to forgetting everything from his past – the good and the bad. It was his way of shielding himself from future pain, a totally irrational and hopeless endeavor. And it was clear they wouldn't be able to convince him to change course. Still, James couldn't leave it alone just yet.

"What's it doing to your heart to black them out like this?"

Shipp stared at the closed box of photos from Risner. James expected another dodge, another attempt to minimize or change the subject. Instead, Shipp told a story.

"When I was seven years old, I had an aunt named Carya Mulwana. My mom's younger sister. She used to come over all the time and play with me. We had a game of Corner the Rat, you remember that game?"

James and Li chuckled and nodded. Every Peterson kid loved playing Corner the Rat.

"My mom got tired of playing it. But Aunt Carya would play it with me for hours. And even when she had an easy shot at cornering the rat, she'd always let me catch up and finish it off. She'd take me out to touch the dome and look out beyond it. She'd tell me about the galaxy and how big it is, and that one day I'd have to choose between living on a planet, or seeing the universe."

"I think you mentioned her a couple times," James said.

Shipp nodded and continued, "One day, there was a war report on the monitor. Westers had broken through our defenses on Rita and annihilated several hundred soldiers. And after that, they took the bodies of our dead soldiers and played games with the corpses. Just gross, unspeakable stuff. Monsters. Carya saw me watching that. She told me she'd been accepted to the Space Force, and that she'd be leaving in a month. This war report was just another reason she was glad she applied."

"Were you sad?" James asked.

"Yeah," said Shipp. "But I knew she had to go. I asked if she was going to kill the Westers that humiliated our dead ones like that. She said she hoped to get the chance."

"Carya was the first person you really lost then, and you lost her when she left to fight the enemy. So it's the enemy's fault you lost her," Li surmised.

"No," said Shipp. "I lost her a year later. She died on Terrasol, from a hive bomb. Her first month there. She never killed a single rat. Just like Juthelle."

James already knew Shipp had lost his aunt and that it motivated him to join the Space Force. But he hadn't heard the whole story before. And Shipp wasn't done.

"My parents held this big celebration to honor my Aunt Carya. They did well at it. But I didn't want to celebrate. My favorite relative was gone forever. I just went in my room and cried."

James realized why Shipp was telling this story.

"This is why you don't want to send updates," he said. "Because you don't want your family to have hope you might survive. They've already lost you, and it's better off staying that way."

Shipp smiled, glad his friend got it. "When the Sorcerer Reborn is built, we're going on a one-way trip into Wester Territory. We're not coming back. I'm going to die in space. So are you guys. And nothing is going to change that. The only question is, how many rats can I take out before that happens. I'm hoping... for millions."

Li marveled at Shipp's lofty goal.

"Your family would still like to hear your voice and see your face. It's the memory that matters. To them. It's why you've kept those photos in that box," said James.

Shipp picked up the box and tossed it in his 'take' box. That was his answer to James. Shipp wasn't ready to sever his past completely, but he wasn't willing to do any more than this to hold on to it.

James thought about how hard it must have been for Shipp to lose so close a relative at such a young age. Pretoria's death was an echo of Carya's. Shipp's life had taken on a pattern of losing women who were close to him. By joining the all-male Sorcerer, Shipp was attempting to shield himself from any possibility of it happening again – whether he realized it or not.

James approached Shipp, clasped his hand and his shoulder, and looked him in the eye. He was with him forever, until the end.

32

Space Mission

The Sorcerer beckoned.

Its one outer door, connected to the mid-level, lay open before Shipp, Li, and James. The door provided the walkway between a girder and the vessel, across a chasm of darkness beneath them inside an attack ship hub.

Normally there would be lights everywhere as workers patched damage, loaded fresh supplies, and fully stocked the weapons supply rooms and caches. But since the Sorcerer was departing today, the workers were gone, and the cavernous hub sat mostly dark except for a few lights surrounding the huge rectangular door leading from the hub into outer space.

Garrison had received a new mission to prosecute while the Sorcerer Reborn underwent construction. To make room for Shipp, James, and Li, he gave three of his usual crew an extended break. They would spend the mission documenting and monitoring the construction of the new vessel, to ensure it was done according to plan and without defect.

That allowed the three friends to embark on their first space mission. All three would work in the Fire Control room officially, and for them this would be as much a training voyage as a real mission. Garrison also needed them to fully integrate with his officers and crew. Every opportunity to get familiar with each other needed to be taken. And, when it came time to fulfill their mission, Garrison needed them to perform in the moment.

Shipp, James, and Li had undergone extensive training during the last few months, so they knew the theory. They conducted space walks. They learned the weaponry. They studied the mechanics of the vessel.

But as with anything, it's entirely different to step across the door, watch it close behind you, and embark into the vast darkness of space toward the Meridian Zone and the Central Frontier – the Void – that surrounded it.

On this mission, the following personnel served alongside Thomas Shipp, Cameron James, and Mansa Li:

General Garrison commanded. Beneath him were First Officer Jennings, Comm Officer Harden, Pilots Blake and Reeves, Chief Medic Locke, Propulsion Supervisor Yao, Weapons Officer Dons, and Mackson, the Mid-Level Control Officer and Medical Assistant.

Beyond them, Yao's Tech Assistant was Wallace. Ewing and Molon served as second shift Pilots. Abe and Marley worked as Weapons Specialists under Dons along with Cardmanov and Jimenez. With Shipp, James, and Li, that made 19 in all. On the Sorcerer Reborn, they would have 24.

Upon departure, Shipp, James, and Li joined Dons' team of Weapons Specialists, but each was expected to pursue at least one additional specialty. Li chose flight, but he very much also wanted to learn from Yao and Wallace about the mechanical workings of the Sorcerer. James chose communications. Shipp chose leadership, intending to spend ample time with Garrison, Jennings, and Mackson.

As for the mission:

Space Force Command had been informed about a recent battle some distance away from the Meridian Zone planets, about halfway between the last of the seven planets and the edge of the galaxy.

Two Peterson attack ships, the Mauler and the Stealth, along with a few convoy ships, had engaged in a furious battle with three Wester attack ships. The Petersons lost two convoy ships, and the attack ships retreated after suffering extensive damage.

What they didn't know, and what the Sorcerer had been ordered to find out, was what happened to the Wester attack ships. The generals of the Mauler and Stealth both insisted they severely damaged at least one Wester ship, and possibly two. They believed the remaining Wester ship might be able to help one of the damaged ships return to their territory, but not both.

If a damaged Wester ship remained, the Sorcerer could finish it off.

The risk was that since the Westers would want to preserve all their ships, they would probably send at least one rescue ship to the area. The question was, who would get there first? The bigger question was, would the Westers anticipate this move by the Petersons and send an armada, or just a single ship?

The Sorcerer would be joined by three convoy ships that would separate from a larger group of ships operating near the Meridian Zone. That armada needed to remain there, but it could spare three convoys for this mission so the Sorcerer wouldn't be alone.

Convoy ships didn't travel as far for single missions as attack ships. Their primary job was to escort and protect attack ships or transport ships whenever the situation risked heightened danger. With several convoys, any attempt to disable an attack ship could usually be thwarted.

Convoy ships held anywhere from four to seven people. These were high-risk assignments, because convoys didn't have nearly as much Blackhead for protection as attack ships. One or two direct hits from an attack ship's best weapons could cripple a convoy. But, being smaller and more maneuverable, they could more easily evade an attack. And with greater numbers, they could gang up on larger ships and pose quite a threat.

Beyond those vessels, the Space Force also utilized single occupant battleships, or SOBs. These got used more rarely, usually only when they knew in advance a battle would happen. Deployed by the dozen, SOBs could be the decisive element in a battle when used smartly. Space Fleets delivered them to battle fronts on transport ships since they couldn't fly long distances.

The Westers had similar versions of all these vessels, and these comprised the bulk of the Space Fleets for both territories, other than transport ships.

Garrison, Jennings, and Harden insisted that a single occupancy battleship should be stored on the prototypical Sorcerer Reborn. This had never been done before on an attack ship, but since the Sorcerer Reborn would be all alone in Wester Territory, they believed it wise to equip it with more than just an escape pod. The SOB would provide another asset if the situation called for it. So, a storage and launch bay for this ship got added to the lower-level designs of the Sorcerer Reborn.

Inside the station hub, the Sorcerer dislodged from its moorings as the vacuum of space filled the darkened expanse. The outer door slid open, and General Garrison's attack ship entered the untamable stillness.

It would take nearly three months to reach the location for this mission.

During that time, Garrison, Jennings, and Harden planned a series of drills for a variety of scenarios. But beyond that and the mission, the secondary goal of this voyage was to integrate Shipp, James, and Li with their crew. The drills and the mission itself would achieve that in terms of combat readiness. But conversation – taking it all the way to the bone, as Garrison put it – was the order of the day.

Once the Sorcerer had put some distance from the space station, the ship prepared to engage the HAT. James and Shipp took up spots on the mid-level to observe the HAT alongside Mackson and Yao, while Li joined backup pilot Ewing in the secondary Pilot Room.

"I just realized," Shipp said to James, "I was in here when we came from Lavoisier. I'm going up to the Pilot Room to watch from there."

"Bored with the HAT already, huh," said James.

"No, just bored with you," Shipp shot back. James smiled. He felt good at seeing Shipp's lighter side show up. It was a rare sight these days.

Shipp bounded up the staircase, catching Li's handwave from the Secondary Pilot Room on his way up. Harden nodded as he passed by Comm-1, and Shipp reached the Pilot Room, where Garrison analyzed the flight path with Blake and Reeves. Garrison nodded him into the one remaining seat in the room while Blake spoke.

"Best path is to arc right around this group of stars, because after that, it's almost a straight shot. That's the fastest route, by about a week," Blake said, as Garrison studied the galactic map on his monitor.

"The risk with that is we come in naked. No planets or stars at all from that approach to the site. If any Wester ships are there, they'll see us when we power down the HAT if not before," Garrison said.

"True," said Blake, "But it's a much smoother approach. Most other routes have more turns, including a couple sharp ones where we might have to disengage the HAT to make them safely."

"Yao isn't going to like that," said Reeves.

"Why not?" asked Shipp. "Don't HATs never break down?"

"Yao's a classic mechanic in every way," Garrison said. "He always wants to put the least amount of stress on the ship, no matter what. That's why I like him. But sometimes the ship's stress isn't the most important factor. Our safety is more. Stay alive."

"Save your friend," Shipp replied. He was surprised Reeves and Blake didn't join him. Garrison noticed Shipp's observation.

"You wondering why our Pilots didn't make the response?" Garrison asked.

Shipp nodded, and looked at Blake, needing him to fill in the blanks.

"All our friends are on this ship," said Blake. "I'm alive because I was saved in a battle on Kora when I should have died. Five other soldiers died to save me, when they could have just left."

Shipp could sense survivor's guilt from Blake. It rubbed him the wrong way.

"Are you saying you don't believe in saving your friend?"

"Do you think it's worth it for five to die to save one?"

"It's not about the numbers. It's about the trust," Shipp said. "James almost died on Lavoisier. He was trapped across a hallway. Injured and bleeding. We ran across to save him, and another soldier got killed. Durman. So one guy died saving another. Durman is a hero because we went into battle with a man who didn't hesitate to save his friend."

Blake thought about Shipp's reply. "That's not how it felt when it happened in real life.""That's how my commander on Risner said it. Commander Vonn," Shipp said. Garrison could see how much Vonn's loss still hurt for Shipp. "It's about the trust in each other on the battlefield," Shipp repeated.

"I just feel like I'm not more important than five men," Blake said.

Shipp nodded. "I get it. Makes complete sense. But with trust, the whole army is stronger, and that means we win more battles and advance farther in the war. In the big picture, fewer Petersons will die because those five saved you."

Reeves looked at Blake, then at Shipp, and then back at Blake.

"The new guy's got some brain fire," Reeves said, using a common Peterson idiom in its usual complimentary form.

Shipp's respect for Garrison inched higher in this moment, because he never interrupted the conversation. He let them both air their perspectives and experiences. After the silence suggested the exchange was over, Garrison finally spoke.

"Shipp, you're going to find that every guy on my ship has a burning pit in his gut. Every one of us is living with an unquenchable fire against the rats. That's Blake's. You still haven't told me yours. Before this mission is over, I need to hear it."

Shipp felt a flush of grief so powerful it reached his eyes. He felt them pulsing. The sudden emotion surprised him and he looked away. Garrison's words felt like a challenge. Shipp's instinct was to fight it. How impossible it seemed to suppress tragedy and move beyond the pain of his losses. Winning battles didn't seem to help. Talking about it didn't either. Yet here it remained, still bubbling right underneath.

Garrison noted Shipp's silence and patted him on the shoulder.

"It's alright brother. We've got three months there and back."

Harden shouted at them from Comm-1, "When you guys are done squawking, how about we push forward here."

At that same moment, Jennings hopped up the staircase and looked down the short hallway to the Pilot Room. "Anything wrong? You guys settle on a trajectory yet?"

"Stop pestering my Pilots. They're a bit rusty after such a long layover," Garrison said sarcastically.

"Rat heads," Harden muttered, loud enough for them to hear.

Blake returned to the original conversation without a beat. "Okay, so you want to take a different route then? Come out of the HAT behind a planet or something?"

"I'd feel a lot better about it," said Garrison. "Plus, that gives the convoys a clearer target."

"Alright," Blake said, "My second-best route would be up and over. Pass over that big star cluster and you're halfway there. But there's an asteroid shower in that area so we'd have to come out of the HAT here and reassess. Eventually, we can land behind this star, PM4523. It's a red giant. From there, it's a week at normal speed to the site."

"I remember those asteroids," Jennings said, now standing behind Shipp. "That's where we wiped those four convoys. Remember that?"

Blake, Reeves, and Garrison all react to the memory. Apparently, it was a close call.

"So the asteroids helped you?" Shipp wanted to know.

"Wester convoys were after us. Four on one. And we were low on weapons," Garrison began.

Jennings picked up after him, "We seeded Mags on several small asteroids and blew them up as the convoys approached. Since they don't have as much Blackhead, two of the ships got partially disabled from the blasts. Then we were able to take out the other two."

"How long ago was that?" Shipp asked.

"Ten years? I don't know, who cares about time." Garrison said. "Blake, I like the plan. Let's do it. Harden, send a comm to the armada and give them this red giant for the rendezvous.

"Who came up with that idea, to put MagTons on the asteroids?" Shipp asked.

"That was all Dons," Garrison said. Shipp was liking Dons more and more. In fact, he was liking just about everyone on the Sorcerer. Except Locke, who seemed to always find a way to bring down the mood. But nobody's perfect. And Locke had proven his medical skill on Lavoisier, so Shipp could put up with his cynicism and sourness now and then.

Blake input the first leg of the trajectory into his flight station.

Attack ships still included actual manual flight controls you could grab hold of with your hands. It had been determined over many decades that this allowed for faster reactions than pressing buttons and pulling levers. So, attack ship technology linked the numerous air burst vents and ignition mechanics directly to the manual controls, so you could turn and bank at will.

When Blake turned the handles to the left, the ship would respond with corresponding bursts from the correct locations to make the ship turn in that direction. Reeves' job was to make sure the pilot console systems correlated to Blake's actions, so he could correct any slight errors since the manual controls were never exact.

Thus, Blake and Reeves had to be in constant communication during a battle, telling each other where they were going in any given moment, using three-dimensional positional charts in reference to the location of the ship. Convoy ships and single-occupant battleships used the same basic technology. However, being of much smaller mass, they were more nimble and could be piloted by one person.

With the trajectory keyed in, Blake waited, ready to accelerate. During pre-set trajectories with the HAT engaged, manual control wasn't usually needed. But Blake still put his hands on the controls because it just felt more natural. Shipp smiled to himself on seeing this. Human control was still preferable to console control, and always will be.

Harden spoke to the crew from Comm-1, "HAT engaging in thirty seconds. Take your positions."

During the initial acceleration period, all crew had to securely fasten themselves, or they'd be smashed against a wall. In the Pilot Room, Jennings stood against the back wall. The other four buckled in. In the Power Control Room, James, Mackson, and Yao buckled into standing braces. There were no seats in this room. In the Weapons Control Room and Fire Control, everyone had seats.

"Go," ordered Garrison.

Blake pried the HAT lever upward.

Shipp had felt this feeling before, but he never got tired of it. His whole body pressed against the seat behind him. The nearest star approached and passed on the right. The next on the left. Pretty soon stars raced by, visible through the small window directly ahead. This visual, Shipp had never seen, and it was the real reason he wanted to come up here, in spite of what he told James.

After about ten minutes, they reached top speed, and inertia resumed, allowing them to once again move about the ship.

33

Fire Control

An hour after reaching maximum HAT velocity and having consumed nutrients, Shipp, James, and Li descended a staircase from mid-level to the lower level of the Sorcerer. That staircase sat not far from the one above it that led from mid-level to the top level. That design enabled anyone to quickly reach any part of the ship.

To the left of the lower-level staircase sat Comm-3, and to the right sat the entrance into the escape pod. If more than four people ever needed to escape, most Peterson ships gave every member on board the right of first refusal. If you wanted to sacrifice to save your friend, all you had to do was speak up first. If ever a final decision was required by someone, the General made the call. Attack ship crew and officers always understood each mission could be the last space flight of their lives.

The Fire Control room opened in front of Shipp as he finished descending the lower-level staircase. The room used an elongated hexagonal design, with three firing stations on each side. Each firing station jutted out from the walls so that the room had six enormous bulkheads extruding from the walls.

If a crew member traced the perimeter of the room, they would have to walk around these six large obstructions. Inside the bulkheads sat the weapons supply rooms that led to the caches near the exterior of the ship. More weapons were stored underneath and around them, and could be accessed remotely from the Weapons Control Room at the far end of the elongated hexagon, opposite the stairwell.

During a battle, Dons would be in that room, which opened up to Fire Control with no door, and was thus within earshot of everyone in Fire Control.

Each seat at the firing stations was situated at the farthest point from the exterior of the ship, at the end of each bulkhead. Looking at the room from above, it would resemble a six-point star or snowflake, with the weapons specialists' seats at the inner vertices of the shape.

The six weapons specialists could speak to each other without their comms. Being far from the edge of the ship, they were well-protected from any blasts that might manage to penetrate the thick exterior and the enclosed storage rooms.

Dons directed Shipp, James, and Li to their stations. Each sat with an experienced weapons specialist between them. Right now, that was Abe, Marley, and Jennings. Garrison wanted his First Officer there while his three new crew members learned the ropes. The remaining crew – Ewing, Molon, Cardmanov, and Jimenez – were off duty and probably sleeping on mid-level.

From the Weapons Supply Room, Dons initiated a series of simple drills. The first featured imaginary targets attacking the ship, which itself was not moving at HAT velocity in the drill.

"Six Krocks from starboard – hit the disabled transport ship at the mark on its bow," Dons called out.

Shipp, Abe, and James were on starboard to Dons' right, since Dons' room sat at the rear of the ship. Jennings, Li, and Marley sat on port, to Dons' left.

Shipp and James both activated their targeting monitors and pinpointed their weapons to hit the mark on the imaginary ship. They activated their K-rockets on the monitor, and fired two shots each. Abe did the same. Just like that, six K-rockets fired and impacted the target in quick bursts. The imaginary ship now showed a small opening as the K-rockets broke through just enough to see some interior.

"Hit it with Mags – ten-second delay – fire five each," barked Dons.

Shipp, Abe, and James kept the same target marked, switched to the MagTon tab, and fired five each. The fifteen weapons burrowed into the ship, affixed themselves to wherever they landed, and blew.

"Port weapons – one nuke each into the hole," Dons commanded.

Li, Jennings, and Marley targeted the same spot and activated the Krock monitor. But they selected the K-rockets marked with an 'N' on the screen – nuclear-tipped K-rockets, often referred to as N-Krocks, or ninks.

The ninks fired and flew straight into the innards of the enemy ship, and exploded from inside. The imaginary ship distorted its shape a bit. The exterior Blackhead-coated hull mostly held firm, but extensive internal damage disabled the ship and would have killed a portion of the crew.

Dons exited Weapons Supply and addressed the room.

"Pretty basic attack package you just ran. Any thoughts on how it could have been done better?"

James began, "Why have port fire only the nukes? Why not have us do all three rounds since we're closer?"

Dons nodded. "Good question. Shipp, Li – got an answer?"

Neither of them could come up with one in the few seconds Dons allowed. "Marley?"

Marley explained, "In a real battle, the Wester ship would likely be moving and attempting to evade. The moment you get the mags in there, you want the nukes to follow them almost immediately. So it's like boxing – a one-two punch, lightning fast, staccato."

"Right," said Dons. "Another thing – when we're sending a barrage of weapons, especially K-rockets, you don't want all six hitting at the same time. That diffuses the impact potential. What's better is to stagger them so each one hits on its own. Maybe a couple seconds between each one, or even less."

"Ahh," said Shipp, getting it immediately. "Sort of like digging a hole. Six separate digs gets you farther than six shovels all digging in the same spot at once."

Dons smiled. "I'm gonna use that. Good analogy. So, when I order a barrage of rockets, you guys need to know who will fire and in what order. You can see weapons firing on your main monitors. The best approach is to follow it down the line from me. So James fires. The instant Abe sees that, he fires, and when Shipp sees that, he fires. James then fires his second, and so on. You guys need to read off each other."

"And," said Abe, "If one of us is unable to fire for some reason, you need to know that so you don't sit there waiting for the guy in front you."

"So you're always aware of what's going on outside the ship," Dons said. "But you must also be aware of everything going on inside the ship. We don't need our comms in this room if you talk loud enough, but top level might be talking to you, and you need to know where we're moving to, and from, and how fast. So there's a constant chatter going on between Harden, me, Mackson, Yao, and Garrison."

Li summed it up, "So we're listening, we're watching, and we're firing, in unison."

"That's it," said Dons. "It takes getting used to, and that fire station needs to become your new best friend. You need to be able to operate it blindfolded. A month from now, you will be."

Shipp looked at him, "You mean actual blindfolds."

Dons nodded. "The Mauler, about twenty years ago or so, had a crew member who was truly blind. He'd been injured on the last mission, total vision loss. But he was an expert weapons specialist. Ten years' experience. He demanded to be sent out on the next mission, but the brass wouldn't let him. His general stood up for him, so they tested him in a simulator. He rated higher than all the sighted guys."

Shipp smiled, "So he got to fly the mission?"

Dons nodded. "Performed exceptionally. Flew for another five years. He didn't need his eyes anymore."

"Awesome," Shipp said to himself.

"I like how we're basically firing the same weapons we use on the ground," said James. "Wizards, MagTons, K-rockets. Other than the standalone nukes, the only new weapon is the TI."

"Basically yes," said Dons. "All our weapons are larger than the ones used on the ground because we don't have to carry them, but the concepts are the same. We hardly ever use wizards so we don't carry very many. Standalone nukes are best used as a death blow, when you're ready to tear the whole thing apart from inside. We'll do a drill with TIs later."

TIs – tracking interceptors – were a defensive weapon primarily used against K-rockets, the only weapon that could break through the Blackhead exterior of an attack ship. They attempted to interrupt the targeting signal between the attacking ship and the K-rocket so the rocket would believe the TI was the ship. A deceived rocket would re-direct and impact the TI instead. A typical TI followed the same trajectory as the ship at first, until it succeeded in co-opting the approaching K-rocket. Then, it would break away from the flight path and detonate the rocket.

"If I'm on the mid-level and using one of those firing stations, do I have to listen to you on the comm, or am I on my own?" Shipp asked.

"Mid-level firing stations usually listen to Garrison and Harden. They can see things up there that we can't see as fast," Dons replied. "But, when you know what you're doing, you can operate those independently, and you can also listen to me. But usually, it's them, or on your own."

Many more drills came after that, mostly simple ones the first several days. Shipp, Li, and James gained a stronger feel for the basics of their firing stations, and grew in confidence and rapport with the other gunners.

In the ensuing weeks, Dons had them rotate positions, operate with one or two stations down, operate against multiple attacking ships, operate as if the Pilot Room was compromised, operate as if the propulsion was compromised, and many more scenarios. They also worked with the backup crews. Later on, they would practice from the mid-level firing stations. He let them be destroyed in some simulations so they would feel the pseudo-reality of simulated death.

In between drills, Li spent his spare time with Yao, learning how to keep the ship functioning. James spent time in Comm-2 to learn the intricacies of the LR, and Shipp went to the top level with Garrison, Harden, and Jennings. There, he also learned Comm-1.

34

Memories

And that was life on an attack ship. Very little downtime, except for sleeping. Downtime meant getting to know the crew. James, Li, and Shipp took this as seriously as the drills, because they knew how important it was. In the ground wars, knowing your fellow soldiers raised everyone's performance, whether on or off the battlefield.

On attack ships, the stakes of life and death were even higher. No reinforcements. No base to run back to. You're it.

Every so often, the three new members of the Sorcerer got some time alone with each other. They spent most of that time discussing what they had learned about the ship and its crew. They had all noticed how little outside information seemed to reach attack ships. They hadn't received an update on the Sorcerer Reborn's construction progress. They received no confirmation their three convoy ships left as scheduled.

Life on an attack ship meant extreme isolation. Keeping busy helped stave off what could easily turn into a pervasive sense of forlorn abandonment, thousands of light years from anything and anyone. Flying in the Space Fleet demanded mental toughness, and the three of them became more and more aware of it as the weeks added up.

One day, Shipp asked Harden if he had received updates from Space Force Command. Shipp assumed Harden did receive them but chose not to pass on the information, because way out here all alone in space, there wasn't much they could do about any of it.

He was surprised to learn that very little information ever reached them. Harden explained how space communication worked. Either enemy could intercept messages, depending on the direction through space in which it was sent. Shipp knew that, but figured a simple code could scramble it.

It could, but that wasn't the value of intercepting a message, Harden explained. The true value came from math. If you did the math right, you could backtrace the direction of the message and get a pretty fair estimate of its origin, including the direction and speed of the ship that sent it. And that meant you might have a shot at finding an attack ship. Of course, this depended on how long ago the message was sent. But simply knowing an attack ship had been in a particular location could give insight into the enemy's movements and tactics, especially if the ship was in an unusual area.

All this to say, attack ships preferred to avoid sending or receiving messages while on a mission.

Harden also explained the Trans-Com system. As far as they knew, the Westers didn't have this technology. They weren't positive about this, but none of their Trans-Com devices had ever been destroyed, indicating the Westers hadn't found any of them.

Seeded throughout Peterson Territory – mostly on the Central Frontier and the other areas around the Meridian Zone – Trans-Com units looked like stationary satellites, orbiting nothing. The purists hated when people called them satellites, since the definition is that satellites *orbit* something. They preferred calling them buoys. But some egghead hundreds of years ago called them that because they looked like traditional satellites, and it stuck.

Trans-Com units just sat there, with one purpose – to receive and pass on messages within the Peterson Territory. When a ship sent a message, instead of heading straight for the recipient, it routed to a Trans-Com unit. That unit might send the message to another Trans-Com unit, or to the final recipient, depending on the location.

The Petersons used the Trans-Com system for two reasons.

First, it added security. If a message were intercepted going between Trans-Coms, the worst outcome would be that the Westers traced the source and found an unmanned satellite, rather than a much more valuable space vessel.

This strategy also protected the security of the message itself. Most Trans-Coms were located on the fringes of the more heavily traveled areas. That meant most messages could travel around the Peterson Territory without ever passing through the Meridian Zone or large parts of the Central Frontier, and made them less prone to interception.

Second, Trans-Coms sped up communications. Each Trans-Com unit could boost the speed of the message and accelerate its journey to the recipient. When the Sorcerer Reborn was ready, and Garrison's crew departed for Wester space on the longest space voyage of the five-hundred-year war, they intended to seed a couple more Trans-Coms on the fringes of the galaxy along the way.

Shipp left his conversation with Harden and headed to his domicile on the mid-level. Each domicile had four beds. He shared his room with James, Li, and Mackson. When Shipp arrived, the room was empty, which he had hoped.

He lay on his bed and closed his eyes. Faces flashed in his mind. He opened his eyes to make them dissipate, and stared at the bed above him. He had never been this far from Risner. There, he had a nicer bed, bathroom, air, grass, water, and ground. He had room to move. And he had her. With Pretoria, he never imagined himself serving on an attack ship. Now, he blasted across the galaxy with eighteen other men. Alone but not adrift.

Shipp reached for his small box of printed photos. He found one with himself, Gugbe, Mixie, and Ramad. Except for himself, a picture of death. Three friends, frozen forever in time. They would never move or make sound again. He flipped through more photos. Several featured himself with Pretoria, James, and Horman at the table where they used to commiserate. Then a few of Pretoria, and several of James.

He flipped through the whole stack. He came to the last one – him and Pretoria the day they left SFU for Risner. It was strange to see himself smiling, especially the way he smiled in this particular photo. Had he really been that happy? Was he naïve for thinking he could retain such happiness while serving in a war? The Peterson commanders wanted friends and married couples to serve together. But did any of these friend groups survive all the way through? Why would commanders want this, knowing friendships and lovers would be torn from each other forever?

He realized this was a dangerous line of thought. What would it mean if the Petersons *wanted* friends and lovers to serve together, knowing that the loss of people you love would provide the greatest motivation for a lifetime of vengeance? Could the leadership actually have ulterior motives this manipulative and cynical?

Shipp dismissed it, because he remembered that lots of married couples survived together. There was an attack ship crewed by multiple married couples. He had met several others at SFU and on various space stations. Plus, James survived. And Li – his only true friend from Lavoisier – also survived.

Maybe the Petersons encouraged friends to serve together because, while it might be inevitable that some would die, others would live, and those would be your lifelong brothers and sisters.

Shipp looked again at his smiling self. Something dark filled his spirit. His former happiness was truly dead. That life would never return. His head felt heavy.

Even if the Peterson Space Force did count on a never-ending supply of rage-filled, bloodlust-driven soldiers, Shipp didn't care. The way to end that was the same way to end everything – win the war. Use this new prototypical attack ship mission to cut off their supply lines. Devastate their resource-rich planets. Kill Elliss and everyone he knows. And this virus...

The darkness within him spread to his limbs. Something changed inside his spirit.

Shipp tore the photo in pieces. Pretoria's face, arms, and torso fell to the floor in shards. He ripped up the photo of his friends all together. He ripped up one of Horman, Pretoria, and James. Then another. Then another. He tore up photo after photo. A small pile accumulated beside his bed. The more photos he tore, the more his emotions roiled and tears tried to break through. But he squelched them with rage.

He reached the last photo. Pretoria, all alone, sitting at her desk on Risner. She hadn't seen him yet when he took this photo, so she wasn't looking at the lens. Just working. At peace with herself. Shipp held it for a while – his last visual reminder of his love. He fixated on it. Then at the pile of torn memories on the floor. He thought again of Gugbe's last words – the 'hex' she put on him.

He decided to keep this one, setting it next to his bed.

Lost in thought, he startled when James came in, ready to wind down for a few hours. James immediately saw the pile of torn photos. He sat on his bed, across from Shipp's. James saw his own face in one of the torn photos.

He got back up and sat next to Shipp. Put his arm around him. They sat in silence for a couple minutes. Shipp lowered his head, swirling in grief mixed with the empathy from James that fed his parched heart. They breathed together.

"Memories are hard to live with. Just as hard to let go," James said.

Shipp nodded almost imperceptibly, "Is this making me a better soldier, or killing me inside?"

James thought about it. He felt like he got a good answer.

"Maybe you don't need to be a better soldier anymore. But I don't want to see you die – inside or out."

Shipp let out a helpless laugh. "But we're going on the Sorcerer Reborn. It's a one-way trip."

"Okay," said James, "Let me revise. I don't want to see you die inside."

Shipp sighed. He picked up the torn photos and condensed them in his hands.

"I think, maybe I already have. I'm sorry." He walked over to a hand-sized door on the wall and pulled it open, tossing in the paper shards. The door closed. This sent them to the incinerator that helped fuel the ship's operations. He stood facing the wall, and hung his head away from James.

"I don't know how to do it Cam. I just want this mission to work. That's all I want. I don't think I'll ever be happy again. Probably don't deserve to be."

"This is what we know how to do," said James. "Maybe someday, we'll be blessed with the chance to find something better."

"Maybe you will," said Shipp. "Not me. I only care about two things now. Elliss, and the virus maker."

35

Pouring Out

Shipp, Garrison, Harden, Jennings, and Yao ate the mid-day nutrients together. This wasn't typical. Normally, they ate as fast as they could by themselves and just kept working. But Garrison had made it clear that on this mission, there would be designated meals for conversation and building relationships. Everyone would share a meal with everyone else multiple times during the mission.

This meal included only officers and Shipp. For Garrison, this was no accident. He'd been looking forward to this one for weeks, because Shipp had 'future officer' written all over him. This man was born to lead. About five minutes into the meal, Locke joined them.

"Sorry I'm late," Locke said as he sat down. "Marley smashed his finger in a door. I've been telling them to stop using those kinds of doors for years, but no one listens."

"Is he going to be alright?" asked Harden, already knowing the answer.

"He'll be good to go by the time we reach the rendezvous," said Locke.

"So," said Garrison, looking at Shipp. "What do you think of Mackson?"

"You got a great crew here," said Shipp. "Everyone talks like this is what they dreamed of doing their whole lives. Mackson wanted to be in space since he was five."

"He fought five years on Kora, but spent half his time studying attack ships," said Harden.

"You trust him enough to go outside with him?" asked Garrison.

Shipp didn't expect this. "You mean a space walk?"

Yao answered him, "We're having intermittent flutter with a shield array device on the port side, lower-level. Someone needs to go out and take a look. That means Mackson and one other."

"And that means you," said Garrison. "You can't have too many space walks. It's different every time and the experience is priceless. And I don't mean how it feels. I mean learning how to function and stay in control of yourself. I want everyone on my ship comfortable going out."

"I'm all in, General," said Shipp.

"Just make sure you triple check your lifeline," said Locke. "You go floating off, and it's a stew of a time trying to get you back. And then I have to break out all the oxygen backups, which is a pain because the storage closet is so badly designed."

Shipp already knew this, of course, so he just gave a simple non-verbal response, not wanting to engage Locke. But Locke kept going, switching the subject to his nutrients.

"That's one thing I always forget about, how bland this stuff is," Locke began. "You ever been to LaMay? Wow, they've got some flavors on that planet unlike anything in the galaxy."

"You can order spice packets," Jennings said. "Why didn't you?"

Locke shrugged, "They'll just run out way before the mission is over because they limit the quantity."

Garrison and Harden gave each other a knowing look. Locke was on fire today.

"You know what I could really go for is some sangria," said Locke. "They had some at the station – first time I've had that in ten years. You guys have any?"

Shipp startled at Locke's mention of sangria. He hardened his heart and fixated on his nutrients. But in spite of his valiant effort, he became more agitated the more they talked about the wine. He pressed his fingers against his thumbs.

"I had a couple cups of it," Garrison said. "Too many ground-based appetites will put me in the wrong mindset for this, so I keep it light."

"I know, I know," said Locke. "I kept it light. For the last couple weeks before we left."

Yao laughed. Jennings tried to change the subject to something more beneficial, "You guys know about the sangria-colored ribbons they use when wrapping remains –"

"Stop it." Shipp cut him off.

Everyone went silent. That awkward feeling. Shipp felt all the eyes on him. He should have kept his mouth shut. But it came out almost by instinct. He looked at Garrison, who was burrowing into him with his huge dark eyes. Shipp looked away. But everyone else was looking at Garrison now, and then back at Shipp.

"It's time, Shipp," Garrison wasn't going to let it go.

"No it isn't, just drop it," Shipp said. Not here. Not now. Not with this many people.

"Every man here has been through hell. It's what bonds us, unites us. Makes us stronger. But only when we know each other's hell," Garrison said. "Rendezvous is in three weeks. Can't wait until the last minute."

"Garrison –"

"Harden – tell Shipp your story," Garrison said.

"Yeah," Harden said, and his complexion altered into a state of protective rage. He suddenly reminded Shipp of Shipp. Harden clearly wasn't a huge fan of suddenly being told to spill his worst moments for the room, but he recognized the importance of Shipp doing so, and that he could set the example.

"I was on Cinque," Harden began. "We charged over a hill, expecting to take out an anti-air Krock launcher. But they also had a Harris array we didn't know about. They mowed us down. We lost thirty soldiers in less than a minute. Including all three of my best friends right next to me."

Harden had Shipp's full attention now.

"Westers took me and three others into their base..."

Harden's voice trailed off. He sought to access the part of his brain that had buried this memory with bloodthirsty vengeance. It was the only way he could keep talking.

"They..." he took a deep breath, and then another. His face twitched. His eyes searched his mind for the words. Finally, he found them, "They cut off a guy's arms when he resisted them. Gave them to me and the other guy. I had the left."

Shipp forgot he was the only one in the room who didn't already know this story. To him, it seemed like the first time Harden had ever shared it.

"Made me move the fingers. Made me use them to fire an AX. I decided I wasn't going to say a word no matter what they did to me. And they did a lot," Harden halted again, his face twitching even more, staring off into the searing memory he had learned to access, from a distance. After another long pause, he continued.

"My base Commander hatched a rescue operation. It was vintage. I heard later they had a huge argument about whether to do it. They came in and got me and one other guy out. Cardmanov, in Fire Control. I found out we were scheduled to be executed in three days. He and I still meet up every week for thirty minutes. Sometimes we just stare at each other."

Harden composed himself and looked at Shipp, "So yeah. We want to know what they took from you. And we're not going to let you rat out on us."

Shipp flinched at the insult, but took it in silence, much to Garrison's admiration. Shipp knew he couldn't hold back any longer after hearing Harden's story.

"Alright," Shipp said.

And then, he began. He started on Lavoisier though, not telling the story in order. He described meeting Li, discovering the virus, and how they had to hole up in the life capsule for weeks. He talked about Rawlic's rebellion, and Mixie's murder at the hands of her supposed friend Shelsie. The blood coming from her head. Her lifeless collapse. He described in gory detail how he beat Shelsie until she was unrecognizable.

Garrison sat astonished. He had never heard of Peterson soldiers murdering each other, or losing their heads in battle like that. This virus must be really gruesome to provoke such a disunifying fear and paranoia. Then, Shipp talked about losing Gugbe, Ramad, and Blasé, men he considered brothers since his time on Risner.

"So you all served together on Risner, and transferred to Lavoisier," probed Harden. "I never knew that part. Why did you leave Risner?"

Shipp couldn't hold it back any longer. This was the question he didn't want to answer. He had never shared his loss with anyone but Li.

He lowered his head so far it almost touched the table. Garrison noted his defeated posture. He glanced at Locke to make sure Locke wasn't about to ruin the moment. But Locke stared at Shipp too, waiting.

Shipp fought it for about a minute. Trying to find a way to tell what happened without losing his composure. It felt like someone was trying to extract words that were chained, latched, and barricaded deep within his soul.

"Flame your supernova," Shipp swore as he wheeled to the door as if wanting to leave, but knowing he couldn't. His glare bored into the table. His hands trembled. His jaw began to quiver. Two more agonizing minutes passed. The others sat in silence. Shipp felt all their eyes an inch away from his head. He clenched his jaw to hold it firm, but that made his abdomen convulse. He grunted to sustain control. Eventually, one eye filled with tears. Then the other. One dripped down his face. He swore again and belched a growl to restrain what could not be held back against Garrison's wordless psychiatric assault. He cried and convulsed, losing the ability to talk.

The other men remained wordless and still. They all knew this would make Shipp stronger, and that made them all stronger together. This wasn't weakness. It was elevation. It was advancement. Together, they could channel his need for vengeance. No longer could he keep that gift to himself.

That was the underbelly of the Sorcerer – harnessing each other's rage and merging each person's losses into a stream of fury with near limitless potential. This was how Garrison united his crew and fueled their work and their devotion to each other and the mission.

Shipp finally recovered enough to share what happened. He began speaking so low they could barely hear him.

"I was married to a base admin on Risner. I met her at SFU. She... always wanted to be a Station Commander. But she... she gave up her dream to go with me." Shipp's voice rose in volume the more he talked. He went on and on about how much he loved Pretoria and all their dreams and desires. By the end he was standing and shouting. "And the rats invaded our base with an underground tunnel. They decoyed us, attacked while I was gone. They killed Vonn. They killed everybody. I got back just in time. To see their commander bitch rat order my wife's death. Right in front of my eyes! She wouldn't be dead if she hadn't gone with me. She should have gone her own way!"

Shipp realized he was yelling. And that he had stood up at some point. He halted, and looked around the room. Each man's eyes watched him. But he didn't see remorse or pity. He saw respect. He saw understanding. He saw brothers.

"I've lost everyone and everything except the people on this ship," he said. "This is all I have left."

He sat back down.

"General Elliss. He's the one who ordered that Wester invasion. He's the one I'm looking for. And, he's got an attack ship somewhere, because there's no way they could have been communicating from that depth in the ground back to their land bases. There was a ship up above us. There had to be."

"Elliss," said Harden, looking at Garrison. "We know about Elliss."

Shipp could barely contain himself and blurted out what he should have known was nonsense, "You do? You know where he is?"

He immediately realized there was no way they knew Elliss' whereabouts. No one knew the locations of any attack ships, most of the time. Now, for the first time, he felt a little embarrassed.

"We think we tangled with his ship once a few years back," Garrison said. "But we've heard his name tossed around here and there. He's one of their most experienced leaders, from what we can tell."

"Hold on," said Jennings. "One more thing. You haven't told us her name. And I hope you have a picture."

Shipp lowered his head again, feeling shame. "Pretoria. I only have one photo left. I tore up all the rest a few weeks ago."

Garrison stood up and walked around the table. He placed his hands on Shipp's shoulders, and gripped him tight. He addressed his men:

"Sorcerer crew – we have a new man with us today. A man who would die for us. A man we would die for. A man with a cause to fight for. A wife to avenge. A people to annihilate. Shipp? You're going to be an officer of mine one day. Stay alive."

"Save your friend!" shouted Harden, Jennings, Yao, and Locke.

Shipp looked up at Garrison's steely frame. He resembled a living statue of an honored war hero who commanded respect, admiration, and brotherhood. Shipp arose and stood next to him.

"Say it again," Shipp said to Garrison.

"Stay alive!" Garrison declared.

"Save your friend!" the others shouted back. And this time, Shipp joined them, leading the response as the loudest voice. They continued repeating the refrain, ever louder, until crew members in the other parts of the Sorcerer heard and came to see what was happening. The entire crew joined in until their spirits united and ascended, and Shipp let out a huge smile and gave Garrison the biggest bear hug of his life.

James witnessed this final moment, through the open doorway. He wondered what Garrison had done to bring out such cathartic emotion from Shipp. And wondered even more if it was what Shipp truly needed.

36

Arrival

"Muzzle the HAT," Garrison ordered Blake and Reeves, sitting behind them a few weeks later in the Pilot Room.

Blake alerted Yao that the HAT would be disengaged momentarily. Yao notched his confirmation, and Reeves began the deceleration process. At top HAT speed, it took about thirty minutes to slow down to normal propulsion speed. The process could be delicate, because if for any reason the original flight path had been miscalculated, the pilot might have to adjust to an asteroid, planet, star, or other object that may have wandered too close to the trajectory. As with acceleration to HAT speed, everyone needed to remain strapped in somewhere during the slowdown. Thirty minutes later, Garrison arose.

"Head for the star and call me when we get there."

"Jonas that," replied Blake, as Garrison exited the top level. He found Shipp with Li observing Yao and his assistant Wallace managing the deceleration process, along with Mackson.

Garrison slapped his hands on both their backs. "We'll be at the star within the hour."

"How long until the convoys arrive?" Li asked.

"Harden sent a comm a few days back, and they should arrive a couple hours after us."

Shipp stepped into the Secondary Pilot Room and watched the Sorcerer's completed trajectory on the monitors. Always learning. Always training. Just like in the ground wars. Garrison and Li joined him.

"And once we hit PM4523, it's about a week to the battle site?" Shipp confirmed. Garrison nodded. "How do we plan for the unexpected in this situation?" Shipp asked.

"Once the convoys get here, we'll coordinate with them," Garrison said. "You have to remember, this is not like a ground battle. We cannot be destroyed with a single shot – of anything. Even if we get detected, fired upon, and hit before we can react, that will be our new on-site intel. Frankly, the Westers would be stupid to fire on us at such a great distance, because they know they can't do significant damage at that range."

"So if they are there, and if they do see us, they'll be attempting some sort of ambush or sneak attack," Shipp presumed.

"More than likely," Garrison confirmed. "Once we locate the damaged rat ship, if it's still there, we'll spend some time confirming we're alone and that the ship is derelict before we get too close. The convoys will make that go much faster."

"Then what? Destroy it? Board it?"

"What would you do?" Garrison turned the question back to him.

"I'd want to board it first, if we determine there's no one alive," Shipp said.

"Good," said Garrison, "Because I want you three to do a space walk if the situation merits."

With that, Garrison strode away. Shipp watched him, then looked at Li, who was very excited at the prospect of inspecting a Wester attack ship.

"I love his leadership style," said Li.

"Well yeah, you were working for Loshea all those years."

A little later, the Sorcerer came to a halt behind the red giant PM4523. Not long after that, three Peterson convoy ships arrived. Two convoys held five-person crews, and one held seven. The seven-person ship included the commander of the trio, Captain Rena.

She had convoyed for Garrison on two other occasions, and he wanted her for this mission because he trusted her and because they were so far from any other Peterson units. Plus, unlike many convoy captains, Rena didn't want to transfer to an attack ship one day. She believed leading convoys to be the best use of her piloting and leadership abilities. And she didn't like long deep-space missions. For Garrison, that meant he could count on Rena for years to come.

Garrison sat next to Harden in Comm-1 as Rena's ship arrived. Shipp stood nearby. Her voice came through the comm.

"Convoy mono-di-tri calling Sorcerer and General Garrison. How you doing you big wuss?" Rena began.

Garrison fired back, "Just fine you cripple," Garrison laughed. Shipp wondered why the insults, even if friendly. He hadn't seen this side of Garrison, and had shied away from this sort of thing in the ground wars, deciding that levity could be achieved through better methods. Garrison turned to Shipp, almost knowing his mind on this – the result of having spent the last several months getting to know him.

"She loves this sort of thing so I play along since we hardly ever see each other," Garrison said, with Rena still listening. "And she's missing her right pinky finger, by the way. Feel free to bring that up every chance you get."

Rena replied, "I've got more courage in my other pinky that you've got in your...oh well, you know the story on that. What do you have to report so far General?"

"We're a week out, as expected. I've got three new crew members – Thomas Shipp, Mansa Li, and Cam James. All vets of ground wars. Some of the best I've encountered. Shipp is an officer-in-training already," Garrison said. "You can talk to Shipp if you want – he's here."

"Pleasure to meet you Shipp. So this is your first attack ship mission?" Rena asked.

"It is, and this is looking like the best assignment of my life right now. Glad to meet you."

Rena replied, "I'll let Garrison fill you in on how we do business if he hasn't already. General, I only know a few details about this mission because they didn't want any chance of a leak."

"Harden will send you the brief, if he hasn't already," Garrison said. "Main thing I need is all your extra eyes. There's supposedly a damaged rat ship out here. If it's really there and if we can take it, we want to board it."

"Got it," Rena said. "And if it's there, there's a good chance the rats will be coming back for their lost toy. Hopefully after we're gone."

"Yeah, hopefully," said Garrison. "That's why you're here."

Over the next week, the Sorcerer led the approach toward the site of the previous battle. During that time, Garrison ran through various scenarios with Rena and the two captains of the other convoys, as well as Harden, Dons, Jennings, and Shipp.

The Sorcerer always took the lead, because if the Westers did attempt an attack from long distance, they'd be more likely to target a much less intimidating convoy ship. So, the Petersons approached the site in a single-file line, with the massive attack ship serving as a shield to the convoys.

The day arrived. The site drew near.

Shipp realized he'd spent months waiting for this day. So much waiting. In that regard, space battles weren't so different than ground battles. Lots of time between conflicts filled with planning and scenario building. Shipp got to watch from the top level as they approached the site. Garrison wanted him here. Later, he'd have him do a shift in Fire Control, but he wanted Shipp to experience their approach to this unique situation.

Harden called out from Comm-1, "LR picking up an object ahead. Size of an attack ship."

"Movement and speed?" Garrison replied.

"Looks derelict," replied Harden.

Shipp whispered to Jennings, who was there to answer any of Shipp's questions because Garrison couldn't afford the distraction, "I thought the LR only picked up motion. If the ship is dead, how is it detecting it?"

"Even dead ships drift," explained Jennings. "The only truly immobile ship is the one that wants to be."

"Would that mean a completely immobile ship would be invisible to the LR?" asked Shipp.

"Depends," replied Jennings. "The light rays would still bounce off it, so it would look like an asteroid, or like a void or blockage in space. But everything in space is moving, so an unmoving blockage we would usually assume to be manmade. That said, appearances can be deceiving. Space is funny."

"Give it a wide berth to the right and circle around," ordered Garrison. "Tell Rena to disperse her ships using scenario 3a."

Harden spoke to Rena, "Scenario 3a – disperse and patrol."

"Jonas," Rena replied.

Rena's convoy, dubbed mono-di-tri, broke from behind the Sorcerer. Rena's ship, the 'mono,' went left of Garrison. The 'di' broke right and headed underneath him, and the tri broke right and angled above him. From there, they had preplanned patrol and search patterns of the surrounding areas. Each convoy was equipped with its own LR sensors, so the whole armada could scan large areas of space with four LRs working in unison.

"Slow down," Garrison said to Blake. "Give me a visual if you can."

Blake angled the Sorcerer such that the front window faced the Wester ship as they passed it by. Garrison wanted to see it with his eyes, not just on the monitor.

"Give me sight," Garrison said.

Reeves activated the telescopic filter, which utilized the window as a visual enhancer, bringing the Wester ship much closer in view.

They could see numerous blast holes all over the ship. Garrison, Blake, and Reeves began an ongoing dialogue about what they could see. Places where K-rockets had impacted the surface. Openings where MagTons probably flew in. The top level on the Wester ship was clearly uninhabitable, because they could see the actual rooms. There, the exterior had been completely blown off.

"Looks beautiful," said Garrison. "Circle us around. Keep orientation constant."

The Sorcerer orbited the Wester ship, facing it the whole time, giving Garrison a clear sense of what he was up against.

"Any signs of attack, defense, movement, life?" Garrison called to Harden.

"None. Looks completely lifeless," Harden replied. "If they are baiting us, they're waiting an awful long time."

"Call Rena and get reports from her every two minutes," Garrison said to Harden. "We're going to Secondary Pilot to plan the space walk and boarding. Get me James, Li, and Mackson. Shipp, you're with me. Jennings, you're up."

In the Secondary Pilot Room on the mid-level, Garrison and the others crammed in and discussed the details of this stage of the plan. Wallace and Locke listened from outside the room.

Garrison began, "We're going to wait at least an hour longer before executing this. Bear in mind, none of us has ever actually boarded a

Wester attack ship. This is an extremely rare opportunity. I wish I could see it myself. Record everything. Take anything you need. Watch out for sealed rooms that somehow stayed intact."

Locke spoke up, "And remember, with the whole interior open to space, you can't hear a thing. So make sure you stay together, and don't be looking in the same direction, ever."

"Comms on at all times, without exception," Mackson said. "I'm in charge, but we're functioning as a single unit. We'll be tethered together, but you'll have a blade at your side. If for any reason you have to cut loose, use it."

"Any questions?" Garrison offered. No one spoke. "Okay – then get in your suits and get prepped."

Prepping for a space walk took a while, and by the time everyone was ready, that hour Garrison mentioned earlier had nearly elapsed. Peterson space suits were black, with neon green or gold stripes going up the sides and around various places. The design concept aimed for a semblance of invisibility, blending in with the blackness of space, but able to be spotted if you moved your arms and legs.

In the exit chamber, the same one the escape pod would use to exit the ship if it ever became necessary, Shipp, Li, James, and Mackson slipped into their space suits and helped each other affix their gear. Each took a pack that clipped to a harness on their chests. They each brought two AX-9s, the smallest weapon in the Peterson arsenal, but perfect for a situation like this because it could easily fit in a casing strapped to the thigh.

It would likely be dark on the Wester ship unless some emergency lights still managed to work, so each man packed several types of lights, some handheld, and some built into the space suit that they could flip on in an instant.

Each soldier brought two MagTons. They probably wouldn't need them. But, if something blocked their way, or if a situation arose where destroying a console or other part of the ship made tactical sense, they needed a quick and relatively safe way to do it.

The space suits included air burst propulsion units, so if any soldier got separated from the others or experienced an oxygen emergency, he could easily fly himself back to the Sorcerer or be flown back by another.

Every Space Fleet soldier underwent hundreds of hours practicing space walking before going on a mission, so this wasn't new to anyone.

Mackson hooked himself to the other three, and each of them to each other. They would fly as a single unit. This way, only one needed to use his propulsion unit, which conserved the air of the other three. Plus, even if three of them got injured or had any sort of trouble, just one remaining soldier could fly all four of them back. This is how it looked to save your friend in outer space.

After waiting in the cramped exit room for far too long, Harden called and gave the green light. Mackson opened the door. Total, dark, emptiness beheld them.

What a marvel.

But this wasn't a sightseeing trip, and they didn't have time to stare too long.

Each man clambered out the exit room and Mackson closed the door behind them. No tether held them to the Sorcerer. They would fly free from the start. The Sorcerer couldn't risk having them attached if it needed to fly off in a moment. They were on their own.

"James, you fly us," Mackson ordered.

The four of them pushed away from the Sorcerer using their legs, and James expertly manipulated his propulsion unit using his left hand. Space suits could be equipped with these controls on either hand, and each person could decide which type they preferred, and which hand they would rather have free. James released the first burst of air, and the foursome glided toward the derelict Wester ship.

37

Discovery

James knew not to fly too fast. Just a gentle approach. No reason to mess with a hard deceleration since they detected no apparent threats.

Garrison's voice crackled through their comms. "Guys are doing great. You're halfway there."

Hearing Garrison's voice oddly reassured Shipp. He didn't realize he needed reassuring, and yet, something about Garrison suddenly interrupting his blissful frictionless moment made him feel like the son of a proud but always watchful father who enjoys letting his children take risks and try new things. Garrison was nearing fifty, so he had almost twenty years on Shipp.

The foursome neared the Wester attack ship.

"Slow," said Mackson. "Crouch."

All four gave a few bursts facing toward the Wester ship so each would slow down. As they did this, they re-oriented their bodies with their legs pointing toward the surface so they could land on their feet and let their legs crouch and absorb the light impact. They landed near the severely damaged and exposed top level.

"Watch out for anything sharp," Mackson reminded. "No fast movements. Look before you move."

Good advice, because shards of metal, including Blackhead and other materials, jutted out from all sorts of places. The ship was shredded.

Once all four made it into the Wester version of a Pilot Room, they did a quick survey. Each man's suit had a recorder on the forehead, so everywhere they looked would become part of Peterson intelligence. This wasn't the first time in history the Petersons had boarded a Wester ship, but it was the first for anyone on the Sorcerer. So, they had some idea of what to expect in the layout. Still, it felt strange to see things in the 'wrong' places.

Mackson couldn't pry the door open to the lower levels. He motioned them back out. Li led the way since he was closest to the exit. They clambered around the ship like wasps on a nest, using propulsion when necessary. They reached the largest area of damage, a gaping hole near the rear, which provided easy entrance into the main level of the ship.

As expected, it was very dark. The farther they penetrated, the more light they needed. It seemed very unlikely that anyone could still be alive in here. After a cursory survey of the exposed area, the group approached an opening that led into an inner section, probably where the HAT resided. Mackson peered inside through a small blast hole caused by a MagTon.

"I can see bodies floating around. The HAT looks dark too," he said. "Let's blow it."

Mackson affixed both his MagTons near the hole he had just looked through, and set the timer for one minute. The four of them then reversed direction and slipped behind a corner to wait for the explosion. They heard nothing. But, after a burst of light, a few chunks of debris flew out from the maw of the ship at various speeds.

"Wait a bit before moving," Locke called over the comm, his voice of experience again jolting Shipp out of the fantasy that the four of them were alone. "Debris flies at different speeds."

Mackson waited another minute, and then led the four of them back around and up to the now much larger opening leading into this inner portion of the vessel. One person at a time could slip through without difficulty. Each of them did. And each of their mouths opened in utter disbelief at what they saw once they flipped on their lights.

The corpses floating around inside the HAT room weren't Westers.

"Uh..." Mackson began, trying to find the right words to say amidst his confusion and disbelief.

"These are Petersons," Li said. "All of them."

James quickly counted. "I count six bodies. All wearing Peterson space suits."

Garrison piped through. "Mack, can you confirm that with absolute certainty?" Garrison and Mackson knew how Wester uniforms should look in all their possible varieties. But there was no mistaking this. Upon closer inspection, they found the small PSF emblem on the backs.

"Yes General. These are Peterson Space Fleet soldiers," Mackson said. "Not a rat in sight."

"Watch out," Harden's voice came next. "There might be rats holed up in a room somewhere."

"I don't think so," said Mackson. "There are zero signs that anything has been touched in here for months."

He was right. Space dust had already collected on all the surfaces. Darkness reigned. Shipp took a closer look at one of the bodies. He flipped it over to see the face.

"Li, James, take a look," he said.

Li and James air bursted over. The Peterson's face shield had been eaten away. So had the face. A foul sight. Shipp looked at Li and James. They knew exactly what this was. Mackson looked too, and he repulsed at the sight of what remained of the dead soldier, so unrecognizable that not a single identifiable facial feature remained.

Shipp hardened. Rage again pulsed through his veins and boiled out through his eyes.

"The virus."

"What?" Mackson said, still not putting it together. "What about the virus?"

"The virus killed this person," James told him while Shipp and Li quickly reached each of the other bodies and looked at what little remained of their faces.

"And all the rest of them," Shipp confirmed.

"Wait a minute, you mean the virus you saw on Lavoisier?" Mackson asked, trembling. "So it's on this ship? It's here?"

He instantly turned into a sweaty mess. But Li, James, and Shipp remained calm. Interestingly, no one from the Sorcerer spoke. They listened, and let the boarding team solve the problem.

"Don't worry," Li told him. "The virus would have diffused out into space through that hole long ago."

"Well," said Shipp. "Not if it's coming from an enclosed room that remained intact."

"So you're telling me the Westers knew they had lost their ship, but before the last person died, they set some kind of delayed virus bomb to go off and kill a boarding crew that might never come?" Mackson said as he worked out the most likely scenario while saying it. He was an external processor.

Shipp nodded.

"That seems likely," said James. "I think we can assume every Wester ship has some sort of virus release mechanism. It might even be automated. It could be on a motion sensor, in which case..."

Shipp and Li got nervous now.

"Yeah, it could. We're not prepared for this. Let's exit the room," Shipp said.

"Can it still kill us out there?" Mackson asked, still petrified but not enough to lose his wits.

"From what we saw, it's based on concentration. So no," said Li.

The four men exited one at a time through the enlarged hole. Outside, in the cratered section of the ship, they assessed the situation.

"Check your suit. Check your face shields. Look at something nearby and see if the glass is blurring," Shipp ordered. He had to take command of the scene, because in this situation, Mackson had the least experience of the four of them. It didn't appear that anyone had been in contact with the virus. All their shields remained clear.

"What do we do then?" asked Mackson. "We want to access their records, collect intel, see if they've made any technical improvements. Can we still do that?"

"We can do it out here for sure," said James. "In there?" That two-word question summed up the hesitancy of the group.

Eventually, they decided to begin collecting detailed intelligence from the portions of the ship they could deem safe, which meant anything broadly exposed to the vastness of space. After a couple hours of this, Garrison's voice interrupted them.

"Update fellas. Just so you know, Rena's team has no enemy contacts. So we're in the clear on that. Harden, Jennings, and I have been talking, and we have a theory."

"What is it?" asked Shipp, still functioning as the new leader, which Mackson didn't seem to mind at all. Ego played no part in his work.

"We think they might be trying to protect some secrets using this anti-boarding virus weapon. Why else do it? Why go to that much trouble, just to kill a few soldiers in a boarding party? Granted, killing any soldiers counts for something, but that's a shipload of effort for a very unlikely scenario," Garrison explained.

"And," Harden continued, "If this weapon really is meant to shift the balance of power in their favor, this is a pretty minuscule way to use it. They can wipe out entire planets with this stuff, but they're using it to kill a few soldiers who will probably never arrive? That doesn't add up for us."

"So they're hiding something," Shipp affirmed. "And that means we need to go back in that room."

"Yes," Garrison said. "If, and only if, you believe you can do so safely."

"Well, none of us have any symptoms or signs of any presence of the virus, and we were in that room for several minutes. If it was there, that's long enough," Shipp said. "Right?" He looked at James and Li, wondering if his confidence was misguided.

James and Li looked at each other, then back at Shipp. Does anyone want to admit they're still afraid?

"How long would it take to make it back to the Sorcerer if we notice symptoms?" asked Li.

Mackson knew this one. "At the present distance, with me flying us, I could have us there in less than a minute, once we're clear of this vessel."

Li nodded back at Shipp, "Good enough for me."

James and Shipp agreed they had enough of a safety margin. So, the four of them entered into the HAT room once again.

They left the Sorcerer with about eight hours of oxygen, and they intended to use just about all of it. Minute by minute, hour by hour, the four men searched every inch of the ship. They examined mechanical differences between the Wester ship and their own. Took photos and video footage. Collected samples when appropriate.

They even turned on any monitors they could make work and tried to navigate through the Wester technology. But, like Peterson ships, very little territorial military information was stored on attack ships, for exactly the reason that was now in play. Attack ships only needed enough to carry out their current missions. No reason to store anything that could compromise any other active missions, locations, stations, ships, or personnel.

But then, after about six hours, Mackson made a discovery.

Against one of the walls in the HAT room, near all the standard propulsion machinery, he found a small, cubic, yellow box, about the size of a human fist. It was wired into the other tech, and would have been easy to overlook for Shipp, Li, and James. But Mackson was the Mid-Level Control Officer. The Wester ships weren't identical of course, but the propulsion areas were fairly similar, and he was able to make pretty smart guesses about the purposes for most of what he saw.

But not this.

Random objects just weren't brought on attack ships. Everything had to have a purpose. The more he studied it, he realized it wasn't actually connected to any of the propulsion technology. Because so much of this area of the room was destroyed, he exposed the remaining wiring leading from the yellow cube and discovered it led to the Wester version of a backup pilot room. In there, it hooked into the main flight monitors. The Petersons had nothing like this on their ships.

With just under an hour of oxygen left, Mackson told everyone what he had found and asked Garrison for an opinion.

"Whatever it does," Mackson said, "Disconnecting it might also disable it. Our best chance to understand it might be to work through the Wester monitors. On the other hand, it might not matter at all."

"I don't want you guys over there again after tonight. Can't take the risk," said Garrison. "Bring it here and we'll do our best to figure it out."

"Jonas that."

And with that, he motioned to the others to hook back into each other's tethers. They had separated while searching around the ship so they could cover more ground. Once re-connected, Mackson led the way back out into open space. With a short air burst, the foursome cleared the ship, and Mackson ordered Shipp to take them back to the Sorcerer at a slow speed. Several minutes later, they were back home, removing their space suits, replenishing their energy, and preparing to rejoin the crew.

A couple hours later, Mackson brought out the yellow cube and placed it before Yao, Garrison, Jennings, Harden, Dons, and Blake. Because no one knew what it did, it made sense to give each expert a look. Shipp, James, and Li went to take a rest. Garrison told them they would hold here for a few hours, and then prepare for the return trip after obliterating what remained of the Wester ship.

Lying in his domicile, just as he was about to close his eyes, Shipp realized something. He bolted up and ran out to address Garrison, who was deeply interested in this yellow cube.

"I got a question," Shipp interrupted as he threw open the door. "Why wouldn't the Peterson ships that came back from this battle have told us they lost crew members here? Wouldn't they have known their guys had boarded the ship and been killed?"

Garrison and the others all sat back from the cube and stared off into space, thinking.

Harden couldn't take it. "Impossible. They'd have no reason not to report it. I can't imagine a single reason."

"Neither can I," said Shipp. "That means there was another Peterson ship that must have shown up afterward. Where did those six guys come from? We have their names and information. Can you check?"

Garrison demurred. "Depends. Attack ships don't keep personnel files about any other ships, as you know. But we could send a message back to SFC."

"Do we really want to wait here for a week or two until they respond?" asked Harden.

"Well, something isn't right," said Garrison. "There's any number of possible explanations. If any of those would require us to come back here, it makes more sense to stay now."

Garrison could see Harden wasn't convinced. He didn't want to stay here waiting for a possible Wester ship to catch them with their pants down. Garrison looked to Jennings for his opinion.

"Let's see what Rena thinks," suggested Jennings. Moments later, they had Rena up to speed on the situation.

"Six dead Petersons on a Wester ship light years from anywhere," she mused. "And our people didn't report any losses. Yes, I can tell you exactly what happened, and why none of you can figure it out."

"You don't say," said Garrison. "You calling me blind, you cripple?"

"I'm calling you an attack ship general who knows everything about attack ships. But not a whole lot about much else."

"Thanks for the compliment," Garrison retorted. "So what's your explanation."

"Six crew sounds like a convoy crew. My guess is one of the two convoy ships that got lost didn't actually get destroyed. They got marooned here, by two careless attack ship generals. Probably damaged, disabled, unable to communicate. Stuck in space. And they realized they might have a chance to survive by boarding the Wester ship."

"I like this lady," Shipp interrupted. "That's brilliant. Jennings, good call getting the convoy perspective."

"Send me the names of the dead," Rena said.

Harden ran over to Comm-2, since they were on mid-level, and sent her the six names. Rena looked at them.

"I know three of these. I've flown missions with them," she said. "And I've got questions for the Mauler and the Stealth. This isn't what it means to save your friend."

Rena's anger bled through the comm. The Sorcerer officers validated it with their silence.

Then, Garrison looked at Shipp. "Now you see why I asked for her on this mission."

"Okay," said Harden. "I'm with you Rena. I assume now we're heading back so we can sort this out?" Harden asked Garrison.

"Yeah," concurred Garrison. "We'll rest for six hours. Second shift can prep the ship. Ewing and Molon plan the return flight. Dons, once we're set to leave, you fire into that hulk and blow it to pieces. Rena? Have your ships park near us so we'll look like one ship to anything that might spot us from a distance."

"Jonas that."

Everyone departed to get some rest while Jennings went to brief the backup pilots Ewing and Molon.

About four hours later, their rest was cut short.

The battle alarm jolted Shipp and everyone else awake. He threw open his door in time to see Cardmanov running through the hallway.

"What happened?" Shipp asked him.

"LR picked up an attack ship approaching," Cardmanov said. "You're in Fire Control."

"I'm already there," Shipp exclaimed while he threw on his uniform as James, Li and others awoke and did the same.

38

Space Battle

Dons already occupied his position in the Weapons Supply Room when Shipp practically jumped down the stairwell. Jimenez sat at one firing station. The other five were empty since Cardmanov had run upstairs to corral everyone. Shipp looked to Dons for where to sit.

Dons pointed to the middle chair on the starboard side, with Jimenez to his left. Moments later, the others arrived. Dons assigned Marley to the right side of Shipp, and Cardmanov, Abe, and Li on port, with Li in the middle spot. He wanted James next to him so he could watch how Dons managed a battle.

When Shipp put on his comm, Harden's voice was already audible.

"LR has them about two minutes away from the derelict ship at present speed. Best guess is they haven't spotted us since we're at a good distance and unmoving."

Garrison cut in.

"We're gonna sit here as long as possible. Prepare for accelerated speed out of the gate on my mark. Rena, you're going to fan out from behind us and give them four targets from what looked like one."

Shipp looked at Dons, then to Marley.

"They always said it's bad to stay still. But since they haven't seen us yet?"

Marley nodded. "Most likely, yeah." Marley then flipped off his comm and addressed the room. "New guys – they're coming in soon with a firing strategy. Be ready."

Dons spoke up from his station, "LR data confirms it's a standard Wester attack ship, just like the destroyed one. Data from the space walk allowed us to pinpoint exact locations of several of their shield array ports. I'm feeding those into your targeting computers."

Shipp watched his monitor, and noticed several points appearing at specific locations on a diagram of a Wester ship. Dons kept talking.

"They don't see us yet, so unless that changes we'll do a bombardment after they start to slow down. If they do see us, same plan just re-mark the target and adjust for higher speed."

Harden's voice came through again.

"Rat ship starting to slow. Thirty seconds and they'll be stopped."

Yao's voice came through next.

"Propulsion set for accelerated jump to max conventional speed. You can fire and then go."

While Yao was talking, Dons gave a second set of orders.

"Starboard side target points S1, S4, and S8. Port target R3, R5, and T3. Two Krocks per station. I'll send a second target package and we'll do the same thing. Once their array is weakened, we'll pound more Krocks, then a glut of Mags once we tear a hole. Fire at my order, in sequence."

Cardmanov shouted to the room. "Jimenez, have TIs ready on your side. I'm ready on port."

Dons spoke again, "Marley – prep a nink so it's ready if we need it."

Shipp realized this was a rare situation, where you could sit here and plan out your entire attack without being spotted. In a more typical battle, both ships would be moving and would know the other was there.

Garrison's voice came through now, addressing Rena.

"Weapons targeted Rena, you be ready for whatever response they send."

Harden interrupted. "Westers veering sharply. Retarget! They've spotted us!"

Dons barked, "Track and fire! 3, 2, 1!"

Jimenez and Cardmanov fired two K-rockets each. Shipp and Li followed almost immediately, and Marley and Abe after them. There was almost no chance the Wester ship could be ready for this so soon, and it was unlikely they could release any TIs in time. This was the Petersons' single best chance to hit them hard.

Dons barked again, "Fire second battery!"

Another dozen K-rockets burst from the Sorcerer and shot toward the second targeting package. All 24 Krocks hit their targets.

Dons yelled to his weapons team, "S4, S8, R3, R5 direct hits. Broke their shields in the red regions on your monitors. Retarget those spots and fire at will."

"Go," Garrison's voice ordered Blake and Reeves as at least thirty more Krocks left the Sorcerer. It accelerated from its stopped position perpendicular to the direction the Wester ship had taken after seeing them. The three Peterson convoy ships fanned out around the Sorcerer and flew toward the Wester ship, in the wake of the K-rockets.

"Send a horde of mags – no detonation!" Dons yelled out.

"Where?" Shipp asked.

"Where their shields are gone," said Marley.

Shipp joined Marley and the others firing at least a dozen MagTons each, and these traveled behind the Peterson convoy ships, matching their speed as they approached the Wester ship.

Meanwhile, the K-rockets burned hyper fast toward the Wester ship. Because the Sorcerer had let them get so close before being spotted, the enemy ship just didn't have time to react. All thirty impacted the surface at six different points. Harden sent fresh data on the Wester ship to Dons. The convoys accelerated past the Wester ship, exposing the approaching horde of MagTons, all of which attached to the surface but did not yet explode.

"Why did we do that?" asked Shipp.

Marley answered again, "Dons set them on manual from his station. He wanted them attached before they could launch anti-magnets. Now we've got them in place and he'll blow them when timing is right."

The Wester ship, realizing it was being pursued by four other ships, quickly accelerated. But it wouldn't be able to engage its HAT for several minutes at the earliest, and the Petersons needed to take advantage of this window.

They could still pursue at HAT speed, but with much more difficulty because they wouldn't know the exact flight path of the enemy. But planning a HAT flight while fleeing four Peterson ships wouldn't be easy for the Westers either, because if they just kept flying in a straight line and constant speed, they might as well be standing still. And as long as their vectors kept changing, HAT calculations would be almost impossible.

Abe fired four more K-rockets at the R3 and R5 areas, on the rear of the ship. Marley followed them with four more, but in a different flight path, with much more arc. About five seconds later, Jimenez fired four more, arcing in a totally different direction.

"Shipp, four Krocks at mark 18," Dons yelled. Arc the flight path to 34 degrees!"

Shipp made the adjustments and fired four K-rockets.

"Li, Card, dump your rocks on my mark!" Dons ordered.

Shipp deduced Dons' strategy. The four of them had all targeted the same spot on the Wester ship, but approaching from different directions, in case the Wester ship launched Tracking Interceptors. Li and Cardmanov would then fire everything left in their cache at same spot again, hoping the Westers wouldn't be ready for a second barrage.

The Westers did release a series of TIs. They fired them to intercept the four K-rockets fired by Abe. Moments later, they fired more at the ones fired by Marley. Abe's K-rockets angled toward the Wester ship, but then two exploded before reaching it, impacting the TIs. The other two flew off in the wrong direction.

"I'll get those," said Dons, able to reacquire control of K-rockets that didn't explode. All four of Marley's got taken out by TIs. But because of the timing and the vastly different approach vectors, all four of Jimenez's rockets hit the Wester ship in rear, and Shipp's hit it soon after.

"Nailed it!" Dons screeched.

Garrison boomed over the comm at Blake, "Close the gap! Catch up! Yao! Are we at full acceleration?"

"Not yet," replied Yao.

But Rena's ships, able to accelerate faster, had already caught up with the Wester ship and were pummeling it from three sides with smaller arms, targeting MagTons at shield array ports, and pounding it with smaller K-rockets.

The Wester ship was overwhelmed with so much coming at it from all directions, and would never escape relying on TIs. Instead, they decided to target one ship at a time. They fired a series of K-rockets at the 'di' convoy ship, forcing it to veer off and circle around. It would be several minutes before it could rejoin the attack. Other rockets fired toward the other two convoys, but didn't target as well, and the 'mono' and the 'tri' evaded them and kept pace.

Rena's ship shot past the Wester ship and angled across its bow, firing K-rockets from its rear directly at the top level of the Wester ship, hoping to blind their visuals. A risky move to fly so close to the ship, but she gambled correctly that they had too much to handle to target her in time. Plus, they wouldn't expect such a bold maneuver so early in a battle.

The Wester ship angled off to the left and unleashed a barrage of K-rockets toward the Sorcerer. Seventeen rockets hurtled toward them, and would impact in seconds.

"TI blanket!" Dons shouted.

Cardmanov and Jimenez were ready, and began firing bundles of four TIs at one Wester rocket at a time. One at a time, the Wester rockets exploded in space. They hadn't had time to target the Sorcerer, so this random spread of rockets was easier to pick up. But, with so many fired at once, five made it through and impacted on the port side of the Sorcerer.

The vessel shook slightly. Shipp looked around the room. None of the other weapons specialists seemed to budge. Laser focused.

"Li, Card," Dons said, "Rena hit them pretty good on the top level. Retarget your rock dumps at her point of impact, T4 to T8 – pick a spot."

But the Westers made a wise tactical move. The 'di' convoy, which had been forced to break off its flight and circle around alone, was by itself. The Westers turned, but not just to escape the attack. They turned to intercept the convoy, all by itself heading back in their direction.

Using TIs to fight off as many attacks as they could from behind and on the sides, the Westers fired a barrage of 25 K-rockets toward the oncoming 'di' convoy. The convoy picked it up and angled away. It released its entire stock of TIs, which intercepted about half the K-rockets. But because the distances were closing so fast since the ships were heading straight for each other, the other half made it through.

Seven rockets hit the convoy. A huge burst of light caused Rena's other two ships to look in that direction, which was much easier than on attack ships since convoys had more of their surfaces occupied by windows.

She knew that wasn't good.

"They're down!" she shouted to Garrison.

The convoy wasn't destroyed yet, but it was badly disabled. The Wester ship angled toward the convoy. They weren't going to fire again. They were going to plow right through it.

Rena's other two ships fired everything they could to stop it, but the Westers bulled forward, realizing their only chance of getting out of this was to take out one ship at a time, rather than try to fight them all at once. And they did. Their much larger, Blackhead-armored attack ship rammed the convoy and shredded it into nothing.

"Flame it!!" Rena shouted.

Because Rena's other two ships hit it so hard on the front end, the Wester ship veered away from them, back toward the Sorcerer.

Dons saw it. This was his chance.

"Li, Card – dump your rocks now! Target!"

Li and Cardmanov emptied their caches of the remaining K-rockets, 22 in all, arcing toward the front of the Wester ship, which had just now turned toward their direction.

"Abe! Marley! Hit the initial targets with more Krocks and I'll detonate the attached Mags!" Dons barked.

That meant Shipp and Jimenez too. All four of them fired five K-rockets each toward the R3 and R5 points on the rear. With Rena's two ships causing so much trouble for the Westers, they were again being fired upon from multiple trajectories all at once.

They released a swath of TIs, dozens of them. But again, with the distances closing so fast because Dons had fired so early, anticipating where the Westers ship was headed, the TIs weren't able to catch more than half the rockets, and only from the group heading for the top level. All twenty of the others hit the rear of the ship. Dons manually released the MagTons that were attached to the Wester ship in that vicinity, and re-directed them into whatever hole had been created by the twenty rockets.

Meanwhile, the remaining rockets that escaped the TIs pounded the top level of the Wester ship so hard that debris broke off – a very good sign.

"Mags! Marley! Send in your nink!" Dons yelled.

The other five weapons specialists fired tons of MagTons into the top level opening they had just created, and Marley fired a nuke-tipped K-rocket at the same spot. Explosion after explosion caused flashes of light to blanket the space around them, like a lightning storm from behind a planet.

"Hit 'em again!" Garrison ordered over the comm.

"Rear of the ship is damaged but not broken through yet!" said Harden.

"Dump your rocks – all four of you!", ordered Dons. Li and Cardmanov had emptied theirs already and Dons was re-stocking them. The other four targeted the rear of the ship yet again.

"Rena!" Dons called. "Take out their TIs coming from the rear!"

The mono and the tri broke off their attacks as the Peterson bombardment of K-rockets approached the Wester ship. The Westers released a huge array of TIs, as Dons expected. Rena and the other ship fired a bunch of their own rockets toward the TIs. Since they were much closer to the Wester ship than the Sorcerer, their rockets reached them first and detonated almost all the TIs.

The Westers must be panicking now, Rena thought with delight.

Nearly every Peterson K-rocket fired from the Sorcerer impacted the ever-enlarging rip on the rear of the ship, and they burrowed in deeper with each impact. Wester munitions spilled out the hole. Dons anticipated this, and sent a nuke-tipped K-rock to each weapons specialist.

All six of them fired. Three entered the enlarging hole in the Wester ship. The others exploded just outside it. The three that made it inside caused a huge explosion to burst out the backside, with debris shooting in all directions. The ship shuddered, slowed, and angled upward from the rear, drifting.

"Dead in space!!" Dons exulted. "They're immobile!"

"I think you reached their HAT, or close enough," Harden confirmed.

"Slow down and give me an orbit around the ship," Garrison ordered Blake, and the Sorcerer began circling the drifting Wester attack ship. The two remaining convoy ships flew parallel to it.

Dons addressed the Fire Control Room, "Well done everyone. Exceptional. It's not every day you get to take out an attack ship. Whoever leads that ship didn't appear to anticipate our presence here at all."

Shipp pondered the unique attributes of the battle, and understood the rarity of their accomplishment. To know the location of a damaged Wester ship is rare enough. In this case, because they capitalized on that opportunity, knowing full well the Westers may attempt to salvage their vessel, they were able to leverage the element of surprise. But the battle wouldn't have been so one-sided without the convoys. Four against one. Just too lopsided.

The most impressive thing to Shipp was how so many men on the Sorcerer could operate as one – they were of the same mind, unified in strategy, even adapting in unison to specific moments they could not have anticipated. They just knew what to do when the moment came. And Dons really was a space battle genius, Shipp decided. He would tell him so after they confirmed the Westers were indeed deceased or incapacitated.

Dons continued talking, "Abe and Marley remain here on alert. The rest of you can depart for now. Garrison will probably run this holding pattern for a while before destroying the ship."

"Don't you think we should board it?" Shipp asked.

"Not my call," said Dons. "I just blow them up."

Shipp wanted to see if this ship also had one of the same yellow cubes. He felt it was worth the risk. He started up the stairwell to meet with Garrison, Jennings, and Harden, to make the case.

39

Yao's Counterpart

"Are you out of your mind?" Harden replied to Shipp when he proposed boarding the Wester ship. "This one probably has the same virus anti-boarding trap that killed the other six. And you want to float right into that?"

"I know how to recognize the virus. It doesn't penetrate or break down materials immediately. There are warning signs. We can easily make it back here in time," Shipp assured him.

"And bring it back here to kill the rest of us?" Harden persisted. "For what? A yellow box that may just be a glorified light switch?"

"The virus doesn't work that way," Shipp told him. "It doesn't multiply or spread. It reacts to surfaces and transmits through the air. Get out of its presence, and any virus on our space suits will stay there."

"How do you know that for sure?" Harden asked.

"Because I marched through air that was filled with it on Lavoisier, and led 24 soldiers to safety. Once inside the life capsule, we were safe," said Shipp.

Harden had heard this story already, as had Garrison, Jennings, Locke, Yao, and Dons, all of whom were meeting to discuss what to do about the Wester ship. Harden cocked his head to Garrison, wondering what he thought of all this. Then he looked at Locke. Locke spoke first.

"Whatever you do, from the sound of it I can't treat this virus at all. I'll be as useless as a screen door on a transport ship."

"But would you authorize a boarding?" Harden asked him.

"Is anything around here up to me?" Locke said, avoiding taking a stand. "He's right. He knows this virus better than me."

Garrison wanted to settle this. "Rena's ships have detected movement on the Wester ship. So have we, right Harden?" Harden nodded. "So the real issue here is, can we board without being killed? If the rats are still alive, the virus is a non-issue for now. Harden – you've got a number of boarding scenarios worked up. Let's use one of them."

"I'm pretty sure Shipp told us the Westers killed their own people with this plague when they got backed into a corner," Harden said. "They don't value life like we do, as if we needed any more proof of that."

"You're saying they'd release the virus to kill us even if it would kill them too?" Jennings said.

"Why not? They know they're gonna die anyway," Harden replied.

"No," Shipp shot him down. "Not a chance. This virus, dying from this thing is about the worst way to go. The Wester prisoners on Lavoisier were almost wetting themselves when they realized what was happening. They were more scared of this than anything we could do to them. Way more. The hallway situation was a chaotic battle, not a calculated move."

"Dying in the vacuum of space is less scary than dying from this virus?" Jennings asked.

"The admins on Lavoisier were cowards," Shipp said. "No one on an attack ship, Wester or Peterson, will do what they did. That's my assessment."

Harden accepted Shipp's assessment, and the decision was unanimous. Not that it needed to be. Garrison could just order it. But that sort of authoritarian approach just wasn't the Peterson Way. Any mission has the highest chance of success when everyone on board fully embraces it. Especially on an attack ship out in the vastness of space.

"Okay," Garrison said. "Harden, break out the scenario that best fits what we're dealing with, and let's master it. Then we'll break for the ship, kill any survivors, and go from there."

A couple days later, Garrison's orders were almost fulfilled. Harden found a scenario for a six-man strike team that worked well for this situation. Harden would lead it, with Mackson, Shipp, Wallace, Cardmanov, and Jimenez rounding out the group. Garrison wanted Wallace there, Yao's assistant, to get better on-site expertise if they found another yellow cube, assuming the nukes hadn't vaporized it. The group simulated the plan a couple dozen times, each time encountering different unexpected surprises.

The plan presumed one important fact – that the Westers would not know they were coming. Harden felt confident about this due to the apparent loss of power. It was a gamble, but he reasoned that any surviving Westers were probably spending all their effort just to survive. Things like securing provisions and air. They might have gotten off an emergency comm to their version of Space Force Command, but no one would make it here for weeks, if not months.

The six men crammed into the escape pod's exit chamber and donned their suits. Mackson would fly the group over this time, because a precise landing zone had been marked out. They would land on the ship in a location where no visual detection would be possible. If the Westers had no functional or accessible LR or other instruments, the Petersons would be totally unnoticed.

Unlike the last trip, on this one each Peterson carried an AX-15, along with a Morse mine. Except Mackson – he had to direct the connected team to the landing zone. Once there, the group untethered from each other, and Mackson armed up as well.

From the landing site, Harden's first task was to see if anyone remained on the top level. One notch, one crevice, one shield array port at a time, Harden made his way around the girth of the vessel, approaching the viewing space through which he would be able to see inside the top level of the Wester ship.

He wanted this task because he knew the top level better than anyone else in the team. The other members held their position in the landing zone, except for Jimenez, who traversed the ship until he found a spot about halfway between Harden and the others. He was the only person who could see everyone. Without Jimenez, Harden would be out of everyone's sight.

Harden reached a precipice, knowing the viewing window would be on the other side. He had near total confidence the room had been destroyed in battle, and they had more or less visually verified it already. But, things look different when you're right next to them.

Harden flipped off his head lamp and gripped the precipice with one hand. He slowly lifted himself up so he could peer over the edge and into the top level Pilot Room. The window was indeed blown out. Rena pelted this part of the ship, and she shredded it.

Harden vaulted himself over the precipice and used air bursts to land quietly near the Wester monitors. All dark, except one. Harden studied it. It took some time to decide which controls did what. His focus consumed him, so much that he startled when Jimenez flipped on his head lamp to get Harden's attention. Jimenez had come the rest of the way because Harden had been out of sight too long. This was part of the plan, and it meant that Cardmanov now held the position formerly occupied by Jimenez.

Harden laughed at his own surprise, and flipped his own head lamp back on.

They weren't using their comms in case the Westers had some kind of monitoring capability. Harden used his hands to direct Jimenez to the monitor. He had determined that one small area of the ship remained habitable. He explained this to Jimenez using hand signals. Tapping his chest with his palm meant someone was alive.

He worked out which area of the ship still had life support and told Jimenez to return to the others. Harden intended to find his way into the belly of the ship from here, and the other five would enter through the large gap in the rear.

With no comms, Jimenez had to communicate to the other four men what Harden had found. They made their way down to the hole in the rear of the ship, and entered it one at a time. Once inside, it didn't take long to figure out where the surviving Westers were.

The whole right side of the ship had been torn to pieces. The nukes must have impacted that side for some reason. They could see patches of outer space through sections of the outer wall. That side of the ship now resembled a crumpled beehive, with various sections bent, twisted, and mangled. Above them, the HAT itself was exposed and damaged, as expected.

All this was typical of a defeated attack ship. Winning a space battle hinged on penetrating the hull in one spot, and then sending as many weapons as you could through that hole. The interior of most attack ships wasn't as well fortified as the exteriors, where most of the Blackhead was utilized. So, once inside, conventional weapons could do far more damage. Krocks tear the hole, and the other weapons exploit it.

A destroyed attack ship often resembled a cracked egg with some of the contents missing. And that's what the Petersons saw.

But above them and to the left, one section in the mid-level remained intact. The surviving section most likely included just sleeping quarters. Perhaps a medical room or a secondary comm station. How did they still have power for this section? That was a mystery, but some fuel cells apparently still operated somewhere. Probably they had them distributed throughout the ship for situations like this, so different parts of the ship could remain habitable.

Shipp and Mackson hunted for the yellow cube in the wreckage of the HAT room. They found it. The same cube. More damaged than the other one, but clearly the same device. They called Wallace over to study it. A little later, Harden pried through debris between here and the top level, and saw his five comrades below.

He made his way down to them and noted the cube. Then, he angled his gaze up to the area where survivors would be. Cardmanov got everyone's attention, and pointed to a partially destroyed closet, part of what used to be mid-level. Inside, they could see a stash of weapons – AX-15s, MagTons, and even a Mossamer-24. What remained of their weapons supply room for the crew.

Cardmanov's point was that, if this closet was still full, it was less likely the surviving Westers had any weapons. Harden gestured back, folding his hands and then tapping his helmet. It meant that personal weapons, like ones stored in a domicile, could still be in the Westers' possession.

But the plan was clear. They would head up to what appeared to be the easiest entry point into the habitable area. Break in, and reseal the door. Breaking in would cause a vacuum, probably rendering any Wester attempt to retaliate impossible. It was also unlikely the habitable area had gravity, since that required a functioning HAT.

The risk of being attacked was getting smaller and smaller.

At the entry point, Cardmanov and Wallace prepared to pull open the door. The other four would force themselves in against the vacuum of space, and Cardmanov and Wallace would close it behind them, remaining outside. That would be the fastest way to get men inside the area and preserve enough atmosphere to remove helmets and be able to talk.

There might also be other rooms in the secured area, and if the doors to those rooms were closed, anyone inside would be relatively unaffected by the entry of the Petersons.

Cardmanov and Wallace gripped the door, wedged their feet and legs appropriately, and pried it open with the aid of specialized tools. Sure enough, air began billowing out. Using hooks, and crawling through the opening around the borders of the entrance, Harden, Shipp, Mackson, and Jimenez made it inside the room in about twenty seconds, and the door shut behind them.

They could feel the air replenishing. That meant an oxygen supply somewhere. The lights worked, and it was warm. But no Westers. The hallway curved slightly, with a clear ending point about ten meters ahead. They could see three rooms with closed doors all on the right side from their position. Harden removed his helmet and ordered the others to do the same.

"Hug the wall," Harden said. Then, he raised his voice and addressed the Westers.

"We're on your ship. We're in your hallway. We're heavily armed. If you're still alive, come out right now and you won't be harmed. Try to hide from us, or play dead, or pretend you aren't there, and we'll blow out one room at a time. You've got five seconds to come out!"

Hooking one leg to the walls or floor to keep from floating off, Harden and the other three held their AX's ready. Three seconds later, the middle door opened. Two men floated out, with empty hands. Right after that, the far door opened, and another man appeared. Three survivors.

"What about this room?" Harden pointed to the nearest one.

"Empty ya," said the man from the farthest room. "Just storage, eh."

"Mind if we confirm that?" Harden asked without taking his eyes off his enemy for a millisecond.

"Be my guest bro," said the same man. "Or ya I'll do it for you."

This surprised all the Petersons. But the man pushed himself toward them, far more casually than you would expect. At this point, Shipp noticed a difference in uniform between him and the other two.

"You're not a soldier," said Shipp. "What are you?"

"Thrust Controller say," said the man.

The Thrust Controller approached, and the Petersons gave him space, as wide a berth as they could in the limited hallway space. The Thrust Controller unlatched the door, entered it, and swung it open, holding it so they could see.

"We barely survived your attack bro. We're just waiting, hoping someone found us, ya," he said to Harden.

Harden looked at the other two. "Who are you? Position and rank."

"They're just gunners. You killed all our officers except me, say," said the Thrust Controller.

"Why don't they talk?" asked Harden.

"Because they think all of this still matters," said the Thrust Controller. At this, without any warning, he drew an AX-9 sidearm from his coat, pointed it as his own men, and shot them both dead.

The Petersons instinctively pointed their weapons straight at the Thrust Controller. But he immediately threw down his weapon, and kept his back to them while it floated away.

"Brave," said Shipp. "That was... very brave. Wow. You guys don't seem to think much of killing your own men though. Not the first time I've seen it."

The Thrust Controller spun around, keeping his hands out to his sides as best he could. "My men?" He asked this in a deadpan tone that suggested he just didn't care anymore.

Harden approached him, felt into his various pockets and around his belt. After being searched, the Thrust Controller pushed his feet down to the floor and held on to the grating, leaning his back against the wall opposite the doors. He lowered his head. A defeated man with no will to fight.

"So? You gonna kill me bro? Take me prisoner? What's the plan ya?" he asked.

"Why did you kill those guys?" asked Harden. "I don't get it."

"I knew they would try to fight you, ya. I knew they wouldn't cooperate. I just didn't want to get caught in the crossfire see."

"Self-preservation," said Jimenez. "That all you have left?"

"You got anything better eh?" said the Thrust Controller.

Shipp grabbed the yellow cube from Mackson and showed it to the Thrust Controller. "What is this?"

The Thrust Controller laughed. "How'd you guys find that? Out of this entire ship ya, you find the one thing we have that you don't."

"One thing?" Harden asked. "Two things. You have the virus on board too."

The Thrust Controller shook his head. "You blew it out into space see. That part of the ship is wasted."

"What is it?" Shipp asked. "Will you tell us?"

"I'll tell you anything you want to know, ya. Just get me off this ship before you blow it to dust."

"Why?" Shipp replied. "We've dealt with a lot of rats. No one ever just talks. Why you? Why should we believe you?"

"What, you still think this war means anything ya?" The Thrust Controller started laughing ruefully. "You know, on our way here, the captain was going on about how someday we were going to retake this whole area see, and it reminded me of this ground battle I was in once on Kora ya. We had just taken this hilly area, and everyone was celebrating ya. Lots o' cheers and ya. But something about that area jogged my brain ya know. I went back to base, right, and I found this video I'd seen in training years before. These guys in the video had taken the same exact area, like sixty years before ya, and were talkin' real big about what a huge big massive strategic whatever nonsense the victory meant to our side. Eh?"

The Petersons stood there gaping in awe. No one talked like this, on either side. The man must be insane, at least partially so. But he kept talking.

"You get the point bro? We've taken, lost, re-taken, lost again, and re-taken again the same hills, the same valleys, the same plains, the same strategic landing zones, the same resource rich areas, the same regions of space see. Over and over and over and over and over and over again. Year after year. Century after century ya. You could make a highlight reel on every Meridian planet of the same places being re-taken by both sides dozens of times see."

Shipp couldn't help entering into the man's craziness. "So you're saying we should just stop fighting because no one's ever going to win?"

"No, bro," said the Thrust Controller, "I'm saying we should bombard the entire Meridian Zone with thousands of nukes say, and render all the planets uninhabitable for centuries with radiation. Then we can go home and be done. Ya."

"Even Rita?" Harden said as he cracked a smile at his own joke.

"Even Rita bro," affirmed the Thrust Controller, not laughing, but saying it in such a way that they could tell he got the joke.

Then it was silent. The Wester looked at the floor again. No one said anything for several seconds until Shipp broke it.

"You're serious," he said. "You really want to nuke all the planets into oblivion. That's your way of ending the war. No one wins."

"There's nothing to win!" the Thrust Controller yelled. "Don't you get it bro? No one's ever going to win, even if they win. What are you going to do if you get control of all seven planets ya? Mine the resources, ya man. Oooh. Mine the precious worthless resources that we both have plenty of on other planets. You win and nothing changes. Nothing!"

"Alright," Harden said, indicating he'd had enough. "You don't care anymore. That's fine. We do. You gonna tell us things we want to know if we take you back with us?"

The Thrust Controller shrugged. "Whatever you want bro. Don't matter to me."

Harden looked at Shipp, then at Jimenez and Mackson. Without a word, they agreed to take him with them. "You have a space suit?" asked Mackson.

"There's some in the storage room right there, ya," said the Thrust Controller.

And with that, the Petersons returned to the Sorcerer. Not long afterward, they planted a series of nukes on the inner sections of the Wester ship, and fired four K-rockets at precisely calculated locations. The Wester ship blew to pieces and chunks. They did the same thing to the other ship that brought them out here in the first place. And then, the Sorcerer began the months-long journey back to Peterson Territory.

Bringing with them the craziest Wester hostage in over five hundred years of war.

40

Secrets

A week passed. Garrison wanted the Thrust Controller to assimilate and get comfortable. If he was going to talk as freely as he claimed, they wouldn't need to put any pressure on him. No threats. No beatings. No exposing him to the vacuum of space for a few seconds.

Plus, Garrison wanted to be sure no other Westers showed up before he sent Rena back to her previous patrol assignment. Now, back behind the red giant, it was time to part ways. Rena turned on her visual to speak face to face with Garrison and the others in the top level, including Shipp.

"It was an honor to fight alongside you again, General," Rena began. "All kidding aside, you're the best attack ship general in the entire fleet. And you've got a brain-fire crew. Even the new guy."

Shipp smiled, "Thanks. My first space battle, but knowing what I know, I'd ask for you again in a millisecond."

"Great seeing you Rena. Very sorry we couldn't protect your other ship. A big loss," Garrison said. Harden removed his hat and rubbed his chest, then extended his hand in salute to Rena, palm upward. Rena smiled, and did the same in return.

A moment of silence from everyone. Then Rena gave a soft goodbye and disconnected.

"Once the convoys are clear, we'll map out the return flight plan and activate the HAT. Once we're moving, we'll question our little furry friend," Garrison said, getting snickers in return. "Shipp, you lead it."

A couple days later, it was time. The Petersons cleared out one of their domiciles, one with only two beds, and stuck the captive in there alone.

Since never more than a handful of the crew slept at any given time, it wasn't hard to manage the altered sleeping arrangements so they could lock the Wester in his room.

Shipp, Garrison, Harden, and Jennings entered the room and shut the door behind them. Shipp brought a chair. The Thrust Controller sat up in bed, realizing his time had come.

"You hungry?" Garrison asked.

He shook his head. "Thanks, I'm fine, no."

Shipp clanked his chair down opposite the Thrust Controller, who leaned back against the wall, across his bed. Shipp sat facing him.

"What's your name?" Shipp began.

"Merriss. Evant Merriss. I've been in space fleet about fifteen years or so ya, if you guys still keep time the same way."

"We do," said Harden.

"What's your role?" Shipp continued.

"I'm the Thrust Controller bro. So I make sure the HAT is running and the ship's systems are all functioning ya."

"So he's basically like Yao," said Jennings. "Should we get him up here so he can verify any mechanical talk?"

Garrison nodded. "Send him up. Mack can run mid-level." Jennings left and quickly returned with Yao, having updated him on the way about Merriss.

"This is Yao," Shipp said. "He's our Propulsion Supervisor, so same as you."

Merriss nodded at Yao, who looked coldly at him in return without a word.

"You said you fought on Kora. Where else?" Shipp asked.

"I fought on Kora, Rita, quite a while on Portia ya. Uh, I was on Terrasol once but only for a stopover," he replied.

"Why'd you end up in space?" Shipp replied.

"Got tired of the ground bro," Merriss said. Shipp said the same thing after Lavoisier. Shipp kept that to himself, but was surprised to find something the two of them had in common.

"Okay," Shipp said. "Those were the easy ones. Now I'm going to ask the stuff we care about. But before I do, I want to hear again – why do you want to tell us all this?"

Merriss shifted a bit and stared in a direction where no one else was. His complexion shifted. Grief. Pain. Shipp wondered if the ten days of waiting had affected him more than expected. Then, Merriss spoke in an unusual manner, different than any Peterson on board had ever heard someone speak.

"Torn asunder, thy galaxy. Wilt that I should extend such loss," Merriss said.

All the Petersons looked at each other. Merriss' eyes watered up, almost as if simply speaking this way had aroused some long-suffering emotion within him.

"What? Why did you say that?" Shipp asked. "You quoting literature or something?"

Merriss shook his head so slightly that if you blinked, you wouldn't have seen it.

"You're not..." Merriss halted, looking a bit nervous. "You're not worthy of it bro. I don't know why I did it, eh."

"I need an answer," Shipp persisted. "Why are you going to share secrets with us?"

Merriss recovered himself and returned to his usual rambling, "There's nothing left worth fighting for bro. Like I told you already. There is no way to win ya. But even if there was, there's *nothing* to win see. No prize. No reward. With no one left to kill, we wouldn't need the resources we're fighting over right?

Garrison nodded. "Some of us aren't in this for the resources. That's secondary."

Merriss looked at him. "You're the captain, huh ya. Took me a bit."

"General. Captains serve on convoys," Garrison corrected him.

Shipp regained his attention. "Tell us about the virus."

Merriss sat up and exhaled. "It's a beast ya." He paused while thinking about how to explain it. "Biological agent that consumes anything organic. Including face shields eh. That was the big advance see. Most agents can be screened out with filters, or shields, or other membranes of various compositions right. But this thing devours them. We haven't found an economical way to box it in yet once it's been activated ya."

"How do you activate it?" Shipp asked.

"It stays dormant as long as it's inside the chute. That's what we call it ya. A metal cylinder, about fifteen centimeters long."

"So it doesn't consume metals."

"Most metals bro. Pure metals. It does enjoy iron, and any metal with iron will weaken eventually. Including Blackhead, though it takes months ya. It also likes copper, silver, and gold."

"Gold? That's surprising," Shipp said.

"All the d9 elements," said Yao, referring to the column on the periodic table where all three of those elements reside.

Merriss nodded at him. "Yeah bro, there's something about that configuration that this thing seems to eat for dessert. So, we keep it in a dual layer chute. Outer layer zinc, inner layer aluminum."

Jennings chortled, "Aluminum finally good for something." The others laughed too.

"How do you get it in there? Where does it come from?" Shipp asked.

"That's beyond my pay grade bro. I just know they found something on a planet, and figured out how to weaponize it say. Decades in development. Quite a few deaths in the process. That's what convinced them this was worth going for, probably ya bro."

"And you have a way to... cleanse it. Kill it." Shipp said. "I saw this happen on Lavoisier."

This got Merriss' attention. "Really? You were there man? I heard they deployed it there, as a test run. How'd you survive?"

"We got underground before it ate through." Shipp flushed at the memory of being stuck in the life capsule, and what Rawlic and Shelsie did. Merriss could tell something didn't go well, but he wasn't about to antagonize anyone.

"I don't know how the countermeasure works bro," Merriss returned to the original question. "They gave us an aerosol chute and told us ya to use it in case we ever had to release the virus in the ship with Westers still alive."

"But why..." Shipp began. "Why put these in attack ships, when it can destroy entire planets?"

Merriss shook his head again. "No idea ya. I guess they got sick of being boarded, not that it happens that much. Hell of a deterrent ya. I'm not military personnel remember? I'm a greaser."

"How long does it take for the countermeasure to work?" Shipp asked.

"They told us about twelve hours bro. But in a larger area more spread out, they recommend three days ya."

Shipp, satisfied regarding the virus at this point, switched topics. He held up the yellow cube. "And what about this? You said it's the one thing your ships have that ours don't."

Merriss laughed at having his words quoted back to him. "Ya that's what we call the Beamer. It beams a signal out of the ship see. Coded. Any other Wester ship, outpost, or base can read it and identify the ship huh. No Beamer. Not Wester. It's pretty flying awesome, I think. We've had these for decades, but they're so good because Petersons can't mimic them like you do everything else we make ya."

"You mimic our stuff too," said Harden, a little annoyed that Merriss had finally revealed some of that well-renowned Wester arrogance.

"I suppose we do," said Merriss, but not convincing enough for Harden to pacify his growing hatred of the man.

"Why can't we mimic it?" asked Shipp.

"Because each ship has its own code, and it changes every time we embark ya man. You couldn't make one because none of our Beamers would recognize whatever code you tried to concoct. There is no way a Peterson ship could masquerade as a Wester one or penetrate our space without being spotted and identified eh. The codes beam out nonstop.

"You're saying that if we tore this thing apart, put our best tech minds on it –"

"You'd figure out all the mechanics of it, ya sure bro. But you can't know the codes. You can't read them with any tools you have," said Merriss. "And even if you could, we change them every launch ya."

Shipp looked at Yao. "You buying this?"

"Gives me a place to start, for sure," said Yao. "Ships have to have a way to communicate the new signal."

"Sure they do bro," said Merriss. "We're using some of that old software tech from few hundred years back in the war. Member that? You guys know your war history ya?"

"Quite well," said Shipp. "You're talking about all the tech that used to run the ships and the stations, and each side kept inventing all these special codes or something that could go in and disrupt the other side's software."

Merriss nodded. "I'm impressed bro. You know what those codes were called say?" Shipp shook his head.

"Viruses," said Merriss, grinning. "Funny how the same concept keeps coming back in new forms ya. We both abandoned software networks susceptible to viruses and infiltration and returned to impenetrable, but isolated, hardware."

"What's your point?" Garrison spoke up. "Why are you coming back to the virus? That has nothing to do with this right?"

"A virus is anything that infects by masquerading as that thing. It's an imposter ya. The Beamer is the anti-virus for Peterson ships. You are the virus."

Merriss realized he was rambling again, and that this time his rambling wasn't exactly endearing himself to them. He quickly course-corrected. "That's how they explained it to us anyway, ya."

The idea of the Petersons being a virus to the Westers wasn't lost on them. It wasn't a bad analogy, and Garrison seemed to enjoy learning the Westers perceived them in this way. Shipp, however, completely ignored the insult and went straight to what he wanted to know.

"Do you know where this new bio-virus is manufactured?"

Merriss figured out what they wanted. "You actually think you can go into our territory and find it ya?" He grinned at the absurdity. But the Petersons weren't laughing.

"I think we can do quite a bit more than you think we can," Shipp replied. "Especially if you know where it is."

Merriss sighed. "This is... going to be a little tricky for me."

"Why?"

"I don't know precisely the planet bro, but I know the system. It's called Hydramol. White sun. I think. Maybe two suns actually eh."

"Where's that? We don't know most of the Wester names for planets or stars in your territory," Garrison said.

Merriss shrugged. "I'm not a navigator. I don't know star charts at all ya. I just know it's somewhere near the border of the galaxy right."

Shipp leaned in. "But we can find out where it is if we get into a Wester station, right?"

Merriss got nervous. "I have a brother and a sister working on an outpost ya. I don't want you to go there. If you actually think you can penetrate our space, they're the only two people left that I care about see."

Shipp hardened. "You've got two more than me."

Merriss read him, and tried to conciliate. "I understand," said Merriss.

"No you don't," said Shipp. "You understand nothing."

Merriss wisely kept quiet. Shipp wanted Merriss to detect the rage bubbling under his skin.

"If I tell you where you can go," Merriss said, "I just want to ask that you don't go to their outpost ya."

"And where are you going to tell us?" Shipp said.

"I'll give you four outpost locations bro, including the one I want you to leave alone."

Harden lost it here. "How do we know he's not making that up, and the one he's telling us to avoid is the one that has what we need?"

All the Petersons glared at Merriss, who realized the predicament he got himself into. He started shifting and sweating, looking at the floor, the wall, anywhere but at them.

"I've been talking freely this whole time ya, and now you don't believe me? I'm not a soldier anymore. I don't do strategy eh," Merriss started babbling.

"What do you expect will happen after we take you back to our territory?" Shipp asked him.

"I guess, I'm hoping you'll let me live somewhere ya, anywhere, because I gave you so much help. I don't want to be in the war anymore huh," Merriss stammered. "Please, I just want to live somewhere. Anywhere. Even a, even a jail ya. Even a jail man."

Shipp spread out his arms to signal to the others to relax. He looked right at Merriss.

"Tell me this then. Tell me what I'm not worthy of," referencing that strange way Merriss spoke earlier, and his evasiveness about it.

Merriss growled, then stammered, then breathed loudly as if trying to hold something back he didn't want to say.

"Why aren't I worthy to know why you spoke that way?" Shipp asked again.

"You Petersons don't know anything about us ya. You've probably got all your propaganda machines working overtime. I'm sure you believe most of it because why wouldn't you? We probably believe a bunch of lies about you too. See, I'm, I'm the only one I've ever known who realizes any of this ya. The whole war is built on lies, revenge for revenge that goes back way before any of our great grandparents were alive."

Rambling again. His insane crazy talk had returned. But Shipp felt he was deflecting.

"Tell us then! Tell us a truth we don't know about Westers."

Merriss lowered his head and after a long pause, spoke softly. "It's. It's.... It's our... It's our formal tongue. Only to be used..."

Merriss started looking around the room, as if he wanted out. "I shouldn't have said it. You won't understand. I don't know why I did it eh."

"Only to be used when?" Shipp said. "You tell me this and I might believe your story about the four stations and the one we're supposed to avoid."

"Tis a language of honor and respect. To be spoken only in such moments when formal expression is due." Merriss blurted out in the formal language again. "And it was not due then, so I don't know why I did it! Now stop asking about that ya!"

He was now fighting tears. Looking away from his captors, hunching over.

Astonished that something seemingly so trivial could matter this much to Merriss, the Petersons sat speechless. Shipp looked to Harden, who had the most experience with situations like this, since he himself had been tortured. He was better equipped to tell when a captive had been broken, and when he might be evading or deceiving.

Harden, barely able to believe it himself, nodded at Shipp that the Thrust Controller was telling the truth. Merriss didn't even notice because he wasn't looking at any of them. So Harden and Shipp kept the exchange wordless.

"Merriss," Shipp said, getting his attention. "Tell us the names and locations of the four stations. We'll leave the one alone with your siblings."

Merriss looked up at Shipp in partial relief, wondering if he could trust him but realizing the impossibility of this – for him and for them.

"This is why I hate this flaming war," Merriss said. "With every capillary in my body ya."

Shipp had no response. He'd never heard anyone say anything like it. All he knew was war. From birth. It was a reality of life in the Space Age. And now, this Wester who hated the war fed them detailed information about the locations of four of his own space stations, which Westers called outposts. And the Petersons lapped it up, like dogs fighting over a water bowl.

41

Dialogue with the Enemy

The trip back to Peterson Territory went mostly like any other. More drills for everyone. More learning for Shipp, James, and Li. Analysis of the previous battle. More quality conversations to deepen friendships. And the growing uneasiness over how to think about this most unique of captives.

As they neared Station Olba, where the Sorcerer Reborn construction had been underway for the many months they were gone, Harden and Garrison began feeding information to the Peterson commanders that Merriss had given them. It was a treasure trove. Over the course of the journey, he gave up much more than just the four space stations. They learned the locations of dozens of new planets colonized since the Petersons left centuries before. Defenses. Populations. Strategic significance. Resources.

Merriss truly did not care about his own side. He didn't care who won the war. Who might die or live based on what he told them. The Westers would call him a traitor, just like the Petersons would if one of their own did the same thing. But traitor wasn't really the right word to describe Merriss.

Merriss had lost the will to care or fight. Apathy devoured him. He didn't see his actions as helping or hurting anyone. He had grown nihilistic. None of this mattered. None of it. People would die in this war regardless of what he did. And because of his actions, the only difference might be that different people would die than ones who would have died otherwise. If ten thousand died who would have lived, but a different ten thousand lived who would have died – did it really matter?

Merriss approached everything with that mindset.

Before they docked, Shipp had one more set of questions for Merriss, but he had to ask these alone, and he'd been waiting for an opportunity. By this point, no one thought anything strange about him entering alone the room where Merriss had spent the entire journey. Merriss had freely divulged whatever they wanted, often more information than asked. So there was no reason to believe Shipp could cause trouble, or end up in a ny.

After closing the door behind him, Shipp could tell Merriss noted the unusual situation before him. One on one. He could tell Shipp had an agenda that didn't need to concern anyone else on the Sorcerer.

"Here to tell me where I'm going to be sent when we dock ya?" Merriss asked, knowing Shipp had come for other reasons, but not willing to let the silence have any dominance, with all its discomfort.

"I need to know something. I need to know about someone. One of your attack ship captains," Shipp said, laying it out plainly, as he had no reason to think Merriss would dodge this one if he knew anything useful.

"I've served with four of them, and I know about several more ya."

"You said you don't know who is behind this virus," Shipp began, wanting to confirm this.

"I can tell you it wasn't a ship captain huh. They don't do development."

"Right, but who found the planet? Who recognized the potential of the virus once discovered? Who suggested the weaponization? Captains don't do the science, but they can set the vision in place that guides it."

Merriss accepted that, but it had become quite clear over the last couple months that he really didn't know much about the origin of the virus. And here again, all he could do was speculate.

"General Garrison thinks a captain named Joseph Arryus probably played a key role. You know him?" Shipp asked.

Merriss smirked at the name. Then shook his head in disgust.

"Arryus. Ya man. That guy, that's the kind of person who wouldn't be in charge of anything were it not for this war. He's a... what's the word? He's a sadist bro. Like I said earlier, if a guy like him captured one of your ships and found a guy like me, we wouldn't be having this conversation eh."

"Did you serve with him?"

"I was on his ship for six months bro, one mission. He's demanding but fair with his crew see. But if you get him in the same room as the enemy, he turns into a monster."

"You saw this happen?"

Merriss looked away. Shipp had touched on a memory, probably one Merriss would like to forget.

"Do you really want the details say?" Merriss began. "It's not worth it. He's a brutal... Yes, I saw it happen bro. He's a very smart battlefield leader. You already have enough hate for us, and guys like him just give you more reasons ya."

"Okay. Could he have had a role in the virus?"

"Very very doubtful eh. He would joyfully use it, without question. He's probably hoping he gets boarded one day just so he can use it and watch their faces melt. But I doubt he had much to do with its development or direction huh."

Satisfied that Garrison's nemesis Arryus wasn't a key player with the virus, Shipp moved on to what he really wanted to know.

"What about another captain named Elliss?"

Merriss eyed Shipp. He deduced from Shipp's attempts to remain stoic that this was the reason he came here alone.

"I never served with Elliss ya. But he's high up in reputation. Has a lot of influence ya. Yes, he could have played a strategic role in the virus. But I don't know for fact that he did," Merriss said, never taking his eyes off Shipp this time, unlike when they discussed Arryus.

"What's the name of his ship?" Shipp asked.

Merriss hesitated. Shipp wouldn't let him. "Don't ask why I need to know. It doesn't concern you."

"You'd be lucky to ever reach a guy like him ya. His ship tends to lead missions. He gives orders to other ship captains. He directs campaigns."

"I know," Shipp said. "What's the name of his ship? And what planet or station does he come from?"

Merriss got nervous. "I know his ship bro. It's called the Eradicator. He's had it about twenty years. I don't know much else that you asked for."

Shipp wasn't satisfied, as Merriss feared.

"Think hard." Shipp said. "People talk. Offhand comments. Something they heard in a training lecture. News reports. Recounting old stories. Think hard. I'll give you time."

"I am thinking hard. But I don't think I know see," Merriss said, now tapping his foot and rubbing his fingers together.

"I'll wait," Shipp said. He arose and then sat in the corner of the room while Merriss remained in place.

An hour later, Shipp still sat there looking at Merriss, having not said a word the entire time. And Merriss still sat there, racking his brain. He hadn't come up with a thing. He really didn't know where Elliss was from.

"Well?" said Shipp.

The sound startled Merriss, who slowly retreated against the wall, still sitting on his bed.

"I've been going over so many points in time see. I just, I really can't think of anything. I don't think it's ever come up. I don't know where most people are from ya. Do you? I don't know where Arryus is from either. I don't even know where the Chancellor is from, or the Premier from my home planet – like what region or city she's from. Once you're on an attack ship, things outside of that kind of disintegrate in your memory, ya?" Merriss rambled, as seemed to be his tendency whenever he was nervous.

Shipp sat for a moment, and then spoke.

"If we take a station, or outpost as you call it, would there be information we could access that would tell us where he's from?"

Merriss nodded. "Very likely bro. You could read news reports ya stored in the archives and would almost certainly find his home planet or station mentioned somewhere huh."

"Do you know if there are any codes or credentials I would need to get into a Wester monitor on a station?" Shipp asked.

"Yes," answered Merriss. "Whenever we dock see, I always have to identify myself when engaging a public monitor."

"How could I get in then?"

Merriss smiled. "I'll give you mine bro."

Shipp shook his head. "If your space admins have half the brains of ours, they would presume you dead and delete your access credentials, right?"

Merriss hadn't thought of this. "I don't know. Never heard of that for anyone ya."

Shipp halted, and his countenance darkened. Then, Merriss got an idea that he knew would satisfy him.

"I can give you mine. And if it doesn't work, you can have my father's code too ya. He's still alive. Lives on Gagarin." Shipp had heard of Gagarin. It was one of the first planets colonized after the invention of the Hyper-Thrust – before the HAT.

But Shipp wanted no possible obstacle in his path. "The station wouldn't know that your father doesn't live there? Wouldn't they know everyone living on the station and only give access to them? You're telling me the consoles in your entire territory all use the same codes and credentials?"

Merriss deflated, thinking he had given a good strategy. But the truth was, he was a tech, and strategic thinking of this sort wasn't required for his work. He didn't view the world this way. But Shipp was right. His father's code probably wouldn't work on an outpost.

Then, he remembered something, and smiled, almost enjoying this collaboration now.

"The Beamer see. You can use that right! It contains a code for the ship itself. Even though our ship is destroyed, the Beamer generates codes for re-entry, and those same codes will work on any public outpost monitor. Use the Beamer to generate a code ya. Send it to the outpost as you approach or even after you land there. And on any monitor, you can access the outpost's archives using that code," Merriss explained.

"There's no way that can fail?" Shipp asked.

Merriss shook his head. "No chance whatsoever bro. Beamers use technology that undergirds Wester life on every planet, outpost, and ship."

Shipp breathed a heavy sigh. Then, he stood and exited the room without a word. After he left, Merriss let out an even bigger sigh.

42

Presentation Day

Shipp brooded for the last few days before reaching Station Olba containing the Sorcerer Reborn. He longed to see how far its construction had progressed. The presentation of the ultimate attack ship would happen before Shipp and the rest of the crew left Olba again. The next time they left, they would be heading deep into Wester Territory. It could very well be the last voyage any of them took.

That meant this station, and any communication and conversation they had here, could be their final opportunity with anyone outside their crew. If they had any final messages to share with loved ones, mentors, their hometowns, home planets, or anyone else, now would be the time.

Shipp decided to send a single message to his parents, that they could distribute to anyone they wished. He told James and Li about it, and they were very happy to see Shipp's change of heart from the last time they brought up this idea. But Shipp wasn't doing it for the reasons they had in mind. He wanted to create a record that would justify what he intended to do so that after it happened, people would know why he did i t.

Shipp's message read thus:

I know you haven't heard from me for many years. You probably learned that I lost Pretoria on Risner. After that, I went to Lavoisier, where I lost all my remaining friends except for Cam James. I found a new friend there named Mansa Li. We are of a single mind. The war against the Westers has taken everything from me, which is why I am giving everything I have left to further its end. Its permanent end.

I'm done with life on the ground. I'm in space for good, serving on an attack ship. I intend to serve here as long as I am able. If you never see or hear from me again, know that what I have done, and what I am about to do, has advanced our cause against Wester aggression. I have achieved some great victories. And now, I intend to achieve our greatest victory in the last five hundred years. Be well. Stay alive. Save your friend. Thomas Shipp

For Jennings, the return to the space station meant a different sort of goodbye. He called a meeting of the officers of the Sorcerer. He invited Shipp, even though not yet officially an officer. Jennings informed them he could not go on the one-way mission with the Sorcerer Reborn. Though he believed in its goals, he simply couldn't bring himself to commit to something that he very likely would never return from. He had always planned to return to SFU as an instructor, and eventually his home planet.

Though he planned to continue serving on an attack ship for several more years, he did not want to die on one. He recommended Shipp be formally promoted to the officer core. Everyone understood Jennings' motives, and no one bore any animosity toward him. His heart and life plan simply didn't include what amounted to a suicide mission. Shipp thought of it more as a one-way trip with a very slight chance of return.

With Jennings gone, Mackson got promoted to First Officer, and Shipp took his place as the Mid-Level Control Officer. With all he had been through the last several months, Shipp was well prepared for the role. His only deficiencies concerned the mechanical aspects of the mid-level. Li had spent much more time with Yao than Shipp had. But since the Sorcerer Reborn introduced a re-design of so many aspects of attack ships, Shipp simply needed to tag along with Yao as he familiarized himself with the new ship. He brought along Li for good measure, because they couldn't have too much expertise – especially on this mission.

Shipp held a sneaking suspicion that Locke would bow out too, taking Jennings' exit as an easy justification. Shipp just couldn't tell what kind of soldier Locke was. But to his surprise, Locke went in the opposite direction. After Shipp's promotion, it was Locke who approached him afterward.

"Welcome to mid-level," Locke said, reminding Shipp that his medical facilities sat right next to the nutrient supplies, dorms, HAT, power supplies, fuel, and other components occupying the mid-level. "I know you're not a medical expert, but neither was Mack. Now that you're in his place, it's time to learn. I'm the guy no one listens to until they get clipped by enemy fire. I could put a man's head back on given enough notice. If it comes to that, I'll need you there to hold the tray."

Shipp smiled. Actual humor from the perpetual crank. This new job was looking better already.

As it turned out, the Sorcerer Reborn still required more work. The internal components – skeleton, wiring, weapons caches, delivery systems, comm, monitor technology – had all been installed. The behemoth attack ship could be ready in a week if only internal work remained. The primary reason they still needed another month or two to finish construction?

Blackhead.

The extra thick layers of Blackhead on the exterior had caused enough challenges, because mining and manufacture of the material hadn't gotten any easier. And because so much material was required for this one vessel, they either had to usurp all the Blackhead being manufactured in the entire Peterson Territory, thereby delaying projects elsewhere that required it, or they had to wait.

So, the Blackhead trickled in. Sometimes in large quantities. Sometimes just a ton or two at a time. But no matter how much came in, the builders of the vessel marveled at how much more was needed. This was a big vessel. And it had so much Blackhead – just on the exterior – that it started to seem like there was more Blackhead than ship. The interior had more too, in case the ship ever became compromised. They wanted to be able to stay alive in multiple sections of the ship.

Progress continued. The Sorcerer Reborn took shape. And then, Garrison caused further delay. But his reason found hearty agreement from Harden, Shipp, Dons, and every other officer once they heard his plan.

Watching the Wester ship tear through the convoy ship in the last battle had given Garrison an idea. Apparently, he kept it to himself the entire journey home. One night, he snuck into Comm-2 when no one was awake on the mid-level, and started a dialogue with Space Fleet Command.

His idea?

Refashion the front of the ship so that it featured a long, sharp, protruding point, stretching across the front of the vessel, made entirely of Blackhead. He wanted to turn the leading edge of the ship into a nearly indestructible battering ram that could rip through any other ships it collided with. His idea required the design team to re-imagine the front-end of the ship. The newly enhanced Sorcerer Reborn now featured what the crew began calling The Joust. If any other ship got in their way, they could ram it and probably rip right through it.

Now, this was insane, of course. No one had ever tried anything like this. Since other attack ships were also coated entirely with Blackhead, what would a Blackhead battering ram constructed like a spire do if it rammed directly into the side of another ship? It would be Blackhead against Blackhead.

Logic said that even though the battering ram was undoubtedly the most impressive visual feature of the Sorcerer Reborn, and would make all the design nerds drool themselves to sleep for weeks, a strong flat wall of Blackhead would still probably hold its own over a thinner protrusion. Kind of like jamming a knife into a concrete wall, the point would probably just crumple, bend, or retract into the ship and cause internal damage. Or, even if the Sorcerer Reborn won the first collision, it probably could only go head-to-head a few times before being weakened too much to continue using The Joust.

But Garrison knew that. A better use of this weapon would target ships that already had been partially damaged. This battering ram dagger provided a much faster and cleaner way to finish off a damaged ship without having to waste precious weaponry that – on this mission – could not be resupplied.

And that's how he convinced the top brass to sign off on it.

So, the Sorcerer Reborn would now become the biggest, baddest, bulkiest, fastest joust in the history of humanity. And woe to any poor little ships that got in its way. When Garrison's officers saw the design taking shape for the first time, they erupted in cheers. Garrison hadn't told them about it, because he knew this would rev everyone's spirits and infuse fresh motivation and excitement about this mission.

Even though everyone was all in, Garrison knew there had to be feelings of regret and uncertainty, knowing this would very likely be the last time any of them saw this place. Even if their new ship didn't get destroyed, at some point they would run out of weapons, or supplies, or something else. At some point, they could be marooned. Or captured. Possibly tortured. Certainly executed.

So his crew needed all the motivation they could get, and The Joust was the best idea he could have come up with.

Yet another delay arose when Shipp, Harden, and Garrison presented what they had learned about the Beamer. Much debate ensued about how they could utilize this to break through the Wester barriers and be perceived as a Wester ship. If they could get the Beamer to transmit a code that the Westers interpreted as one of their own ships, they could avoid any battles until they got deep into the territory.

The problem was, as Merriss had emphasized, this Beamer's code would be long obsolete by the time the Petersons could use it. But the Peterson Space Force didn't make it through five hundred years of war without amassing some pretty big brains. After a few weeks working on the problem, they found a solution.

The Beamer could be enhanced with its own version of a software 'virus,' that long abandoned technology that had no use anymore due to the simplification of Space Force technology on both sides of the war. But here, the virus wouldn't be causing any damage to the Wester monitors. It first would secretly send a new code into their system, make sure their consoles logged it as the code belonging to a Wester vessel recently launched on a new mission, and then receive that same code from the Sorcerer Reborn.

In essence, the Beamer would tell the Wester monitors what code to look for, and then send that same code. The best thing about this was that they could create a new code every month or two if necessary.

Much vitriolic debate then followed about whether to tell Merriss about any of this. But they couldn't escape the fact that, as great as this idea sounded, they needed to get his confirmation that it could work.

And he gave it. In fact, he gave them even more. He showed them a couple tricks to ensure their initial beam containing the virus with the manufactured code would succeed in implanting in the Wester monitors. This type of work was Merriss' specialty.

Some Petersons worried he was telling them exactly what they wanted to hear. But due to the overwhelming amount of intelligence he had already given, some of it since independently verified, enough Petersons believed he could be trusted. The entire Sorcerer crew believed him.

It was even agreed that Merriss would not be executed, an extreme rarity for an enemy prisoner. Merriss would live out his days on a Peterson planet at the far backside of the territory, and under constant supervision. That day would come after the Sorcerer Reborn completed its mission, they told him. That gave him extra motivation to share everything he could to help them.

Garrison, Shipp, and Harden also kept their promise to Rena, and reported to Space Fleet Command that the Mauler and the Stealth had failed to conduct an adequate search for the lost convoy ships during their last battle, resulting in the gruesome deaths of six Petersons. The top brass could decide how to handle it, but at the very least, this would ensure a little shame and a good dose of new trainings.

During the final couple months of construction, Garrison's primary task was to recruit the remainder of his crew. He needed extra bodies on this much larger ship. Garrison wanted a 24-man crew. Plus, in addition to Jennings, the other three crew Garrison had left on the station so Shipp, Li, and James could take their places for the previous mission decided not to return. They enjoyed their extended time outside the attack ship, with so much room and so many places to go. Diving back into the confines of an attack ship – and for a mission they would probably never return from – proved too much to stomach.

So, Garrison had the Station Commander put out a call for volunteers, and sent it to all attack ships when they returned to Peterson Territory. Internally, they now referred to this as the Galactic Mission. Volunteers came.

Garrison, Harden, Mackson, Locke, Shipp, and Dons met every one of them.

They were questioned about their motives. Evaluated for their psychological sturdiness. Assessed about their war experience, whether on the ground or in space. Garrison wanted only people who had lost someone close to them. And he wanted to hear the story of that person. Every applicant needed attack ship experience. No one fresh off the ground was invited. Ideally, he wanted people who had served together on the same attack ship.

Eventually, the new crew members got introduced to the existing crew.

A fifth pilot named Winston joined backups Molon and Ewing. Winston had served as the main pilot on a different ship, but this mission inspired him so much that he decided now was the time to switch ships, even if it meant taking a backup pilot role behind Blake and Reeves.

Locke found himself a beneficiary of welcoming Cruz onto the ship. Cruz served on the same ship as Winston, which pleased Garrison, and on that ship he had gained a fair amount of medical experience from their Chief Medical Officer. So now, with Shipp in line to learn under Locke's guidance, he also had Cruz, giving himself a team of three – a first for any attack ship.

Lastly, Dons added four new weapons specialists to his team – Mitz, Zum, Drummond, and Algiers. Drummond and Algiers knew each other well, having served on the same attack ship for five years. Garrison was delighted to add two men with such a long friendship to his ship.

The Sorcerer Reborn had eight Fire Control stations instead of the usual six, so he needed a lot of new gunners. Now, he had Abe, Marley, Li, James, Cardmanov, and Jimenez, plus the four new crew members.

With Yao's assistant Wallace staying on board too, that gave the Sorcerer Reborn its crew of 24 men, all committed to giving their lives, if necessary, to locate and annihilate the Westers' new weaponized virus.

Garrison ordered the entire crew to spend as much time as possible together in the final weeks of preparation. At times, they were permitted to board the ship and spend considerable time there. Several nights, they slept there. They chose domiciles. Worked out sleeping schedules. Learned each other's habits, personalities, and humor. Shared stories of loss, anger, and triumph.

It was one of the greatest experiences of their lives – preparing together to embark on a mission that, in Shipp's mind, could lead to the end of the war and a Peterson victory. The others struggled to see it going that far, but at the very least, everyone believed that this mission, if successful, could well be the next great Pivot in the war, something both sides would look back on centuries later.

This was history in the making.

If the Westers were allowed to freely expand their usage of this virus, eventually they would figure out a way to deploy it on Peterson Territory planets or space stations. That would mean the end of everything. So this campaign had a defensive purpose, but was entirely offensive in nature. And it had been nearly three years since the virus first appeared on Lavoisier. The Westers had to be planning a second attack with it.

Presentation Day arrived.

With limited fanfare due to not wanting to risk any leaks about the mission, the space station residents and key leaders from Space Force Command and Space Fleet Command took their places in the largest circular room in the station, one that stretched across the entire diameter of the station at that section. They formed three large concentric circles of people.

In the center of those circles stood the 24-man crew of the Sorcerer Reborn.

One by one, each member received a eulogy of sorts. Their life story, their reason for joining this mission, their conviction about it, their pain, their friendships, their home planets – whatever story they wanted told about them, plus more that SFC wanted to say – was spoken on record in the hearing of everyone present.

It took several hours to get through all 24 men. But not a single attendee left the entire time. Not even for a bathroom break. And no one sat down for the whole ceremony.

When it finished, the encircling audience clapped and cheered as the crew and officers of the Sorcerer Reborn filed out, one by one, through a tunnel that led to what most believed to be the last vessel they would ever board.

The last man out – General Garrison – looked around the room and held his hands out, almost as if embracing them all. He appreciated their support and the work that led to this moment, and believed they would be with him on this journey all the way. He quieted their applause, and spoke these words:

"We cannot fail. We will not fail. Stay alive."

A cacophonous "save your friend" erupted, sounding like the combination of a choir and a war cry. The audience repeated the chant. Garrison withdrew as they continued the chant, so the crew could hear it echoing through the hallways until they reached the ramp.

The crew crossed the ramp and entered the Sorcerer Reborn. The ramp, which doubled as the door like on other attack ships, retracted upward and sealed behind them. The huge station doors opened, and the greatest, most ambitious attack ship ever built departed, heading for The Region of Rats.

43

The Trip

One of Garrison's favorite things about his new ship was that it contained a Meeting Room. It was actually just one of the domiciles, but it included a table in the middle with stools that rose up from the floor. Seating for up to six. And, it included a wall monitor for larger visual displays, more like what the ground bases had. Perfect for strategy and planning meetings.

After the Sorcerer Reborn had been away for several days heading for the Central Frontier, but angling away toward the faraway edge of the galaxy, they held a meeting to finalize the course. At the meeting, Garrison worked with Blake, Harden, Mackson, Shipp, and Yao.

"The general plan for the last several months has been to exit the galaxy in a parabolic course and then re-enter it at a point of our choosing, somewhere in the heart of Wester Territory," Garrison began. "We now must choose that point. Ideas."

Blake began, "Based on the data from Merriss the Traitor, we know these locations hold Wester outposts. And we should start referring to them as outposts instead of stations since some of us will be talking to Westers before too long."

He noted the locations on the wall monitor, which included a map of Wester Territory. It was a remarkable thing to see, because so much of this region of space was unknown to the Petersons, and had been for centuries. So much had changed since their ancestors left, and none of the old data could be relied upon. Most was discarded before the war even began.

But now, because of Merriss, points of light dotted the formerly darkened expanse typical of most space maps featuring Wester Territory. They knew the approximate locations of eighteen planets, five outposts, and a number of planetary space defense facilities. One outpost, marked in red, was the one Merriss had pleaded with them not to harm. And they would keep their word to him. That left four remaining choices.

Blake continued, "I'm just a pilot, but the shortest distance between two points in space is usually the best one to pick. So, as an initial proposition, I say we go with what he called Outpost Raheem. It's closest. Shorter trip."

"Is there any advantage we know of between any of these stations? I mean outposts," asked Mackson.

"Not really," said Harden. "The main question is, which can be reached with the lowest amount of risk, from what little we know. Risk can come from any number of sources."

"Wester convoys," Shipp said.

"Asteroids, stars, space phenomena," added Yao.

"Unknown Wester threats and defenses," said Harden. "The list is infinite. I'm looking at what we know, and we know there are four inhabited planets within proximity to Outpost Raheem. To me, that makes it too great a risk. I want something more isolated."

"Agreed," said Garrison. "What about the other three?"

A lengthy discussion ensued. After an hour spent hashing out the variables, they settled on Outpost Ulrich. Each location had its pros and cons, but they liked Ulrich because of the four outposts they know about, it sat closest toward the edge of the galaxy. It sat a bit farther back into Wester Territory than the others, but likely with less resistance in its path because they would never expect to encounter a Peterson ship so far from their border.

Blake returned to the Pilot Room and worked out a course with Reeves, under Garrison's supervision. They laid out the path. From here, they would head toward galaxy's edge. At a certain point, they needed to steer clear of an asteroid shower and a cluster of stars. From there, they could set a clear parabolic course that would shoot them temporarily outside the galaxy, arcing back in and entering at a point about one third of the way along the Wester border.

From there, they could reach the outpost in a few weeks if they wanted to. But they expected to slow it down and spend time collecting mapping data and other intelligence, since no Peterson ship had ever been to this area. Instead of a few weeks, they would likely spend a couple months traveling from the edge of the galaxy to Outpost Ulrich.

They also planned to plant three Trans-Com units along their path – all three would reside outside the galaxy. With three units in place, they could send a message and have it reach their home Territory in a few months, rather than the several years it would otherwise take. Every day, they would send fresh data back to Space Fleet Command.

Yao planned on a HAT speed of around one third full once they entered Wester Territory. How long would it take to reach the point of re-entry into the Milky Way in Wester Territory?

Eight months.

They'd be riding the HAT at full speed the entire time before re-entry, which would be easy once clear of the galaxy because the space would be nearly empty and pose almost zero risk. It would also be one beautiful view – something hardly any human had seen – a view of their galaxy from outside it.

Four months into their journey, they reached the vertex of their parabolic course – the farthest away they would travel from the Milky Way.

Garrison didn't want to slow the ship down and turn to face the galaxy and give his crew a view through the windows, because that would add to their trip time. The monitors could show the external camera views well enough.

Shipp opposed him.

"General, this is our voyage. Possibly our last voyage. It's the ultimate starlight," Shipp said.

Garrison knew what starlight meant to Shipp – even more than it meant to the typical Peterson. He relented, and ordered Yao to power down the HAT so they could angle the ship toward the galaxy.

And what a sight to behold.

They weren't far enough away to see the galaxy in its fullness. But, spreading before them, they could see a wall of stars, with blackness above and below. It almost resembled an epic sparkling sword being drawn from its sheath, ready to be thrust into darkness.

When his turn came, Shipp stood speechless for ten minutes. He asked for James and Li to be there on his shift. About four at a time could stand behind the Pilot seats, and Garrison left Winston and Molon in place the whole time, while everyone else filtered in and out to look at the view.

James put his arm around Shipp on one side, and Li on the other. Together, they held vigil.

"Goals aren't etched in stone. They're drawn with starlight," Shipp whispered to himself. James heard him quote his wife's favorite saying, and rubbed his back.

"Time to shift," Garrison called from behind after the allotted fifteen minutes had elapsed. James and Li stepped away, but Shipp remained. Winston, sitting in front of him, noticed.

"No one has said anything except you," Winston said. "Sixteen guys, and not a word the entire time. It's like I'm driving a ghost ship."

"No words do it justice," Shipp replied. He gripped Winston's shoulders. Then, he stepped out and let the next group in.

Shipp had bonded with Winston over the last four months. Winston had a purity of mind about him, almost as if the war couldn't touch him or throw him off course mentally or emotionally. Extreme loss seemed to just run off his body like oil and water. And he knew extreme loss. His father died in the war when Winston was just ten. He never knew him. His best friend died right next to him in a battle on Kora. But you'd never know it watching Winston conduct himself. Shipp envied him for that, but his admiration overcame his envy. It felt good to have new crew members.

"Thank you General," Shipp said to Garrison on his way out.

Before re-amplifying the HAT, Garrison took this opportunity to plant the second Trans-Com unit, with the first one having been deployed soon after exiting the galaxy. He would plant the third one about a week before they re-entered the galaxy on the Wester side.

As the months went by, and the galaxy's edge drew closer and closer, drill after drill and strategy session after strategy session filled up the time.

For the first four months of the trip, Garrison actually went light. He gave significant time off – far more than on the last mission. Crew had time to spend with each other. They even brought a couple decks of cards and other games. Garrison wanted his men to have something good to recall once they re-entered the warzone. He wanted a time of peace before the coming onslaught.

But on the second half of the trip, the intensity steadily accelerated.

They had one shot at this. They needed to know each other. They needed to know their stations blind. They needed a plan for how to infiltrate Outpost Ulrich. If this vessel ever did return to Peterson Territory, it would be filled with the most agile, skilled, versatile experts ever assembled on a single attack ship.

Shipp oversaw much of this, so consumed with empowering every man with full working knowledge of the ship. But not just the ship. Since they would need to physically dock and board at least one Wester outpost, some of them needed a refresher on ground weapons.

While every man on board had served the ground war at one time, Shipp was renowned as a weapons expert, and he wanted everyone to know everything he could teach them. On this trip, the Sorcerer Reborn had been equipped with far more ground weapons than a typical attack ship. They might need them on Outpost Ulrich and wherever the virus originated. At some point, they might have to land on a planet. They might find themselves in a ground war, something many of the men on this ship hadn't experienced in more than fifteen years. For Shipp, he was only a few years removed.

So, he wanted to refresh their memories, remind them of the situational awareness that would keep them alive. Garrison, Harden, and Dons attended every session and treated Shipp as if he were a general. But that's because they and Cardmanov had spent more time in space than anyone else on board, other than Locke. They needed this training as much as anyone, and they ate it up.

The four months passed quickly, because every day was filled up with trainings, drills, and meetings. But spirits remained high. No one complained, except Locke. Everyone was all in. They had nothing else to look forward to. And, nearly eight months after engaging the HAT, the Sorcerer Reborn crossed the edge of the galaxy and entered Wester Territory, making Space Age history. Blake's course trajectory was spot on
.

"Muzzle the HAT," came Garrison's familiar order, a couple days later.

Yao decelerated the HAT and they began using the LR to study their new surroundings, take note of any natural obstacles, and work out a plan to reach Outpost Ulrich. Harden began collecting data immediately. Dons began working two shifts of five weapons specialists at a time in six-hour intervals. Yao, Wallace, and Cruz, along with Shipp, made sure all the Sorcerer Reborn's core functions were in full working order. No space walks were necessary. This ship was built better than any before it.

To endure an eight-month stretch of the HAT at full power, with one small sightseeing break in the middle, and to arrive here with so few problems, made Yao exhale in amazement. He loved his job, and going on this mission took him less than a second to decide.

Yao lost his entire family to this war. Both his parents served together, much like Shipp and Pretoria, with one exception. They had Yao. Normally, married couples in the Space Force were forbidden from having children. But Yao's parents married before entering Space Force University and Yao was already four years old. When they applied to join, both scored higher than just about anyone else in their applicant pool. But they had Yao, and kids weren't allowed.

So, SFU made an exception. Yao would be allowed to live with them while at SFU. But after that, he would have to return to his home planet under care of a relative. Four years later, that's exactly what happened.

At age eight, Yao had to say goodbye to his parents. They had been telling him since he could speak that this day would come. So, even as a young child, Yao knew that one day, he would be separated from his parents and go live with his uncle and aunt on New Pompeii. That final year, he spent many hours communicating with his uncle and aunt, to smooth out the transition.

But the day his parents said goodbye left a lifelong impression. He cried more than he ever had before or ever would again. At the same time, he knew why they did it. They had to fight. They had to win.

Six years later, Yao's family received news that his parents had been killed on Terrasol, in the same battle. Before that, he'd received letters over the years, and updates from Space Force Command. But on that day, it ended. And Yao decided he would follow them into the Space Force. Two of his cousins – the children of his uncle and aunt – went with him. Later, both of them would die too.

The Sorcerer Reborn was all Yao knew, and its crew the only family he had left. If this mission were to be his last, he wanted to know he had played a major role in a future Peterson victory.

Just after initiating the HAT's deceleration process, Shipp entered the room, carrying the yellow Beamer cube along with the hookups and attachments the Petersons had added to adapt it to the Sorcerer Reborn.

Yao turned and saw it in his hand. "Ready to install it now?" he asked Shipp.

"No," said Shipp. "I need something else from this thing first. And I need your help to figure it out."

44

First Contact

Several days into Wester Territory, the Sorcerer Reborn already recorded one inhabited planet not given to them by Merriss. Yao installed the Beamer, with Shipp assisting him in place of Wallace. No one thought anything of it, but Shipp now had what Merriss had promised him – access credentials to the Wester monitors when they reached Outpost Ulrich.

He tried to quell it, but at nearly every spare moment as the outpost drew closer, Shipp found himself ruminating on General Elliss. Learning his face. Finding out where he lived. Picturing his family, his wife, his parents, his friends, his house. He wanted to find the location of his ship, the Eradicator. The names of his crew. Shipp knew the point of this ultimate mission wasn't about Elliss. But Elliss occupied an ever-larger share of his mind. The man who murdered his wife and so many others on Risner was coming within reach.

From Comm-1, Harden sent the latest update to the nearest Trans-Com unit, which would send it to the next unit and eventually back to Space Fleet Command. Shipp arrived on the top level at that moment, interested in seeing actual Wester space. Right afterward, the LR picked up a signal, and Harden read the data. Garrison turned at the familiar sound.

"What do you got?"

"Based on size, structure, and speed, it's a transport ship. Probably on a supply run. No convoys. It's all alone," Harden said.

"Of course it is. The war never touches this part of the galaxy," Garrison said with a mocking self-assurance.

Harden smiled. "Until now."

"This is a great opportunity to test our new vessel. See what it can do," Garrison said. "Alert Dons. I want to wreck that ship and then ram through it."

Shipp flushed with adrenalin. "Want me on mid-level for this? Or can I stay here and watch?"

"What would you rather do?" Garrison asked. "This will be a mop up job. Your choice."

Shipp decided to stay. He wanted to see how it looked to tear straight through an enemy vessel.

Down in Fire Control, Dons assigned his five-man crew specific points to hit on the transport ship. These ships were huge, far bigger than attack ships, but coated with a much thinner layer of Blackhead to protect against space debris, and only one layer of shield array ports. A concentrated barrage of K-rockets on one of the broad sides, followed by a swarm of MagTons, would blow it open and expose the interior.

With no weapons on transport ships, and no reason for the Westers to suspect anything, Dons' scripted plan had near absolute assurance of success.

And it did.

The Wester ship may have attempted to contact the Sorcerer Reborn. Harden picked up a signal that didn't read like anything he'd seen before. But not long after that, Dons unleashed his calculated firing plan. Six K-rockets introduced the Sorcerer Reborn to Wester Territory, and pummeled the side of the ship. The entire crew must have been shocked and bewildered, with no time to respond or do anything.

A huge hole ripped open on the side of the ship, and a stream of MagTons burst through it and exploded from within, causing untold damage. The ship lost propulsion and began to drift. The Sorcerer Reborn accelerated away from it, tracing a wide arc and picking up speed the whole way.

"Hit the hole Blake," Garrison said as he leaned toward his lead pilot. "Right through that rat ship."

Shipp peered into the blackness of space. Blake was still curving around and the actual vessel remained far out of sight.

Garrison spoke to Harden, "Get Yao ready. Burn the HAT on my mark."

"Yao reports ready," Harden replied after a moment.

Silence. The Sorcerer Reborn barreled through space. Shipp could see the location of the transport ship on Blake's monitor, coming closer to their path. Blake set the controls to head straight for the gash in its side.

"Here it comes," Blake said. "Hit it."

"Burn the HAT!" Garrison called out. Shipp and Garrison held on to the pilot seats in front of them as the HAT activated. Though only about one tenth speed, the acceleration still pressed on them. The Sorcerer Reborn shot forward. At almost the same instant they visually saw the derelict transport ship, they plowed right through it.

They felt the impact, like a strong windstorm hitting against a house, and saw debris and twisted metal dangling in front of them.

"Muzzle it, circle back," Garrison said. "Let's see what we did. And Mack? I want you out in space to inspect the Joust. See what that collision did to it. Take someone with you."

Mackson left his post, grabbed Mitz, and the two of them prepared for a space walk while the Sorcerer Reborn made its way back to the Wester ship. Mackson would later report the Joust suffered minimal damage.

What the Peterson officers saw when they approached the point of impact with the transport ship delighted them. They had carved right through it, practically obliterating it. Large and small sections now drifted in all directions. An expanding debris cloud. They passed several chunks as they slowed down, but most had already exceeded visual range. Harden displayed the LR readings on the monitor. Multiple fragments flew off in a spray-like pattern.

"Incredible," Garrison said. "That ship was three times our size. If we inflicted that much damage without suffering much ourselves, we're more powerful than I think anyone realized. We could take out an outpost with this thing."

"And we should," Shipp said. "Once our main mission is complete, we should go on a spree. All these back sections of their territory will be unguarded, at least for a while."

"It won't take them too long to figure out something isn't right," Harden said. "But they'll have no idea where we are, if things go our way."

"You think that transport got any messages off?" Garrison asked Harden.

"Hard to say," he replied. "I did get a funny reading, like they were trying to send us a comm before we attacked them. I don't think our comm tech is compatible with theirs. Didn't think of that before we left. We've never attempted to communicate ship to ship so it's never come up."

"Right," said Garrison, raising an eyebrow at the thought. "I wonder if you can figure out their tech from that data and maybe we can communicate next time."

"Possible, but don't hold your breath," Harden said.

"But they have a Beamer probably," Shipp said. "And ours isn't sending the virus-laden code yet, because we didn't want to turn it on until we approached the outpost."

"Right again," Garrison said. "We should turn it on now. Don't want to accidentally give any rats the cold shoulder."

Shipp went down to mid-level and found James and Li in their domicile. Several other crew members also took a break now that the excitement had died down. It was just the three of them in the room, and Shipp took advantage of the opportunity.

"Guys," Shipp said. "I've got a code from the Beamer that Merriss says will get me access to Wester media and archives. I'm going to search for General Elliss when we get to Ulrich. No one else knows. I need you to know, so if I run into any trouble, you're with me."

Li was stunned. "Shipp, everyone here is with you, not just us."

"I know. But Elliss is personal. Our mission is the priority, and I'm not going to screw that up. But in case something happens to me, I need you guys to be sure and get his location or whatever else I find."

James affirmed Shipp's plan. "This is the best chance we have to learn anything about him. It's worth it. I'm with you."

Shipp reached out and grabbed his hand. Li grabbed Shipp's other hand, and they stood together in a quick moment of unified silence.

In the ensuing weeks, the Sorcerer Reborn made its way toward Outpost Ulrich. They slowed down to a crawl several times to survey various regions and send the data to the Trans-Com. They found another inhabited planet, plus 71 that couldn't support life. No more space vehicles crossed their path.

Finally, the day arrived. Outpost Ulrich would be within sight in a few hours. Garrison huddled his officers in the meeting room to finalize the plan, which they had been honing to perfection the last several months.

The goal was simple and twofold – find Hydramol and destroy the outpost. A team of eight, led by Shipp, would wear Wester attack ship uniforms, which the Petersons manufactured to look like those observed on their last mission. The team would board the outpost and break up into pairs. Shipp's pair would find a monitor and locate the Hydramol star.

The other three pairs would plant MagTons on the levels closest to the docking bay. These specialty MagTons were a bit larger than normal, and had been upgraded with shards of Blackhead. This way, when they exploded, they might penetrate the hull.

The bigger challenge would be a cultural one. Other than Merriss, the Petersons had spent very little time with any Westers. There could be language cues, jokes, or common cultural references Westers would take for granted that everyone would know. The formal tongue Merriss accidentally used in front of them served as one example of this.

Mackson stressed this problem during their planning work, and emphasized the importance of talking to as few people as possible, and to avoid using odd expressions that only a Peterson would understand. They would keep comm chatter to an extreme minimum because they had no way of knowing if the Westers might be monitoring.

The most immediate worry concerned what would happen at the entrance, right when they opened up the door of the docking station. What if the Westers asked about their unusually shaped and oversized attack ship? In addition to the eight, another team would remain by the door and do whatever they could to keep the Westers from doing any sort of inspection. That could prove challenging if there were standard procedures for this, so the Petersons had worked up several plausible excuses to try and delay the Westers from boarding.

Even the Petersons who wouldn't be entering Ulrich understood these excuses so if called upon they could verify whatever the Petersons might be telling the Westers at the entrance. In particular, this required Blake, Yao, and Dons to be well versed in all the prevarications they had devised.

Shipp reviewed his boarding team with Garrison, Harden, and Mackson, one last time.

"Li is going with me, and Winston and Cruz will be another pair. Then Algiers and Drummond, and Zum and Ewing. Mackson is staying by the door with Mitz and James."

"Taking mostly new guys," Garrison noted.

Shipp explained his reasoning, "Pilots should stay here as much as possible, and I don't want to break up Dons' core team of gunners. I'd also like Harden to hold the entrance with Mackson's crew," Shipp suggested.

"Negative on that," Harden said. "My face and name are probably in their records from when I was captured. I can't be seen."

"We'll be fine," said Mackson. "My group knows the stories we developed, and I know this ship as well as anyone."

Harden and Mackson left to make final preparations.

Garrison turned to Shipp. "You're the best man for this. You've been in Wester facilities more recently than any of us. You sure you want just the small AX-9s?"

"That's the main thing I don't like about this," Shipp said. "But if their outposts are anything like our stations, no one walks around carrying weapons. We can sneak the AX-9s in along with our cases of Mags. I just hope they don't have any sort of search protocol."

"If they do?"

"Then we abandon the weapons planting job. Hydramol is top priority," Shipp said. And finding Elliss, he thought to himself.

45

Classified

With the boarding teams disguised in fabricated Wester attack ship uniforms, the hulking Sorcerer Reborn approached Outpost Ulrich. Interestingly, its external construction didn't look that different from most Peterson space stations. The most sensible scientific and space engineering approach to building space outposts relied on a circular stacking of levels of various diameters assembled in a somewhat random but aesthetically pleasing fashion, and it had been that way for centuries. No two outposts looked exactly the same, but this one resembled the typical construction. Some sections were much narrower, others wider.

Blake quickly identified the docking entrance. The Beamer, already transmitting the Petersons' virus-laden signal, made contact with the receptors on Ulrich. Harden picked up on this when what appeared to be an acceptance stamp flashed on his monitor where they had connected the Beamer's display to appear. He exhaled in relief.

"Looks like the Beamer is working."

Then, Harden received a strange comm signal, just like with the transport ship they destroyed.

"I think they're trying to call us. I still can't interpret it."

"Try to send something back," said Garrison, "So they know we made the attempt. Keep trying so it's persistent."

"Jonas," said Harden.

"And don't say Jonas," Garrison stressed.

Harden almost said it again, and then checked himself. "Right."

Harden began speaking, "Ulrich, we're trying to reach you but something's wrong with our comm. You receiving this?" Then, he sent a keyed message saying the same thing. He kept repeating this several times as the Sorcerer Reborn neared the docking station, which protruded from one of the widest layers of the outpost, about one third of the way from the top and two thirds from the bottom.

"Docking in five minutes," Blake said. "Boarding team ready?"

Garrison looked at Mackson. "Go check on Shipp and stay there until he and Li are on board. Keep your comm on when the door opens."

Garrison ordered all crew remaining on the Sorcerer Reborn to arm themselves with AX-15s, or to have one very close by.

Mackson made his way down to the mid-level and exit door, where Shipp and Li waited.

"Watch your language, Shipp," Mackson reminded him. "Yah?"

"Ya man," said Shipp, doing his best to mimic the way Merriss and other Westers spoke.

The seconds ticked by, and the Sorcerer Reborn crept closer to the outpost docking station. As the ship slowed to a crawl, Blake positioned it so the airlock balloon could extend from the outpost and form a temporary seal against the ship's exterior wall. Once he got the green light that the space inside the balloon had equalized air pressure, Reeves released the mechanism for the door so Shipp could open it.

Shipp turned the three handles, and the door extended downward, forming the ramp connecting them to the outpost entrance. Unlike Peterson docking stations, this exterior door had no markings at all. Just plain metal. It opened, and a Wester attendant awaited them on the other side, through a dark tunnel about ten meters long.

"Hey ya," said the Wester. "Don't believe I've seen you fellas here before, ya? Where you coming from?"

"We just finished a run at Kora, and then an extended mission in the frontier, ya," said Shipp.

The Wester looked at him a little funny. Shipp deliberately avoided eye contact, wanting the interaction to seem as pedestrian as it should be. But Li watched him, and got a little nervous at the Wester's reaction.

"This is my first time at Ulrich see," said Li. "I want to check messages from my family once we get settled. Can you point me in the right direction ya?"

"Yeah bro," the Wester replied. "There's a bunch of monitors two levels down for general usage eh."

"We've been in space a while," Shipp blurted as if distracted. "A bunch of our guys want some time to relax, ya?" Then he interrupted himself, turned back into the Sorcerer Reborn, and called with a loud voice, "Hey Winston, Cruz – you guys ready?" Shipp turned back to the Wester, "Winston and Cruz are managing our re-supply run."

"Sounds good ya," the Wester replied.

Shipp and Li started ahead. Li looked back to see Winston and Cruz emerging from the tunnel, wheeling a supply crate that had been manufactured to resemble ones found on Wester attack ships. Of course, this crate wouldn't contain supplies, and it wasn't empty. It was filled with MagTons. Then, Li whispered to Shipp, "So far so good."

They scanned the hangar. It was huge. Much larger than similar rooms on Peterson space stations. Large crates, stacked six levels high, extended far back into lower-lit fringes of this level. Almost as if they used this level for storage for the entire outpost, as well as incoming ships. The Petersons had a minimum of three such storage rooms on every space station, in case an area became uninhabitable. This Wester outpost could also be a hub of sorts, and thus require a larger storage capacity. Either way, they both looked forward to destroying it and killing as many Westers on board as possible.

Li and Shipp walked with a casual gait, which wasn't difficult as this was their first time off the Sorcerer Reborn in about a year.

A few other Westers seemed to be walking in similar directions toward one area, so Shipp and Li presumed that must be the way out of this level. They were right. Around a corner, they found an elevator. But beyond that, they saw a slanted walking pad. Shipp had seen photos of these in history books, but never in person. Apparently the Westers still used them.

Rather than stairs or an elevator, the slanted pad moved under your feet, so you could traverse down to the next level without having to take a step. They probably used these to make it easier to move larger objects to different levels, as opposed to cramming them in an elevator.

To avoid getting stuck with a bunch of Westers in an elevator, Shipp and Li took the walking pad. Shipp also spoke quickly into his comm, which had been pre-set only to send and receive from the eleven Petersons who would set foot on Outpost Ulrich. He told the other Petersons about the walking pads, and suggested they use those instead of elevators.

"That guy looked at you a little strange, back at the entrance," Li told Shipp.

Shipp turned as they rode the walking pad, "Really? Strange as in suspicious? Should I warn the others?"

"I don't know. It was hard to read. I didn't think you said anything unusual," Li said.

Shipp and Li passed through a number of other Westers on the next level, but like Peterson stations, there was plenty of room and no large crowds. Most people seemed to be walking with a purpose. No one was just standing around. They found the walking pad to the next level, and rode it down to where the Wester told them they would find monitors.

"Hold on," Shipp said. He noticed a corner area that seemed out of the way enough to contact Mackson. The whole team would hear the conversation.

"Hey Mack, how are things looking back there? We're two levels down, near monitors."

Mackson was still on board the Sorcerer Reborn, which Shipp presumed he would be, so he could speak freely there.

"Winston and Cruz are off, Algiers and Drummond are heading out next. I'll send Ewing and Zum in about five minutes, or longer. Hoping that Wester twerp goes somewhere soon if we can sell this as a routine stop."

"Well done everyone." Shipp ended the comm, and began searching the level. Li already found where to go. He pointed Shipp ahead, and they strode deeper into the center of the outpost. Up ahead, Shipp noticed a series of four monitors along one wall, embedded in the wall and with small standing level tables jutting outward. One Wester stood at one of them, but the other three were unused.

Li stood between that Wester and Shipp so Shipp could retrieve the code he had generated from the Beamer without looking silly, since it was likely Westers never needed to write their codes down.

He examined the monitor. Touched the field where it looked like you could enter a code. A keyboard appeared on the screen. Shipp typed in his code. He looked at Li before submitting it. Then, he whispered, "Keep an eye out."

Li watched the room as Shipp sent the code.

"Not registered, please retry," the monitor taunted.

"Merriss. If that rat was lying after all this time..." Shipp muttered.

Before re-entering the code, he studied the screen some more. So did Li. Li pointed to a symbol on the bottom right corner. "What's that?"

Shipp pressed it. "Special format accreditation – please enter" read the monitor.

Shipp and Li nonverbally agreed to try it. Shipp typed in his Beamer-generated code again.

Accepted. The monitor opened access to all the Wester archives, whatever was stored at this outpost. Like the Petersons, the Westers had abandoned software networks centuries before. Not just on ships, but on outposts too. Viruses and poison pills were just too easy to create and could cripple entire defense systems without ever entering any facilities. So they returned to a method where information was brought by hand, on storage cartridges, whenever a ship arrived from a different planet or outpost.

For this reason, news tended to travel planet to planet, and outpost to outpost. It was standard procedure, whenever you docked anywhere, to upload your info box, as the Petersons called it, to the destination's archives.

Shipp typed 'Hydramol' into the entry field.

A screen appeared with a photo of a white star, along with a nearby planet and several paragraphs of text. The planet had a reddish, purplish hue covering most of the surface. Were those clouds? Strange. Either way, it didn't appear to have any water.

"Sangria," Shipp remarked about the color of the planet, feeling the prick in his mind that this color evoked. He couldn't seem to escape it. Li knew the story, and sympathized. They were in this together.

Shipp and Li quickly read the text, skimming past all the general information. Then, near the end, they read something that set them both on edge:*Due to recent military developments, the location of Hydramol has been classified since 980 S.A.*

Shipp and Li froze. They needed to keep quiet because of the Wester at the nearby monitor. But their faces gave away the sudden tension. Both stood there for a moment, trying to work through what they could try next.

Shipp decided to regroup later and plow ahead while he had the time. He typed "General Elliss" into the entry field. A photo appeared, along with text.

Shipp devoured it. General Brelan Elliss served almost thirty years in the Wester Space Military. Born on Faraday, one of the most densely populated planets in the galaxy with almost two billion inhabitants. Serving as a general in the Space Military, with many years as an attack ship captain, but now more often as a strategic planning overseer.

Shipp kept searching. He found the location of Faraday. The city and address of his place of birth. He found the location of the Wester Space Academy, as they called their version of Space Force University. He found photos of Elliss' family of origin. He confirmed the Eradicator as the name of Elliss' ship.

Shipp kept searching and searching as more questions came to his mind, puzzles to solve, blanks to fill in, things the Space Fleet would find useful. He lost track of time. Li stood by without a word the whole time. Almost two hours passed. Finally, the Wester left the other monitor. Others walked by now and then, so they still couldn't talk in normal voices most of the time. But they managed.

At one point Li activated his comm, "Team 1 hit a snag. Finding information, but still missing the key. Any updates?"

Li waited. The silence made him nervous. He knew the strong possibility that no one on any teams could speak at the moment. But for the three teams planting MagTons and the team at the entrance to the Sorcerer Reborn to all be silent for this long was very disconcerting. Several minutes passed. Li whispered to Shipp.

"I have no response yet. From anyone. That doesn't seem good."

Then, someone responded. It was Algiers. "Ya Li, sorry for delay. We've planted 65%. Out."

Each team carried twenty MagTons on board, so 65% meant Algiers and Drummond had planted thirteen of theirs. That was good progress for a couple hours. A bit later, Winston spoke up. They had planted nine. Ewing and Zum later called in, reporting eight planted Mags.

But Mackson, James, and Mitz never spoke up for over fifteen minutes before Li switched off his comm. "Never heard from the entrance team," he told Shipp.

"That's not good," Shipp said. But he barely said it, and barely realized what he was saying, so engrossed in his archive exploration. He had become a vanadium miner, living his moment with just one thing on his mind – more. More information. More locations. More data. More secrets. More maps. More names. More. More. More. More. More.

At one point, Shipp stumbled on something quite shocking. He gestured Li to take a look.

Andromeda.

Apparently, the Westers were developing a new type of long-distance spacecraft that allowed for an increased HAT speed, and they believed they could reach the nearest galaxy in about twenty years. A plan was already in the works to build several such vessels and initiate a permanent exploration and colonization mission to Andromeda.

"Twenty years," remarked Li, astounded at the short amount of time. "Why would they want to colonize Andromeda?"

"I don't know," Shipp said. "Sounds like a one-way trip, so it's not like it would help them win the war."

After a moment of reflection, Shipp returned to his data mining. Finally, after a third hour had elapsed since they accessed the monitor, Li had to intervene. With no Westers nearby at the moment, he took his opportunity.

"Shipp, you need to stop," Li began. Shipp barely heard him. Li put his hand on Shipp's shoulder, and lightly pushed him out of his information-fueled trance. Shipp reacted like he'd been caught with his pants down.

"What? What? What is it?"

"We need to find Hydramol. We have to find that. That's priority one."

Shipp breathed a heavy sigh. Almost like coming down from a high, back to reality. "Yeah, we do. Right. I think we'll have to find a person to ask maybe."

Li shook his head. "If this has been classified for that long, none of the young guys here are going to know about it. A military person with age."

Shipp nodded in agreement. "Or, maybe anyone with age. Food service guy. Someone near the end of service. Problem is, how do we bring it up?"

Shipp and Li began pondering their way through this unexpected challenge. After a quick brainstorm, they concluded that no reasonable way existed to approach a Wester and ask for the location of a classified outpost or planet.

With the digital archives likely scrubbed, one possibility emerged – old physical star atlases. Most Peterson stations contained physical maps and records, so Shipp and Li expected something similar on Ulrich. They were right.

A quick monitor query turned up the location of a library six more levels down. Shipp and Li hurried off and made their way down, now eight levels below the dock to the Sorcerer Reborn. Once they found the library, they began examining books and atlases, visually scanning them to find Hydramol. With over a hundred occupied planets in Wester Territory and thousands more uninhabitable, it would take time.

But up to this point, they had no reason to believe their time was limited.

46

Entrance

Once Ewing and Zum exited the Sorcerer Reborn, Mackson made his way out, along with Mitz, later joined by James. They sauntered around the cavernous storage hangar, never straying too far from their vessel.

The Wester attendant departed not long after Ewing and Zum went through, so for now, the Peterson trio had the area to themselves. Mackson and James noted Li's message that the Beamer-generated code had worked. So, they milled around and waited. Garrison and Harden sent periodic updates about things they were picking up from the outpost and beyond. Nothing out of the ordinary so far.

About thirty minutes passed.

Then, a group of four Westers rounded a corner and approached. One of them was dressed differently than the other three, who looked like grunt workers. James had been studying a monitor nearby, which displayed manifests for the various cargo stored on the outpost. He stayed there, remaining within eyesight and earshot of Mackson and Mitz, who kept near the entrance to the tunnel leading to their vessel.

The Westers neared. The distinguished one spoke when they reached Mackson and Mitz.

"Hey ya, got your checklist for me bro?"

Uh oh.

This was their worst fear – some sort of Wester procedure they couldn't have known about. But Mackson played it smooth.

"Did you not receive our comms when we entered proximity?" he asked.

"We heard nothing," said the Wester. "Your ship checks out, ya, but we had no word of a second attack ship heading our way, and the Dogfighter still isn't here see."

"Yeah, I figured. Our whole comm system failed a few weeks back, ya. We've been working to fix it, but no success. We couldn't hear any of your comms either," Mackson said.

"Eh?" said the Wester, seeming truly surprised. "Well that explains a lot eh. We just saw a huge dark shape approaching in total silence. Got a little nervous."

"Ya man, sorry about that," Mackson shook his head, aping frustration. "It's been a pretty stressed-out couple weeks huh. We passed a transport that I think was also trying to talk to us, and they got nothing but static probably."

"Got it," said the Wester. "I can corral a band of decks and have them take a rip at your comm systems, eh."

"That'd be great," said Mackson, picking up the lingo that 'decks' must be the Wester word for tech or mechanical experts. "How soon can they be here?"

The Wester, who must have been an admin, looked over his portable monitor, which displayed some scheduling and personnel information. He putzed around for a bit, then looked up at Mackson. "I can have a band here in about two hours. That work?"

"Should be fine. We might want to push it to three. We'll be here for several days, so no rush. I'll check with the captain. He doesn't always like to let the decks on so soon after docking from long missions, ya?" Mackson said.

Mackson then called Garrison and Harden on his comm, whose responses only Mackson would be able to hear. "Captain bro, they wanna send on some decks to work on our comms in a couple hours. Two hours okay with you? I was thinking more like three, ya?"

Garrison chuckled, hearing Mackson talk so stupidly. Harden shook his head in disgust, "He's good."

"Yeah, let's do three. The more delay the better," Garrison affirmed.

Mackson nodded and relayed that to the Wester admin.

The Wester admin then returned to the topic Mackson had been trying to avoid, "You got your checklist for me say? Since we weren't expecting you, I don't have anything ready for you bro."

But James chimed in here, having studied the monitor in the storage area the whole conversation.

"Gotcha bro," James said. "I'm in charge of the checklist. You've got a big reserve of fuel cells here, and we'll need some of that. Plus a re-supply of rations and water ya. I'll get you the figures in a bit. We have a few guys out taking care of some personal business. I don't want to re-supply until they get back because they like to do things a certain way, if you know what I mean, ya."

The Wester admin nodded in understanding.

"Alright bro man. I had a question about that. My lead says you sent eight guys out right after docking. That's a lotta personal business, as you call it bro," the Wester said.

James got a little nervous, but was able to conceal it because he wasn't even facing the Westers, still pretending to work on figures on his personal monitor.

"Well, with no comms for weeks, that's the situation, ya," James said, hoping to diffuse further inquiry.

"Yeah," said the Wester admin. "Our situation is, what the flame is the name of your ship, bro? I'm standing here waiting for the first thing you shoulda been telling us ya. I got no specs on an attack ship with these dimensions."

"Obliterator," said Mackson, giving the fake name the Petersons had agreed to use if this came up. "We're a little larger than normal, but we're also the latest ship."

"Latest?" asked the puzzled Wester admin. "Whaddaya mean say? Were you supposed to be somewhere sooner?"

Mackson realized the Westers didn't recognize his use of that term, which surprised him. "Latest, meaning the most recently built attack ship. The newest. Ya."

"I see," said the Wester admin. "Obliterator. Right ya." He returned to his monitor, remaining there for some time.

Then, Mackson, Mitz, and James all heard Li's voice in their comms:

"Team 1 hit a snag. Finding information, but still missing the key. Any updates?"

They had to ignore it, but the 'snag' worried them, because it meant they had to prolong this charade even longer than it had already gone, and this Wester admin was prying a bit too thoroughly for comfort.

"I'll be back in a few," the Wester admin said. The other three Westers stayed put, and began pulling small crates and other materials out of a large nearby storage unit. Mackson thought about what a dumb statement that was. A few what? He figured he must have meant some unit of time, but clarity demanded a specific unit. Seconds? Minutes? Halves? The Wester propensity for cavalier language was downright pathetic.

It was also interesting that only the admin spoke. None of the others said a word, even after he left. But with these three rats crawling around, the Petersons couldn't relay any messages to Shipp or the others. James thought about heading inside the Sorcerer Reborn, but decided it was better to remain here to make sure nothing went bad. Right now, any conflict would happen with three on three.

After about twenty minutes, one of the grunts spoke up, to Mitz.

"You like listening to all the big men talk bro? They go on like a military lecture," said the grunt. He stood the tallest of the three. Mitz was ready.

"The big men talk and we can daydream. Been thinking about the lady I met last year on leave," Mitz said.

"The lady?" said the second grunt, the only woman of the three. "Is that what you call us, bro? You know, I heard you guys talked funny right after you broke from your Obliterator ship. But lady is about the funniest line of the year, say."

Mitz didn't give in. "That's what I call her because that's what her friend called her. Good enough for me ya."

She smiled at him, seeming to accept his response, but then turned back to her crate work.

"What I wanna know," said the third grunt, "Is why you're wearing the last generation uniforms if you're from the 'latest' attack ship. You guys don't seem to know a whole lot about much around here, bros."

"Well," said Mitz, "If you'd been on this last mission with us, you'd know. These are our backups. Bunch of us had to switch up a few weeks back ya. You ever serve on an attack ship? Or you always ask such stupid questions bro?"

While Mackson and Mitz kept stalling, James reached into his pocket and activated his personal AX-9. He was ready to fire. This conversation wasn't heading in a positive direction.

"Hey bro stay light, eh?" said the tall grunt. "Just makin' conversation. You stuck in that bucket for months you get a little anti-social, ya?"

Mitz laughed, and Mackson joined him. Amidst more small talk, the woman left when she got called off to another task. But the other two remained and continued the bantering.

Finally, the tall grunt turned to Mackson. "It's odd, you say you got no checklist to give us, and your bro over there says he's working on it. But ya'll out here the whole time."

"Bro? We run our ship the way we run it," Mackson said, trying a stronger tactic to get them to pull back again. "You don't like it, take it up with the captain. We're waiting until our guys get back."

Then, the woman returned, along with two other women and the original Wester admin who greeted them. The other two women were dressed like him, presumably as admins, or whatever the Westers called them.

James noticed one of the new women admins wore a yellow band around the wrist of her jacket. She's the one who spoke up first.

"We need your stack, sis," she said to Mackson. "Right now. Your new Obliterator ship isn't in any of our records, so we need to update the archives see."

Mackson was unnerved. She called him 'sis,' the first time he'd heard any Wester use the opposite sex slang to refer to someone. Was she taunting him? Second, he didn't know what 'stack' meant. His best guess was that 'stack' was their term for the info box, which the Petersons used to update the archives on any outposts and planets whenever they landed or docked.

"Right," said Mackson. "Hold on." He switched on his comm for Harden and Garrison. "They want the stack to update the archives. Can you get that out here ya?"

Garrison looked at Harden. They both sunk. This detail had been overlooked. No one thought about it when this Galactic Mission was planned. So many details had been worked through. But not this one.

"What do we tell them?" asked Harden.

"Tell them our 'stack' got corrupted when our comm system failed and we tried to fix it. So we don't have any new updates," said Garrison, pretty proud of his answer.

Mackson held back a smirk at Garrison's clever response, then shook his head at the wristbanded Wester admin.

"Ya sis he says the stack got corrupted when we tried to fix our comm system, ya know?" Mackson said to her, hoping she'd buy it.

"I see," she said. "You know, you've been here almost three hours and we have nothing at all from you, let alone any record that the Obliterator even exists. What is this, a secret ship say? I checked with Space M. You wanna explain yourselves a little better? You let us on your ship right now, or I'm going to bring down a whole band of arms and do it our way. Your fish stink."

Just then, Ewing and Zum emerged from the walking pad off in the distance and headed toward them. What a welcome distraction, thought Mackson. He nodded them over. The Westers all turned to see them coming.

"Hey there Ewing, Zum. All taken care of?" said Mackson, hoping they'd pick up on the tension and not make it worse.

"We're good," said Ewing. "Hey ya bros, you got some great facilities here," he said, as they passed right through the group and boarded the Sorcerer Reborn.

The wristbanded Wester admin turned and smiled at Mackson.

"How many more guys you have wandering around on Ulrich, sis?" she asked.

"I don't know, six I think. Right man?" He looked at James as if needing confirmation. James confirmed it.

She squared up with Mackson and looked right at him for several seconds, saying nothing. Enough to make him fidget. Then, she spoke, as if it required great effort to say these words:

"Thy place of origin speaks to thee, dear sir."

Mackson trembled a bit in his spirit. This was that formal tongue thing Shipp had told them about. The Wester seemed almost troubled, even after she finished speaking. A similar sort of profound emotional fallout like Merriss had exhibited after speaking this way. But she never broke eye contact.

When Mackson said nothing, her expression turned dark. Her face firmed and turned resolute.

"Sergeant of arms," she said.

The tall grunt faced her immediately. "Yes ma'am." Apparently, he wasn't a grunt at all.

"Take these men into custody, and put out an alert for the other six. Report their outdated uniforms so they're easy to spot. You can also triangulate their locations based on any more foreign comm transmissions the intel room picks up eh. Bring them to detention level eight. We have questions say," she ordered.

Before the Petersons could react, all six Westers pulled AX-9s from their belts and pointed them at Mitz, Mackson, and James.

The Wester leader, who wasn't an admin at all, but apparently a military expert instead, spoke into her comm. "Send in your band of arms to board the ship."

Inside the Sorcerer Reborn, Harden and Garrison had been listening the entire time. But this happened so fast they had little time to react. Plus, Harden's eyes widened as he looked with growing alarm at the LR.

"General, there's another attack ship coming. It must be that Dogfighter one the other guy mentioned."

Garrison arose. "Call Dons. Tell him to prepare an attack on the Dogfighter – after it docks. The rest of us need to prepare to repel the boarders. We need to act now before her 'band of arms' gets here."

He started down the stairs to mid-level, then turned back to Harden.

"You need to risk a call to Shipp. Tell him to get back here immediately. We can try again at another outpost."

47

SEARCHING

In the library, Shipp and Li had been scouring atlases and star maps for nearly an hour when Shipp received a private call from Harden.

"Can't talk long. Rats are on to us. Taking three prisoners, planning to board us. They know your uniforms. Get back here now." Then he disconnected, which Shipp knew meant he wasn't allowed to call back. He quickly told Li the message.

"We don't have the location yet," said Li.

Shipp looked around the room. In their vicinity sat eight tables interspersed with counters, monitors, and chairs. Beyond were numerous corridors filled with records and documents. It was sparsely populated. Just a few people studying and shuffling around here and there. Shipp picked out a Wester sitting by himself. He nodded Li in his direction.

"You bring that guy to that back corner, the darkest place in the room, after I buzz your comm," Shipp told him. "Tell him your friend needs help."

At this, Shipp arose and strode over to the library admin, who was wearing a shirt with a jacket over it, open in the front, "Hey bro, I'm having a tough time finding a document that's supposed to be back here, can you help me?"

"Sure," said the library admin. "What's the resource?"

"Hold on," Shipp said, since he didn't have a title, "I'm getting a call." He pretended to be annoyed with the interruption and spent the rest of the walk to the back corner telling the non-person that he couldn't talk right now and arguing about why. Finally, they reached the corner. No one could see them.

"Okay, we're here," Shipp said. Then, without a word, he drew a blade from his belt and drove it straight into the Wester's heart, then slammed him to the floor and covered his mouth with his palm until the man died. Shipp had never killed someone with his blade before. A strange experience to watch the life drain from a face. He made sure no blood from the wound touched the man's jacket.

Then, Shipp buzzed Li. Li arose and approached the other Wester.

"Hey bro, my friend needs a little help reaching something in the back, can you come help her?" Li said.

"Help with what?" the Wester said as he stood up to go with Li.

"She's short," Li said, laughing. "Having a tough time reaching the top shelf. I'm too short too."

The Wester rounded the corner and saw the dead library admin on the floor. But because of the fairly low light, it wasn't immediately clear that this was a dead body.

"What's that? Are you okay bro?" the Wester said, as he approached the corner.

Right when he reached it, Shipp stepped from around the shelf and clocked him in the head with the butt of his blade. Then, he knelt on his chest, clasped his hands around his throat, and choked him to death. The Wester struggled, but Li held down his legs. Together, they suffocated him. Again, Shipp felt something strange inside, watching a second man die in his grasp.

Shipp crept to the end of that corridor to ensure no one had heard anything. All was calm.

He rushed back to Li, who was already changing his clothes. Shipp ripped off his own outer clothes, and they proceeded to put on the Wester civilian clothing – just the jacket and pants from the man Shipp knifed.

"Wipe your sweat," Shipp said. They dried off the sweat from their heads, necks, and hands. They waited until their bodies calmed.

"Just gonna leave their bodies?" asked Li.

"Place is pretty sparse. Doubtful anyone will go back there before we find Hydramol."

And with that, they returned to searching the physical maps, more frantically than ever. Ruling out one sector after another, looking at each planet, each star, and each outpost.

"He said it was toward the edge of the galaxy somewhere, right?" Li confirmed.

"Yes! I don't know how close, but it has to be there. Where are you?" Shipp asked.

"I'm in what they're calling sector 18, near the back of their Territory," Li said. "I've already scanned 14, 31, 8, and 6."

"I've done 21, 24, 30, and 32," said Shipp. He looked at the larger map of the whole Territory at the front of one of the space atlases. "I see six more on what seems like the edge to me. I'll take 20, 35, and 36."

About five minutes later, a loud buzzing sound jolted them both from their fixation on the star maps. A voice came over a comm somewhere in the room.

"Attention outpost residents and military personnel. There are unauthorized persons inside. They are wearing the last generation attack ship uniforms. If you spot them, contact outpost security immediately. Do not attempt to engage them yourself."

The voice was that of the wristbanded Wester leader. She repeated the message again.

Shipp and Li kept searching. A Wester walked over to them. "I'm positive I saw two guys wearing those old getups come in here a while ago ya? You guys see them?"

Shipp feigned ignorance. "I've been buried in books all day bro. I haven't seen anybody."

The Wester started looking around the room. He headed toward the corridors, and started looking down each one. He neared the last one, where the two dead bodies lay.

Shipp looked at Li. Then, he scanned the rest of the room. There were two Westers in sight, other than the one about to make a disturbing discovery. Shipp and Li knew what they had to do. Both men pulled out their AX-9s. Li snuck down a corridor to the back wall and made his way toward the dead bodies, taking care not to cross into a corridor before the suspicious Wester had passed it.

The Wester reached the last corridor. From the other end, he saw the two dead bodies.

"Hey guys," he said, looking back toward the table where Shipp and Li had been. But they weren't there anymore. Shipp was across the room, preparing to kill the other two Westers in the room.

Li stepped out across the dead bodies, and fired three shots at the suspicious Wester. Immediately afterward, Shipp raised his weapon and killed the two other Westers in the room. Li ran back to the open area with all the tables. Shipp stood across from him.

They waited.

Silence.

"Rip out the pages of the remaining six sectors. We'll take them with us," Shipp said.

"What if it's not on any of them?" Li said.

Shipp halted. He had to risk it. He called Harden.

48

Firefight

The Wester commander, or whatever she was, turned away from her subordinates, who were pointing their weapons at Mitz, Mackson, and James. She headed toward the elevator at a brisk pace, and turned around to confirm that her people were indeed directing the three suspicious attack ship crew members forward. She neared the elevator. Her people had escorted the other three about halfway there.

But then, she heard the sound of AX-15 fire, not the AX-9s her people were carrying.

She wheeled around to see her people falling down dead. They were being shot from behind, from within the Obliterator. It was Cardmanov, Jimenez, Garrison, and Harden. They fanned out of the tunnel, gunning down all five Westers before they could figure out what was happening.

She bolted the rest of the way and closed herself in the elevator while yelling in her comm, "Send in the arms! More came out of the ship and just killed all my men say! There's at least seven of them in the cargo bay!" She switched to another channel and spoke to someone else, "These must be Peterson dogs! I don't know how they coulda made it all the way here or why, but this cannot be anyone else see."

Back in the cargo bay, Garrison, Harden, Jimenez, and Cardmanov spread out and took up positions behind large crates near the tunnel entrance, knowing that a second attack would be coming soon. James, Mackson, and Mitz began running back to re-unite with them.

Up the walking pad streamed a band of Wester soldiers. Twelve of them. The moment they reached the top, they opened fire.

Mitz got hit multiple times and crumpled down dead. Mackson fell too, hit in his calf and above the hip. James jumped off to the side and took cover within the walls of crates. Mackson lay vulnerable out in the open and could be killed easily.

Harden and Jimenez fired back from about ten meters to the left of the tunnel. Garrison and Cardmanov were situated twenty meters to their right. The crates, made of thick metal, gave ample protection from AX fire, but if the Westers brought anything more severe, they'd be in big trouble. But, using more severe weapons would also risk puncturing the exterior walls of the outpost directly behind them.

Still, the Petersons needed to be ready.

Harden called Zum, "Get a Mossamer or hive bomber and get out here! We're pinned down."

Zum marched through the tunnel moments later, took a knee, and fired two hive bombs toward the Wester positions. Each prop whizzed through the air and then exploded near the targets. They could hear some Westers screaming and cursing about hive bombs being fired on an outpost and how insane that was. They called for greater firepower.

Then, Zum lost his balance and crashed to the floor as the tunnel between the outpost and the Sorcerer Reborn shook violently. Something had hit the Sorcerer Reborn. Harden heard it too.

Reeves called him on comm seconds later. "Harden! That other attack ship just hit us with K-rockets. Direct hits both. Unprovoked!"

Garrison intervened, "Reeves – tell Dons to fire back. He can lead the attack without us. Get everyone available down to Fire Control and hit them hard. You're sitting ducks. But you have three times the armor!"

Then, he yelled to Zum in the tunnel, "Zum! Get back in the ship and head to Weapons!"

Cardmanov had superb shooting skills. He sighted a Wester who kept peeking over a crate at the same spot. The next time his head appeared, Cardmanov nailed him. Dead.

"Nice shot Card," Garrison said. "How many you think are left?"

"At least eight. The hives took out a couple, maybe injured more."

Two more Westers rode up the walking pad, bringing electric pulse rifles. Harden spotted them first. "Pulse rifles! We're not prepared for that!"

The Westers began firing electric pulses toward the Peterson positions. At that range, it was tough to hit a target with a pulse. And they had to wait to recharge. But it put the Petersons on the defensive.

Mackson lay bleeding in the middle of the floor. He kept still, playing dead, hoping the Westers wouldn't finish him off, which they would easily if they knew he was still alive. He grimaced, clenched, but held still, breathing in and out the intense pain from his wounds.

Garrison called Locke. "Locke – Mack is down from AX fire. I can't tell if he's dead. Mitz is gone. Be ready when we reboard."

"I'm ready to go," replied Locke.

Harden had been firing the most, mainly to keep the Westers too nervous to advance. His weapon ran out of rounds first. Jimenez ran out next.

"Garrison! We're out." Harden said on his comm so as not to alert the Westers.

"We can't bring more out. Everyone on board is fighting the Wester ship," Garrison replied.

"Send Yao!" Harden said.

"Not a chance Harden, you know better than that," Garrison replied.

Risking the life of the Chief Propulsion Officer was the last thing Garrison would do. No matter the situation. If Yao died, that would mean everyone had died, in Garrison's mind.

"We're almost out! What then?" Harden said louder.

Then, he and Jimenez felt a very sharp tingling. They got hit with an electric pulse. He and Jimenez both fell to the ground contorting, twisting, grunting, and hardening up in bizarre, fetal positions from hell. Immobilized.

Garrison could hear the Westers celebrating, knowing they had pulsed them. For the first time, he started getting nervous. "Fireballs," Garrison swore.

The Westers arose and advanced, nine of them firing continuously, pelting Garrison and Cardmanov's position, forcing them to stay behind the increasingly misshapen crate protecting them. The Westers moved briskly, from one protected area to the next, covering for each other, firing ahead, and closing the distance to the general of the Sorcerer Reborn. They passed the halfway point in the cavernous cargo room.

But James was waiting.

He had taken the opportunity to surround himself with crates. Though all he had was an AX-9, he gambled the Westers had forgotten about him or assumed he would keep running. As they passed his position, he opened fire from behind his crates. One down. Two down. Three. Four.

The Westers saw their fellow soldiers dropping all around them, and turned to see James firing at them.

Five down.

They reeled, and ran back out of James' sight. Just four remained. Garrison smiled. "James, you're a beast! Harden and Jimenez are pulsed. They'll be out for a while. We're low on rounds. Can you get back here? They'll be coming for you."

"I can run farther back and maze my way around to you," James replied.

"Do it. You can't stay there," Garrison said.

Right then, the Wester commander's voice sounded throughout the outpost, the same warning Shipp and Li heard at this moment:

"Attention outpost residents and military personnel. There are unauthorized persons inside. They are wearing the last generation attack ship uniforms. If you spot them, contact outpost security immediately. Do not attempt to engage them yourself."

James bolted from his spot, and ran away from the battle toward the huge storage crates looming in the recesses of the cargo bay.

Harden's comm came to life. It was Shipp.

"Harden – we still haven't found it. Can we have more time or do we need to come back?"

But Harden couldn't answer. He sputtered. Spat. Roared in rage at his inability to respond. Harden knew Shipp wouldn't risk calling someone else. He had already risked his position with this first call. But he couldn't respond or tell Garrison about Shipp's predicament. He spewed out all his impotence trying to will his body to move. But it wouldn't.

Garrison saw Harden trying to move and could tell he was about to explode in fury. He couldn't risk exposing his position, because the Westers had gone quiet.

Cardmanov looked over the crate, trying to find them. No movement. "I think they're searching for James," he said to Garrison.

They were. Moments later, they kicked aside what had been James' hiding place. Not wanting to hunt for him in the recesses of the cargo bay, they returned to the main thoroughfare, firing again at Garrison and Cardmanov from behind a twenty-meter-tall crate. They were now parallel with Mackson's position. He was still trying to play dead.

Dons called Garrison, "General, we're getting hit hard. Armor is taking a beating. We need to get out of here. Reeves picked up convoys heading toward us. I'm blowing a ton of TIs."

"Jonas that," Garrison said. Then his body tingled. "Oh, fireballs," Garrison swore again. He and Cardmanov were hit with a pulse. "nnsifphieshuqsh!"

They crumpled and writhed. The Westers celebrated again. Harden and Jimenez were still down. The tunnel to the Obliterator was empty. James was somewhere else. Mackson was playing dead and had no weapons near him.

The four remaining Westers emerged from cover, and marched toward Garrison and Cardmanov. Sitting ducks. They could now see their Peterson uniforms.

"Petersons ya. Dog meat intruders," said one of the Westers, while the others kept an eye on Harden and Jimenez. "How'd they get this far into our space, eh?"

Another Wester spoke up. "They'll regret it. Forever."

They stepped toward Harden and Jimenez, intending to kill them first since they would be the first to recover from the pulses.

But then, AX-9 fire erupted from behind them. Multiple weapons. One Wester went down, then another. Winston and Cruz had just made it up the walking pad and fired repeatedly at the Wester soldiers.

Caught in the open, the two remaining Westers ran for cover and returned fire. But now, it was them caught in the middle. A bit later, Algiers and Drummond arrived as well, joining Winston and Cruz. The Westers retreated, and decided to risk running into James and hide within the caverns rather than be caught in the middle. Too many variables in play for them to stay put.

James saw them run by his position, but decided to let them go. He made his way to Garrison and Cardmanov, distressed to see their immobilized bodies. He called Locke.

"Locke, we have four guys pulsed out here. Get out here and get them inside," James said. "We can cover you," as Winston, Cruz, Algiers, and Drummond approached.

"Be there in ten seconds," Locke replied.

Locke emerged from the tunnel wheeling a strange contraption. A single steering post rose up to about hip height, with several buttons and switches going down the neck. At the bottom, it fanned out into a set of four wheels. Locke flipped two switches. From within the post, two sets of belts and hooks shot out, still connected at one end of the post.

He wheeled over to Garrison and Cardmanov, and quickly strapped the belts and hooks around each of them, threading under their shoulders and between their legs. Then, he turned on the power, and steered the post back toward the tunnel. With this, he was able to drag the two men into the tunnel and back into the Sorcerer Reborn.

By that time, James and the other four Petersons reached their position and kept an eye out for the remaining two Westers and any more who might come up the walking pad.

James looked at Winston, "You hear from Shipp? Where is he?"

Winston shook his head. "We haven't heard from anyone for a while, until that alert went out. We planted one more Mag and then made it back here. We found an emergency stairwell and got almost all the way without being spotted."

James glanced at Algiers and Drummond. They hadn't been as fortunate. Algiers had an AX wound in his shoulder, and a bruised and bloodied Drummond had entangled in personal combat. But they all made it. Except Shipp and Li, James' two best friends in the world.

Locke returned, and started strapping up Harden and Jimenez.

"They're going to send way more than this the longer we sit here," Locke said. "And our ship is taking a beating out there. We have to leave now!"

James knew this wasn't a military outpost, so it wouldn't be staffed with a huge supply of soldiers, most likely. But Locke's warning wasn't empty. Non-military Westers wouldn't just sit around while Petersons were burying dog bones in their outpost. James had to risk a call. He called Shipp.

49

Escape

Shipp and Li were running out of time, and running out of sectors to search for Hydramol on the paper atlases. Each still had two more sectors to comb through after finishing the ones they were searching. Losing patience as his heart beat steadily faster, Shipp was finishing his search of his third to last sector when he got a comm from James.

"Shipp – what's your status? We need to pull out immediately. As in, right now," James said with measured urgency.

"James, we ran into a nettle. Big prickly one," Shipp said. "Still haven't found Hydramol. Looking at paper star maps and atlases eight levels down."

James stumbled in his mind at the terrible news. The one thing they came to do still hadn't been done.

Shipp kept talking, "I called Harden but got no answer. I've heard nothing from Mack, you, or Garrison for hours."

"We've had a lot of trouble up here. Our vessel is getting pelted by other ships. Lost Mitz. Mack is hurt. I don't know what to recommend," James said.

Shipp and Li had to make the decision. And they did.

"We're bringing the star maps with us," Shipp said while he and Li began ripping out pages of the remaining sectors, and other reference materials they had been using, then folding and stuffing them in their clothes.

"Watch out," James said. "They're picking up our comms. This was a long call. You better move fast. Let me know if you need help."

Shipp and Li weren't assigned to plant any MagTons, but they each brought three just in case. Shipp decided to plant one in the library as a means of misdirection. They slipped out of the library right as three Wester admin-looking types rounded a corner and saw them. But Shipp and Li had changed outfits, so at first glance, they didn't look suspicious.

"Anyone else in there say?" one Wester asked.

Shipp nodded, "Yeah, a couple more."

The Westers picked up the pace, and asked, "What were they wearing?"

"I wasn't paying attention," said Shipp, as he and Li strode quickly toward the nearest walking pad, looking back to see the Westers enter the library. A moment later, Shipp ignited the MagTon he planted.

The explosion rattled the whole level, tearing through one interior wall, and leading to screams from inside the library.

Shipp and Li bolted up the walking pad. Seven more levels to go. Doing their best to look normal, they kept a steady clip, finding each path up to the next level and then ascending. They reached the fourth level down. From the third level, a group of six armed Westers raced down the pad, no doubt responding to the explosion. On seeing Shipp and Li, they approached them and blocked their path.

"Credentials please? Where are you headed?" The lead Wester asked them.

"Right now, we're headed up to the next level. After that, the possibilities are limitless bro," Shipp said, figuring he couldn't talk his way out of this. He and Li just kept walking, going right around them.

But one of the Westers pushed Shipp against the wall, and two others grabbed Li.

"I asked for your credentials and your destination. You answer me, civilian," said the leader.

"I'm just doing my job," said Shipp. "Why are you hassling us like this, ya?"

"You gonna play stupid like you didn't hear the Overseer's alert bro? She picked up a transmission from down below and now there's been an explosion. We're checking everyone. Everyone we see. Now show me your credentials or we're taking you down to detention see."

"Fine," said Shipp. "Fine. I didn't know it was that serious. Hold on."

The Westers released him so he could retrieve his 'credentials.' Of course, Shipp had no idea what they were actually expecting. He played stupid.

"Oh yeah, I gave it to Li earlier. He's got mine and his," Shipp said.

"What? Are you stupid?" the Wester said. "Show me your flaming wrist."

"Li! Show him your wrist," Shipp said.

In his pocket, he'd been arming another MagTon. Li had been doing the same, and they both knew it.

"I got my credentials here," said Li.

Li threw one hand up while tossing the MagTon down the hallway to the other side of the Westers. Shipp tossed one in the same direction. Then, he and Li both grabbed a Wester and used them as shields. The MagTons exploded, sending everyone to the floor.

No one got killed, but two of the Westers cried out in pain and writhed on the floor. "You dogs, what the hell man ya!" screamed one of them.

Shipp and Li pushed away their stunned human shields and rolled to their feet, drawing their AX-9s. They fired as they ran away, and hit several Westers until they rounded the corner and bolted up to the next level.

Shipp called James, "We're three levels down now, getting closer!"

Shipp and Li kept going, and found the walking pad up to their original level, where they stood at the monitor looking for General Elliss.

When they got there, they saw a throng of Westers near the same monitors, led by the Overseer, identified earlier by her wristband. She turned and saw them. They walked forward, acting normal, counting on their clothes to protect their identities again.

The Overseer looked at a screen capture of their faces, gleaned from their time spent at the monitors just a few meters away from her. Then, she looked back at them.

"That's them," she said. "Kill or capture them."

Shipp and Li stopped and fired at the group and took off running. The horde of at least twenty Westers chased after them. These weren't military, and Shipp knew it. Some sort of outpost security detail the overseer commanded directly. While possible some could have actual military experience, more likely they were Wester Academy washouts, not quite good enough for actual combat, but suitable for outpost security.

But all that being true, nobody looks forward to twenty against two.

Shipp called James again, "James – they're on to us. They know our faces and we got about twenty after us. Can you get me out of here?"

"Yeah, Winston told us about an emergency stairwell on the fringes. He's right here, I'll add him to the channel," said James.

Winston began directing Shipp and Li, telling them about several access points to this stairwell that he and Cruz had observed or used.

"We're in civilian attire," Shipp said. "Don't shoot us when we get there."

Shipp and Li reached an entrance to the stairwell. Shipp planted his third and final MagTon on the reverse side of the door, and they bolted up the stairwell three at a time.

"They're gonna split up and head to our level for sure," said Li.

"I'm counting on it," said Shipp.

Still in the stairwell, they reached one level down and kept going. When they reached the level of the cargo bay, Li planted his second MagTon on that door. Two levels down, the door opened. Shipp detonated his MagTon, inflicting untold suffering on however many Westers had followed them to that point.

Shipp could hear the Overseer screaming at someone through the din, "Cut them off above I told you! There's only one place they can go!"

Shipp and Li ascended one more level, now being above the one where the Sorcerer Reborn awaited. But they didn't open the door to that level. They waited. Li noted two MagTons attached to the outer wall, and pointed them out to Shipp. Probably planted by Winston and Cruz.

"Fix your eyes on the door below," Shipp said. "They know we're in here."

Eventually, the door to the cargo bay level opened. A Wester tentatively stepped in, AX-9 raised, and began looking around. Shipp and Li waited, their own AX-9s at the ready. They could see everything below because the stairs were made of metal grating. The Wester stepped forward, within their line of sight. Another entered. They looked up.

The moment they did, Shipp and Li fired, killing both of them. Then, Shipp detonated the MagTon at that same door. It was close to their position, and they felt the blast. Shipp even took a piece of shrapnel in his quad. He called Winston and James again.

"What next? We blew doors level and minus two."

"Go three levels up," Winston said. "From there, you can run along a level with glass walls. They won't risk firing at you with glass behind you. Get to the middle. Use your lines to rappel down. It will land you right in the cargo bay. I can see that level from our position."

Shipp was amazed. The cargo bay had looked like an enclosed room. But according to Winston, at least part of it ascended up several levels. Why?

"Jonas," said Shipp, as they bolted up the remaining stairwells, Shipp straining against his wounded leg. Reaching the third level, Li affixed his final MagTon to the side of the door that would face the stairwell. They opened the door. Winston was right.

This was a viewing level of some sort. Across the way, Shipp could see stars, along with catwalks running along the exterior wall, and one across the middle. He called Winston again.

"Which catwalk? You said middle!"

"Sorry – the one against the far wall – the middle of that one," Winston replied.

"Jonas," Shipp said. He and Li stepped out the door, closed it, and then ran along the glass wall separating them from outer space. The nearby planet came into view as they made their way around the slow turn. As they reached the halfway point, the Overseer arrived, along with six security personnel.

But she was too late. Li and Shipp attached their lines to the railing and secured them tight. Shipp looked at the Overseer from across the expanse between them.

"Better luck next time," Shipp said. "Better run too. You're not going to want to be on this level for much longer."

"Who are you! How did you get here?" She called out to him.

Shipp smiled, though she probably couldn't see it, and taunted her, "I'm a virus, invading your space."

Then, to the great astonishment of the Westers, he and Li hopped over the railing and quickly descended three levels down, landing safely in the cargo bay, where Winston, Cruz, James, Drummond, and Algiers had been waiting at the elevator and at the top of the walking pad, holding the line against any Westers that would try to approach them.

"Nice of you to drop in," James quipped as they severed their lines.

The group raced back to the Sorcerer Reborn. Locke had long since brought Mackson safely inside, and they brought Mitz's body too so the Westers couldn't learn anything from it.

Once everyone had made it back on board, with the door latched and sealed, Blake and Reeves immediately severed the connection and accelerated away, while being pelted by K-rockets from the Dogfighter and three nearby convoy ships. A fourth one had already been disabled by Dons.

50

Dogfighter

Garrison was still barely mobile and not yet lucid from getting pulsed. With Harden also still putting his head back together, and Mackson injured, Shipp had to take command of the Sorcerer Reborn. This came as quite a surprise, but suddenly he found himself tasked with leading them away and defeating four attacking ships.

His first and greatest instinct was to trust the expertise of the men around him.

He sent everyone who had just returned with him down to Fire Control, figuring Dons needed everyone there so he could fill up all eight firing stations, and the pulsed Jimenez and Cardmanov weren't yet able to perform. Turned out Dons had nine men available, so he sent James up to mid-level to man one of the firing stations from there. And Wallace could take another one in the mid-level if need be.

Then, Shipp put Reeves in charge of Comm-1, where he already was sitting anyway, and brought Molon up to the second Pilot position, since he was the only backup pilot who hadn't gotten fatigued running around on Ulrich.

"Blake, give us distance from Ulrich," Shipp said. "Dons – increase your returning fire as we pilot away. I'm going to detonate the outpost and we'll swing back around."

The Sorcerer Reborn broke away from the Dogfighter, taking fire from the convoys on the other side. Dons was expelling tons of TIs. As they picked up speed, he shelled one of the convoys with a barrage of K-rockets, followed by two ninks and a dozen MagTons. This focused fire caught the Westers off guard, as up to this point the Sorcerer Reborn had been mostly acting defensively, firing sporadically at all the ships coming against them to keep them at a distance.

But that was before Dons suddenly found himself with nine gunners and Shipp's new plan.

The targeted Wester convoy was completely unprepared for such a focused assault. The K-rockets broke through, the nukes blew it to pieces, and the MagTons weren't even necessary. Dons had Abe and Marley redirect the mags to a different convoy, which was forced to flee and destroy them before they could affix to its hull.

With one convoy destroyed and the other fleeing, Dons found himself facing only the Dogfighter attack ship and the remaining convoy.

At that moment, Shipp turned to Reeves. "Activate the detonation sequence." They had linked the MagTon bombs in Ulrich to the comm system so Harden, now Reeves, could blow them from the ship. Reeves lit it up. A series of nearly sixty explosions, extending about twenty levels within the central section of Outpost Ulrich, burst with light before the vacuum of space extinguished the flames.

The damage was done.

Ulrich teetered, with its middle sections unable to support the still-intact ones above and below it.

"Veer around and ram it," Shipp said to Blake. He knew the Dogfighter would never expect this, so he figured they would give chase, and then realize they were about to crash into their own outpost. This would force a sudden and awkward redirection, and give the Sorcerer Reborn a chance to bear down on the Dogfighter.

"Dons, after we ram the outpost, fire two ninks into each of the upper and lower sections."

The Sorcerer Reborn accelerated away from Ulrich, which quickly fell out of sight. The Dogfighter pursued them, but the remaining two convoys held back. The Westers may be thinking we're fleeing, Shipp thought. Even better.

The Dogfighter fired a barrage of Krocks. But now, at speed and distance, Dons was able to deflect all but two of them with TIs.

Blake steered them in a slow arc back around, as the Dogfighter attempted to hit them with more K-rockets. One impacted on the exterior of the top level, startling Blake a bit.

"Faster," Shipp said. "Find the weakest point."

"Already targeted it," Blake said. "Light it up in ten seconds."

"Yao, we want to fire the HAT in ten seconds," Shipp said, which Reeves repeated.

Ten seconds later, the HAT activated and reached 10%, its lowest speed, careening the Sorcerer Reborn back toward Ulrich at hyper speed. It tore right through the outpost at the weakest point, right around the level where Shipp and Li had stood at a monitor for several hours.

"Muzzle it and bank," Shipp ordered.

The HAT darkened, and the Sorcerer Reborn banked left and came back around. They returned to see two large intact sections of Outpost Ulrich drifting away from each other. One of the convoys headed toward the upper section, apparently planning to help a transport ship that must have been docked inside a hangar bay. It was struggling to exit, and the convoy headed in to assist.

"Burn it with ninks," Shipp ordered.

Dons launched four nuke-tipped Kampraseuth rockets. Two shot into the exposed area of the lower section, and the other two entered the upper section. They detonated from within, causing considerable damage since the interiors of outposts were not built to repel this sort of thing.

To the Petersons' great surprise, Ulrich's upper section ruptured, and nearly the entire fragment went dark inside. Only perhaps three or four levels at the very top shone any light. The lower section, which was larger, held up better, but the damage had been done. The transport ship took damage from the explosion as well.

"Wipe out the convoys and ram the transport," Shipp said.

Blake turned and accelerated. The crippled transport ship would be easy pickings even at a non-HAT speed, they presumed. Dons began a coordinated assault on the convoy that had been attempting to help. They must not have seen the Sorcerer Reborn when it returned, because they weren't moving much. Perhaps they were just stunned by the sight of a splintering outpost – something none of them had ever seen, even on video.

This was historic.

Dons destroyed that convoy with a series of K-rockets. The Sorcerer Reborn accelerated, and its Blackheaded bow ripped through the side of the weakened transport ship, sending its contents floating off in space, and likely killing everyone on board. All that remained was one more convoy and the Dogfighter.

Reeves called out, "LR picking up the Dogfighter. They stopped following us when we headed back here. They're just now coming into range."

"Play chicken," Shipp said to Blake. Blake turned to look at him, as if to say, are you serious?

"You know what that is right?" asked Shipp.

"Yes, but we're not actually going to ram them head on are we?" Blake needed to confirm.

"They've seen what we can do, and they'll be far more afraid when they see us coming at them. When they bank, be ready, and hit them on whatever side they show us," Shipp said. "Reeves – relay the plan to Dons so he's ready. Accelerate in ten seconds"

The Sorcerer Reborn accelerated toward the Dogfighter, and the gap closed very fast. They'd ram each other in seconds. Shipp was right. The Dogfighter peeled away, probably in a panic, exposing their underside.

"Hit them with everything Dons!" Shipp yelled loud enough that he might have heard him audibly.

Dons fired a barrage of twenty K-rockets at the Dogfighter. All twenty made contact with the underside of the ship.

"Send Mags inside if we made a hole!" Shipp ordered. "Reeves? Is there an opening?"

Reeves wasn't as quick at this as Harden. He had to study the LR data a bit longer than Shipp was used to hearing. "Reeves! Is there an opening?" he asked again.

"Maybe a small one. I think their underside might be the most armored section. Surface is uneven. Hard to tell if there's an actual opening," Reeves said.

"Dons," Shipp called him directly. "Can you see an opening yet? Did we make a hole?"

"Data is fuzzy and they're at extreme distance, probably looking to team up with the remaining convoy. I don't think the hole is big enough for Mags, but we took out parts of their array," said Dons.

"Recommendation?" asked Shipp, leaning on Dons' experience.

"They had to attack slowly when we were docked, because they couldn't risk harming their outpost. That's one reason we were able to fight off most of their attacks. Now that we're out in the open, they'll be coming for us. I'd expect a serious barrage coming our way soon," Dons began.

"It's two on one now," Shipp said, "Should we take out the last convoy first?"

"If we get a chance, yes. Otherwise stick to the beast. After we evade their first assault, head back for Ulrich because they'll think we want to finish it off and they'll try to protect what remains. Plant yourself behind the biggest chunk and they won't be able to see us. Hit their ship on the opposite side from before. Then they have two wounds to protect."

Shipp loved it. "Let's do it. Prepare for an assault. TIs ready."

Dons liked it too. Always great to be listened to and have your plan accepted so quickly. His admiration for Shipp vaulted in that moment, because Shipp wasn't overstepping his lack of experience with command or space combat.

The Sorcerer Reborn veered back toward Ulrich, but slow enough that the Dogfighter would likely attempt an attack. Sure enough, here came the rockets. Twelve of them in three groups of four, arcing toward them and tracking their movements.

"TIs," said Shipp.

"Probably another barrage coming after this one – much larger. They want us to waste our defenses here. Just like I did to that other ship," said Dons. Shipp remembered – Dons had indeed done this exact same maneuver.

And he was right. So Shipp let the twelve rockets hit the Sorcerer. Their ultra-thick armor seemed to be holding up well. And then, here came a larger barrage of thirty K-rockets. Dons launched a huge array of TIs, filling up the space in front of them.

As the TIs made contact with the oncoming rockets, they shot off in various directions and began to take them out, one at a time. In the end, only four of the original thirty made it through and impacted the Sorcerer Reborn.

Soon after that, the two ships passed each other, and the convoy paralleled the Dogfighter. The Dogfighter no doubt realized their attack had little effect, and that the Sorcerer Reborn was headed back to Ulrich.

"Outpost approaching," Blake said.

"Settle down right up against that big lower section. Drift with it," Shipp said.

"Wouldn't survivors inside the outpost see us? Try to contact them?" Blake asked.

"Are they able to do that easily? For all we know, their comms are dead. Everyone in there is probably just working on staying alive," Shipp surmised.

Blake decelerated and hugged the backside of the lower section of the drifting Ulrich chunk. From here, they could see into what remained of the upper section drifting above them. The nuke caused extensive damage. The upper section resembled a hollowed-out melon husk.

"Beautiful," said Shipp. "If that Overseer went up instead of down after we left, she's dead."

A few minutes later, the Dogfighter returned and slowed to patrol speed.

"Dogfighter is back," Reeves said. At this point, Harden stumbled up the stairs. Reeves stood up.

"No, you stay," said Harden. "My reflexes are still dulled. I just want to be here. Second set of eyes."

"Dons," Shipp said.

"I see him," Dons replied.

"Target the upper opposite side, I'd say... I marked a K in the area to hit," said Shipp, making a mark on his monitor.

"Got it," said Dons. "Give me a minute. We want to plan this one right."

Being able to plan out a specific attack sequence provided such an enormous advantage. As with their last mission, this was the fastest way to cripple an attack ship.

"They're wondering where we are," said Shipp. "Might they see us soon?"

"Pretty tough," said Harden. "To their LR, that drifting mass is already an irregular shape with no precedent, surrounded by debris. So even if it picked up a section of our hull, it wouldn't recognize it."

Shipp nodded in appreciation at the expert information. "You ready Dons?"

No response. That meant 'no.' Shipp had learned that Dons didn't usually respond with 'Jonas' or other small talk language unless the message confirmation carried great importance. As long as he was at his Weapons Control station, Dons always heard every message.

“LR picking up the convoy. Looks like it’s coming closer to Ulrich. They might see us,” said Reeves.

Shipp tensed up. Dons wasn’t ready, and the convoy could ruin their plan.

“If he spots us, he spots us. We’re not abandoning this opportunity,” said Shipp. He glanced back to Harden to get his non-verbal opinion. Harden nodded back his approval. The right move.

A couple minutes passed. Luckily, the convoy did not circle the outpost fragment. Instead, it started to patrol back and forth. The Dogfighter began angling away, probably intending to get clear of Ulrich’s fragments to scan the wider area for the Sorcerer Reborn. The convoy angled the other way.

“We’re set,” said Dons.

“Fire it up,” said Shipp.

Dons’ attack began with twenty K-rockets. They shot out from behind the outpost fragment in twenty unique trajectories. The smoke streams looked like a spiderweb encircling the huge structure. All the rockets, traveling independently, angled toward the Dogfighter.

Before they reached it, twenty more K-rockets fired. But this time, all twenty followed a parallel trajectory – one huge thick band of K-rocket fumes burning as one.

The Dogfighter launched a few TIs which took out eight of the initial barrage, but the remaining twelve all impacted in the region marked by Shipp. Because all twenty were traveling in unique flight paths, each TI had to target an individual rocket. This would take more effort for the Wester gunners to defend.

While that occupied them, the group of twenty more headed for the same spot and pounded into it before they could mount a defense.

A huge explosion of debris and light burst out into space, and the Dogfighter accelerated away, now pursued by the Sorcerer Reborn as it emerged from hiding. The convoy pursued them too.

“LR – convoy giving chase from behind,” Reeves said.

“Brave little rat,” said Shipp. “Blow him off course. Use the mid-level gunner if we have one.”

That meant James and Wallace. James reoriented his targeting controls and released three K-rockets, sending them out from behind, toward the pursuing convoy. It managed to dodge all three and then destroy them with TIs, but it had to abandon the pursuit to avoid being hit.

"Convoy broke away. He's out of the picture," Reeves said.

"Dogfighter's advantage is he knows this space and we don't. He could be leading us somewhere we don't want to go," said Shipp.

Harden nodded in agreement. "Hit him now before he gets there. Can't let them share too much about us."

"Yao," Shipp said, "What happens if we fire the HAT and ram them from behind. Wouldn't be the same as a head-on crash, right?"

Yao replied immediately, "Correct, a rear collision should bump them off course, and our armored bow should protect us. They'd never expect that sort of move."

"Prepare for impact," Shipp ordered. "Everyone belt in."

The Petersons harnessed themselves to their seats or to nearby wall harnesses.

"Reeves – call Locke to confirm he's ready," said Shipp.

"Locke – are the patients strapped in for an impact?" Reeves asked on comm.

"Impact? You guys are nuts up there. Yeah, we're ready," replied Locke.

"Blake? Activate when ready. Dons, get ready to hit them hard. I think our second attack did more damage so we should target that side again," Shipp said.

"Already done," said Dons, apparently having anticipated this move, which meant Shipp was thinking along the right track.

"Five seconds," Blake said.

The HAT lit up, and at 10% speed, the Sorcerer Reborn shot toward the escaping Dogfighter, bumping it in the rear and jolting it into a spinning, tumbling projectile. The Sorcerer Reborn also shuddered at the impact, and they could hear creaking metal and sparks somewhere on the ship.

Harden and Reeves laughed at what they saw on the LR. "I bet they didn't train for that one," Harden joked.

But Shipp felt nervous at the sound. "I hope we didn't overstep on that." He could hear Yao yelling at Wallace to go check something out.

Dons had to wait for the Dogfighter to regain control of its flight path. No way to target any section with that spinning. But internally, if their crew hadn't strapped in, they were suffering some serious bodily injuries with all that irregular motion.

The Sorcerer Reborn began trailing the Dogfighter, waiting for it to right itself. Harden ran play by play on this, because he could see them trying one step at a time to get out of the spin. It wouldn't be easy.

"You could do it, right Blake?" Harden joked.

Blake shook his head. "That would not be fun."

"They'll be dazed and disoriented. Don't give them any time to regain their bearings once they stop spinning," Shipp said.

"We're ready to fire in a millisecond," said Dons. "Location is targeted."

Finally, after several minutes, the Dogfighter's pilots managed to regain control of their vessel. The second they stabilized their motion, Dons sent an eruption of K-rockets and hit the same damaged spot on the upper side. All of them impacted, so many rockets the barrage lasted 20 seconds. This time, the rockets burrowed a hole and penetrated the vessel. He followed it with a swath of MagTons, all of which entered the ship. Lastly, he fired a single nuke tipped K-rocket inside, and the job was done. Attack ship disabled.

"Let's get out of here before the convoy decides to catch up to us," Shipp said.

The Sorcerer Reborn escaped the area, heading in a direction toward the edge of the galaxy. Everyone exhaled and sat back to reflect on recent events. Harden congratulated everyone and then said, "Amazing we got out of there only losing one man.""Still one too many," said Shipp.

Shipp pulled out one of the star maps he had taken from Outpost Ulrich. Molon, Harden, and Reeves all came over to study it.

"Where are we?" asked Molon and Harden at the same time.

"Brain-fire move, Shipp," Reeves said. "A map of their whole territory. Epic brain fire."

Eventually, the Petersons found their location on the atlas. They headed toward an uninhabited planet where they could lay low, assess damage, regroup, heal up, resupply their weapons caches, and most importantly, find Hydramol on the star atlases.

51

Division

Shipp made his way down to Locke's infirmary, which doubled as a domicile. He needed to get his shrapnel wound taken care of.

"Pretty effective escape there, from the bowels of a Wester outpost," Locke said when Shipp entered the room. Garrison was attempting to move his limbs again, and Cardmanov was standing.

"We might have to do it again at Hydramol. Not going to be easy," Shipp said. "How's Mack?"

Mackson hadn't moved at all since Shipp entered the room. He lay on one of the bunks, with a couple tubes attached to him.

"He's alright. Bled out quite a lot though, so I'm rehydrating him while his body repairs itself. Put him out so he could sleep," Locke said. "You got something for me too?"

"Shrapnel," Shipp showed him the wound. Locke waved him over and began working on it. He worked fast and without much talking, which surprised Shipp. Once he had completed repairing, cleansing, and bandaging the wound, Locke spoke.

"You did well. It was a tough mission. I'll update you on Mack in a couple hours. Garrison should be good to go soon."

"Thanks," Shipp said as he exited the room. He saw why Garrison liked Locke, in spite of his usual negativity. When it came time to work, Locke was all business, and he worked faster than any of the medics Shipp encountered on Risner or Lavoisier.

Shipp made his way back to the top level, where Blake waved him over.

"We took a lot of hits while sitting in the dock. Those four ships pelted us with K-rockets and MagTons for at least ten minutes. We fought some of them off, but you need to go out there and assess our exterior damage," Blake explained.

"First I'm going to check with Yao and Wallace about that noise we heard during the collision. Then I'll take out a crew of four," Shipp replied. "Harden – you can send an update to the Trans-Com from here, right?"

"Jonas that, already working on it," Harden said, now feeling back to full mental and physical strength.

Shipp went down to meet with Yao and Wallace. Both were inspecting the structure of the ship near the stairwell as Shipp came down.

"What's the story?" Shipp began. "I heard what sounded like a bad noise when we rammed them."

"It did put some stress on the ship," Yao said as he showed Shipp a schematic of the vessel. "Structural integrity appears sound, and I think the Blackhead layers absorbed the majority of the shock, which I anticipated. So much thickness combined with malleability. Acted like a big metal cushion, sort of."

"Was that a bad decision on my part? If we're weaker now..." Shipp wondered.

"A quick end to that skirmish was probably worth it. We're in good shape for what we need to do. But I wouldn't recommend ramming any more attack ships that are still largely intact," Yao cautioned.

"Got it," Shipp nodded. "I'll brief Garrison and Mack once they're recovered. Were any weapons storage sections impaired?"

"Dons said no. I already asked him that. Most of those are in the underbelly and in the sides. It's this area here" – Yao waved his hand around the structural elements forming the front end of the mid-level, the parts most closely connected to the Joust – "that seems to have taken most of the stress."

"And the HAT's okay?"

"100%. Not a scratch."

"Thanks Yao," Shipp said as he descended to the lower level to debrief with Dons about the attack.

About an hour later, Shipp took Wallace, Cruz, and Ewing out into space to examine the exterior of the Sorcerer Reborn. A couple hours after that, they were back inside, and the officers prepared for a strategy meeting. Shipp arrived with a bunch of atlases, which drew some chuckles from the group. Li came with him.

In the meeting room sat Garrison, Harden, Locke, Blake, and Dons. Yao stood to one side, where Li joined him. No one objected to Li, the only non-officer, being present. They figured Shipp had his reasons.

"Li's been studying these atlases for the last couple hours. He found Hydramol," Shipp announced, as the room brightened with claps and exultation.

"Outstanding," Garrison said. "Let's see it."

Li spread out a star atlas showing the entire Wester Territory. He let everyone take a few minutes to absorb the incredible significance of this find. No Peterson general, in five hundred years, had seen this level of detail about Wester space.

"Harden?" Garrison said, knowing he didn't need to say anymore. He didn't, because Harden replied immediately.

"Oh yeah. This is going back with my next transmission. Be the best comm received by the big brains in, forever."

"They better appreciate it," Shipp said. "It comes at a cost. And if we don't do anything with it, it's useless."

Shipp's aggressive comment surprised several of the others.

"What do you think they should do with it?" Garrison asked.

"We'll get there," Shipp said. "First, let's get clear about the situation. Where's the star Li?"

Li pointed to the planet the Sorcerer Reborn had settled near, and then used his other hand to point out Hydramol. It was indeed near the edge of the galaxy, relatively speaking, about in the middle of Wester Territory along that edge.

"Merriss said it was a white sun. He was right. It also has a companion star about half a light year away. Close enough to cause some interesting gravity, but not that big a deal because the second star is much smaller. According to this map" – Li unveiled a second map that featured only the sector containing Hydramol – "Hydramol's system has four planets."

Everyone leaned in to study the space terrain. Li gave them a few moments.

"And the second one has the outpost, am I reading this right?" Harden asked.

"Right," confirmed Li. "These maps are dated about ninety years ago, so while some things could have changed since then, we all know space construction doesn't happen very fast. It's highly doubtful there would be two outposts in a single star system way over here."

Several officers nodded in agreement.

"How long will it take to get there?" asked Locke, showing a bit of impatience. He hated meetings, but he had to be at this one in case anyone asked about Mackson. Everyone turned to Yao, who laughed at the attention.

"HAT is ready. The only question is, can we plot a course through unfamiliar space with enough safety factor, given what we see on these atlases?" Yao said. "That's Blake and Reeves."

"I'll need some time," said Blake.

"Fine. We have it," said Garrison. "I want to commend Mid-Level Officer Shipp for taking command in the midst of a high-stakes situation. You performed with excellence, took out an attack ship, destroyed Ulrich, and got us out of there. Superb work. And Dons – another outstanding attack plan. You guys are the best crew in the galaxy."

Everyone felt good to hear that. But then, Garrison changed his tone.

"I do have one question though. Shipp?" Garrison paused to get everyone's attention. "What took so long? You were down there almost four hours. We've been wanting to know what you ran into."

Shipp shifted in his seat. "Right," he began. "Li and I found a monitor pretty quickly. Once we got the code to work, we found Hydramol almost immediately. But the listing had a message. It said recent military developments led to the need to make the location a secret."

"Rat turds," Harden said. "Hiding their stuff from their own people. When was it classified?"

"About forty years ago. I think they must have discovered this virus back then and realized they didn't want anyone to stumble on it," Shipp said.

"So what did you do?" Garrison asked.

"We decided to find actual physical maps, and there was a library archive six more levels down. So, we went down there and started searching through atlases. All we could do was go star by star, because other than knowing it was somewhere toward the edge of their territory, we had no way to narrow it down."

"We spent a long time staring at maps," Li concurred. "Then, when the outpost Overseer sent her alert over the comm—"

Garrison interrupted him. "Overseer? They call station commanders overseers? You have to be kidding me."

"Anyway," Li continued, "We realized we were in trouble, because no one was responding to our comms. We figured you guys must be having trouble too."

"An understatement in the extreme," growled Harden, still fuming over getting pulsed.

"So, we had to quietly kill two Westers in the library so we could take their clothes," Li said, finally finishing his thought.

"How'd you kill them so quietly?" asked Garrison.

"Knife, then bare hands," Shipp said, which impressed everyone. Even Locke. "Then, we resumed looking at maps until James called and told us we had to get back immediately. Stuffed our shirts with the remaining ones and made it back."

"So you were staring at maps for over three hours in the library?" Garrison asked. "It took that long?"

Shipp realized he couldn't dodge the full truth any longer. "No, General. I also spent time at the monitor looking for something else before we headed to the library. It was a mistake. I should have kept Hydramol the priority. I got flustered by the classified piece and didn't know what to do. The monitor was right there, and I had to know."

Garrison nodded. He seemed to somehow know Shipp and Li had been hiding something. Shipp couldn't imagine how. But the four-hour timeline just didn't add up for Garrison.

"Elliss. You looked up that rat prick Elliss didn't you?" Garrison said.

Shipp lowered his head and nodded at the floor.

"Well shoot the stars, I sure hope you found something, considering your delay nearly unraveled our entire mission and could have gotten us all killed," Garrison said, mocking the officer he had just commended. "Look at me."

Shipp raised his head and looked at Garrison, who seemed to want him to own it. Shipp labored to speak, and finally found the words.

"I let my rage compromise my judgment at the worst possible time." Shipp's emotions leaked out. His grief from letting down his crew mates merged with his obsessive fury against Elliss' role in killing Pretoria, his other friends, and Vonn.

They all understood, and their silence gave Shipp room to process the gravity of his error.

"You want to demote me General? I'll understand and I'll accept it without protest," Shipp said.

"Why did you come on this mission, Officer Shipp?" Garrison asked.

Shipp realized Garrison had a knack for sniffing out any hint of deception.

"I came because I want to win the war by annihilating as many rats as possible back where they aren't expecting to be attacked – after we find the virus. I want to destroy Elliss' home planet of Faraday. I want to kill Elliss. Then, we go planet by planet, leveling cities, killing millions, wiping them out until we get destroyed, or until we finish the job, win the war for good, and go home," Shipp said, exhaling.

He felt relieved as much as afraid to finally say all this to the only people he wanted to serve with for the rest of his life. But he refrained from sharing the one detail he hadn't yet told anyone – including James or Li – an idea still brewing in his mind.

Garrison stood so he could address the room with authority.

"Thank you for the truth. I understand why you would aim for that plan, and why you concealed it from us. But that isn't the plan. Our plan is to find the virus, destroy the outpost, eradicate the records associated with it, and go home."

Garrison paused and looked around the room to gauge the nonverbal reactions of everyone present.

"Does anyone in this room object to our directive?" Garrison asked, searching the room again until he reached Shipp, who bore the brunt of his glare. "Anyone?"

Shipp arose and faced Garrison. "I'm with you General. My idea is too risky." He started for the door. But Garrison grabbed his arm and shook his head.

"You're not leaving. We're not done with the meeting. And my Mid-Level Control Officer must be present until its end."

Garrison had a way of validating and condemning Shipp all at the same time. It felt painfully good. Shipp nodded and returned to his seat. So did Garrison, and then he looked up at Li.

"I presume that you and James knew about this the whole time, am I right?" Garrison asked.

Li nodded his affirmation. "You are correct General."

"You all see why it's good to bring people on board who know and trust each other?" Garrison spoke to the room. "These guys were willing to see this plan through together, because they would rather die together trying to win the war than lose their friendship. Li – did you agree with Shipp's decision to search for Elliss after you couldn't find Hydramol?"

Painfully, Li looked at Shipp as he shook his head. "No. I knew we needed to move on."

"But you didn't. You stayed there and stood by his side for, what, an hour?"

"Two hours," Li said.

"Two hours, watching your friend dive off into a rabbit trail clouded by bad judgment. Why?" Garrison asked. "And how did you guys end up in the library?"

Li stammered a bit, not enjoying having to expose disagreement with Shipp, but accepting that this was probably healthy for the officers to witness.

"I did it because he's my friend and I know how much he has suffered. And I don't want him to live with that the rest of his life. And in that moment, he had a chance to do something about it. Something really incredible. So..." his voice cracked.

He took a moment to recover. The others gave it to him. Shipp watched his friend, realizing now how great a friend he truly was.

"So I gave him the time. And I'd do it again in the same situation."

Harden, Garrison, Dons, Locke, Blake, and Yao sat transfixed as Li poured out his heart, his devotion to his friend, regardless of the potential cost.

"You've all lost people close to you. So have I." Li shook his head, as the image of Shipp beating Shelsie to a pulp replayed in his mind. "But not like what happened on Lavoisier. I wasn't there for Pretoria. But I was there for the others."

Garrison waited while Li kept himself composed. Then, Garrison asked his final question.

"And, the library?"

Li nodded. "After a while at the monitor, I pulled him out of it and we made a new plan. We then began searching for the library."

"So you did eventually redirect your friend, because you realized he would stay there forever. He was lost in his own obsession."

Li nodded. "Yes, General."

Garrison turned to the others. "How many of you think I shouldn't let Li and Shipp, or James and Shipp, work alone together again while we're on this mission? Be honest or I'll kill you."

Locke raised his hand. So did Harden. No one else did. Garrison didn't seem to mind.

"A ship divided, in the belly of Wester space," he summarized. "That's okay. I believe in having all the cards on the table, as most of you know. But you don't discuss any of this with the rest of the crew. They don't need to know. We made it out. We're whole except for Mitz, and his death isn't on Shipp as that happened much earlier."

Garrison paused, put his hands on the table, and seemed to indicate he was satisfied and ready to move to the next item on the agenda.

"Now – let's talk about the next few weeks. What is the status of the vessel's exterior?"

Yao was ready. "We took heavy damage on five spots, which you can see here." He put up a diagram of the Sorcerer Reborn on the monitor. "Two areas bordering the lower level, one on mid-level, and two near top level. Portions of the Blackhead are warped, dented, and cracked. The deepest crevice goes about halfway through the armor, with a diameter stretching about a meter across. That's the one on the lower left. We also lost about 30% of our shield ports, mostly in those same areas."

Yao paused, giving everyone a chance to absorb the information. Then, he continued.

"We're intact, and we're still way stronger than any conventional attack ship. My recommendation to Dons is to use TIs to protect those areas as much as possible. And the pilots need to keep the crevice out of direct lines of attack," Yao concluded.

"Thank you Yao. Very good information," Garrison said. "We will do our best to follow your recommendations as always. Dons? What do you have?"

"Well first, as to Yao's point, any other ships we encounter won't know we have a few weak spots. So unless they have time for detailed scans of our exterior, we have a good probability those areas won't get directly targeted."

"Good point," said Garrison, and Harden nodded in affirmation.

Dons then presented his own charts on the monitor with data on weapons supplies.

"I've got bad news and good news. The bad news is, we used a lot of TIs while we were stuck at the dock. I simply had no choice with four vessels firing at us. We used 55% of our supply. That's not good. If we get surrounded by a fleet of vessels again, we might exhaust what remains."

"What's the good news?" Garrison asked.

"The good news is, with our ramming the outpost and other tactical maneuvers led by Shipp, we still have a meaty supply of all our weapons. 77% Krocks, 80% Mags, 84% ninks, and 100% of everything else. Personal combat weapons inventory is also doing great, in part because of Winston, Cruz, and James turning the battle in that room in our favor."

"Good. So all battle tactics and options are still available to us. Our ship is damaged but still stronger than any of theirs. We know where Hydramol is and nothing can stop us from getting there. All things considered, our mission is a success so far, and I have absolute confidence in every one of you that we will complete it," Garrison said, wanting to end the meeting on a unifying, motivational note.

"Blake?" Garrison said, as people arose and departed. "Get Reeves and all the backup pilots in here. We'll use these atlases and see if we can puzzle out a HAT course to get to Hydramol faster."

"Jonas," said Blake.

Soon, everyone left except Shipp and Garrison.

Garrison looked him in the eye. "I think you're the best Mid-Level Control Officer in the fleet. It was a mistake. Perhaps a foolish one. But not an insane one. I hope you haven't lost anything that makes you you, because I need you at your best at Hydramol."

"You'll have me, General. Thank you," Shipp said, and he left the room to get some much-needed sleep time.

Before he dozed off, his brain ran through the avalanche of Wester intelligence he had viewed on the monitor at Ulrich. He knew it was a bad decision. But the more he thought about it, he realized how valuable all the information would prove to be. And the fact is, they did get away. Now, Shipp knew much more about how to find Elliss. With Hydramol coming up next, the plan forming in his mind quickly consumed any lingering embarrassment at being found out by Garrison. Yes, he wanted to eradicate this virus and murder the man who invented it in the most painful way possible. But after that?

Shipp pictured planets on fire. Outposts splintering in space. Cities of corpses. He began drifting to sleep somewhere around this time. The corpses all had the same face – that of General Brelan Elliss. Each face then began decomposing as the virus ate away the skin, muscles, and blood vessels. Then Pretoria's face filled his mind. "Goals are drawn with starlight," she said. "With starlight." Then Gugbe. "She put a hex on you. A hex on you. Hex on you."

52

The Approach

The group of five pilots with Garrison determined a reasonable course through Wester Territory that would enable them to use the HAT at 30% capacity for several segments of the journey. With their plan, it would take about five weeks to reach the smaller companion star to Hydramol, which they planned to approach from behind, in relation to the outpost.

In that time, they met multiple times to discuss possible scenarios.

Based on what went wrong at Ulrich, they struggled to find a way on this next outpost without similar conflict. Something gave them away last time, apparently to the very first attendant who met them at the tunnel. He must have gone off and reported it, and the overseer sent some sneaky rats to act like grunts. But their real purpose had been to tease out the truth about the strangely oversized ship at their dock.

The Petersons went back and forth in meetings for days trying to guess what could have given them away. It might have been not mentioning the 'captain's' name, which one Wester commented about. Maybe they didn't open with some kind of customary greeting. One Wester even told them they should have announced the name of their ship.

Mackson, now regaining his strength enough to participate in talks, wondered about the use of the word 'sis.' They had never heard that used in place of 'bro' from a Wester. And it was even stranger when she used it in reference to Mackson. Was she trying to insult him with a female term? That seemed really childish, and beneath even a Wester. Why go for such a petty insult? His point was well taken, but they couldn't decipher the meaning behind her use of that term.

Finally, Harden summarized the situation.

"Here's the last sheet. They're never going to let us dock. We have a Beamer, but we have no business being at an outpost they made secret forty years ago. They surely receive advance notice of any vessel coming nearby. Beamer or no, they're not going to be friendly. I don't see any way around that other than brute force."

"Plus," Shipp followed, "If they have heard about Ulrich, they might have gotten warning of an extra-large attack ship with a functioning Beamer. If they know that, they'll expose us from a light year away."

"Our one advantage," Garrison said, persisting with a line he had been using for several days, "Is that they have no idea we're coming. That means, even if everything you're saying is true, it's still just a lone outpost against us. In all the vast Wester Territory, from the Wester perspective, we could go anywhere. They cannot defend their entire space with twenty attack ships, and they can't know we're going to Hydramol – especially because it's classified."

"Unless they know I searched for it somehow," Shipp said.

"Very doubtful," replied Harden. "And even if they did, that intel died with them on Ulrich."

"I agree," said Mackson. "So what then? You want to break onto the outpost with Harden's brute force, find the virus production lab or whatever, and neutralize the threat?"

"Why not just destroy it without boarding it at all?" asked Dons.

"Because we need to know what they know about this virus," Garrison said. "Space Force Command wants to know. Shipp wants to know. Probably even Locke wants to know."

Shipp remembered the remains of Rawlic and his mutinous companions when he found them consumed by the virus on the surface of Lavoisier. He kept quiet, not wanting the others to perceive how much vengeance still fed his actions, words, and intentions. He could not and would not accept comfort, solace, or closure for all his dead friends until the maker of this virus was dead, followed by General Elliss.

"They might have another outpost, or a facility on the planet, or something else with more records, samples, production capabilities," Harden said. "We need to get on board and figure that out."

Dons accepted the argument. "Okay. We have the weaponry. We have superior military capability. It's likely just a bunch of scientists and admins with minor security, right? Way out here and classified?"

Everyone nodded. This had become the consensus over the last few weeks. Even though it held such a valuable research prize, it was deep in the backwater of Wester Territory and classified. How much security do you need for a place no one knows about?

The atlases didn't identify the name of the outpost, which disappointed everyone. But they knew the name of the sangria-colored planet it orbited – Wrath. An unusual name for a planet, for sure. Most planets were named after famous scientists or war heroes, with the occasional government leader or early space pioneer. Why name a planet with a descriptor? And why wrath? It couldn't be named that way due to the virus, because its name was printed on the 90-year-old space atlas.

After much more discussion, they settled on a plan. They decided to use the single occupancy battleship – the SOB – that Garrison and Harden had insisted be installed on the Sorcerer Reborn to provide an additional asset.

With an SOB, they could approach the outpost and blast a hole in one section. The occupant of the SOB would emerge wearing a space suit and take control of the destroyed area. Since any nearby Westers would be dead from the vacuum of space, the Sorcerer Reborn could approach that spot, and more Petersons could space walk to the same opening. From there, they could break into the rest of the outpost, comb the corridors, and locate the virus production facility.

Most outposts didn't have much, if any, exterior weaponry, especially this far back in their own territory, because an enemy attack was simply unthinkable. Being classified, that might not be the case here. But Harden felt confident they'd be able to determine that before sending out the SOB. Plus, Dons explained that he could surround the SOB with tracking interceptors and have them match speed and direction. If any outpost defense weapons fired on it, the TIs could take them out.

It was a bold plan, but it bypassed the need to play a bunch of games trying to board the outpost the usual way. Plus, it would catch them by surprise, and would kill a number of inhabitants right from the start.

The next question became, who should fly the SOB?

Not many pilots knew how to fly these vessels since they weren't used that frequently. Anyone could fly it if it were just a simple docking or boarding flight, or an exploration mission of some sort. But heading into possible combat, and needing to exit the vessel into outer space – that wasn't something for a newbie.

Only the five pilots seemed likely to have any possible experience. And one of them did – Winston. Harden took credit for this, recalling that he pushed for Winston to be accepted for the mission above other volunteers in part because of his SOB experience. Garrison liked that he had served with Cruz, so they got the nod. When they told Winston about the mission idea, he didn't hesitate. He was all in. They then began building the rest of the strategy around Winston's SOB capabilities.

Another week passed, and the Sorcerer Reborn disengaged the HAT and approached the smaller companion star, a white dwarf. On the other side of it half a light year away sat Hydramol. Harden located the four planets, including one with an orbiting outpost, and Blake positioned the Sorcerer Reborn with the white dwarf between them and that plane-t.

Through the enhanced vision scope, they could see the planet and the outpost. It was indeed colored like sangria, the mix of blood and wine. The outpost was about half the size, perhaps even smaller, compared to Ulrich. A good sign, confirming their belief of its mostly scientific nature.

But they also discovered something unexpected – an array of defensive sentry outposts encircling the primary one.

The Peterson Space Fleet had encountered sentry outposts on other occasions when venturing too close to Wester Territory. The first such encounter happened about 150 years ago. Space Force Command wanted them destroyed whenever spotted. But somewhere, the Westers were manufacturing hundreds of them, because they quickly dotted entire regions of space, acting as a formidable barrier.

The Petersons had nothing like them because they didn't see the purpose, not believing the Westers would ever reach far enough into their territory for sentries to be worth the effort or cost.

At their secret research outpost near Hydramol, the Westers had chosen to use this automated defensive technology. Sentries could fire rockets and extra high caliber AX-style rounds. Their rockets weren't likely tipped with Blackhead, so even a barrage from a couple dozen sentries didn't pose much threat to the Sorcerer Reborn.

But the SOB was a different story. They couldn't possibly risk Winston alone with what Harden determined to be at least fourteen outpost sentries. Six of them formed a ring around the outpost's planet, with four more positioned above it, and four below. The only option was to destroy all the sentries. But this would alert the outpost to their presence, eliminating the surprise advantage they were counting on.

Garrison made the final decision:

"The surprise has been ruined. But consider the likelihood that these sentries were put here precisely because the outpost has no other outer defenses. These *are* the outer defenses, and we can take them out easily. Then, we send in Winston, and proceed with the plan."

And that was the final word. Harden fed the locations of the sentries to Dons, and he worked out a plan to destroy them using minimal arms.

Meanwhile, Winston piled himself into a space suit, and crammed a Mossamer – much to Shipp's delight – two AX-15s, an electric pulse rifle, and a slew of MagTons into the SOB. They would launch him the moment the last outpost sentry got taken out.

53

Lightway

Blake piloted the Sorcerer Reborn out from behind the white dwarf and approached the outpost at a speed expected of a vessel intending to dock. Yao had altered the Beamer to produce a new code, just in case the previous one had been reported as counterfeit. It appeared to work, because as they approached the closest two sentries, nothing happened.

Harden then received an attempted comm from the outpost, and the incompatibility of Wester and Peterson comm technology again prevented his receiving it. Garrison knew it was only a matter of time before their peaceful welcome changed. He decided not to wait.

"Dons, light them up," Garrison ordered.

Dons had worked it out so that each sentry could be destroyed with two carefully placed K-rockets followed by a half dozen MagTons. For fourteen sentries, that meant 28 K-rockets, more than Garrison wanted to use. They decided to use the much weaker and seldom used pair of AX guns that were mostly ineffective even against convoy ships. Attack ship AX rounds were larger than the ones used in the AX-15s, but they still couldn't do much against Blackhead. But, attack ships still had them in case situations arose where weaker firepower could get the job done.

Like this one.

The revised plan was to hit the closest group of sentries with K-rockets and Mags to thin them out, and then pound the remaining ones with AX fire, even if it meant exhausting their entire supply, since they wouldn't likely need it again.

Having passed the closest two sentries and entered within the 'circle' of all fourteen of them, the Sorcerer pushed ahead, now with two sentries behind it, two above it, and two below it. Perfect spot. Dons ordered his six active weapons specialists to target their assigned sentries.

All at once, twelve K-rockets shot out from the Sorcerer Reborn at the most extreme speed possible. The six closest sentries exploded with bursts of light and debris. MagTons followed close behind each pair of rockets, affixing themselves to what remained of each sentry, and then exploding.

In an instant, six more sentries began firing on the Sorcerer Reborn. Two of them sat off to each side, and the other four fired from above and below the planet, but at greater distance.

The Sorcerer Reborn quickly accelerated and began what amounted to an orbit of the planet. As it arced around the globe, Dons unloaded a massive battery of AX fire at each sentry, erupting from each side of the hull in such quick succession that it looked like a continuous stream of jagged lightning.

They tore the first sentry to pieces. Then the next. Then the next. Circling around behind the planet with the outpost out of sight, Dons' team wasted the next two as they feebly attempted to return fire. Dons didn't bother wasting any TIs on this. Any hits on the Sorcerer Reborn would do minimal damage, even though the Petersons were surprised to find the sentries were equipped with K-rockets, in addition to AX rounds and a few MagTons. But the K-rockets were the size of those used in ground combat, not nearly as large as the attack ship variety. And Harden reported these sentry rockets also had less Blackhead in their tips, likely because the Westers didn't see the need to waste the precious metal this deep into their territory.

Coming back around the other side of the planet, Dons dispatched the remaining three sentries, and then zeroed in on the chosen entry point for Winston and the space walkers who would follow him.

"Send him out!" Garrison called.

Winston's single occupancy battleship shot out from the Sorcerer Reborn, and he took immediate control, swiftly piloting it toward what the Petersons had determined to be the weakest point of the outpost. Winston pounded it with AX rounds until he tore himself a little opening. Then, he fired all four K-rockets in his arsenal, blowing apart a much larger opening.

He quickly decelerated and entered into the destroyed area. He had taken out portions of four levels, and he could see automated walls closing at various points of each level, to protect the inhabitants from the vacuum of space.

Winston expelled the air from his ship and opened its only door above his head. He landed his ship on the destroyed interior of the outpost, jumped from his seat, and retrieved his weapons. Since he was exposed to space, the usual gravity compensators didn't affect him, so everything floated. That's why, before leaving, his shipmates connected all his weapons with a belt. All he had to do was yank the belt, and he had multiple weapons at his disposal, more than he could have carried on his own.

Winston used air bursts to thrust himself toward the nearest remains of a hallway with an automated door in its path, situated one level up from where his ship sat. He switched on his comm.

"I'm in, and I'm in the remains of a hallway, outside an emergency wall. No return fire as of yet. Send over the rest. I doubt they know I'm here, because no interior windows are facing the void I just created."

Back on the Sorcerer Reborn, Harden snickered at that description. "The void. He just created a void. I love it."

"Move closer," Garrison said.

Blake and Reeves metered the Sorcerer Reborn closer and closer to the outpost, receiving no return fire, as Garrison anticipated. When they got within about a hundred meters of the void, they halted.

"Let's go. Team 1 away. We'll be behind you in five minutes," Garrison said. "Mack – you're in charge."

Already in the escape pod with their space suits on and weapons strapped, the first assault team opened the hatch and climbed out. Linked together as one, they burst their way toward the void and entered it in less than a minute.

Team 1 consisted of Shipp, Cruz, Algiers, Drummond, and Zum. Team 2 would be led by Garrison himself, and included Cardmanov, Jimenez, Li, and James. Almost half the crew would be leaving the Sorcerer Reborn, unthinkable in any normal mission or combat situation. B ut this *was* their entire mission, and they weren't going to risk under-estimating what may lie behind the emergency walls.

Shipp's team reached Winston, and the six of them prepared to break through. Cruz, the technical expert, unveiled a collapsible canopy. These acted like portable emergency walls, usually used when rescuing people off damaged space vessels. They allowed the formation of a temporary wall, and included a supply of compressed air that would fill the space created between the canopy and the interior of the vessel being boarded.

Here, they used canopies to cause the Westers' automated door to detect the re-pressurization of the hallway on both sides, conclude the threat had been diffused, and thus reopen without the Petersons needing to fire a shot. Cruz extended the canopy across the broken end of the hallway, affixing it to the remaining smooth sections of the walls. Once successfully sealed with all six team members inside, the canopy's pressurization process commenced.

The 'room' flushed with air. No gravity existed, but the Petersons could feel the air pressing against them. The air compression ceased. They waited.

Moments later, the automated wall opened before them. All six men pushed their way along the wall and entered the outpost. Team 2 would use the same entry process but at a different location. With two teams operating independently, the Westers would have a much harder time fighting them off.

Once they reached far enough inside, gravity took over and they could walk normally again. They removed their space helmets. One man at a time, they removed their space suits while the others kept watch.

The initial plan was to shoot anything that moved. Though the Petersons didn't yet know the location of the virus production facility, it certainly wouldn't be near the exteriors of the outpost. And though they assumed the vast majority of Westers living here had little combat experience, anyone with a weapon can kill someone, even with a lucky shot or an accident. The Petersons weren't taking any chances. And they didn't want to lose a single man.

Winston had chosen a narrow hallway along the perimeter of the outpost, curving to the right. Occasional windows on the left reassured them they only had one side of the hallway and straight ahead to worry about. They started along the edge of the outpost, and would later work their way into the middle.

Two Westers opened a door up ahead and stepped into the path of the Petersons. They saw them, and seconds later, they were dead, torn up with quick AX bursts.

"Move ahead!" Shipp ordered, knowing they needed to clear out the room those two had just exited from. Algiers and Drummond rushed forward and kicked open the door. Shipp ran right through them and started shooting, with Algiers and Drummond following. This room appeared to be a workspace, as it contained monitors, chairs, counters, and desks.

Five Westers stood panicking as the Petersons entered. All five got killed with minimal rounds fired.

"You want to start searching these monitors to find the virus lab?" Cruz asked.

"We clear out this area first and then come back. Not going to be ambushed. We'll clear levels above and below too." Shipp said.

Shipp received a comm from Garrison, "We're in. What's your status?"

"Just killed seven. Found a room with monitors," Shipp replied.

"Assume they're triangulating on us. Minimal comms," Garrison said as he ended the call.

Shipp addressed his team. "We need to find a different set of monitors. If they are picking up our transmissions, they'll check here at some point, and we don't want to be here when they do."

Shipp and Garrison both led their teams one room, one area, and one level at a time, killing any Westers they saw, and encountering no serious resistance. They anticipated a relatively easy initial phase, because having your outpost attacked for the first time in your life would cause some panic, especially among non-military personnel. At first, the Westers would be working to survive and communicate. That's probably what the seven they just killed were doing – communicating with other monitors.

But given a couple hours, whatever Wester authorities and leaders remained would attempt to mount a counterattack, or at least a robust defense. They knew they were all alone, and they wouldn't just roll over. And even though the eleven Petersons probably outmatched every Wester on the outpost in terms of combat skill, the Westers outnumbered the Petersons at least a hundred to one. And there would certainly be emergency weapons stashed at various locations. So, inflicting maximum damage and maximum casualties these first couple hours was critical to the success of the mission. Thus – shoot to kill, everyone you see.

Not knowing the layout, Shipp led them up stairwells, down corridors, through large rooms and common areas, and room to room. The Petersons kept their attacks precise, and used only AX rounds for now. Shipp also directed his team to plant an occasional MagTon. Never know when you might need to have a surprise up your sleeve. Each Peterson had to pay attention to where they affixed each MagTon, so any soldier could detonate one at any moment.

The body count rose, surpassing a hundred after a couple hours. They hadn't encountered any large groups.

"Strange," Algiers said. "No alerts. No outpost alerts or base-wide comms at all."

"You're right," Shipp said. "That is surprising. Are they worried about giving something away? Or maybe they lost the capability?"

"Or they have some other way to communicate personally," said Cruz. "Probably every resident has a personal comm device and they're using those."

"Right," said Shipp. "Let's lift one from one of these dead rats."

Shipp hurried to a Wester they had just killed, and ripped the shirt from the neck down. He found a thin rectangular receiver affixed to his hip. Shipp unlatched it. Then, he turned the Wester's head to the side and checked his ears. He extricated a small comm device, commonly used on outposts because no one wanted to wear helmets or headsets all day. Shipp attached the receiver to his belt and placed the comm device in his ear. He listened. Yes.

"You hear them?" Cruz asked.

Shipp nodded, but didn't want to risk being heard. He pried the comm from his ear and removed the receiver from his hip, placed them on a counter and then walked a good distance away.

"We don't know their tech that well. I can't tell if it's still transmitting or not, or how many channels, people, or instructions are sending and receiving," Shipp said. "Here's the plan. We all get a comm from a dead rat, and together we listen for ten minutes. Then, we take them off and plan the next phase."

A little while later, all six Petersons stood listening while watching their surroundings. Most of the chatter sounded like one man talking to numerous others in various places throughout the outpost. They kept hearing the same voice giving directions and orders. There was fear, confusion, and panic. That was good. But several Westers also said they would rather blow up the outpost than let the Petersons reach the 'weapon,' as they called it several times.

The leader told them they weren't going to blow up the outpost, in part because they had no way to do so. The leader's name was Bguyen. The longer they listened, they learned the Westers intended to fortify sections of the outpost that would protect the weapon and other key facilities.

After a while, Shipp had everyone disconnect.

"Winston," Shipp said. "Get back on their comm and just keep listening. Step away from us a good distance." Winston went into an enclosed room and wrote down anything he heard that might be useful.

"Okay. Let's find a monitor and do a search on Bguyen," said Shipp. "I think it's a safe bet they aren't coming after us. They're expecting us to come to them. And they're right. We need to know how many live here, how many levels, and the basic layout. Then, I'd like to find Team 2. Algiers, can you locate them while we head to the monitors?"

Algiers started a comm with Garrison while Shipp and Cruz started searching an outpost monitor.

The outpost's name was Lightway, named after a famous scientist from six hundred years ago. Lightway had 43 levels. Far less than half the size of Ulrich. The listed population said 924, quite a bit smaller than the Petersons expected. They decided that with a classified location, the Westers had probably minimized the number of personnel who needed to work here. Plus, being so far on the fringe of the territory, it would be rarely visited.

"I got Garrison," Algiers said. "He thinks he knows our approximate location based on where we both entered. They're on their way."

"Let's be ready with a plan," Shipp replied.

Lightway's construction wasn't that different from any other outposts. Circular levels with varying diameters. But specifying the virus production facility location proved tougher than they hoped. The

Lightway schematics they found had no mention of a high-security laboratory.

These Petersons had entered at level 33. Shipp decided to count from the top down, with level one above them at the upper most point, and level 43 below them at the bottom tip. Team 1 had cleared out most of levels 35 through 32, and parts of 36, 37, 31, and 30. Team 2 probably entered around level 28 or so. Since they hadn't encountered much resistance either, it was a safe bet the virus lab waited above them. But it couldn't be at the very top either. You wouldn't put your most important facility at the most vulnerable spot in the outpost.

"Should we go down first and just wipe everyone out, so we know our backsides are safe?" Cruz asked Shipp.

"Not a bad idea, honestly," said Shipp. "Maybe a better way is to have the Sorcerer Reborn do it for us. Shear off the bottom five levels. Then, we go up, level by level, until we meet resistance. Then we know we're close."

Team 2 rounded a corner, and the teams spotted each other simultaneously. A friendly reunion. After a quick recap, Garrison was up to speed. Combined, the two teams had killed about 250 mostly unarmed Westers. Garrison's team encountered a couple larger groups, all heading up to higher levels, confirming Team 1's presumptions.

"So we have about 650 left. And they're walling themselves in up there, you say," Garrison summarized for himself. "Well Shipp? You're the ground war expert. What's the plan?"

Shipp laughed. Was Garrison serious? No. Just injecting some levity into a totally new scenario for all of them. Shipp knocked on Winston's door and motioned for him to come out. Winston removed his Wester comm and left it in the room.

"Listening to Wester broadcasts Winston? You're not falling for their propaganda I hope," joked Garrison.

"I'm a lucky dog," said Winston in total deadpan.

Everyone laughed.

"What have you heard?" Garrison asked.

"From what I can tell, they've got MagTons guarding several corridors up there," Winston cautioned. "I noted the names of some of them, so maybe we can find those corridors in the schematics. I also know there's a big horde of Westers on what he called the cafeteria level. I don't know what cafeteria means, but hopefully it's on the schematics too."

Shipp and Cruz studied the layout of Lightway on the monitor they had been using.

"Right there," Cruz said. "Cafeteria. Looks like.... level 22."

Shipp shook his head. "This is bad, General. MagTons can be planted just about anywhere with metal. Behind walls. Above ceilings. There are tons of corridors between here and level 22. And the virus is definitely above that if that's where they're barricading. I don't know how we'd make it through all those levels without serious losses."

"Send a couple nukes up from Winston's void?" Garrison suggested. "At least ten levels between us and the virus, probably more like fifteen. Nuke damage wouldn't reach that high."

"True," said Shipp. "But then how would we get up there?"

"We don't," said Li, part of Team 2 and very pleased to be reunited with Shipp again. "We go back outside and space walk it to the top level, break in there, and work our way down. All their barricades will be below the virus location. We come in from above."

Garrison looked at Li and then at Shipp. "You've got good friends. I love it. That's outstanding."

"What if they see us climbing up the side through a window?" asked Drummond, who had made it clear back on the Sorcerer Reborn he didn't much enjoy being out in space.

"I think there are enough sections with no windows that we can climb all the way up undetected," said Li. "Unless they have external sensors. But why would they? No way they ever anticipated a scenario like this."

"Shipp," Garrison said, "Call Harden and Mack. Relay the plan while we head back to our two entry points and get back in our suits. We meet back in the void."

"I got a better idea," said Shipp. "Let's send Winston back to the Sorcerer Reborn. They'll see it, probably. Make them wonder what's going on. They might think we're leaving. Whatever they think, it'll distract and misdirect them. When he gets there, he can update Mackson in person so we don't have to risk a transmission."

"Even better," said Winston. "After that I can fly back and forth a couple times, as if I'm taking back one person at a time. Like injured ones."

"I like it," said Garrison. "Do it. Enter the Sorcerer Reborn each time. Stay there a few minutes. Then return. The rest of us will be climbing up the other side of Lightway. I'd estimate we can reach the top in under an hour."

54

The Climb

Garrison was wrong. The climb took longer than an hour. Way longer.

At first, it started out okay. After getting back in their space suits, strapping on weapons, linking together, and re-entering the destroyed region of the outpost – Winston's void – the Petersons easily air-bursted their way up and collected themselves along the upper edge of the wreckage. Winston flew off in his battleship, and they climbed around onto the undamaged exterior of Outpost Lightway.

They knew it would be a challenge to find grips to hold onto. But there were none at all. The exterior surface curved, rolled, and extended before them. Just smooth metal and glass. No corners. Nothing to grab. Nothing to push off from.

The Petersons found plenty of areas without windows, so they easily avoided getting spotted. But from the very start, they struggled just to stay together and keep from floating off into space. Constant air bursts to keep close to the group. Softly bursting forward a few meters at a time. But then, the curvature would bend away, forcing them to regroup.

Were it just one man trying to ascend the 31 levels to the top of Lightway, he could have done it relatively quickly. But the ten Petersons had to stay together and move as one. They couldn't risk letting anyone drift off alone and get seen through a window. They couldn't risk an air burst malfunction or even just a mistake. They couldn't tolerate the loss of a single man, let alone the mission. Not here. Not when they had come this far and now floated so close to the prize.

Staying together mattered more than conserving oxygen. Each soldier brought eight hours' worth when they left. After surmounting the first five levels and spending almost an hour to do it, everyone started doing the math. They were beginning to figure out a rhythm for this, and the pace picked up a bit. But this climb, at best, would take three hours. Probably more like four.

Shipp missed Mackson. He had learned that Mackson was the very best space walker in Garrison's crew. Without him, the clumsiness of Shipp, James, and Li showed up right away. They kept over-bursting, or bursting from the wrong side of their bodies. Left is right. Up is down. Forward is backward. And the terrain prevented them from having just one person lead them all the way there. Every man had to do it right. Every centimeter of the way.

Even more challenging, they had to do all this without talking. Hand signals, head nods, eye movements, arm waves, and hip shakes – whatever each man could do to communicate with whoever needed to be told something – he had to figure out how to do it. They couldn't risk the possibility that Wester surveillance might pick up a transmission, even from outside Lightway's walls.

So, up they went. Centimeter by centimeter. Rivet by rivet. Level by level.

Shipp found himself fixating on where he was, and the incredible path he had taken to get here. When he told his parents he intended to apply for Space Force University, they celebrated and rejoiced that he had felt the call to devote his life to the eradication of Westers. At that time, still a young teen, he imagined himself roving through the hills of northern Cinque, unleashing death upon Wester rats.

His understanding of Space Age warfare evolved from that youthful idealism and self-centered brand of heroism, but his heart never wavered or weakened. He knew the evil they faced, and he could think of no better way to use his considerable abilities – physical and mental.

He imagined journeying through battle after battle, forging lifelong friendships with fellow soldiers. Bonding. Saving. Relying. Trusting. Fighting together and becoming stronger and stronger. He imagined passing on what he would learn to other young soldiers. He watched footage of famous Peterson soldiers who had taken this path, and he emulated everything he could learn about them.

When to wake up. What to do first thing in the morning. What to tell yourself every day. How to think about your fellow soldiers. Sacrificing carnal desires and the 'normal' life that soldiers made possible.

Eventually, of course, his mind returned to Pretoria. She wanted to one day become the chief administrator for a space station, just like the one he now climbed. She wanted the job of the overseer who probably got killed by the nukes on Ulrich. She would have been so good at it too.

I never should have loved her. He had never planned to love a woman in any way other than the way he loved all his fellow soldiers. He went to SFU single-minded, fixated on one thing. But the more time he spent with her, the more he felt as if she had taken all his greatest qualities and made them even better.

How could he not love her back and try to give her the same? Risner was a paradise. He could not imagine a better life than ambushing a squad of Westers, watching them die, and then returning to base to watch his beautiful bride supervise the rearming of weaponry and make sure the returning soldiers had adequate provisions. And after all that, he got to sleep with her every night. They had such a life together, and such big dreams.

And now...

Alone, climbing up a Wester outpost halfway across the galaxy from his home planet. In the dark and cold. Above a planet that housed a hostile virus. Running out of oxygen. Dependent on nine other men to reach the top.

Now, he cared about just one thing: Find the virus that destroyed his sense of confidence and trust in his own people, and kill its maker. He again pondered Rawlic tearing apart his own unit with fear, cowardice, and selfishness, and taking eight others down with him. Mixie. Shelsie. The pain hadn't subsided whenever Shipp chose to dwell on it long enough. There was no getting over it. It was heightening. Deepening. Consuming him.

All that mattered now was pulverizing Westers. He greatly admired Garrison. He had been honest with Garrison in the meeting when his mistake on Ulrich came to light. He was committed to this mission. But deep down, he still harbored a desire to find a way to do something... genocidal. Something that would alter the course of space history forever.

Shipp also wondered if Garrison suspected anything like this. Garrison seemed to have a special ability to sniff out secrets.

So what would happen if Garrison and he were to find themselves opposing each other over what to do? Shipp didn't know. He didn't want that. Hopefully it wouldn't happen. But being so close, right outside the walls of the only place in the galaxy where a war-ending weapon sits right there for the taking – Shipp knew a moment was coming soon that would never come again.

Shipp found himself bringing up the rear of the ten linked Petersons clambering their way up Lightway's surface. His thoughts had probably slowed him down, and he just followed the lead of whoever was in front of him.

Garrison had told everyone to try and count the levels as they passed. Shipp lost count. He tugged the leg of the guy in front of him. It was Drummond, which Shipp realized only after Drummond jerked his head around to make eye contact with Shipp so they could communicate.

Shipp held up his fingers and used them to count one, two, three. Then waved both hands in the air as if to ask, "How many?" Then, he tapped the surface with a finger and asked how many again. Drummond got it. Shipp wanted to know which level they were on.

Drummond held up two fingers with one hand and then four fingers with the other. Level 24. Shipp got the attention of two more Petersons by yanking the belt connecting them. He wanted to get everyone's attention. Eventually, he had it.

The web of Petersons huddled against Lightway's surface, and Shipp pulled out a MagTon. He pointed to the surface with the weapon and nodded. Then he put it away and held up his fingers, two in each hand. 22.

Then, he made a motion with ever widening hands and arms, suggesting something getting bigger and bigger. Did anyone get it? He looked around and waited. James got it. Of course he did. James could read Shipp better than anyone, and it made perfect sense to him.

Shipp wanted to plant a swath of MagTons against the wall on Level 22, because Winston had told them about a large number of Westers massing on that level. And on the schematics of the outpost, the cafeteria appeared to occupy pretty much the entire level – just one big room.

Blow a big hole in the side, and they might push a whole bunch of Westers out into space.

James found another way to say the same thing to Garrison. Once he got it, he instantly approved it. He directed each man to affix three MagTons each across an area of the 22nd level, once they got there.

But once they climbed up to level 23, they discovered a big problem with Shipp's plan. Almost the entire level 22 featured floor-to-ceiling windows. Planting MagTons would be easy enough. But how could they cross the windows without being seen? If tons of Westers were holed up in there, it would be impossible.

Everyone took a much-needed break to think it over.

After about ten minutes, they started discussing it. This looked pretty silly – ten men floating outside an outpost on the fringes of colonized space waving their arms and legs at each other trying to communicate. Eventually, after at least thirty minutes, they finally settled on what seemed like the only possible plan. And there was no reason to wait to implement it.

The Petersons spread apart, forming a cluster of two rows of five men. Each one took just two MagTons, one in each hand. With a light air burst from each of them, at Garrison's hand signal, all ten pushed upward and into full view of whoever might be inside this level.

As they floated upward, each man affixed and armed both his MagTons to the window frames. Then, he continued bursting upward. They got a quick glimpse inside the room. It looked like a mess hall. Filled with Westers.

A few of them saw the Petersons outside the windows and pointed at them. But it didn't matter. A couple more air bursts and the Petersons were gone. They then accelerated up and away from Lightway. No reason to go slow anymore.

Once far enough away, Shipp gave the signal, and each Peterson blew his own pair of MagTons. The glass – strong as it was – couldn't withstand this, and it shattered into chunks, blowing away a set of windows about ten meters wide and two meters tall.

Seconds later, a flood of screaming, flailing Westers spilled out into the vacuum of space. The panic of imminent death, very soon afterward met with the agonizing reality of it, filled the silent darkness. The Petersons watched as dozens of Westers belched from the outpost without any protection. A parade of bodies, with arms and legs flailing in searing pain as the water throughout their bodies turned to vapor, which spewed out their mouths as they contorted themselves trying to breathe.

Very soon afterward, their internal organs failed, and they went still, hardening into an unconscious stupor from which they would never awake.

To an average person, what looked like Lightway vomiting a cascade of writhing human bodies would have been pretty horrific. But to these Petersons, they watched it all with profound gratification. Almost in awe. A lot had happened in this five-hundred-year war. But no one in all those centuries could claim to have seen anything like this. What a sight.

To Shipp, it reminded him of the corroded faces he had seen on Lavoisier who died from the virus. Those bodies were just as deformed as the human mass pouring out the side of Lightway, once all their limbs went still and cold. To him, since these were the very people who had discovered, invented, weaponized, and mass-produced this virus, this death was fitting and right.

Garrison reacted with bemused annoyance. He wanted to know how many they had killed, but it was impossible to keep track since there were so many, and they drifted away with surprising speed. Whatever the number, it was high. And he knew Harden would be very jealous to have missed such a sight.

The Petersons floated in space for about ten minutes, watching and waiting, because an occasional Wester would fly out each time they thought the parade had finished. A few Westers somehow managed to hang on to tables, chairs, doorways, and counters, eventually losing the strength to withstand the forces and the cold of depressurizing space.

Finally, all the air in level 22 escaped, and any remaining Westers died inside. At that moment, the Petersons realized how much this benefitted them. Level 22 was impassible without a space suit now. Would any Westers below level 22 dare to attempt it? Very unlikely, since these weren't combat specialists.

They had now cut off all remaining survivors below level 22.

And that meant only the final assault awaited them. The Petersons air bursted back toward Lightway, found a dark and empty room on level three, exploded the lone window with two MagTons, and climbed inside one at a time. Cruz attached the canopy to the wall bordering the destroyed window, and the pressure equalized. They removed their space suits and prepared to hunt down any remaining Westers, and then locate the virus production facility. It had to be somewhere between here and the hollowed-out cafeteria.

55

War Virus

Before going anywhere, Garrison decided they needed to break comm silence and update Mackson and Harden on their progress. It didn't matter now if anyone was still capable of detecting their location.

Harden's elation at Garrison's update could be heard across space. His ebullience at the mental image of Westers tumbling out into space like a swarm of deranged bees was contagious. Everyone felt pretty proud of what they had just accomplished. Ten against 924 had probably whittled down to ten against less than two hundred. They couldn't be sure, of course. Could be four hundred. Could be one hundred. All that mattered was how many remained above level 22, and the virus.

Garrison ordered Mackson to move the Sorcerer Reborn closer to Lightway so Dons could target specific levels, even specific rooms if necessary. The Sorcerer Reborn provided the ultimate fail safe in virus destruction weaponry. There was no way Lightway would survive once the Petersons had finished with it.

But before they destroyed it, they had to ensure the virus could pose no further threat.

"Our first task," said Garrison, "Is to kill every Wester still breathing above level 22. Let's go."

At that, the ten Petersons merged and mutated into a single murdering machine, roaming through the halls, breaking down doors, and killing anyone they encountered without hesitation.

Five Westers had holed up on the very top level. Several more hid in a storage room on level two. Algiers found six more that seemed to be trapped on purpose, almost like prisoners, on level six. Weird. Why would there be prisoners way out here, on Lightway of all places?

Most if not all the Westers they found were non-military personnel. Researchers. Admins. Support. But all played a role in the production of the most deadly viral weapon in human history. Thus, all had to die. The Petersons worked through every level from one to fourteen, and left not a single man or woman alive.

Then, when they breached level fifteen, the layout of Lightway shifted dramatically – differing from the structural charts Shipp and Cruz had found earlier. Levels fifteen through nineteen consisted of a few corridors circling the periphery. But every time they tried to move inward, they encountered walls. Walls, walls, and more walls.

Until they reached level eighteen. There, they located a solitary door leading into the inner areas of Lightway. They broke through the door and entered a vast enclosed facility that stretched vertically from levels fifteen through nineteen.

Shipp stepped through first, and Garrison followed. They walked onto a metal gantry with railings. The gantry split off in opposite directions and encircled a large structure, enclosed with what appeared to be very dense, hard glass, probably the same kind used in the windows of attack ships. Within that structure, they saw more sealed doors at various locations, leading to inner rooms enclosed with more glass. It looked like a cylindrical glass maze for experimenting on rats. How fitting.

From the Petersons' position on the eighteenth level, most of this four-level enclosed facility sat above them, with one level beneath. And even though they could mostly see through the glass and could observe all sorts of scientific and laboratory equipment, they did not see a single person.

Had the Westers abandoned the virus production facility entirely?

"They might have released the virus in there, so we all die if we enter it," said Shipp. "I wouldn't put it past them."

The other Petersons agreed.

"Li, take six men, and go kill the remaining Westers through level 21. But first, send us a lab rat," Garrison ordered.

Li took Algiers, Drummond, Zum, Jimenez, and Cruz with him to carry out Garrison's orders. Within moments, Algiers returned and shoved a terrified Wester through the outer door onto the gantry. He fell at Garrison's knees. Shipp hauled the Wester to his feet and marched him toward the nearest door that led into the first inner room. There appeared to be a total of three concentric rooms enclosed within each other.

Shipp shoved him against the door and pointed to the handle.

"Open it, or I'll blow off your limbs one at a time," Shipp said. To his surprise, the Wester opened the door and then waited for more instructions. Shipp nodded him in, and they explored the area carefully, keeping the Wester close.

Tons of supplies, body suits, respirators, masks. Boxes of metal chutes for storing the countermeasure, like Merriss had described to them. More equipment and devices these Peterson military experts couldn't even make a guess as to their purpose, or even how to describe them. But it didn't matter. All Shipp wanted was one thing: The next door. Once they found one leading into the second inner room, he ordered the Wester to open it. Again, he did it without question.

This inner room was of course smaller than the last, and it completely enclosed the third inner room, which the four Petersons – Shipp, Garrison, James, and Cardmanov – approached and observed through the glass.

They found a door into that room. Sealed with a coded entry lock. The Wester shook his head, "I don't know the code say."

"But you do know if the virus has been released inside there," Shipp said.

The Wester looked at him like he was crazy. That was all Shipp needed. He shot the man in the head and shoved his body aside. Then, Shipp adjusted his Mossamer and prepared to fire at the locked door using the K-rocket attachment. Cardmanov, the only other Peterson with a Mossamer in the room, did the same. Garrison and James took cover behind some supplies, while Shipp and Cardmanov got on one knee at as safe a distance as they could manage in the confined space, and prepared to fire.

But before they could, the door made a few beeping sounds. The lock disengaged and opened. Red lights turned to green. It was unlocked. How? Who? Why?

"It must be Bguyen. He's probably somewhere around here, guarding his death baby," Shipp said.

Then from around an obstruction within the most inner room, a slender upper middle-aged woman stood up and moped around a corner. She sneered at the four Petersons about to fire at the door leading into her room. She gestured toward the door. Shipp and Garrison looked at each other, perplexed. She's inviting us in?

Knowing for sure that no virus had been released within the area, Shipp and the others marched up to the door, opened it, and walked right up to her.

"Who are you?" Shipp asked.

"I'm Wren. Didn't you know? How could you have found this place and not know who I am? And how did you find this place?"

"That's not your concern anymore," said Shipp. "We're asking the questions. Who are you? Why are you in here? Why did you let us in?"

Garrison didn't care so much about that. He approached a silvery rectangular metal chamber, about three meters wide and two meters long, with viewing ports.

"Aluminum?" He speculated. "This must be where you keep it, or where you make it."

Wren squinted at him in disbelief. How could he know this much about the virus? Garrison picked up on it.

"Yeah, we know a lot more than that."

"I let you in because I didn't want your weapons to expose me to it," Wren said, answering Shipp while scowling at Garrison.

"You're in charge of manufacturing it?" Shipp asked.

Wren smiled at his ignorance in that condescending manner typical of Westers. Even Merriss had exhibited the same attitude at times.

"I invented it, you mongrel," Wren seethed. "And my only regret is that it didn't find its way to you in time."

Shipp flushed with rage and started toward her, fingers clenching into fists, still composed but ready to bash her head into the wall. Garrison pushed him in the perpendicular direction.

"Not yet, my friend. We're not done yet. Don't let her get to you," Garrison calmed him.

"You've obviously seen its effects," Wren surmised. Then, looking at Garrison, "And you obviously haven't."

At that moment, Li entered the innermost room to update Garrison. All remaining Westers above level 22 were dead. That included Bguyen, which Li seemed particularly proud to report, hinting that his death would be a great story to tell. But Garrison just gave a perfunctory nod of appreciation, told Li Wren was the real mastermind, and ordered him to return to the other Petersons and keep watch. After Li left, the conversation resumed.

"I was on Lavoisier," Shipp said, nodding almost imperceptibly. "It killed your own as well as ours."

Wren curled a sort of whimpering smile. She really was proud of her invention. But she couldn't conceal her profound disappointment at having her life's work about to be cut short.

"It would have killed billions more," she said through her own brand of rage and regret that mirrored Shipp's. "How did you find this place?" She asked it again, barely getting the words out through her fury. "I wanna know."

"Ya," Shipp mocked. "Where are all those useless words all the others tack on to everything they say, sis?"

"Sis? Nobody says 'sis,' you wormbrained mutant," Wren responded.

Shipp laughed at her insult. "We hold your life in our hands. I would think you'd be a little more cautious."

But then he realized, if Wren was being truthful, the Westers on Ulrich must have used that term to see if the crew of the 'Obliterator' would use it back. And because they did, the Westers knew they were Petersons. Shipp looked at Garrison and James. They realized the same thing. They may be rats, but they're cunning rats.

"You think I care about my life now?" Wren said. "This is all I have left. Inside this room. My mother, you killed when I was twelve. My father when I was sixteen. My husband when I was 27. My two best friends the year after. And each time..." Wren paused – disbelieving she was saying any of this to the people she hated more than anyone else in the universe. But she couldn't help herself.

"Each time, it was worse than the last. More cruel. You don't just kill. You torture. You inflict pain without cause. You maximize suffering. I saw my best friend breathe his last breath, but he didn't see me because your hive bomb blinded him."

Shipp wasn't about to share his own source of rage or counter the propaganda she'd been spoon-fed. But he realized in that moment Wren was in many ways his polar opposite. She had been through what he had been through, only on the other side. For that, he respected her, for a very brief moment. But then his lifetime of conditioning reminded him that her pain was of her own doing, because the Westers were the ultimate cause of the war. They perpetuated it from the beginning. They broke truces and treaties early on. They violated the unwritten rules of war, over and over throughout the centuries.

Her pain wasn't due to the Petersons, he knew. It was self-inflicted.

"So you invented this virus to fight back," Shipp said, trying to keep his head in charge of his emotions.

"Where is it?" asked Garrison. "I want to see it. Your records. Your manufacturing process. The science behind the suffering."

Wren clammed up. "You do whatever the flame you want to me you hominids. I wouldn't give you a drop of water if I had an ocean of it."

Garrison, unlike Shipp, had remained passive and methodical this entire time. Her resistance didn't phase him at all. Instead, he activated his comm.

"Harden, you got me?" Garrison said. "Send Locke over. We need a scientific mind here. All the Westers are dead. Except one, and she's not going anywhere. Send him to the canopy we placed over a window on level three. He'll see it."

56

Vulica Septica

By the time Locke finally made it over to Lightway – having to put on a space suit, pack relevant gear, do his first space walk in years, take off a space suit, and do it all without complaining which was impossible for him – Shipp, James, and Garrison had spent considerable time rummaging through data records on the Wester monitors. They also rummaged through the physical contents of the room. Cardmanov kept a constant eye and his AX-15 on Wren, who was seated and looked bored.

The one thing all four of them could observe with absolute certainty was that her intelligence was matched only by her revulsion and hatred for all things Peterson. So Cardmanov had one job, and he wasn't about to slack on it.

At one point, James found several photos of a reddish purple spongy thing, but Wren wouldn't answer any questions, or even look at the monitor. Garrison found cinematic records of someone dying from the virus. It was gruesome. The man screeched and wailed almost nonstop, begging to be killed. But he appeared to be alone, and no one else ever set foot in the frame. Garrison never looked away.

Again, Wren said nothing when asked, and didn't budge even when Garrison replayed the video, turned up the sound, and watched her. Garrison had never seen what the virus could do until this. It was hard to watch and equally hard to look away from. He wanted to know the identity of the dying man – Peterson or Wester. She wouldn't say.

They found a ton of data. Chemical equations. Mathematical calculations. Analysis. Schematics for various instrumentation. The Petersons could make guesses about it, but they needed someone like Locke to fill in the blanks.

Locke finally arrived and entered the innermost room, coming face to face with Wren. "Nice vermin," he commented. "Why haven't you knocked her silly yet, Garrison? Seems unlike you. I'm sure Shipp would do it happily."

Garrison ignored him. "Come over and look at this stuff. She's as quiet as a rocket in space."

He directed Locke to the photos of the spongy thing. Locke approached the monitor and looked around the area.

"Why does no one else sit down at monitors anymore? I want a chair." He lowered the adjustable height monitor and waited, then saw Wren's chair. He looked at Garrison, as if to ask if he could have hers. But Garrison was already rummaging for another one. He found it and set it down with a clang. No words. Garrison wasn't in a light mood, and Locke picked up on it.

He sat and began examining the records. Before saying anything, he looked up several other references and research reports. He did a fair amount of reading. Even though it was Wester technology and infrastructure, there are only so many ways to organize and store information. What it takes is a person who knows what questions to ask.

After about forty minutes of total silence other than Locke's typing, note-taking, and occasional annoyed grunts, he turned in the chair and addressed the group.

"This is an alien species of fungus. We would place it in the septica family, probably, which may be why they named it vulica septica. Resembles and behaves enough like fuligo septica." Locke leaned back toward the monitor and snickered at the meaning of the name. "Dog vomit slime mould. No wonder they liked this so much. But it's not like any other fungus, including that one, for several reasons that apparently even the Westers still haven't figured out."

"What do you mean?" Garrison asked.

"It appears to be cannibalistic," Locke said. "They sent multiple expeditions down to that planet. Several observed the life form appearing to consume its own. A slow process, but they documented it. Seems to kind of absorb them. And in the process, its color and other features change."

"How could it survive if it eats itself?" Garrison asked.

"It also drinks water, eats other life forms. It looks like this planet has a functioning ecosystem with a number of different organisms totally unknown to us. But the vulica septica dominates. It rules this planet. Its only predator appears to be itself. Very weird."

"And these expeditions went down there without dying? How is that possible?" Garrison asked.

"I haven't found that yet. Hold on," Locke said, and began researching again. Then he stopped and turned around again. "But they did try to kill it a few times. Turned into a whole research project from what I can see. It survived fire and heat up to 437 degrees. Survived total absence of water for 194 days. This thing is a survivor. Oh interesting... until you remove it from the planet. Then, it dies in a few weeks without water."

Garrison nodded and looked at Wren. She just sat there, watching Locke expose her secrets one at a time. Garrison decided she would change her stoicism if they found something that truly threatened her invention and its preservation.

"Locke, forget that question. Look at this video we found." Locke watched the video of the infected person dying of the virus. He turned to look at Wren with contempt while he listened to the victim scream in agony. She met his gaze for a while, and it wasn't clear if she was proud of the video, disturbed, or embarrassed. But she finally looked away before he could decide.

Off the video, Locke began another round of research. Another twenty minutes later, he turned to face Garrison but made sure Wren was in his sights too.

"This woman should be torn limb from limb," Locke said, much to Garrison's surprise, because Locke wasn't typically one for gruesome treatment of prisoners.

"That man was a Wester. A prisoner of some kind. They tested this weapon – *her* weapon – on their own people. They watched them go through that. Dozens of them. Until they could perfect, predict, and control it," Locke spoke with his usual self-righteousness. But this time, every Peterson felt his delivery was spot on.

"I'm getting so tired of seeing Westers killing their own people. We don't do that. But you seem to do it all the time," Shipp said, neglecting or forgetting the episode with Rawlic.

"You do so," Wren finally spoke with derision. "You would kill your own wife if it gave you a big enough advantage over us."

Shipp cracked a little, but held still and kept quiet. James watched him closely, ready to intervene if Shipp lost it. Wren could tell she touched a nerve, but wisely left it alone.

"What did they learn?" Garrison asked Locke.

"From what I've seen so far, this is how they developed the countermeasure that Merriss talked about," Locke said, letting the rat out of the bag and only realizing it after he said it.

Wren jumped on it. "Merriss? Who is Merriss? Is that one of ours? Did you pick up one of ours and torture him until he gave away everything?"

Shipp took one step toward her and knelt to get at eye level, "No. We didn't. He spoke freely, because he hates you and hates everything about this war. He doesn't care who wins anymore. And no, he didn't know where this outpost was. We found this rat hole on our own."

"Shipp – it doesn't matter. Locke, continue," Garrison said.

"The countermeasure takes at least 72 hours to effectively consume the virus. In a larger area, they recommend a week," Locke said, shaking his head. "They really did invent this thing. The virus is unnatural. They combined elements of vulica septica with some old-style bioweapons dating back centuries that no one uses anymore. This is a manmade weapon. But they couldn't manufacture it without the fungus. And they have to be close to this planet to make it."

Here, Locke seemed to be talking and reading at the same time.

"Wow," he said, shaking his head. "This is a direct quote: 'Conclusion confirmed. Weaponization requires initial human host. Spores escaping from deceased take on new characteristics that enable safe hibernation and deployment.'"

Wren began chewing her tongue, almost as if she wanted a piece of gum but had to make do. Locke turned to face her again. "You wrote that. You have to kill someone to make your weapon."

Wren's face soured and hardened. She rubbed her nose and furrowed her brow looking at the floor. She was consumed with guilt but had been forcing it far down into her subconscious for years, probably decades. This was the first time anyone had attempted to call it back up. "I wrote a lot of things."

"Prisoners huh," Shipp said. "Not as important as regular people. You should see Peterson prisons."

"You have no idea what it took," Wren said, speaking as if someone were forcing her at gunpoint, even though no one was. "What it cost. What I had to give up. What I had to... what I had to approve. I gave up my soul for the greater good."

"Right," said Locke, but Wren cut him off.

"You monsters stand there in judgment over me like you're born on a planet of angels. As if you haven't butchered and murdered thousands, taken joy in death, written songs and poems about the fields of dead you leave behind. I've seen the footage from 745. I've seen the images from 892. I've read what your artists wrote about them! You can't make that up. And you try to outdo them every time you go out to war."

She stood to her feet, raising her voice.

"So don't stand there and tell me what I've done is any worse, because you – had you sat next to this planet – would have done the exact same thing!"

"I wouldn't have," said Locke. "I'm in this for my own reasons. But bleeding out entire planets isn't one of them."

"I would have," said Shipp, drawing Wren's attention. His honesty calmed her. She sat down again. Cardmanov never moved, and never took his weapon off her. Shipp continued, "You're right. You are 100% right. I would have done it, and I would have done it faster. But I wouldn't have used my own people to make it work."

"Right of course," mocked Wren. "You would have used us, because that, that would be justifiable."

"Where is the virus now?" James asked, speaking for the first time. "We haven't found it in here yet."

Wren started giggling uncontrollably, but in a tragic sort of tone. She couldn't seem to stop herself. "No you haven't..." and her laughter got even more out of control so that tears started forming. But these didn't seem like typical tears of laughter. Wren was not in a good state of mind.

Garrison again intervened, though he let this interaction go on longer because it was fascinating to hear her finally talk. "Locke. Can we use the countermeasure on the planet? They have reams of it over there," he said, pointing off to his right.

"It would be easy to test it," Locke said, "But I would imagine they already have. I'll keep looking."

At this, Wren's eyes widened with alarm. Garrison had finally found that tender nerve he'd been looking for. She stood up again and took a step toward them.

"You can't do that! That's outside our conflict. That's a native species. Alien. Undiscovered until less than a century ago. There's no telling what else we can learn from them." Wren rambled.

Garrison nodded to Cardmanov, who stepped toward her and pointed her back to her chair. Then, Garrison spoke.

"Them?" he said thoughtfully. "I would have said 'it,' not 'them.' Do they have intelligence?"

"You'll never know if you use that on them. They have something we don't have. They expand and consume an area, but then stop when another helpless area lies before them. Instead, they eat their own, get stronger, but less prolific. Then they move in a different direction. They check their progress. They let themselves die off. One section turns a dark purple color while the rest turns pink. Then, the pink sections die off and the purple spreads. There are patterns and bizarre behaviors we haven't even begun to understand," she went on and on, until Shipp interrupted her.

"You haven't begun to understand them, because you're too busy using them to murder billions," he said to silence her. "I on the other hand, have no problem at all wiping out the entire planet, alien species included. You're not going to poison one more Peterson after today."

"I destroyed all the remaining weapons on Lightway," Wren said. "To keep them from you. There's none left. We'd have to start over."

"Meaning, you need a new human volunteer," Garrison said. "But you know how to do it. Just plug and play."

"Not after you blow up Lightway. All the records and data are here for security purposes. No one else has it," Wren pleaded. At this point, they couldn't be sure if she had become a normal scientist again, horrified by the loss of a historic discovery, or if she was still hiding something.

"Card?" Garrison said. "Tie her up to that post in the chair. We're done." Then, he called Dons on his comm, "Dons, we are going to deploy the countermeasure across the entire planet and wipe out the source of the virus. Can you come up with a way to make that happen?"

"No! Nooo!! Stop!!! Please stop!" Wren screeched as Cardmanov tried to wrap her against the chair with a stretch line. "This isn't about the war! You can't just kill them!" She struggled against Cardmanov, but he was much stronger, and tightened a line around her waist and across her arms and chest, pinning her in place.

"You want me to muzzle her too?" Cardmanov asked.

"No, I like the sound," Garrison said. "Very reassuring." He called Dons again. "Locke is sending you information about the countermeasures. Let me know once you have a plan."

Garrison, Shipp, James, and Locke commenced documenting everything they could while Dons worked up a plan. Cardmanov watched Wren, who quieted down again, helpless. Looking at her, Shipp got the sense that in her brain, she was working through every possible option she could fantasize about for how to stop the Petersons from carrying out their plan.

Almost two hours went by. Wren urinated on her chair, and herself, when Garrison refused to give her a bathroom break. Dons apparently had his work cut out for him. Garrison brought in Li and Drummond to help Locke assemble all the countermeasures they could find and prepare to transport them through space to the Sorcerer Reborn.

And there was a lot of countermeasure. Apparently, Wren really had incinerated the virus. Locke found the mechanism for it. She had done it inside the metallic chamber they observed when they first entered the room. The other Westers on Lightway who had been planning to make a stand against the Petersons were indeed buying time – for Wren to prevent any virus from falling into enemy hands. She succeeded on that front.

But Garrison didn't care. All he wanted now was to wipe out vulica septica and destroy Lightway. Finally, Dons called Garrison back with his solution.

"It looks like, once this thing gets in the air, it just consumes the viral spores. And from what Locke is saying, it will kill the fungus too because it attacks a key cellular division process?"

"That's right," Locke verified. "The Wester researchers found that it reverses cell division in the sponges, and leads to cell implosion. It withers and dies."

"We just need enough of it," said Dons. "It's not a huge planet, but it's hard to say if the supply you have will be enough. Can you make more?"

Garrison hedged. He looked at Wren for a clue. She wasn't looking at him, and didn't budge. He gambled, and his intuition often proved correct, so he went with it.

"I think it will be enough. They have enough of this stuff to kill an entire planet, like they tested on Lavoisier, and then cure it so they can inhabit it. I think there's enough here for ten planets."

"Good. Makes sense," said Dons. Shipp nodded in agreement and admiration. Garrison's sharp mind had reached the right conclusion again.

Dons continued, "In that case, what I think will work is to affix these to our hive bombs. Since these don't use heat or fire when they burst, the effect should be to quickly produce a cloud of countermeasure that will settle on the fungus. Send down bombs at pre-determined intervals across the planet, and it should spread everywhere."

Garrison nodded. He looked at Shipp for affirmation, because Shipp knew hive bombs the best of anyone on the Sorcerer Reborn.

Shipp gave it, "Should work. Good plan, as long as we have enough bombs."

At that, the final act of the mission of the Sorcerer Reborn got underway. Locke left to finish packing up the countermeasure and send it to the ship, where Dons and Yao would work on merging it with their hive bomb supply.

A lot of waiting. The Petersons ate the nutrients they brought with them as emergency supplies.

While eating, Shipp just stared at the images of this fungus that had the potential to wipe out entire civilizations without causing any environmental or structural damage. He started thinking again about the Westers deploying this virus on his home planet of Saul, where his parents and 300,000 other people live. He reasoned they must have a continuous production process in place, and that they must need new human hosts at regular intervals. And that must mean they have something else on Lightway, somewhere, at all times.

He finished his last nutrient and then turned to the utterly exhausted Wren.

"The prisoners on level six that we found. Those are yours aren't they?" Shipp asked. Wren came out of her sleepy stupor. She didn't answer.

"Were," said Garrison. But that wasn't Shipp's main focus.

"You have a sample of the sponge up here," Shipp told her. "You'd have to. Otherwise you couldn't make more virus without a trip to the planet."

Wren was so tired it was hard to control her reactions strategically. Shipp was certain of it.

"You have to," he repeated. "It's here somewhere. We just didn't find it yet."

Right then, all four Petersons turned toward the entrance at the sound of AX fire.

"Let's go," Garrison said. "Leave her," and he, Shipp, James, and Cardmanov darted through the doors leading back out to the gantry and through the only entrance to the virus production facility.

Zum lay dead on the floor. Li and the others had retreated down the corridor.

Garrison called him on his comm. "Li! We're at the entrance. Where the flame did these rats come from?"

"They must have broken through level 22 from below, brought a bunch of weapons across," Li responded. "You can get out if you spray cover fire to the left and come our way."

Garrison looked at his three comrades and then at the deceased Zum, "Okay, we're going. We can get back to the ship, kill the fungus, destroy Lightway, and go home. No reason at all to lose anyone else to this fight."

Garrison, James, and Cardmanov stepped out into the arc shaped corridor and fired to the left, running toward the right until they re-united with Li and the others. From there, they began ascending back up toward level three where their space suits awaited.

On Level seven, James looked around at every Peterson in the room while Algiers opened a door.

"Where's Shipp?"

57

Shipp's Mission

Right after Garrison gave the order, he, James, and Cardmanov bolted into the corridor using their own cover fire and never looked back.

But Shipp stayed. He watched them leave. He realized this was his chance. The Westers would chase them. All he had to do was close the door, and he would be all alone with Wren. If his plan succeeded – and it had only a small chance of doing so – Garrison would have to accept it because, how could you pass up the opportunity?And even if he didn't accept it, Shipp would find a way to force him. All his grief, rage, fury, and agony had coalesced and condensed into a sharpened point, and he was ready to drive that point as far as he could take it – all the way to Faraday and General Elliss.

He closed and sealed the outermost door to the production facility before any Westers reached that point. They would run right by, having no idea what was transpiring behind it. Then, Shipp made his way back through the series of concentric rooms and doors until he reached Wren.

She eyed him, and her jaw quivered a bit, because this was unexpected. Why was he alone? What was he planning? Shipp got right to business.

"I know you have a sample of the fungus here somewhere. You tell me where it is, and I'll untie you." Shipp didn't expect her to take him up on this weak offer. But, he tried it because he figured she was looking for any chance to break out and stop the Petersons from annihilating her mass genocidal creation. Being untied is infinitely preferable to being tied down.

"Why?" Wren asked. "Why would you want to see it? What can you do with it? You're not a scientist."

"I like to know my enemy face to face," Shipp said. An obvious dodge.

"You're staring at her," Wren replied. She wriggled a bit in the chair and winced, trying to sit straighter. "Your boys didn't send you back here. You're going rogue aren't you?"

"I'm giving you an easy chance to tell me what I already know. If you don't tell me, I have all day to keep searching these rooms. It's a matter of time before I get what I want," Shipp said.

"Why don't you torture me?" Wren taunted. "Or are you too squeamish and soft to hurt a woman?"

"You don't want to go down that road," Shipp said, letting her see his rising anger.

"Tell me what made you like this. I told you mine," Wren said. "Tell me that, and I'll tell you where it is."

Shipp almost spoke, but held back. He wiped his hand across his mouth, picked up a tape dispenser, and walked toward her. He ripped off a section of tape.

"Why are you doing that? I want to know! You're taping me because I want to know your mmmpph?"

"You don't deserve to know," Shipp said, as he pressed the tape across her mouth. Then, he threw her chair to the floor, with her still tied to it, putting her in a very uncomfortable position.

At that, he began searching the room. He searched for about ten minutes. After that, he broadened his search to the second layer of rooms. Garrison, James, and him had pretty much scoured the entire innermost section, but they hadn't done much with the middle or outermost sections, which were both far more spacious, and with multiple levels. The second layer completely enclosed the innermost room, all around, below, and above. Almost like the protein of the egg surrounding the yolk.

Shipp found a drawer of syringes and small knives. He brought them out and laid them on the floor surrounding Wren's face. She had been struggling to free herself. Shipp made it clear that she should stop struggling, without saying a word. He placed them around her, pointing blades and needles toward her, and then looked in her eyes for a few moments, making her stare at his.

He left again and searched another room in the second layer of rooms. Came back with nothing, knelt before her and stared at her some more. This time, he took a scalpel, and pressed it against the tape, in the middle of it, about where her mouth would be.

He pressed the blade deeper. She pulled away.

"Open your mouth, and it won't hurt. Resist, and it will," Shipp said without a hint of remorse or empathy.

Wren stopped and tried to open her lips. Shipp cut through the tape. The blade entered her mouth, but didn't make contact. Shipp removed it, then stuck two fingers into her mouth, and ripped the tape off. She yelped in response to the stinging sensation.

"What do you want, you sadistic dog lover?" Wren belched.

Shipp slapped her. "I told you want I want. You wanted to play games. You wanted that. So I'm playing them. You don't like the way I play, then tell me what I want."

"Why would you keep your word if I tell you? You'll just walk over and...do whatever you want to with it, which won't amount to much."

Shipp nodded in agreement. Why should she trust him? So, he decided to give her something she wanted.

"My wife, was an admin on Risner. We served together. She was better than me, in every way a person can be better than another one," Shipp began. But then, his eyes fell, and he couldn't bring himself to say this to the most vile Wester he had ever countered. She really didn't deserve to know.

But he'd already said enough to clue Wren in. "And we killed her, and you couldn't stop it."

Shipp's hands trembled. His face began vibrating as he sat right next to the adversary he had sought for so long – someone he had always imagined being a man. He wanted to strangle her. He wanted to hang her by her feet in a dungeon filled with rats biting at her face from below.

"Was it the virus?" Wren asked. "You said Risner, not Lavoisier. We haven't released on Risner."

Shipp looked at her, realizing she wasn't actually responsible for Pretoria's death. He had blended all his targets together, and his rage had cost him his mental clarity.

"Elliss," Shipp blurted. "I want General Elliss."

"The fungus is... you were really close last time. It's behind the glass to the left of the door you reached. In a sealed, environmentally stable receptacle."

Wren gave him his answer, feeling satisfied she could trust him. And he kept his word. He lifted up her chair. Kicked aside the blades and syringes. And used his own much larger blade to cut the binding around her legs and torso. Then, he stepped back and held out a hand directing her to show him the fungus sample.

Wren took a moment to re-animate her fingers and other extremities that had been confined for several hours. She arched her back, kinked her neck, and breathed a sigh of relief. Shipp gave her the time. Then, she started ahead, step by step, watching him. Shipp sheathed his blade.

She walked ahead of him, but looked back his way every half second, looking more toward him than where she was going. He followed at enough distance to make her feel as comfortable as could be.

Wren reached the room she had referred to and opened the door. At this, Shipp quickened, not wanting her to play some trick and seal herself inside. Now, both inside, she rolled aside a small table and pulled a dark blanket off a mostly transparent cubic container.

Inside, Shipp saw a living, breathing, pinkish, spongy life form.

Its sudden companionship at such close proximity startled him. His breathing quickened. He looked in Wren's direction, knowing she had to be plotting some sort of escape plan.

"Open it," Shipp said.

"Are you insane?" Wren retorted. "Open that and we both die."

"Your research said the virus was manmade, not directly from this thing."

"Your science expert was dumbing it down for you. It's not that simple."

Shipp lunged for her without any warning and pinned her by the neck against the glass wall opposite the chamber holding the fungus. He squeezed enough to lightly choke her.

"I'm not dumb, and you will tell me what you're talking about, or I'll open that thing and stick your head inside. I don't care if I die too!"

Now truly scared at his evident total sincerity and realizing he was her polar opposite, Wren spoke quickly.

"The virus kills. It's part of its natural reproductive cycle. Our weapons just work exponentially faster and with far greater lethality. And they're easy to store and deploy at will. You can't just throw the sponge on a spaceship and fly it ten thousand light years."

Shipp released her as she spoke, finally satisfied with some real information. He took a step back.

"So your first expeditions to the planet must have all died."

"Yes, eventually. Long ago. Decades. Maybe even a century. But it takes weeks. And the effect isn't as acute."

"Good," said Shipp. He drew his AX-9 from his belt and shot her in the thigh. She screamed and grabbed her leg, falling backward along the rear wall and knocking over some equipment that clanged to the floor.

Shipp pulled out a MagTon, his last, and affixed it to the outside of the fungus chamber, on the corner to minimize damage to the organism inside. He knew this glass was the same as that used on exterior windows, and that the fungus would survive it for sure.

Then, Shipp stepped outside the door leading into this room, and blew the MagTon. It tore a hole in the chamber containing the fungus, and sent up a cloud of dust and debris, removing the fungus from sight for a moment.

Wren cried out, trying to crawl to her feet. Shipp found a burning torch he had seen hours ago in a previous room, and began welding the metallic door handle, sealing it closed with the metal strip bordering the otherwise transparent door and walls.

"What are you doing??" Wren screeched. "I told you it takes weeks! You can't leave me here that long without food or water! I'll die before it kills me!!!"

Shipp leaned against the glass on the opposite side, nodding.

"I wanted to be sure you were telling the truth. Now I know."

Then, Shipp returned to the innermost room, while Wren watched him through the various walls and doors, trying to determine his next move. He turned on the monitor, searching for something. She couldn't see the monitor well enough to be sure. But her terror grew with each passing minute.

She darted her eyes at every object in the room, looking for any possible means of escape. But Shipp had planned well. He correctly presumed this room would have only one entrance, and he sealed it shut.

And by shooting her, he limited her strength and mobility, even if she did manage to find something that might pry open the door. Every so often, he looked over to be sure she remained helpless and trapped.

About twenty minutes later, Shipp arose. He was reading something on the monitor and saying it out loud, almost as if trying to understand it, or remember it.

He checked Wren again, and then stepped over to the metallic box where Wren claimed to have incinerated the remaining virus samples. He pressed a couple buttons and adjusted a gauge. Then, he returned to the monitor again. He was following some kind of procedure.

Wren's jaw quivered. Her eyes widened in terror. Her fingers tensed up and started sweating. She knew his plan. Her breathing quickened into panicked, short spurts. She fell to the floor crawling around looking for anything she could use to escape. She found a flat metal scoop they used to dissect the fungus when it got too large. She crawled to the door and tried to jam it between the door and the wall. She dug it in hard, her fingertips turning white with pressure, her joints spiking in pain. She finally got it to stay, and tried to pry the door, but the metal dislodged with a ching.

"Arrrghhh!!!!" Wren screamed. She dug it in again and got it to go a little deeper. She pried it and got some leverage this time, but the door wouldn't budge. She tried again and again, but couldn't break the seal with such a thin piece of metal.

Suddenly, Shipp's feet appeared right there at her eye level on the other side of the door.

She wheeled over on her back and pushed away with her good leg and arms, a crippled crabwalk.

"You can't put me in there!" she screamed at him.

Shipp now wore a face filter, another item they found while searching the area. He picked up his torch again, and melted the seal. Once it softened, he kicked open the door, marched over to Wren, and picked her up under the arms.

He carried her writhing, kicking, screaming body over to the blown-open fungus container, grabbed her by the back of the neck, and shoved her face against the opening.

"Breathe it in deep!" he growled at her.

In her heightened emotional panic, she couldn't do anything but exactly that. The spores from the fungus entered her lungs in a far higher concentration than they had so far. After ten seconds with her screaming and struggling, and then finally relenting, realizing her fate was sealed, Shipp yanked her to her feet and dragged her out the door. He closed it behind her, picked up the torch with one hand, and sealed it again.

He dropped her on accident while fumbling with the torch. She fell and started scooting away, trying with all her strength to escape. She got on her good leg and opened the next door. Shipp saw her hopping away and up the stairs, but had to finish sealing the door. Just as she reached the door leading into the outermost layer of rooms, he shut off the torch.

Then, he raced through the rooms and caught up with her as she climbed a set of stairs.

"Please!! Don't put me in there!!! Please I'll do anything I'll tell you anything!!!"

Shipp ripped off his mask and held her against another wall. "You didn't seem too concerned when you sat there, taking notes, while your prisoners screamed like that. Ya?"

"I was wrong for that. I knew I wrong from the very beginning. This is war and after five hundred years we do crazy and terrible things. But LOOK WHAT YOU'RE ABOUT TO DO! You're no better! You're no better if you put me in there! You're worse!! Because you know exactly what will happen! You could just kill me with the AX!"

Shipp was unmoved. He dragged her back to the innermost room and crammed her into the metallic chamber, locking the door while she pounded on the sides and screamed and screamed and screamed.

Shipp returned to the monitor. His breathing was like someone trying to climb a high mountain without enough oxygen. Tears burst from his eyes but he kept wiping them away to see clearly. His fingers trembled so much he had to clench his hand before he could work the monitor. He tried to block out her screams and the deafening sounds of her body and limbs slamming against her impenetrable cage. What he intended to do to her was monstrous, but he simply could not miss this one and only opportunity to finally end the Westers – all of them. That meant she had to suffer far more intensely than any Wester he had ever killed.

He went through the remaining steps of the procedure he was following, and reached the last one.

He walked over and looked at her through the window. She saw him.

"I'm gonna flip that lever over there, and turn you into the virus. You're the new host. I'm not doing this just to kill you. I'm doing it to turn you into my own new virus weapon. I'm going to collect it in that container over there, just like the procedure says, and take it back to my ship. And then, we're going to end this war, one Wester planet at a time. Starting with Faraday!"

She held still, mouth agape, knowing finally his actual plan. She looked for words to try to change his mind. She found them.

"This will still work if you kill me first. My blood will still be warm. Kill me first you can still do it. Please kill me first."

"Right. You think I'll believe that?"

"It's true! Look up the file. It's number... uh... Show me the screen I'll walk you through it!"

"Your virus cost me everything! One of my best friends was killed by HER friend, after they went crazy because of what you invented. You're going to become the instrument of the death of your own entire territory. You are going to win the war. For us!"

"Nooo!!!!!!!!!! Please kill me kill me kill me first!!!!"

Shipp held back his own anguish enough to reach the lever, while Wren bawled and screeched and kicked and crashed inside her prison box. He placed his hand on the lever.

But then, to his complete astonishment, another hand reached around his chest and threw him across the room, crashing him into the wall right next to the metallic chamber that held the bawling Wren. She looked out and saw Shipp in pain, stunned, unable to process what just happened.

Then, James stepped into view, and knelt beside Shipp. He looked up and saw Wren in the chamber. He stood next to her window, and withdrew his AX-15 to get ready to kill her.

"Nooo!! I need her!" Shipp screamed. He bolted to his feet and crashed his body into James against the metallic chamber holding Wren, knocking away the weapon.

Shipp and James began fighting, punching, and shoving each other around the room, crashing into all sorts of things. Shipp punched James in the face. James hit him in the belly and then uppercut him. Shipp bowled into him, crashing against some crates which spilled empty countermeasure containers across the floor. Wren watched, wondering who to root for. But Shipp's exhaustion from having expended so much emotion and vigor to get this far enabled James to overpower him.

James punched Shipp one last time and sent him sprawling on the floor. Then, he retrieved his weapon, opened the metallic chamber and pointed it at Wren.

"Sorry," he said, and then he shot her in the head.

"James! What are you doing?! James!" Shipp lay screaming at him from the floor, half crying and half shouting. James knelt by his side. Shipp continued in a softer tone, a mixture of defeat and despair, "I had it, James. I had the answer in my hands. I could have ended the war. Do you know that? Do you know what you just did?"

James put his hand on Shipp's chest and spoke in a calm, measured tone, through his own tears. "Yes, I know what I did, Thomas Shipp."

James looked up. Garrison, Li, Cardmanov, and all the other Petersons stood there, having watched the entire fight. They had fought their way back through all the Westers who breached the 22nd level, without losing a man. Just to get back here.

James placed his hand on Shipp's head and turned it toward him so their eyes would meet.

"I came back to save my friend."

Shipp knew what James meant. It cut him to the heart. He started sobbing, much like Wren had been doing moments before. James cried too, and pulled his friend to his chest, hugging him by the head while Shipp released.

Garrison strolled over to the metallic chamber and looked at Wren's body. An odd look crossed his face. He glanced at the procedure on the monitor, and read the final step that James had interrupted. Then, he turned to Shipp and James and waited.

Epilogue

After he recovered himself, Shipp and the others returned to the Sorcerer Reborn. Dons' plan worked. They fired an array of hive bombs – their entire supply – at evenly spaced intervals across the planet's surface. Then, they obliterated Outpost Lightway.

They waited around for a couple weeks to verify the plan had worked. After fifteen days, the color of the planet itself began to change from a cloudy sangria to light gray, almost like ash. After a third week, the gray appeared to have consumed the entire planet.

Satisfied they had neutralized the threat of the virus and the alien fungus, Garrison went to give Shipp the news. Shipp remained in his domicile for most of these weeks, not wanting to watch or hear about it. He asked James to give him time alone, because he wasn't sure how to feel. He barely ate.

Shipp slowly grew to accept that James had saved him from becoming the same monster he came to slay. Wren wasn't just his opposite. She was also twenty years older. She was him, twenty years from now. And James halted his descent.

"It's done," Garrison told him as he entered the room, with a flat expression. "Mission accomplished. Now, the war can continue as it always has."

Shipp shook his head. "You really want that? You want it to continue forever? Is that what all the Peterson leaders really want? Endless war, even stretching to Andromeda if that's what it takes?"

Garrison curled his lip just a tiny bit.

"Not exactly, no."

Shipp got a little confused, and then realized Garrison was appealing to Shipp's idealism again.

Garrison continued, "We're over here, where no Peterson has ever been before. We have maps of their territory. Strongest attack ship in history. Huge supply of weapons. You think I came all this way for a little virus? I'd wager we can do quite a bit of damage before we finally give out."

Shipp managed a smile. His mind turned toward the possibilities.

"Are you in?" Garrison asked.

Shipp cocked his head and gave Garrison a nod. They weren't done. And it was time to go.

Also by Daniel Magill

War Virus is just beginning!

Book 2: War Virus: Waen Hex

Waen Hex will upend everything you just learned about Thomas Shipp, the crew of the Sorcerer, and the Galactic War. Shipp and his crew meet Epaga – a female from a strangely undiscovered race who won't stand by and let the Human war destroy her people...or the Humans.

Book 3: War Virus: Earth

The third book takes Shipp back to where human life originated, where they meet the loneliest man in the galaxy.

Book 4: War Virus: Gagarin

The next story sees a small surviving quartet land on one of the most populated Wester planets, where Shipp and James face perhaps their greatest test yet.

Future In Doubt

This standalone sci-fi thriller, set in the present day, is available now on Amazon. Also receiving a 5-star review from Reader's Favorite, this crowd-pleaser features Essie Palantir, who meets a dying man claiming to be from the future who warns her and her fiance Jonah about a coming global disaster. He even gives a specific date and predicts two coming earthquakes. Essie believes him. Jonah does not. And she gives up everything – including her love – to try and piece together the clues left by the man to save the world from disaster. But, what if she's wrong, and the man was just a lunatic?

Follow me on X (Twitter) – @dmagillwrite

Get updates about future books

Join the Magill Storyteller Newsletter – danielmagill.net/contact

Help Independent Authors – Leave a Review!

Please leave a review for War Virus and my other books on Amazon, Goodreads, or other sites you prefer to participate.

www.ingramcontent.com/pod-product-compliance
Lightning Source LLC
Chambersburg PA
CBHW032139050726
47591CB00001B/25

* 9 7 8 1 9 6 9 2 7 9 0 3 4 *